Melanie La'Brooy lives in Melbourne with her husband and son. Although she wrote *Babymoon* shortly after the birth of her first child, she would like to make it clear that this book is fiction, as the thought of making love while dressed in a football jumper makes her feel ill.

When Melanie isn't writing, doing the laundry, trying to find the 'off' switch on the singing Winnie-the-Pooh, cleaning the high chair or having balls thrown at her head by her beloved toddler, she likes to pass out unconscious against the nearest available surface.

Babymoon

Melanie La'Brooy

PIATKUS

First published in Australia & New Zealand as *The Babymoon* by Penguin Group (Australia) in 2008
First published in Great Britain as a paperback original in 2009 by Piatkus

A CIP catalogue record for this book is available from the British Library.

ISBN 978-0-7499-4172-7

Typeset in Ehrhardt by Action Publishing Technology Ltd, Gloucester
Printed and bound in Great Britain by Clays Ltd, Bungay, Suffolk

Papers used by Piatkus are natural, renewable and recyclable products sourced from well-managed forests and certified in accordance with the rules of the Forest Stewardship Council.

Piatkus
An imprint of
Little, Brown Book Group
100 Victoria Embankment
London EC4Y 0DY

An Hachette UK Company
www.hachette.co.uk

www.piatkus.co.uk

For my beloved Charlie & Dashiell,
both of whom taught me how to fall in love
in an entirely new way.

Babymoon

Prologue

I was never one of those girls who always knew that they wanted to be a mother someday. I never leaned over prams and cooed at babies on the street or caught the gaze of their proud parents and offered them a warm smile. Through a mixture of disinterest, fear and, I have to admit, distaste, I rarely offered to hold the newborn offspring of friends and family. Dropping them on the crowns of their partially formed skulls was only one of my many concerns. Infinitely worse was the thought that at any moment I might be hit by a projectile form of liquid waste from either end.

In short, I wasn't really interested in babies. Babies can't tell jokes, they don't have opinions, they smell and they're more demanding than, well, I am.

Which was why I was now staring in abject terror at the newborn babe in my arms, wondering what the hell I was going to do with it.

Because, for once, I couldn't hand it back to its parents after the obligatory five minutes and a pathetic stab at which parent it most resembled.

This time it was different.

This time it was mine.

First Trimester

1
The Beginning

'God. Oh God. Oh! Oh! Oh! OOOOOOOOOOHHHH-HHHHHHHH!!!!!'

After thumping the shopping down on the kitchen table, I went to investigate. It was as I had expected. Carlton were losing. Again. Why Jack didn't give up and support the local netball team, I had no idea. They certainly had a better chance of winning the Australian Football League Premiership one day. However, as Jack had sternly informed me at the beginning of our relationship four years ago, some things were genetically programmed into you at birth, and these included eye and hair colour, height and which football team you supported. To abandon Carlton simply because they were, without a doubt, the crappiest team in the League was unthinkable. The only flaw in his argument was that Jack hadn't been a Carlton fan from birth, as he had only discovered AFL when we'd moved from rugby-mad Sydney to Melbourne (the home of AFL) two years ago.

Jack had taken to Melbourne like a duck to water. Which was an appropriate simile because, it must be said, the defining feature of Melbourne is water. Not the sparkling blue Sydney Harbour type of water that he had grown up with and which I had become accustomed to during the four years that I had lived in Sydney, but the grey, falling-from-the-sky-in-a-relentless-drizzle, Chinese-water-torture type of water. Jack loved the trams, the city laneways, the football code. He marvelled at the friendly staff in restaurants and cafés. For the first six months he had acted like a naïve farmhand, straight off the train from Albury-Wodonga. He was enchanted with everything and everyone Melburnian. Initially I was happy that he loved my hometown so much, but then it started to get a little annoying. The day that he had beamed at me and said, 'Will you look at that!' when another driver had courteously allowed us into their lane, I had come perilously close to pushing him out of the car and into the path of an oncoming tram.

We had settled in a rented house in the inner-city suburb of East St Kilda and publicly demonstrated our commitment to one another by adopting a dog from a shelter. Jack worked as a surgeon at the Royal Women's Hospital and I had a job at a very posh art gallery in Toorak, where all of the paintings had at least four zeros on their price tag and people who wandered in by chance got a very frightened look in their eyes as they took in the plush carpet, the soft music and the expensively lit artwork. They would then back out as soon as they reasonably could before they were coerced into putting a deposit on a painting that was roughly equivalent to what they had paid for their house.

Jack and I had had a complicated beginning to our romance. When we'd first met in Sydney, he had been a compulsive serial dater (he liked to date brunettes). As a brunette, I naturally caught his attention but initially I wasn't interested in him as I had been going through a rough patch following the break-up with my ex-boyfriend Charlie. For differing reasons, we then both lied to each other about our names, jobs and pets (leaving Jack under the impression that I was an air hostess named Annabelle who owned a cat called Hamish, while I thought he was a stockbroker, surname Norbert, who possessed no less than four horrible miniature dogs). However, once we sorted out the truth, it took only a few dates for me to establish that Jack Boyd was the well-read, articulate, witty man of my literary dreams, while Jack was simultaneously reassuring himself that I was not the deranged, hair-brush-throwing, underpants-stealing, tutu-wearing, catastrophe-attracting lunatic that he had initially mistaken me for. From that time on, our romance had proceeded in a thoroughly satisfactory manner, entirely worthy of a horse-and-sunset-combination ending.

Notwithstanding our domestic bliss, we had no plans to marry, which suited me perfectly. While you would have been forgiven for thinking that a girl who was still hoping that archivists would unearth a happy ending to *Wuthering Heights* would be frothing at the mouth for a legitimate reason to don a hooped dress and tiara and swoon around carrying on about Wuv for an entire day, nothing could have been further from my mind.

For, despite being so in love with Jack that it wouldn't have surprised me to discover that I had a spider's web attached to my head that offered pithy comments on my love-struck state such as 'RADIANT!' or 'TERRIFIC!' à la Wilbur the pig from *Charlotte's Web* (although knowing my luck I would probably also have to endure 'SOME PIG!' hovering over me for an entire fortnight), I still hadn't entirely conquered my innate fear of commitment.

I had been in a long-term, live-in relationship before – with Charlie. I already knew what it was to plan a future with someone, only to have all of those dreams snatched away. I had also been in love before – as had Jack. And although it did feel different this time – I adored Jack and knew that we were far better suited than

Charlie and I had ever been – a stubborn doubt refused to budge from my suspicious heart.

I had been deeply committed to Charlie but he had left me alone in Sydney, with no warning, to pursue his career in Adelaide. Several months later I had discovered that long-distance relationships were not my strong suit when I embarked upon the one and only one night stand of my life. I had confessed to Charlie, resulting in the inevitable messy break-up over the telephone, and then, with what I still considered unseemly haste, Charlie had started a relationship with the oboe-playing Liesel (who I had instantly christened Sleazel). And my whole world had splintered.

While I had gradually rebuilt my life, first by myself and with my friends, and then with Jack, marriage remained a commitment that I still wasn't quite ready for. It was too final; too binding. (Well, it was unless you believed in divorce. Which I didn't.)

Anyway, given my mistrust regarding the permanency of relationships, it only made what happened next all the more surprising. Because I was about to embark on the most irrevocable relationship of my life.

I hovered in the doorway, taking in the scene before me. Jack was watching a pre-season Aussie Rules match on the television, while our dog Rufus was curled up near by, trying to sleep, but jumping out of his skin every time Jack yelled abuse at the umpires.

I knelt down beside Rufus, stroking his soft ears, and he looked at me wearily as if to say, 'Only seven months of football to go for the year.'

'Are they losing by less than fifty points?' I asked optimistically.

Jack grunted and then cursed as the final siren blew, signalling an end to his team's humiliation.

'Why on earth didn't you pick a better team? It's not like they were winning two years ago either, when we moved to Melbourne and you started watching footy.'

He looked at me scathingly. 'I work in Carlton. There are some things you can't choose, *they* choose *you*.'

'But we live in St Kilda and St Kilda win lots more than Carlton do,' I pointed out.

'Yes, but Bert goes for St Kilda.'

Bert was an obstetrician and a colleague of Jack's from the hospital who had also become his best friend in Melbourne. To the best of our knowledge, he was the only Bert under the age of sixty-eight in the whole of Australia.

'So?'

'So you can't barrack for the same team as your best mate. It's unheard of.'

I gave up. They had a whole elaborate system worked out. Whenever Jack called Bert's mobile phone, Bert had it programmed so that the phone played St Kilda's club song. Bert thought this was hilarious.

'They only lost by seventy points. I think they're reaching a plateau,' he said glumly, pointing the remote control at the television and switching it off.

'But last week you said that they'd reached their nadir. I don't think you can plateau when you're at your nadir.'

He looked at me accusingly.

'I just mean to say – a plateau suggests raised ground and a nadir is a low point so it doesn't really make topographical sense,' I explained helpfully.

'Belle?'

'Mmm?'

'You're not helping.'

He really did look miserable.

I gave Rufus a final rub behind the ears, as a plan to

cheer up Jack occurred to me. I disappeared into the bedroom, and five minutes later re-entered the living room.

Jack looked up morosely and then his mouth dropped open.

I smiled and sashayed over in as sexy a manner as I could while wearing nothing but a Carlton football jumper. I felt about as sexy as a used Band-Aid in a sweaty-smelling locker, but it was obviously doing it for Jack. His blue eyes had lit up and he opened his arms.

'Oops. Wait a moment.' To his consternation I stopped mid-sashay and headed back towards the door. I held it open and Rufus gazed at me pitifully. 'Sorry. Can't have sex in front of the dog. Way too weird. Out.'

Rufus heaved a sigh and then staggered to his paws and slunk out of the room. I closed the door firmly behind him.

I collapsed into Jack's lap and nuzzled his neck. 'Wanna play? You can be the doctor and I'll be the player with a groin injury.'

'Too much like work,' he murmured, running his hands up and down my back.

'Oh. Well, how about I pretend to be the naughty club mascot and you can be the strict umpire?'

'Carlton's mascot is a male puppet with an oversized head, called Captain Carlton.'

'Not so sexy?'

'Not so sexy,' he agreed. 'Honey?'

'Yes?'

'You look gorgeous. How about you just be you, only quieter, before you ruin the mood?'

Not being the maternal type, I hadn't given a lot of thought to the matter but I suppose I'd had a vague idea that conceiving a child would take place on a bed scattered with rose petals, surrounded by flickering candles and that the lovemaking would be gentle and tender and like the sort of euphemistic sex they have in Mills & Boon novels where nobody ever grunts and the starring role is played by 'his firm manhood', because anything as vulgar as a penis must never be mentioned.

But as it turned out we had a raunchy session right there and then on the couch, with me in a football jumper and Jack with his trakky-daks around his ankles in a quite undignified manner.

Afterwards, we lay in each other's arms and he explained to me just why Carlton's coach ought to be sacked; I told him about the time my best friend Cate's dog had eaten a used condom out of her bedroom bin and she had taken him to have his teeth professionally brushed every day for three weeks and even then she had screamed when he licked her face. Then we just lay there quietly for a very long time, both of us secretly pondering what we had just done.

Of course, we hadn't just launched into a session of football-themed procreation with no prior discussion. Jack had (ahem) planted the seed about our having a baby for the first time about a year ago. While it had taken me a little by surprise, I had been reassured by the way that Jack had casually mentioned it then just let the subject drop, leaving me to digest the idea. Since that initial hint, our discussions on the topic had gradually grown longer and more frequent, until finally it had become accepted between us that we would try to have a child, without either of us ever actually having to say aloud, 'Jolly good, let's go forth and multiply', which was just as well, considering that the only thing that terrified me more than giving birth was mathematics.

One of the things that I loved about Jack was that, even though he had always made it plain that he wanted kids one day, he didn't show it by behaving in a stupidly sentimental manner around other people's children. My closest friend from Sydney, Fran, had told me that, for months before they started to try for a baby, her partner attempted to cuddle pretty much any baby that they passed on the street, while heaving mysterious sighs. Fran had been quite sure that on at least one occasion he had come perilously close to being arrested.

I quite liked young children but babies remained a mystery to me. Their heads always needed supporting, which irritated me no end. It was as though they just couldn't be bothered. Nah, I think I'll just lie here and be floppy for another few months, if it's all the same to you. Now get me some more milk or I'll double your sleep deprivation.

The thing that worried me the most was that I had never been *certain* that I would have children one day. I had distinct memories of a conversation at a dinner party with a group of girlfriends when we were all in our mid-twenties. These were all party girls, mind you, whose idea of commitment at that juncture meant drinking only vodka and cranberry juice for six months.

But when the topic of motherhood came up, to my complete bewilderment, all of them confidently asserted their desire – no, their certainty – that one day they would be mothers.

'But how do you *know*?' I demanded.

Jayne smiled. 'I just know that it's something I'm going to do. I'd be miserable if I didn't have kids.'

'But what if you don't meet the right guy?'

She shrugged. 'I'll worry about that if it happens.'

And there was the inexplicable crux of the matter. These girls, who would go on to spend the better part of the next decade alternatively obsessing and despairing over meeting their real-life version of Fitzwilliam

Darcy, nevertheless retained an unshakeable belief in their maternal futures. It made absolutely no sense to me at all.

For me, having children had always been inextricably bound up with finding the person I wanted to have children *with*. Only once I was happily settled down with Jack I still didn't feel any impulse towards motherhood. Not only was my biological clock not ticking, I had apparently had a sundial inserted instead.

And then, one day, Fran rang me from Sydney to say that she was pregnant. We had become friends when we worked together at an art auction house in Sydney. Fran was an artist who worked part-time as the auction house's receptionist. She had been a hopeless receptionist but an utterly wonderful friend when Charlie had left me. We still emailed each other often and spoke on the telephone, but I missed her terribly.

She sounded very happy and I congratulated her and her partner who worked with computers but who had pretended to be a botanist when he'd first met Fran in order to impress her. Prior to meeting the fake botanist, she had always dated creative types, and there were still times when I wasn't entirely sure if she remembered that her partner was a fake botanist, such as now when she mentioned that it was auspicious that their baby was due in spring, and that its birth flower would be the aster, which symbolised patience. But, then again, botanical symbolism didn't have to be confined to professionals, so we spent the next few minutes coming up with names like Daisy, Violet and Lily.

But, after we'd chatted for a few minutes, my curiosity overcame me and I burst out, 'Frannie, I am happy for you, you know I am. I'm just ... surprised, I guess.'

'Why?'

'Because – because *you* don't particularly like babies either,' I finished helplessly.

There was a pause, and in that pause I could practically hear Frannie smiling. 'I know,' she said mildly. 'But I'm pretty sure it's different when it's your own. And, anyway, it's not like they stay babies forever.'

In the scheme of things, it wasn't a particularly insightful or deeply philosophical comment. But, for me, it struck home. Babies, those alien creatures that, to be honest, I was quite fearful of, *didn't* remain babies forever. It was something that I hadn't really considered.

The second thing that helped to change my mind was the death of my grandmother. I had adored my grandmother and I missed her terribly. How much I hadn't quite realised until about two weeks after her funeral. Jack and I had gone over to my sister Audrey's house for dinner and I was reading a bedtime story to her eldest son, Felix. Felix was three years old and obsessed with *The Lion King*. So, for about the forty-fifth time, I was reading the story aloud to him.

Only this time, when we got to the part where the old lion king, Mufasa, died, all of a sudden I was bawling, sobbing my eyes out. I didn't want to upset Felix so I started to babble something about being hormonal, but then he asked me what 'hormonal' meant and I started to cry even harder when I envisaged the scene that would ensue if Audrey came into the room and caught me trying to explain the concept of female hormones to her three-year-old son. But, amazingly, Felix didn't get upset or start to cry. He simply crawled further into my lap, put his arms around my neck and said wisely, 'Don't be sad about Mufasa, Auntie Belle. It's the circle of life. Look, I'll show you.'

He flipped over the pages until he reached the very

end and he showed me the picture of Simba and Nala with their newborn cub, while Mufasa smiled benignly down on them all from the starry sky. I gazed at the picture through my tears and emitted a hiccup and a long, shuddering breath.

Felix was looking up at me patiently, smiling trustfully, as though waiting for me to realise there was really nothing to be scared of or sad about when it came to either birth or death.

I caught him up in a fierce hug. 'Thanks, Felix. Hey, do you think maybe your great-grandmother is up there in the stars with Mufasa?'

He looked again at the picture. 'Maybe,' he said cautiously. 'But I think lions eat old people.'

So that was the undignified way in which I started to embrace the concept of motherhood. Thanks to *The Lion King*, a three-year-old and Frannie all pointing out the obvious, something within my psyche began to shift and the idea that I might one day become a mother started to seem not so improbable after all.

2

Fetid For ever

I'd spent so many years trying *not* to get pregnant that having unprotected sex felt almost abnormal. Like all of a sudden deciding to let the hairs on my legs grow to plaiting length. Or politely saying, 'No, thank you, I'm full,' when someone offered me chocolate anything.

After years spent obsessing over condoms, the occasional mad dash to the doctor for the morning-after pill, struggling to remember to take the pill every day and then Googling the Billings method in a panic after a sudden realisation that I had forgotten to take it since Easter, it was hardly surprising that having unprotected sex seemed almost kinky.

Unfortunately I've never been a spectacularly raunchy kind of a gal. As much as I like the image of me swingin' naked from chandeliers, shouting, 'Watch out down below!' before plummeting into an orgy taking place in a swimming pool, the reality is that I always get bogged down by details. Like how or why there would be a chandelier above the swimming pool. I tried to watch a porn film once but couldn't get past the fact that one girl had very bad ingrown pubic hairs, the men looked like they'd snort when they laughed and all the close-ups looked like meat-tray raffle night at the local Rotary Club.

Given this, it was probably unsurprising that having unprotected sex made Jack and I extremely polite all of a sudden. Honestly, one moment we would be ripping shirt buttons off with our teeth and tumbling backwards on to the bed and then the next it was all, 'Do you mind?'

'No, not at all. Please go right ahead.'

'Well, if you're *sure* ...'

It was as though Sir Galahad had taken to having sex with Emily Post. There was just something so indescribably *rude* about a naked penis going about its procreating business that we felt the need to compensate with bizarre levels of courtesy.

Added to all of this was my certainty that I was already pregnant. We had only been having unprotected sex for just over a week now and I knew that there was every chance that it would take us months to fall pregnant. Nevertheless, I was convinced that we'd conceived that very first time on the couch and, as a result, a hidden doubt had started to plague me.

The doubt was linked with our first Melbourne anniversary. We had celebrated in true style. Dinner at ritzy restaurant Matteo's in North Fitzroy, followed by copious amounts of champagne at The Supper Club. All of which meant that we were extremely hungover and tired the following day. But we had decided that, instead of buying each other presents, we would jointly purchase a painting that we could keep forever. Thus it was that we had spent the entire day, both of us in filthy moods, trawling through galleries, with neither of us daring to say, 'Bugger it, let's go home and have a sleep and do this when we're not so hungover.'

Naturally, the inevitable happened and we had ended up buying a painting that we both secretly hated but thought the other liked. It wasn't until about six months later that we both finally admitted that we thought the picture was a heinous crime against art, but by that time it had acquired the status of our First Anniversary Present and we were stuck with it. We tried moving it to the spare bedroom so we didn't have to look at it every day but that prompted an endless stream of anxious enquiries from relatives and friends, who were then convinced that our relationship was troubled. So we had to move the bloody thing back.

My friend Cate, who in addition to being a highly successful management consultant was also a trained counsellor, said that we ought to think of it as a symbol of mutual love and sacrifice hanging on our wall. This was a nice thought but little help, as you couldn't really get past the fact that it looked like an angry substance-abusing artist had simply thrown a can of house paint at the canvas, rolled in it and then written the word 'FETID' in fluorescent-green letters across the centre.

Which was why I couldn't help wondering if the baby would be like the FETID painting. That maybe what we had thought was a good idea at the time we would later realise was a terrible mistake. Only then it would be too late because we'd be stuck with it for the rest of our lives.

But it was still too early to tell.

So I went about my daily business: going to work, having incredibly polite sex, walking Rufus and seeing friends, while inside me the sundial started to move faster and faster, until it became a blur of time and motion, counting down to the moment when everything would change for ever.

I had first taken up yoga when I lived in Sydney. Since moving to Melbourne, I had been to the occasional class here and there but I had let it lapse, and nowadays my main form of exercise consisted of throwing a ball for

Rufus in the park and then running to get it myself, as Rufus stubbornly refused to grasp the concept of Fetch.

But for the first time in a while I felt the need for a yoga class. I needed something to help me relax in order to stop focusing on my spinning sundial.

I had taken a class at the yoga school on Acland Street on a Saturday afternoon several months ago and the instructor had been lovely. Only this time, when I walked into the room, I was greeted by Diego, the sort of yoga instructor who always made my heart sink.

Within ten minutes, it was apparent that Diegó belonged to the hippy, healing-crystal-wearing, borderline creepy, touchy-feely school of instructors. He was the sort who was forever adjusting his students; a slight pressure on the sacrum here, a rub of the inner thigh there.

I put up with it because at least he was being non-discriminatory in his groping, but Diego's hands wandering all over me during backbends was ruining the whole point of my coming to yoga for relaxation in the first place. It was an immense relief, therefore, when we made it to savasana, the final, and my favourite, part of the class. Savasana basically comprised lying down and taking a nap. Strictly speaking, you were meant to meditate, but I usually just ended up asleep.

Only this time I couldn't properly relax. Because from somewhere near by came the sound of Diego singing. And it was moving closer.

As the singing got nearer and nearer, I desperately wanted to open one eye to see what was going on but I just knew that I'd end up in trouble.

And then, Diego was on me.

Literally on me. Sitting on me. Singing. Or chanting was probably the more accurate term. And it wasn't comfortable either; he had a very bony bum for starters, and it hurt.

All I could think at first was: Please God, don't let him squash my baby. My second thought was that, if I *was* pregnant, surely I was meant to have the maternal instincts of a lioness or something. If a lioness had returned home to find a smelly yoga instructor sitting on her cub, she would probably have eaten him for dinner, wandering hands and all. But I was just sitting there and taking it because of my over-socialised fear of being rude. Which was ridiculous.

I opened my eyes. 'Excuse me?' I whispered, as everyone around me was still meditating or sleeping, depending on how advanced they were in their practice.

At the sound of my voice, Diego jumped violently, which naturally meant that his bony bum rebounded on me. Hard.

He looked at me, outraged that I had interrupted his chanting.

'It's just—' I couldn't say that I was pregnant. I might not be, and anyway it felt too weird. I compromised. 'I've got a stomach ache. Would you mind?' I did a little movement with my hands to indicate that I'd like him to shift.

He didn't. Instead he made himself more comfortable, looked at me intently and nodded.

'Manipura,' he said aloud, not seeming to mind if he disturbed the meditation of the other students. 'Yes. I can see now. You have definite problems with your ten-petalled lotus.'

I had absolutely no idea what Diego was talking about but the lotus part I understood. Show me a yoga class anywhere on this planet and I'll show you a lotus flower being mercilessly flogged for every last drop of its symbolism. It had happened in every single class that I had ever attended. What the poor lotus had done to deserve this I didn't know, but I could just imagine a lotus airing its grievances down the local pub, saying bitterly to the English Rose, 'You think *you* got a working over by the Romantic Poets? Try propping up the entire global population of yoga devotees. See how knackered you are after a day of *that*.'

Diego was moving his hands around me in a gesture that I recognised from a holiday at Byron Bay as 'sensing my aura'. 'I can see the yellow vibrating around you. You're angry, aren't you? You're feeling a sense of victimisation.' He abandoned his aura-channelling voice to add, in a decidedly matter-of-fact tone, 'Manipura is the solar plexus chakra. These feelings are very common when it's blocked.'

The peculiar part was that he was absolutely right. I was feeling angry and victimised and my solar plexus was definitely blocked. But I felt the strong urge to point out that all of those things were due to the fact that HE WAS STILL BLOODY WELL SITTING ON ME!

Diego looked down at me pityingly. 'You need to activate your chakras and allow your Kundalini energy to flow to your crown. It's not something you can do once and then just forget about. You have to really work at it.'

I nodded and admitted that I had been very remiss, but, henceforth, directing the flow of my Kundalini energy would become an indispensable part of my daily hygiene routine, slotting in somewhere between flossing and moisturising. Anything to get his bony bum off my unborn lotus.

Maybe Diego had tapped into the signals from my higher consciousness because he finally heaved himself up. I waited until I was sure that he had moved on to his next victim and then I breathed freely once again while patting my tummy anxiously to check for dints.

The next night I took Rufus to the park and played Fetch by myself for forty minutes. Much less stressful.

3

The Plastic Oracle

'Belle, hurry up! We're going to be late!'

It was ten past seven in the evening and Jack and I were meant to be meeting Bert and his new girlfriend at a restaurant in Prahran by quarter past.

Jack stopped in confusion at the doorway to our bedroom as he took in the sight of me sitting, half-dressed, on the edge of the bed.

'What's wrong with you?'

'I think I'm pregnant,' I said in a small voice.

His face brightened. 'You do?'

I nodded.

'Do you feel nauseous?' he asked anxiously.

'No. But my period's late.'

He sat down beside me and took my hand. 'Why haven't you said anything?'

The correct response to this was: WHAT THE HELL ARE YOU TAKING ABOUT? WE'VE BEEN HAVING UNPROTECTED SEX FOR OVER A MONTH NOW! DO YOU MEAN THIS *HASN'T* BEEN OCCUPYING YOUR MIND TWENTY-THREE AND A HALF HOURS A DAY? WHY HAVEN'T YOU ASKED?

Instead of which I muttered, 'I don't know.'

'Well, let's do a test.'

I swallowed and nodded again.

[illegible]k one up tomorrow,' Jack said excitedly.

'I bought one already.'

'Then what are we waiting for? Let's find out!'

God, it was horrible. I felt as though we'd ended up at two different events. Jack was waiting for the lottery results and I was in the dock, about to hear a verdict of life sentence.

'Let's do it after we get back from dinner.'

'Why?'

'I just – I just want to do it after. Look, we're already running late. And, besides, I don't think I'll be able to sit there and make conversation if we know.'

Jack gave me one of his patented 'I-know-you-Isabelle-therefore-I-know-that-there's-more-to-this' looks, but instead of pushing it he handed me my skirt so that I could finish getting dressed.

Throughout the dinner with Bert and his new girlfriend Mona (cue sex-noises jokes ad nauseam), I couldn't concentrate. For starters, I was worried that Bert could tell via his obstetrician's sixth sense that I was pregnant. Secondly, I was already confronting the difference that potentially being pregnant could make to something as simple as having dinner at a restaurant.

I didn't know very much about being pregnant but I had picked up a few basic nuggets of information when Fran and my sister Audrey had gone through their pregnancies. I knew that you weren't supposed to drink alcohol or eat raw fish. This would wipe out eighty-five per cent of my diet, leaving me to subsist on chocolate and cups of tea alone. I also knew about something called 'mother's guilt', which Audie said was the primary emotion she had experienced since becoming a mother.

Guilt over trying to balance paid work with your child's needs, guilt over bottle instead of breast feeding, guilt over not being able to competently bake a birthday-cake replica of Hogwarts, complete with revolving staircases . . . apparently, the list was endless. Audie would no doubt have been thrilled to learn that I had discovered a new branch of maternal guilt that could perhaps be christened 'anti-antenatal guilt'. This type of guilt occurs when one believes oneself to be pregnant but still defiantly drinks a glass of wine. Feeling evil, I tried to rationalise that it didn't count as I hadn't *officially* found out and, if I wasn't going to drink for the next eight or so months, I bloody well deserved a last hurrah. Then I decided to dig the ditch a little deeper. As I'd already doomed my unborn child to foetal alcohol syndrome and continuing with the 'If I don't know it doesn't officially count' thesis, I decided to order prawn sushi for entrée.

On the way home we made desultory conversation, comparing our thoughts on Mona and her compatibility with Bert, with Jack making his obligatory sex-noises joke, and then that was pretty much it. We were home. There was no escape or hope of further prevarication.

I made my way into the bathroom and broke open the box containing the pregnancy test. It must be said that, as a means of revealing the fateful course of your life, peeing on a plastic stick is right up there in the dignified prophetic stakes with sacrificing a goat and sorting through its entrails. I feel reasonably confident in asserting that the Oracle at Delphi would probably not have commanded the respect of the whole of Ancient Greece if, in answer to the queries put to her by kings and generals, she had emerged from the loo with an errant splash of wee on her hand, brandishing a plastic stick and cheerfully declaring that it was an excellent day to invade Sparta.

In my opinion, this was one of the few things that Christianity had got right when it came to women. Sure, we're the cause of original sin and Christianity is responsible for the whole Madonna/Whore dichotomy, but personally I'm a big fan of the Annunciation, Fra Angelico style. Finding out that you're pregnant *ought* to take place in a cloistered garden and involve a male archangel wearing robes of crimson, descending in all his glory from heaven to blow his trumpet and solemnly inform you that you have to lay off the sushi for the next nine months. The bit about it being the Son of God and having to account for every night you've spent apart to your bewildered partner is less attractive I'll admit, but I'd even prefer that to the indignity of peeing on a plastic stick.

I opened the bathroom door. Jack looked at me. I took a deep breath and then held out the test.

'Three stripes,' I announced breathlessly. 'What does that mean?'

'What do you mean – three stripes? It's meant to show two!'

I stared down at it. There were two dark lines in the panel. And fainter, but unmistakably, there was a third line.

I brandished the stick at Jack. 'You're a doctor! What does this mean?'

Jack could hardly contain his grin. 'I'm pretty sure it means we're having a baby.'

He caught me up in a fierce hug and showered kisses all over my face.

'We're having a baby,' I repeated. I tried to name what I was feeling but I wasn't really feeling anything. It felt unreal.

'But why are there three lines?' I persisted. 'Does that mean we're having twins? Or—' I gulped and continued weakly, '*Triplets*?'

'It doesn't work that way,' Jack explained patiently. 'It's not a line for each baby. One line is no baby, two lines means you're pregnant. It simply tests for HCG – human chorionic gonadotropin hormone.'

'There was absolutely nothing simple about that explanation. English please.'

'It tests for a specific hormone. Maybe your hormone levels are just a little – higher – than average. Look, we ought to have the pregnancy confirmed by a doctor anyway.'

'You are a doctor.'

'Yes, but you should be seen by an obstetrician. You'll need to book in to the hospital too.'

'Fine. I'll make an appointment with Bert.'

'With Bert? Nuh-huh. No way.'

'But you always say that he's the best!'

'Call me old-fashioned but I'd rather have a stranger become intimately acquainted with your gynaecological area than my best mate.'

'So it's nothing but second-best for our child?'

'In this instance, yes. I'll make an appointment for you with one of the other Obsties. They're all very good.'

I watched as he made his way over to the kitchen sink and opened the cupboard door underneath.

'Wait a minute!' I yelled in alarm. 'You're not throwing the stick away?'

Jack paused. 'You want to keep it?'

'It's the first official proof of our baby's existence!' I protested. 'We can't just throw it out!'

'Belle, it's a bit of plastic that you *peed* on. What do you intend to do – frame it?'

'Of course not,' I said, crossing my fingers behind my back. 'But give it back. It feels . . . wrong to just chuck it out straight away.'

Jack sighed but acquiesced. I slipped the plastic stick into the pocket of my skirt and snuggled into his arms, while one thought replayed constantly in my head.

Baby. We were having a baby.

But, no matter how many times during the following days that I mentally repeated this phrase or gazed at the three lines on my plastic oracle, it still didn't seem real.

4

Whoa Baby

One of the reasons that Jack and I had moved to Melbourne was that I had been offered a job at Durville Gallery. The gallery, which specialised in contemporary Australian art, was owned by Carmela Durville. Carmela had henna-red hair, a propensity to wear black leather everything and was clinically insane, which wasn't entirely her fault as it was kind of a prerequisite for owning an art gallery in the first place. Naturally, we called her Cruella behind her back, after Cruella De Vil from *101 Dalmatians.*

Becoming a gallerina had never been part of my career plan. My experience of gallerinas was that they were snooty, condescending and financially exploited by their bosses. But Cruella was one of only a handful of gallery owners who properly remunerated her staff (she had to as that was the only way she could still get staff, given her reputation) and, while I had loved working for an art auction house in Sydney, auction houses dealt with art collectors far more than with artists. The opportunity to work more closely with Australian contemporary artists had therefore been irresistible.

The great advantage of working for Durville Gallery, however, had been becoming friends with Doug, the other gallerina who worked there. Doug was like a relic of a British colonial outpost crossed with a flamboyant Sydney gay boy. He somehow managed to be excessively prudish about certain things and utterly outrageous about others, depending on his mood. Doug was also a former Sydney-sider who had worked for Cruella for six years. This in itself was a record as Cruella tore staff apart and got rid of them in the same casual manner that other people tossed half-eaten apples out of car windows. Doug had survived by being a brilliant salesman who could convince a collector of nineteenth-century romantic watercolours to invest in a death-metal-inspired installation piece, but also due to the fact that he treated Cruella with utter contempt.

In my early days at Durville Gallery, I thought that perhaps this was the key to gaining Cruella's respect. So on one memorable occasion I had tried a bit of attitude myself. This had resulted in my almost suffering heart failure when Cruella responded by executing the verbal equivalent of skinning me in order to turn me into a Dalmatian-puppy cloak.

But, given that she had gone to the trouble of recruiting me from Sydney (evidently she had burned her way through all the eligible staff in Melbourne), Cruella wasn't really in a position to fire me outright. Besides, I was made of sterner stuff. So, from that point on, if I needed to confront Cruella, I simply made Doug do it. This worked perfectly as Doug was able to get away with most things because he had the complete self-assurance that comes with being from the sort of extremely wealthy background that also meant he could wear things like cravats and velvet smoking jackets with impunity.

The day after the pregnancy test, Doug was enlivening the very boring task of updating the stock database with a story told to him by his outrageously good-looking boyfriend, Zac. Zac was so gorgeous that even

Cruella was nice to him. He worked in film and television production, so Doug always had fabulous gossip about well-known actors, which had carried us through many a slow day at the gallery.

But, despite today's juicy revelations from the set of *Rolf Harris: The Movie* (famous Australian actors doing lines of coke off the wobble board, followed by lewd acts with Jake the Peg's extra leg), I couldn't concentrate. I desperately wanted to tell Doug my momentous news, but Jack said that we had to wait until after week thirteen as miscarriage was quite common before that date.

Eventually, I interrupted Doug just as he was saying, 'Talk about "Tie me Kangaroo Down", according to Zac, it's a wonder she's ever *out* of handcuffs—'

'Doug, I'm so sorry but would you mind if I took my lunch break now?'

'It's eleven thirty!'

I nodded. 'I skipped – er—,' I had been going to say breakfast but belatedly remembered that I had raced into the gallery that morning, late as usual, clutching a half-eaten piece of toast '—brunch.'

Thankfully, Doug didn't seem to find anything amiss, merely commenting, 'You know, I blame brunch for all the Brangelina and Bennifer nonsense that we have to put up with these days. When you think about it, brunch is where it all started. I ask you, what's wrong with the term "Morning tea"?'

I murmured my agreement, grabbed my bag and made my exit in a manner that I hoped was the same as any other normal, non-pregnancy-confirmed day.

Feeling as though I was on a secret mission, I quickly walked the short distance to the Borders bookstore on Chapel Street and, after a few furtive circuits to make sure that nobody I knew was there, I scurried over to the parenting section.

I had never been in this part of the bookstore before and I wasn't entirely sure that I liked it. There seemed to be a severe lack of Penguin Classics and an oversupply of American gurus. It was also situated smack bang in the middle of the self-help section.

I hated self-help books. The whole concept was ludicrous. If you were in a situation that required you to ask for help, then trying to help yourself would have to be about the most self-defeating thing you could possibly do. Furthermore, if you were relying on a book to help you, then technically it wasn't self-help anyway.

I was about to pick a few books at random and flick through them when a sales assistant suddenly appeared at my elbow. Everything about Beatrice (she was wearing a name tag) shrieked 'serious literary credentials'. You could tell that she resented having to leave her ostentatious perusal of Dante's *Inferno* to come over to the section for people with low self-esteem and a desperate need for motivational quotes in bold font.

'Looking for anything in particular?'

Gee, I dunno, Beatrice. I'm in a bookstore. Do you sell hammers?

'Er, no. I'm fine, thank you.'

This was my standard response to avoid conversations with sales assistants because I had a tendency to attract the most useless one in the store, who invariably had halitosis and a borderline personality disorder.

Beatrice heaved a deep, smelly exhalation, as though I had inexcusably wasted her time and energy. As she turned to depart, I realised that I was being stupid. I *did* need help. I had no idea what sort of information I was looking for.

'Excuse me?'

She turned back.

'Sorry, but I think maybe I do need some assistance.'

Beatrice cast a longing glance at her copy of *The Inferno,* lying face-down on the counter and then reluctantly walked back towards me.

'Is there a particular book that you would recommend for a first-time—' I struggled to say the word, '—mother?' That sounded weird. Mother. *I* was going to be a mother.

'What's the problem?'

'There is no problem,' I said in surprise.

'If you need a book, then there's a problem. Otherwise you wouldn't need a book.'

Hooray. Today I had scored the passive-aggressive shop assistant.

She started pulling a couple of books off the shelf. 'Behavioural problems? Toilet-training philosophies?'

There were books dedicated to the philosophy of toilet training? How complicated could it get? To wee or not to wee? How could that even be a question?

There was so much I didn't know. It was terrifying.

I managed to gather my wits. 'Pregnant,' I said faintly. 'I'm—' I couldn't bring myself to say it. It was stupid, but until we were safely past the magical thirteen weeks I was too superstitious to say it out loud. 'My friend,' I said lamely. 'I'm buying a present for my friend. She's pregnant.'

Unsurprisingly, Beatrice was overwhelmingly disinterested in my 'friend's' exciting news. With a decidedly grudging air, she put back the books she had selected and pointed at several lower shelves. 'That's the pregnancy and childbirth section.'

She started to walk off and I gazed, aghast, at the array of titles available.

'Wait a minute – isn't there one you personally recommend?'

'I don't have kids.' She sounded both horrified and

insulted by the idea that she would ever do anything as disadvantageous to her literary life as procreate.

'I didn't mean that. But isn't there one book that's more popular or something?'

Beatrice thought for a moment. '*Woah Baby!* is a bestseller. It's a compilation of stories and photographs of freaky babies from around the world.'

'What do you mean "freaky babies"?'

'You know, human–eel hybrids. Babies born with a full set of teeth. That kind of thing.'

By now, Beatrice had slid so far down my list of least favourite people that she was officially *below* touch-feely yoga instructor Diego.

'There are human–eel babies?' I asked faintly.

Beatrice nodded. 'Happens all the time in El Salvador.'

'That's near Mexico, isn't it?' I was grasping at whatever comfort I could get. Mexico was a long way away, I rationalised. Just because El Salvador had human–eel hybrids didn't mean it happened in Australia.

Beatrice cast me a withering look. 'El Salvador is bordered by Honduras and Guatemala.'

'Do the babies with full sets of teeth come from any of those places?' I asked desperately.

She shook her head. 'The one on page thirty-five of *Woah Baby!* was born in New Zealand.'

I let out a little shriek. New Zealand was just across the Tasman. Actually, it might have been Tasmania that was just across the Tasman, but either way New Zealand was practically Tasmania for all geographical intents and purposes. This was getting a little too close to home.

Ignoring my distress, Beatrice pulled *Whoa Baby!* and two or three other books off the shelf and handed them to me. 'We sell a lot of these ones too.'

'OK, thanks.'

Clutching the books, I headed for a nearby armchair to peruse them before making my purchase. I waited until Beatrice had departed and then buried the evil that was *Whoa Baby!* deep under the cushion of the adjoining chair and made the sign of the cross over it.

I had only turned over a few pages of the first book when something else Beatrice had said suddenly sank in. These weren't just pregnancy books. They were also about childbirth.

I was terrified of giving birth, which was probably at the root of why I had never been certain that I would be a mother one day. I blamed it all on a Year Eight science class. At the culmination of the unit on the human reproductive system, our beleaguered science teacher, Mr Perkins, exhausted after a week spent making frisky fourteen-year-olds roll condoms on to carrots and putting up with immature questions along the lines of 'Excuse me, Mr Perkins? I can't quite understand the diagram on page *sixty-nine*', extracted his revenge by making us watch a birthing video.

And I had been completely and utterly traumatised by it. The screaming. The blood. The sheer animality of the woman in the video and the terrifying rawness of her pain.

I could still remember Mr Perkins snapping the light switch back on and staring in satisfaction at our shocked faces. He had then informed us that the video concluded the unit on sexuality and reproduction. We would be sitting a test in the next class so he advised us all to spend the weekend boning up. So to speak.

Since that fateful science class, I had managed to avoid the gritty details of childbirth, which wasn't that hard as long as I didn't loiter around the maternity wards of Jack's hospital or linger too long at petrol stations. (It seemed to me tabloid newspapers reported on some poor soul giving birth at a petrol station at least once a month.)

But now there was no escape. One of the books was replete with glossy, full-page colour photographs of everything from stretch marks (ugh) to something called a prolapsed uterus, a glimpse of which made me feel as though I was back watching the meat-tray porno movie. I flicked through the pages rapidly, trying not to look too closely at the photographs, until I reached the section on childbirth.

I gulped and snapped the book shut. It had only now started to dawn on me that the baby I had just discovered was inside me was going to have to come *out* in just under eight months' time. And, quite frankly, that freaked me out. I would have been much happier living in an earlier, more euphemistic century. Confinement and lying-in both sounded so much cosier than pregnancy or childbirth and gave the impression that you took to your bed and snuggled under the duvet for nine months. I didn't want to know where babies came from. I wanted the stork to deliver mine. Failing that, my ideal birthing scenario was the Cabbage Patch Kid adoption method. Sure, you were stuck with a kid with a head like a pumpkin for the rest of your life, but at least the process of acquiring it didn't hurt.

I closed both eyes, took a deep breath and then opened the book. Holding it at arm's length, I squinted through half-closed eyes at the photographs and then tried blinking rapidly as a compromise between looking and not looking.

A few seconds later, the book had been slammed shut once again, but this time I retained a vague impression of blood, something purple that might have been the baby, a father who had a moustache that was almost more frightening than the unidentifiable purple thing, and the startling 1980s permed hairstyle of one of the midwives.

I reshelved the book, aware of an emotion that felt a lot like cowardice. Fine. So I was an enormous girl's blouse with pink frilly bits when it came to giving birth. I'd deal with that in due course, thank you very much. I had enough to be getting on with for the moment as it was. Right. Process of elimination. There would be no buying of books with gory photographs.

Fortunately, I mustn't have been the only squeamish pregnant woman out there, as drawings, rather than photographs, did seem to be the illustrative medium of choice in most of the pregnancy books. One book, evidently trying to avoid as much detail as possible, had month-by-month drawings of the developing foetus that were so basic the casual peruser could have mistaken the pictures for an incomplete game of Hangman.

I put the Hangman book in my buy pile and then flicked through another one. A blur of information and unfamiliar terms sped before my eyes. Amniocentesis. Braxton Hicks. Pre-eclampsia. Surfactant. Meconium. I had absolutely no idea what any of these things were. Possibly they were the five most popular Australian baby names. I didn't know.

Realising that it was stupid to try to make an informed decision about which pregnancy book to buy when I was utterly and without question uninformed, I made my way up to the counter, clutching the Hangman book and another that I picked at random called *The Secret: Seven Habits of Highly Effective Mothers*. It wasn't until I was on my way back to the gallery, carrying the bag containing my purchases, that it occurred to me that I was only a few weeks pregnant and already I was so confused that I had been brought down to the level of needing self-help.

The following day, I started to read the books. By about

page twenty I was pretty certain that the secret-habits book wasn't for me. For starters, it spent chapters detailing how women should think about the pain of labour as positive pain and deal with it. But then came a carefree little half-pager in which the author suggested that men should be excused from being present during the labour and birth because many men found it difficult, if not unbearable, to see their wife (the author was quite strict on the fact that anyone having a baby must be heterosexual and married) in pain.

So basically women were expected to deal with the pain of labour but men were excused from merely *witnessing* their loved one in pain. But the double standards didn't stop there. The index ran to several pages but didn't contain an entry for either Dads or Fathers.

Both of the books also seemed obsessed with something called the pelvic floor. The Hangman book described the pelvic floor as a sort of trampoline that sits underneath all of your internal organs. Apparently it was very important to exercise the pelvic floor during pregnancy or else you'd end up weeing every time you sneezed or laughed after childbirth. The only problem was, despite following all of the book's instructions to the letter (these variously involved pretending to stop a wee, not clenching my buttocks and using a miner's lamp and GPS), I still couldn't find my pelvic floor. Typical. It was bad enough that my G-spot was partial to hide-and-seek without the additional burden of having to locate a pelvic floor that was apparently in a witness-protection programme. I would have been more than happy to buy my pelvic floor a gym membership but neither of the books explained how I was meant to exercise something that I couldn't for the life of me find.

Then there was the sensitively named birth canal. They (whoever they were but I intended to blame Jack as he was a member of the medical fraternity) could have called it the birth rivulet or the birth trickle, but oh no, *they* decided to go straight for the Venetian-type-get-me-a-gondola-to-the-other-side metaphor. For any woman who may have harboured secret concerns that having sex after childbirth would be like flinging a banana up Bourke Street Mall, it was more than a little insensitive.

On the plus side, what with all the room for a trampoline and a canal inside me, it was hard to believe that childbirth could be that painful. It almost seemed like a design fault that the baby didn't intend to roll out sideways.

Hitherto, my perception of pregnancy had largely comprised of having a big tummy and morning sickness. Thanks to the books, I now discovered that that was a little like describing the symptoms of the Bubonic plague as a headache and pimples. In the coming months, apparently I could look forward to nausea, vomiting, heartburn, indigestion, constipation, tender breasts, headaches, dizziness, fainting, flatulence, bleeding gums, a stuffy nose, swollen ankles and hands, leg cramps, varicose veins, nosebleeds, backache, an itchy abdomen and insomnia. And that was the list of bearable side-effects. The unbearable list included skin tags, haemorrhoids, rectal bleeding, something called the 'mask of pregnancy' which resulted in dark patches on the forehead, nose and cheeks, leaking breasts and vaginal discharges. But both books were very firm that one shouldn't ever think of pregnancy as a sickness. Heaven forbid.

I couldn't help recalling all of those stories that one heard from time to time about women who were admitted to hospital complaining of stomach pains and were surprised to find a baby popping out of their vagina. 'Goodness gracious, I had no idea! Well, now that you mention it, I *haven't* had my period for nine months, and I suppose I did gain thirty kilos, and, well, yes, I have been feeling like a plague victim crossed with a rabies epidemic, but who'd have thought? A baby! Dearie me.'

It was unsurprising, therefore, that, by the time Jack walked through the door that evening, I was in a nervous frenzy, having spent two hours familiarising myself with the new language of pregnancy and childbirth, which contained pairings of adjectives and nouns that ought *never* to be used together. (Example: 'vaginal' and 'stitches'. And 'split' and 'nipples'.)

I accosted him with the Hangman book, waving it madly in his face. 'I haven't had morning sickness!' I screeched.

'So, that's good, isn't it?'

'Not necessarily. Some experts believe that nausea is a sign of a healthy pregnancy.'

He calmly took the book from my grasp and read the page. 'It also says that about half of pregnant women don't get it at all.'

I refused to be consoled. 'That's not all. I've been drinking about three or four cups of tea a day.'

'You always do that.'

'Apparently three or more cups of tea or coffee can double, some say even *triple*, the probability of miscarriage.'

'There's not much you can do about it now,' he said sensibly. 'Just cut down to one cup of tea a day.'

'And what if I'm having an ectopic pregnancy, where the baby is growing in the fallopian tubes, not the womb?'

'Maybe you shouldn't read this book any more. It seems to be having a bad effect.'

'If I don't read it I'll probably keep doing the wrong things.' I burst into tears. 'I've drunk alcohol, I've eaten sushi, I've been having way too much caffeine, I haven't taken a single folate supplement, I don't have morning sickness or cravings and I'm not constipated. I'm a bad mother.'

'On the positive side, you don't use drugs, you don't smoke cigarettes, you don't own a black velvet Alice band and you haven't started calling me Daddy.'

'We're not ready for this. I don't know which Wiggle is which. I don't even know what colour their skivvies are. And I still couldn't care less when I look at pictures of babies. Shouldn't I *feel* something?'

'It'll be different when it's ours,' he said, putting an arm around me, which enabled me to discreetly wipe my nose on his shirt.

'What if it's not? What if I don't like it? What if it doesn't like me?'

'Then we'll take it back to the hospital and you can eat a big chocolate mousse and forget all about it.'

'I'm *serious*.'

'Well, what's the point in worrying about things that might not happen? If it *does* happen, we'll deal with it then.'

Why didn't he understand? Jack *always* understood me. 'Jack, I'm scared stiff. I mean it. I don't know if I can do this.'

He laughed and enfolded me in his arms. 'Belle, stop being such a drama queen. Once you get used to the idea, you'll be fine.'

I nestled into Jack's arms, deriving comfort from his embrace, even as I pushed away the awful feeling that he really didn't understand exactly how terrified I was of losing the life that I knew and loved.

5
Constant Craving

The following day, at least one of my fears was allayed when morning sickness kicked in with a vengeance. Although, strictly speaking, it might not have been morning sickness. There was a fairly good chance that it was actually nausea caused by a couple of paragraphs in one of the books, which described how at around twenty weeks (I had skipped ahead) the foetus was covered in something called vernix caseosa. Vernix caseosa was comprised of fat and dead skin cells and apparently looked like a coating of cheese. It was at this point that I threw up.

Four days later, I was still gagging, retching and vomiting whenever I encountered a poetic phrase such as: '*Rectal bleeding may also stem from fissures – cracks in the anus caused by constipation, which can accompany haemorrhoids or appear independently.*' Good grief. It was like reading a haiku penned by a particularly warped geisha:

Rectal bleeding flows
From cracks in poor, blocked anus
While piles sit alone.

I knew that I really didn't have too much to complain

about in the old morning sickness department, as friends of mine had related horror stories in which they had taken conference calls and attended dinner parties with their heads down the toilet for the entire first trimester. One of my friends, Kazz, who had two children, claimed that she had been ill for the entire nine months of her first child's pregnancy, which had culminated in her throwing up during labour. Apart from the baby-book-induced vomiting, the worst part was the queasy sick feeling that I got, which went away if I ate something. But still.

All my life I'd had erratic eating habits. I wasn't anorexic or bulimic or anything silly like that, but it was a fact that I only ate when I was hungry. If that meant two meals a day, then that was fine by me. Occasionally, it meant four meals a day plus snacks in between. But this new era of me as 'host organ' was horrible. I had to eat whether I liked it or not. And I most definitely did not like it.

Worse, I had to eat specifically when I felt sick. The thought of food made me sick but I also knew that eating something was the only thing that would take the sick feeling away. So I sat there, like a sullen, masochistic cow, chewing on a snot-flavoured cud.

Added to all this fun was the fact that I couldn't tell anyone that I was feeling terrible or why. We had to wait until the mystical thirteen weeks. In the close confines of the gallery, it was impossible to hide my frequent trips to the loo from Doug, so I told him that I had a urinary tract infection. He very kindly went out and bought me an enormous vat of cranberry juice and kept encouraging me to drink it, which only made things worse as the strong smell of the cranberry juice made me feel even queasier.

I kept expecting to have the passionate urge to eat ice-cream and pickles but that's not quite what happened. As it turned out, my cravings were for Cheezels, fried dim-sims and Coco Pops. Basically all of the stuff that my parents had forbidden me to eat, and that I had had to watch my schoolfriends devour while I ate soggy salad sandwiches and fruit.

The problem was that I worked in Toorak, which is hands down the snootiest, most cashed-up suburb of Melbourne. It's the type of suburb where the local convenience store stocked gluten-free chocolate figs instead of Mars Bars, and squid-ink pasta and porcini, as they were widely considered to be emergency items. Whenever there was a natural disaster in some third-world country, I always imagined the compassionate denizens of Toorak generously arranging for air-lifts of artisan pasta and washed rind cheese.

Craving crappy junk food in Toorak was like hoping that Paris Hilton would use her fame and fortune for altruistic ends: it was both foolish and futile. The only vaguely healthy food that I still wanted to eat and that was in abundance in Toorak was sushi, and I wasn't allowed that.

The situation became so desperate that I began smuggling contraband into the gallery. Every time Doug went to the toilet or out for lunch I'd frantically pour Coco Pops down my throat or reheat something deep-fried that I'd purchased on my way to work.

By far the most intolerable part, however, was the fact that I couldn't get bloody K.D. Lang's song 'Constant Craving' out of my head. It was driving me mad. To put it in perspective, 'Constant Craving' has thirty lines of lyrics. Only nine of these lines are the verses. The other twenty-one lines are the chorus, which consists solely of the words 'Constant craving / Has always been', which doesn't even make sense. Just in case her audience started to get bored, occasionally K.D. threw in the phrase 'Craving / Ah ha'. It is fair to say that, when it comes to repetitious lyrics, 'Constant Craving' comes second only to 'The Wheels on the Bus Go Round and Round'.

Compounding the problems of my new 'Elvis in the seventies' diet and K.D. Lang torture was exhaustion such as I had never before experienced. I was so damn *tired* all the time. I started sleeping in later and curling up on the couch for a nap as soon as I got home from work. I went to bed at eight o'clock. But nothing seemed to make a dint in my voracious need for sleep. I felt like the narcoleptic character that River Phoenix played in *My Own Private Idaho*, except that sadly I just had the 'falling asleep at inappropriate moments' tendency without the 'riding around on a motorbike with my arms wrapped around Keanu Reeves' bits.

One night, as Jack and I watched a television documentary on bears (oh how our social life had already changed), when they reached the part about hibernation, I startled Jack by punching my fist in the air and shouting, 'Yes! Yes! Sleep for three months! Do it! Do it NOW!'

It all became overwhelming one morning as I stood staring dully at the shower. The mere thought of having to stand up while I washed my hair was too much. I got back into my pyjamas and went back to bed.

For three days.

Because just when I thought it couldn't get any worse, it did. I got gastro-enteritis.

Suffice to say that having gastro concurrently with both morning and sleeping sickness is not one of the life experiences that Louis Armstrong had in mind when he sang 'What a Wonderful World'. I wasn't allowed to take any medication in case it harmed the baby, so I just had to let the repulsive virus run its course.

I reached my nadir while sitting on the loo and simultaneously retching into a bucket. Pregnancy sucked. If you believed the trashy magazines, pregnancy was a riot of designer maternity wear, glowing for the paparazzi and posing naked while Lucian Freud painted your portrait. My experience of pregnancy so far was cheap, bad food, hanging out in the toilet and throwing up. Either the tabloid magazines lied (say it ain't so) or else there had been a mix-up with my patron saint of pregnancy, and instead of getting Kate Moss I'd been given Pete Doherty.

Jack knocked on the bathroom door. I threw up in response, flushed the toilet and staggered out of the bathroom into his waiting arms. He helped me back into bed and gave me a sip of water.

'Can I get you anything, sweetheart?' he asked tenderly, brushing my hair back from my fevered brow.

'Potty,' I murmured.

The brushing abruptly stopped. 'What was that?'

'Potty,' I said insistently. 'Chamberpot. Bedpan. Whatever you call them these days. Can you borrow one from the hospital?'

'No I can't! What the hell do you want a bedpan for?' I couldn't help noticing that his tender bedside manner had vanished.

'I want to make a sculpture,' I said petulantly. 'What do you think I want it for? I want to go to the toilet in it.'

'What's wrong with using our actual toilet?'

'Because it's too far away,' I wailed. 'I'm so *tired*, Jack. I thought that maybe if I used a bedpan then I wouldn't have to keep getting out of bed. Maybe I could just sleep until I woke up feeling better.'

'Belle, I've been a doctor for quite a while now, and believe me I am yet to meet the patient who can sleep through the sort of bowel movements that you've been having.'

'Could you *please* not use the phrase "bowel movements"?' I begged. 'It's foul.'

'You're asking me to steal bedpans and *I'm* disgusting?'

'I didn't ask you to steal bedpans plural, I asked you to *borrow* a single bedpan which I have every intention of returning once I'm finished with it.'

'Belle, I forbid you to use a bedpan. Pregnancy only lasts nine months but our relationship has to last a lifetime. I don't think it will survive if you start using bedpans.'

'Does that mean you won't love me when I'm old and wrinkly and incontinent?'

'Not if I have to change your bedpan.'

I burst into tears.

'Isabelle, that was a *joke*,' Jack said, exasperated.

'I kno-ow,' I sobbed. 'It was ve-ery funneeeee.' I ended on a wail.

He sat down beside me on the bed and I snuggled into his arms and continued to sob.

'Belle, you have to try to calm down,' he said softly while he stroked my hair. 'Your body is doing a lot of extra work right now and your hormones are all over the place and—' he paused, then added resolutely, 'You're not the most stable person in the world at the best of times either.'

Fair point.

'It's just the tiredness that's depressing me,' I said, wiping my eyes. 'Everything is such an *effort*. How am I going to function like this for another seven months? I can't keep missing work but I can hardly even get out of bed.'

'The tiredness will go soon,' he consoled me. 'Your

body is making the placenta and that's what's sapping your energy.'

'What does the placenta do again?'

'You don't know?'

'Why should I know? I got taught all this stuff in Year Eight science. About the only thing I remember clearly is that Gail Bernhoff brought liver sandwiches to school and tried to make us believe that she was eating the placenta from her new baby brother.'

'How do you know she wasn't?' Jack asked, interested.

I looked at him in consternation.

'I'm just saying that placentophagia is a well-documented practice in some cultures,' Jack began, but stopped when I abruptly leaned over the side of the bed in order to heave into my bucket once more.

When I raised my head, Jack had opened my bedside packet of Cheezels and started to munch as he patiently waited for me to finish throwing up.

'If you ever, and I mean *ever*, mention—' I stopped and shuddered '—*eating* the placenta again, I swear I will throw up in every single pair of shoes that you own.'

Jack eyed me, decided that I was serious and threaded some Cheezels on to my fingers as a peace offering. 'Maybe you should start reading the pregnancy books again,' he suggested.

'You're the one who thought the books were doing me more harm than good and told me to stop reading them,' I reminded him, as I ate my radioactively coloured snack. 'Besides, they make me feel sick.'

'Well, now I'm changing my mind. And you're sick all the time now anyway. I think you need to know that what you're experiencing is perfectly normal.' He paused. 'Except for wanting a bedpan. That's still weird.' Before I could say anything he quickly added,

'And I'm going to make an appointment at the hospital for you. You need to see an obstetrician and book in to the midwife clinic. In the meantime, promise me you'll try to give in to the tiredness and go easy on yourself. You've never done this before, remember?'

'I promise,' I said obediently. 'I'm sure I'll be much calmer when I've been to the hospital and have more of an idea of what's going on inside me and what to expect.'

Pleased with my acquiescence, Jack kissed me. Basking in his affection, I decided against telling him that it had just occurred to me that the hospital appointment might provide the perfect opportunity to swipe a bedpan.

6

Isabelle the House

Thankfully, I had recovered from my illness and a bedpan was no longer required by the time my hospital appointment rolled around. My first appointment at the hospital's Pregnancy Booking Clinic took about three hours; two hours and forty-five minutes of which consisted of my filling in administrative forms in triplicate.

When they finally called my name to go in to see the doctor, I hastily paged Jack and then carted my nine million completed forms into the consulting room.

I stopped short when I saw Bert's familiar face. He looked equally shocked, so Jack obviously hadn't told him anything. However, Bert recovered quickly, and, after ushering me in, he closed the door behind us.

'But why have I got you?' I asked in confusion. 'Jack was going to make an appointment for me with one of the other obstetricians. He did say you were the best,' I hastened to add, in case Bert got offended, 'it was just the idea of you touching . . . and my . . . well, you know.'

Bert sighed. 'This is a public hospital. Jack probably did try to pull some strings but, when it comes down to it, you get who is available on the day and you have to be grateful for it.'

He then gave me an eloquent little talk about how, even though we knew each other on a social basis, it wouldn't compromise his professionalism. While this all sounded very reasonable, I still didn't think I'd ever be able to face him calmly over the dinner table again once he'd seen me in stirrups and probed around my labial folds.

We finally agreed that we would make the best of an awkward situation by promising not to look at the other's face during the intimate bits. I would also call him Dr Bert when seeing him in his professional capacity. He said it was unnecessary but if it made me feel better then by all means I should go ahead. Then we got down to the nitty-gritty of why I was there in the first place.

A big smile spread over Dr Bert's face as I told him about our pregnancy test but he quickly regained his professional demeanour. He then performed a supposedly highly technical version of the test that I had already taken, only his version involved me peeing into a specimen jar followed by him poking a plastic stick into it. I honestly would have preferred to see him sort through goats' entrails.

'Would you mind not telling me the result until Jack's here?' I asked quickly. Even though we already had the proof of the positive home test that I'd taken a week ago, as well as the pregnancy symptoms that had swamped my body, I still hadn't been able to shake the strange feeling of unreality surrounding the pregnancy. But I just knew that it would feel real when Dr Bert confirmed it, with the full weight of a professionally analysed urine sample to back him up. I didn't want Jack to miss out on the formal announcement.

He smiled. 'Of course. But do you mind if we keep going with some of the other routine tests while we wait for him? As a public hospital we're always under pressure time-wise unfortunately. Now, Belle, when was the last time you had a Pap smear?'

'A few years ago,' I mumbled.

'All right then, let's get you up on the bed.'

I gritted my teeth, lay back and thought of England, which was an annoying thing to have to think about under these circumstances as it reminded me of Prince Charles saying that he wanted to be Camilla Parker-Bowles's tampon, which has to be the most revolting expression of affection in the history of the world. Dr Bert then had a quick grope of my breasts, to check whether my milk glands were in. I couldn't help feeling that this was all very disorderly. In a matter of mere minutes, Dr Bert had gone from third base to second base with me. As I got up from the bed, I felt as though we should at least kiss.

Luckily, I didn't try to put this plan into action, because at that moment there was a brief knock at the door and Jack poked his head around. 'Mind if I come in?'

The next few minutes were spent going over the whole 'best mate delves into girlfriend's private bits due to pressures on public hospital system' debacle. It almost threatened to get nasty until I pointed out that Jack was too bloody late anyway, as Dr Bert had already been to second and third base with me, and it obviously wasn't going to affect our relationship as I felt nothing for him but professional respect. Bert hastily reciprocated my feelings but unfortunately he overdid it a bit, which meant we then spent the next five minutes watching Bert try to dig himself out of the 'I didn't mean that I don't think your girlfriend is attractive' hole. Jack then turned on me and demanded to know why I was calling him Dr Bert. I responded by saying that if they didn't both shut up I was going to ask my dentist to deliver this baby. And now that I mentioned it, did Jack want to know whether we were actually having a baby?

This finally made everyone calm down. Jack sat

meekly in the chair next to me and Dr Bert cleared his throat. 'Are you ready?'

We nodded.

'Well, the test you did was correct. You're having a baby. According to the dates Isabelle gave me, I'd say you're about six weeks pregnant. As a standard pregnancy lasts for forty weeks, that means that you're due around the fourth of December.'

Jack caught me up in a hug and showered me with kisses. 'We'll celebrate tonight, OK?'

'You have to go right now?' I asked, dismayed.

'I really have to. But I'm leaving you in very good hands.' He turned to Bert. 'Look after her – *them* – for me.'

Impending fatherhood seemed to have had a mellowing effect on Jack already.

Dr Bert grinned and they shook hands and punched each other on the shoulder and did all those things that blokes do when they're feeling affectionate and emotional but can't squeal. I also couldn't help staring thoughtfully at Bert's hand as it was clasped by Jack's and thinking that it was very odd that, simply because I was pregnant, having both of those hands up my so-called birth canal at varying times would be perfectly acceptable to all involved.

Jack shut the door behind him and Dr Bert resumed his professional voice. 'Do you have any questions?'

I nodded. 'How many stripes were there on the test that you just did?'

Dr Bert looked confused. 'Two.'

'You're sure?' I persisted.

'Very. One stripe means you're not pregnant, two means—'

I gestured impatiently for him to stop. 'What does three stripes mean?'

He stared at me. 'There's no such thing.'

'There *is*. Jack can back me up on this. The pregnancy test that I did showed three stripes. Does it mean I'm having triplets?'

'The only way of determining a multiple pregnancy is via ultrasound. I'll book you in to have one when you reach twelve weeks. But unless there's a history of twins or multiples in your families I think it's unlikely. Anything else?'

I hesitated.

He looked at me and grinned. 'Let me guess. You drank alcohol during the past six weeks before you knew you were pregnant?'

'Yes,' I said gratefully.

'How much?'

'I'm not entirely sure. I definitely drank some wine at dinner with you and Mona the other night.'

'We'll be able to tell more after the first ultrasound when we get the measurements back, but I'm quite sure you haven't done any damage.'

Growing bolder, I ventured, 'I also ate some sushi. A few weeks ago.'

'How much?'

'A couple of salmon and avocado and prawn handrolls,' I said, my eyes growing dreamy at the memory.

'Again, unlikely to have done any harm. But generally it's not recommended for pregnant women to eat raw fish. So no more from now on.'

'And I had bacon and eggs and the egg yolk was runny and I ate brie and I haven't been taking folate supplements and a yoga instructor sat on my stomach and squashed me,' I disclosed in a rush, deciding to make a clean breast of it.

Dr Bert blinked. 'I beg your pardon?'

'I said I ate a runny egg yolk and—'

He waved his hands impatiently in the air. 'No, no. The last bit. Your yoga instructor *sat* on you, did you say?'

I nodded miserably. 'Right on my stomach. And he was quite heavy.'

'But . . . but *why* did he sit on you?'

'Not sure,' I mumbled. 'I had my eyes shut and was lying down so I didn't know he was about to sit on me or I would have asked him not to. But by then he had already sat on me and it was too late because I didn't want to interrupt his singing.'

'He was singing?'

'Yes.'

'While he sat on you?'

'Yes.'

'But in the name of God, *why*?'

'No idea.'

Dr Bert pondered this for a long moment. 'What was he singing?'

'Pardon?'

'What song was he singing?'

'"Dancin' On the Ceiling",' I said, annoyed. 'Look, what difference does it make what song he was singing? Did he hurt the baby?'

'How pregnant were you when this happened?'

I thought hard. 'Not sure. Maybe five or six days.'

His lips twitched suspiciously. 'Oh. Ah, then I think you're probably fine. But probably best not to let him sit on you again. And no more brie for you either.' As I nodded, Dr Bert looked at me kindly. 'Would it be fair to say that you're a bit anxious about this pregnancy, Belle?'

'Not really.' I most definitely wasn't a *bit* anxious. I think it was fair to say that I was rapidly approaching the level of fear and paranoia normally reserved for internet conspiracy theorists.

Dr Bert leaned back in his chair and steepled his hands together. 'You need to think of yourself as a house for your baby. Any emotional or physical disturbances are like earthquakes, shaking the house. So the calmer you can be during the coming months the better it will be for both you and your baby. It's very important that you try to stay calm and don't get upset about things that don't matter.'

I looked at him and nodded in a calm, Zen-like fashion while terrifying images from the childbirth book, the even worse horror of having to tell Cruella that I was pregnant and the memory of being sat on by a chanting yoga instructor chased each other through my mind.

Dr Bert picked up a pen and started to make notes on my file. 'Have you had morning sickness?'

'Yes.'

'Simple remedies are often the best for morning sickness – always keep a snack on hand and try drinking ginger tea and staying away from the things that trigger your nausea.'

'So I shouldn't read the pregnancy books?' I asked, anxious to be perfectly clear on this point.

'I beg your pardon?'

'I'm having trouble reading the pregnancy books because they make me throw up,' I explained.

'That *can* happen,' Dr Bert said tentatively. 'Some women find the photographs of the developing foetus and childbirth too graphic.'

I shuddered at the memory but had to set him straight. 'The photographs do gross me out, which is why I avoided the books with photographs. I bought one with line drawings instead.'

Dr Bert looked perplexed. 'So how are the books making you sick?'

'It's the text. It's when they talk about things like the embryo's eyelids developing. Just thinking about a pair of eyelids growing in my stomach makes me feel like I'm going to vomit.'

Wisely, Dr Bert avoided the whole freaky eyelids tangent and focused on the germane issue. 'Isabelle, we're going to keep a close watch on you and your baby, so try to remember that everything that's happening to your body and your moods is perfectly normal and happens to every pregnant woman.' He paused and then added, 'Although, I must say, you are the first patient of mine to voice concerns about three stripes on your pregnancy test and being sat on.'

I found Dr Bert's advice extremely calming and, as I left his consulting room, I felt ridiculously pleased with myself that I hadn't seriously maimed or injured our baby through my bad dietary habits or carelessness in allowing yoga instructors to perch on my abdomen while they serenaded Hindu gods.

Perhaps there wasn't only a new baby growing inside me. Maybe, just maybe, nestled deep down, somewhere close to our baby and my worn-out sundial, there was the faintest beginnings of my maternal instinct.

7
Are You Ready, Boots?

Being Melbourne, even though it was only the middle of April, crisp autumn days had already started to give way to seriously cold mornings. During my years in the far balmier Sydney I had almost forgotten how the first cold snap in Melbourne heralded shopping expeditions for electric blankets, beanies, gloves, scarves and all of the accoutrements needed to survive the bitterly cold Melbourne winter. This year, at the top of my shopping list was a new coat and a pair of boots. The only problem was, as I would soon resemble a reverse camel, the sort of coat that I would usually purchase (brightly coloured with a tie around the waist) and the sort of boots that I would normally head straight for (knee-high, black leather, high heels and kick-arse) were clearly not going to cut it.

After several miserable hours spent trawling through endless racks of coats and dismissing all those that were too stylish (i.e. had a flattering cut so wouldn't do up over an ever-inflating basketball), in desperation I finally paid for a coat that resembled nothing so much as Paddington Bear's duffel coat. It might actually have been Paddington Bear's duffel coat. By this stage I didn't care. I needed something to keep me warm, and this was the only one that would do the job in the coming months. This fact alone outweighed the considerable negatives of it being navy blue and having hideous buttons as well as the ability to house a small family in the event of a natural disaster.

By the time I reached my favourite shoe store in Collins Street, I had a fair idea of how the 'shoe shopping while pregnant' mission was going to pan out. One of my pregnancy books had been extremely strict on the subject of shoes. According to the author, if I continued to wear high heels I would be endangering the life of my unborn baby (falls down stairs caused by my unwieldy body teetering on stilettos) as well as increasing my risk of backache and sciatica. (Not that being pregnant meant you were sick of course.)

So while all around me hordes of shiny young things were trying on strappy sandals (with winter approaching, I ask you), I was the one pointing dully at a pair of extremely boring, sensibly soled, flat-heeled 'Ugh' boots.

With my feet encased by practicality, the sales girl and I regarded the boots solemnly. For the first time in my life I understood what a horse felt like when it was shod. At the sales girl's suggestion, I clumped unenthusiastically around the store a few times while merry banter flew around me.

'Do you have these rhinestone-encrusted Chinese slippers in a size seven?' asked a girl who looked uncannily like Aussie supermodel Miranda Kerr.

'No. Sorry. We've almost sold out of those. And we're running low on the gold wedges and the turquoise stilettos too.'

'That's such a shame. They would have gone perfectly with the coat that I just bought,' Miranda said regretfully, pulling out of her bag the softest, most beautiful white woollen coat, complete with cute faux-fur-lined snow-bunny hood.

'I think I need a half-size smaller,' I said in a voice that was also half its normal size, gesturing towards the boots I was trying on, while trying not to compare Miranda's stylish coat with the navy tent that I had just purchased.

'What? Oh, sure thing. We've got millions of those boots in stock.'

Somewhere inside me, the hotpants-wearing, table-top-dancing party girl that I had once been started to bawl. This was not *me*. I was not an ugly coat and flat, sensible shoes girl. Goddammit, I was a turquoise stiletto kind of a girl. The last sensible shoes I had bought were gumboots to wear to take Rufus walking in the very muddy park. And even those had been designer gumboots with a pink Pucci swirl pattern.

I looked wistfully at a pair of Charlie's Angel, sexy, kick-arse boots that I would have normally paid for without even trying on.

The sales girl saw my look and smiled. 'Aren't they fabulous? Would you like me to get your size in those?'

As they were also considerably more expensive, before I could answer she bustled off, before returning a moment later with a large box.

I swapped the horse shoes for the Charlie's Angel boots and rejoiced for a brief moment in my reflection in the mirror.

'I think you should get those ones,' Miranda said firmly, as she pulled on a pair of gloriously impractical peep-toe pumps in lemon suede.

'Normally I would,' I said regretfully. 'It's just—' It felt very odd to say it aloud, and in the back of my mind was the thirteen-week prohibition, but somehow I forced the words out. 'I'm pregnant, and I don't think it'll be very practical to be tottering around on these with a big belly.'

It was as though my fairy godmother had waved a magic wand. All of a sudden bad-taste girl disappeared and in her place was a potential yummy mummy.

'You're pregnant?' The sales girl looked genuinely excited for me. 'Congratulations! When are you due?'

'Um, December. Right at the beginning.'

'My sister just had a baby,' Miranda chipped in.

'Boy or girl? What did they call it?' The sales girl had hardly drawn breath.

'A little boy. His name's Darryl,' Miranda said proudly. 'Do you know what you're having?'

'Er, no,' I said, startled to find myself the centre of attention and reeling from the knowledge that in this day and age there were still people naming their kids Darryl.

'It's much better to have a surprise,' the sales girl said, nodding her head.

'I suppose so. But if you know what you're having it's easier to buy clothes and nursery things,' said Miranda wisely.

I sat there in silence while they batted around the pros and cons of finding out your baby's gender. It was peculiar. Sometimes I forgot that just because I wasn't terribly interested in babies other people were. Whatever it was, I didn't care. Because now I was no longer bad-taste girl. I was bad-taste girl for a specific reason and duration.

It was while musing on this last point that something occurred to me. So I was going to be pregnant for most of this year. These boots should last longer than one season, and there was really no reason I had to conform to some vague mummy composite that I had conjured up out of my own mother, my sister Audrey, Carol Brady and, for some unfathomable reason, the woman on the Brand Power commercials.

'I've made up my mind.' Resolutely I took off the Charlie's Angel boots and packed them back into the box. I beamed at the sales girl and Miranda, as I picked up the box. 'I'm taking these ones.'

'Those ones? Are you sure?'

I grinned. 'I'm positive. They're exactly my style.'

After the shoe shop, it just got easier and easier to say it.

'I'm pregnant,' I said reprovingly to a bemused man in the Bourke Street Mall who was handing out flyers for free cups of coffee. 'I'm not allowed to drink coffee.'

'I'm pregnant,' I informed the girl in the café who was making my sandwich, when she asked in a perfunctory manner how I was. She looked startled and I patted my still-flat tummy. 'That's why my coat is so ugly,' I confided.

She nodded thoughtfully and moved all the knives a little further back on the bench.

I decided to experiment. 'I'm expecting,' I confided to the man sitting next to me on the tram home. 'A baby,' I added, just to be sure that we were absolutely clear on the crucial point. He smiled in a distant way and then put up his newspaper as a barrier between us, the way that normal people do when they find themselves in close proximity with a nutter on public transport.

While it was quite fun voicing my secret aloud to strangers, after weeks of silent suffering with morning sickness, I had to admit that, after only a few hours of saying it aloud, the stock phrases were already starting to get a little repetitive. However, I couldn't quite bring myself to say that I had a bun in the oven or that I was up the duff. 'With child' and 'begetting' sounded quasi-religious, while 'knocked up' suggested a violent accident and 'in the family way' sounded like a bad American television sitcom.

There were more poetic phrases I could have used, such as 'I'm blossoming' or 'I'm propagating', but, when coupled with hand gestures indicating my lower regions, they may have left my confidant in some confusion as to whether I was having a child or had unnaturally flowering pubic hair.

'I'm gestating' had a semi-scientific sound to it, as did 'I'm parturient', but that wasn't strictly accurate until I was much further along. 'I've been inseminated' seemed like entirely too much information and was repulsive to boot, as was 'fecund' and 'burgeoning'. Spawning was downright demonic, while 'I'm breeding' suggested that I would be giving birth to a well-mannered horse.

There really ought to be some other word or phrase for it. Something a bit more dignified and important sounding. Like 'progenitoring'. Or 'descendanteering'. Luckily, providing none of the strangers that I had confided my secret to knew my friends or family in a spooky six-degrees-of-Kevin-Bacon kind of way, I still had about seven weeks to find the perfect phrase with which to break the news to my nearest and dearest of one of the most momentous events of my life.

Second Trimester

8
Pregnancy Pictionary

It was both the start of June and a bitterly cold winter and I was now about thirteen weeks pregnant. As Jack had predicted, the morning sickness, tiredness and endless trips to the loo had all abated. Apart from having breasts like flexible concrete, most of the time I felt almost normal, physically speaking. On the emotional front, even a toilet-paper commercial could bring me to tears, and keeping a secret did *not* agree with me psychologically, but by continuing to inform complete strangers of my delicate condition I had managed thus far to resist the temptation to spill the beans to anyone who actually knew us. Luckily, we would be able to tell everyone next week, once we received the test results back from the ultrasound that was scheduled for today.

Waiting for Jack to join me, I was filling in more forms at the hospital when I was startled by the receptionist pleasantly enquiring as to whether I'd like to purchase a DVD.

'Of what?' I asked, looking around for suitably hospital-themed entertainment such as *Grey's Anatomy* or *House*.

'Of your ultrasound.'

'You can buy a *movie* of the ultrasound?'

'Of course. They're very popular. Especially as we

don't offer the 4D ultrasounds in the public hospital system.'

I didn't consider this a disadvantage. I had seen images from 4D ultrasounds in some of the pregnancy books and all of the babies looked like the mutant offspring of Mr Potato Head and a car sponge.

'But – but what's on the DVD?' I floundered.

The receptionist looked at me as though I was mad. '*Your baby*,' she enunciated very slowly.

'Yes, I realise that, but it won't actually be *doing* anything, will it?'

Why she was still giving me the Crazy Lady stare I had no idea. I mean, really. It's not like the foetus was skulking around the womb carrying on like Robert De Niro in *Taxi Driver*. We were talking about a creature whose major accomplishment during the past fortnight had been to develop nostrils.

While clearly there was money to be made from new parents' excitement about their offspring, things were going too far. Before we knew it we'd be compiling DVDs of our child's life in which the ultrasound video would be preceded by Mummy and Daddy's sex tape of the conception. And in a civilised society, only Pamela Anderson's children ought to have easy access to their parents' sex tapes.

I didn't like my chances of conveying my strong feelings on this subject to the receptionist, however, so I politely declined and paged Jack once more, wishing, not for the first time, that he had the sort of job that meant he could be on time for appointments once in a while. But, before I could get stroppy, he rushed in, kissed me, and then we were shown into the room for the ultrasound.

Being pregnant was starting to feel a little like being a sex worker. One was forever being ushered into dimly lit rooms to allow complete strangers (or, in the case of Dr Bert, my partner's best friend) to do intimate things to you. Now, for example, despite the fact that the operator hadn't even introduced himself, I meekly followed his instructions to lie down and then lay quite passively as he pulled down my skirt and spread something cold and sticky on my stomach.

The operator applied an instrument to my belly. There was a muffled static sound and then, a few moments later, we heard it for the first time.

It was a heartbeat.

To my complete and utter surprise, my eyes filled with tears. Jack, who was sitting in a chair next to the bed, grasped my hand and squeezed it tightly. Neither of us said a word.

We just sat there, holding our breath, listening to our baby's heart beating away and waiting for the picture on the monitor to come into focus.

Which I'm not sure that it ever entirely did. Because, quite frankly, looking at an ultrasound is a bit like playing Pictionary. You screw your eyes up, focus on something vaguely recognisable and then project wildly. The only problem was, for someone who worked in the art world, I was quite crap at Pictionary.

I squinted and made a concerted effort. 'Is that, um, hair?'

The operator and Jack looked at me doubtfully.

'You wouldn't be able to see hair,' the operator intoned, with what could only be described as malicious satisfaction. He then turned to Jack and launched into a conversation where medical terms such as 'amniotic fluid' and 'nuchal fold' were flung around far too jauntily for my liking.

I gave up trying to follow what they were saying after about two minutes and focused on the strange little pulsating and glowing jellybean on the screen instead.

There is something very weird about the fact that our idea of what an extraterrestrial looks like is firmly grounded in the appearance of a foetus. It's all there – the oversized head, the translucent skin, the visible vertebrae and the spooky waving limbs. So, when we had to come up with the most alien thing from the human race that we could possibly imagine, that's what we based it on. A developing human baby. This was not an especially comforting thought.

The operator broke off from his conversation with Jack to ask, 'Do you want to know what sex it's going to have?'

I couldn't help thinking that this was a weird way of putting it. Would you like to know whether your child is gay, straight or has an inclination towards small furry creatures called Larry? Why, yes, thank you, that would be lovely so we know to buy it a goldfish rather than a hamster called Larry for its thirteenth birthday.

I looked at Jack. 'Do you want to know?'

He shrugged. 'Dunno. Do you?'

'Dunno. What do you reckon?'

Good lord. We sounded like teenage hoodlums discussing whether to hang out in front of the local Subway or 7-Eleven on a Saturday night.

The operator cleared his throat loudly but I spoke over the top of him. 'It might be nice to wait. Sort of like a Christmas surprise.'

'Oh. OK.' Jack looked disappointed.

'But if you want to find out . . .'

Jack brightened. 'OK.'

'What do you mean – OK?'

'I mean, that's a good solution. I'll find out but I won't tell you.'

'No frigging way.'

'Why not?'

'Do you honestly think I'll let you find out if I don't know?'

'I don't see why not.'

'Well, you wouldn't be able to keep it a secret for all that time anyway.'

'I would too.'

'But I'd try to get it out of you. Every minute of the day.'

'You don't want to know! You just said so.'

'Yes, but if you knew I'd want to know.'

'That's completely irrational. Why should you want to know what I know when you said that you didn't want to know?'

The operator heaved a deep sigh. I turned my head towards him and said, with as much dignity as it was possible to muster while lying flat on my back with my tummy smeared with jelly, 'Could you just give us a few more moments please? I'm sorry but we hadn't considered this yet.'

He started to object but this time Jack interjected. 'If we know whether it's a boy or a girl we can start calling it something other than "it".'

'Personal pronouns are not a good enough reason. Anyway, we can give it a nickname.'

'You're the one who practically threw up every time Audrey and Henry referred to Felix as Bambino.'

'Yes, and that was bad enough, but then they shortened it to Bambi. I kept looking over Audrey's shoulder in case there was a hunter lurking near by who was trying to shoot her.'

'If we don't know what sex it is, what are we going to call it for the next six months?'

I thought for a moment. 'We could call it Cruella.'

'Why on earth would you want to name it after *her*?'

'Because, right now, the only thing that freaks me out more than this baby is Cruella. It seems sort of appropriate.'

'What if it has some kind of unconscious effect and the baby grows up to be like Cruella?'

'Oh *God*. All right, you choose a nickname.'

'How about Elvis?'

'*Elvis?*'

He nodded happily. 'Think about it. When you've given birth, we can say—' he cupped his hands around his mouth to make a funnel '—ladies and gentlemen, Elvis has left the building.'

'Bert said I'm a house, not a building,' I said crossly. 'This is ridiculous. Let's just call it bèbè.'

'Why does it have to be French? Neither of us is French!'

'Because it sounds more like an affectionate nickname that way. We can't just call it "baby".'

'Technically it's not a baby until twenty-seven weeks,' Jack pointed out.

'If you'll *excuse* me,' the operator snapped loudly.

Surprised by the frostiness of his tone, Jack and I both fell quiet and looked at him.

'If you had only let me finish, I *was* going to say that, if you do want to know the sex, I'll make a note on your file for the week-twenty ultrasound. We're unable to determine gender accurately until then anyway.'

Crestfallen, Jack and I were subdued for the rest of the examination.

Several minutes later, we emerged from the room clutching a blurry photograph of the Pictionary squiggle. I paused in the hospital corridor and peered intently at it. 'Do you think we're having a boy or a girl?'

'Dunno. What do you reckon?'

Oh for Pete's sake. We were back to hanging out the

front of the 7-Eleven again.

Not wanting to get sidetracked into another disagreement, I instead demanded, 'How could you not know about the twenty-week thing for finding out the sex? You're a doctor!'

He looked sheepish. 'Of course I knew. You just have a unique talent for making me forget the salient points during an argument.'

Deciding that this sounded like a compliment if I didn't think about it too hard, mollified, I allowed Jack to pull me close and rest his chin on my shoulder. Together we gazed at the photograph of our baby alien. It was then that I had an inspiration.

'Let's call it Fetid. I don't mean as its proper name,' I added, as Jack recoiled in horror. 'I just mean as something to call it until it's born.'

'But why? You hate that painting as much as I do.'

'Cate says that we should look at it as a symbol of our mutual love and sacrifice.'

'The only thing that painting symbolises is the stupidity of shopping when you're hungover. When *we're* hungover,' he amended hastily, taking in the expression on my face.

'But it's ours,' I insisted stubbornly. 'And even though it was scary at first we've learned to live with it and we're used to it now.' As the words tumbled out of me, I gradually became aware of why I was pushing so hard for this nickname.

However, Jack, who was coming at the having-a-baby situation from a far less fearful angle than I was, still looked unconvinced. 'If you want to name it after something that's a part of our lives, why don't we call it Rufus?'

My face filled with disappointment. 'You want to name our child after our *dog*? Jack, how could you?'

Jack looked at me helplessly. 'Only you,' he muttered. 'Only with you would I ever end up in a conversation having to defend myself for wanting to name the baby after the dog. Only you would make me even *think* about naming our child after the dog.'

He sighed as his pager went off again. He looked at me apologetically and I smiled. 'It's OK. Go!'

He kissed me, then tilted my hand that was holding the ultrasound photograph so that he could have another proper look. 'You know, it kind of looks like a Fetid.'

I beamed. After he'd gone I gazed at the photo once more. I didn't care what that operator said: I could definitely see Fetid the foetus's hair.

9
Show & Tell

The ultrasound tests had come back normal and I was now a week past the sacred thirteen-week taboo, so we were finally allowed to tell everyone that we were having a baby. But, while Jack was excited, I was suddenly ambivalent. Breaking the news to complete strangers had admittedly been fun, but I had seen what happened to friends of mine after they came out of the pregnancy closet. The pregnancy became the sole topic of conversation for the next six months.

I couldn't put it off forever, though, so we rang Jack's parents in Sydney first. They were thrilled and excited and wanted to know when we were getting married and if we weren't whose surname the baby would take. Then we rang my parents who lived in Broome in Western Australia. They were also thrilled and excited until my mother asked me who else we had told.

This was a minefield and we both knew it. 'Who else have you told?' really meant 'Who do you rank higher in importance than your own parents?'

I thought about replying: my doctor, a shoe-shop assistant, a customer who was in the shoe shop at the same time, a guy who offered me a free coffee, a sandwich maker in a café, a man on the tram who thought that I was a nutter and the ultrasound operator. And about a dozen other random strangers. But somehow I didn't think that would go down very well.

I mumbled something about having told Jack's parents only ten seconds before, which still seemed to be ten seconds' worth of preferential treatment too much for Mum. My father then asked whether we intended to get married, and, when I said no, my mother asked whose surname the baby was going to take.

'I don't know. Jack's, I suppose. Boyd is easier to spell than Beckett.'

'So you're going to have a different surname from your child? Oh dear.'

'That's about as undesirable as getting married simply to change my name,' I retorted, starting to get annoyed. This was not how I had envisaged the breaking of the news to the grandparents-to-be. I had thought it would result in general jubilation and promises of hand-knitted bootees.

Of everyone I had to tell, the person I was least looking forward to sharing the news with was Cate. I knew it made no sense. She was my best friend. She would be thrilled for me.

And yet – I was dreading it.

Cate and I had been friends since primary school. We had been through everything together. Slumber parties, using make-up for the first time, overseas holidays, relationship break-ups, job changes, moving house . . . the list was as long as our lives.

In fact, only two things had ever come between us. The first was when I had moved to Sydney, which hadn't really mattered much as we'd still stayed in touch over the telephone. But the dogs had been a different matter entirely.

Cate had a spoodle called Shnoodle whom I adored. He was the single exception that proved my dislike of little dogs rule. Cate and I had often talked about how much fun it would be when I had a dog too, so that we could take them both to the park and go for long walks on the weekend together.

Only it hadn't turned out that way. From the moment they first laid eyes on each other, Rufus and Shnoodle hated one another with an internecine and implacable enmity. You would have thought they were respectively descendants of the Montagues and Capulets the way they were constantly at each other's throat. We attempted one or two Sunday-afternoon walks together, but the constant snarling and eruptions of hostility were unbearable.

Our dogs' hatred of one another hadn't driven a wedge between us, but it had been weird to have something that was an important part of my life – in this case, Rufus – and not to be able to share it with Cate.

My chief concern with breaking the news to Cate about our baby, though, was that Cate didn't want children. This didn't mean that she disliked children or being around them – in fact, quite the reverse. As a trained counsellor, Cate had a soothing presence that kids responded to well, and she was far more comfortable holding small babies than I was.

But I also knew that, however much Cate would be happy for me, this was something that we would not be doing together. And it was going to be a much bigger part of my life than adopting a dog. I also knew what happened to friendships when one friend had a baby and the other didn't. Despite the very best of intentions, it signalled a lifestyle change that couldn't be fought against. Friends who had previously been up for drinks or a movie at a moment's notice now required a week of advance planning to get out of the house. Long conversations on the telephone became brief, harried exchanges, which were instantly abandoned if the baby started to cry or woke up from a nap. If I hadn't exactly lost friends who had become mothers while I maintained my carefree existence, it was fair to say that they had slipped away. And I most definitely didn't want to slip away from Cate.

As we hugged hello and sat down at one of the little tables in the Carlisle Street Wine Bar, I was still trying to figure out the best way to tell her. I was about to launch straight in when the waiter came over to take our drinks order.

'I'll have a glass of the Margaret River shiraz,' Cate said, after a brief glance at the drinks menu.

I sighed wistfully. 'I'll have a – um –' I cast around wildly in my mind for a non-alcoholic drink. 'A cider, please.'

The waiter looked at me in disbelief. 'A *cider*?'

'Yes,' I said defensively. 'Apple cider. The sparkling kind. No ice. With a twist of lemon.' As he departed, every little sommelier fibre in his being twitching with outrage, I called out, 'A '92 vintage if you've got it.'

I turned back to Cate, intending to comment on the pretentiousness of wine bars, but stopped when I saw that she was staring at me with her mouth wide open. 'Oh my God,' she said slowly. 'You're pregnant.'

'You can't assume that just because I ordered a non-alcoholic drink!' I protested. 'I'm not that much of a lush.'

'Belle, we're at a *wine* bar. And I've known you for over twenty years and I have never in my life seen you drink cider. You are, aren't you?'

I took a deep breath and then nodded.

Just for a moment, the merest split second, I saw in her eyes the expression that I had been dreading. It was sadness. But then it closed over and she sprang up and enfolded me in a hug. 'Darling, that's wonderful! Congratulations! When are you due?'

'December.'

'Is Jack over the moon? He must be.'

'Of course he is. But, Cate, I want you to know, I don't want this to change things. I don't want to end up one of those women who can only ever talk about babies or being pregnant.'

She looked relieved. 'Thank God. I know you won't be like that, of course, but I really don't think I could bear it if all you ever talked about was teething or playgroup and all the rest of it. It's so *boring*.'

It was exactly what I thought. It was exactly how I felt when parents waffled on to me about the achievements of their offspring. I changed the subject quickly. 'I had to see Bert to have the pregnancy confirmed.' As she opened her mouth to ask the obvious question I cut her off. 'No, Jack couldn't do it for various reasons. Don't ask. I'm not sure I understand. But it was a good thing anyway because it reminded me that I still think we should try to set you up with him.'

'Belle, I know he's Jack's best friend, but his name is *Bert*, for God's sake. I always picture him at the lawn-bowls club.'

'Playing lawn bowls is very cool these days,' I protested. 'And I know he has a ridiculous name but that can't be the only reason that you're not interested. You keep saying that you're sick of being single and dating people with no long-term potential, and Bert's lovely and he says *exactly* the same thing to Jack.'

'I thought you said he had a new girlfriend called Mona?'

'He does. But she's definitely not going to last.'

'Why not?'

'I think they both realise that alone their names are

bad enough but together they're ridiculous. I mean – Bert and Mona? It just reeks of carpet slippers and Horlicks.'

'He is cute,' Cate conceded. 'Which just makes me think there must be something hideously wrong with him if he's still single at his age. Are you sure he doesn't have a wife stashed away somewhere? He probably does wear a wedding ring and you just haven't noticed.'

'You're only a few years younger than he is and you're single and there's nothing wrong with you,' I retaliated. 'And of course he doesn't wear a wedding ring. Not only have I looked, I'd know because I would have felt it when he – never mind.'

Cate blanched. 'Why do I feel as though I'm getting your leftovers?'

'Don't be silly. We're intimate for purely professional reasons.'

'Still. I'm not sure that I want to be in a relationship with someone who's put their hand up my best friend's—'

'Who's talking about a relationship? That's half your problem! You always fly ten steps ahead. Just go on a date with him.'

'No thanks. I don't want some cheesy semi-blind-date set-up. And I certainly don't want to "drop around" when he and Jack are watching the footy. If I want to be ignored by a man whose attention I'm trying to get, I'll attempt to order food from the waiters at Ladro like everyone else.'

'You could come to my next appointment with me,' I suggested.

She gave an eloquent shudder. 'Forget it. I don't date men with girlfriends.'

'If he breaks up with Mona, will you reconsider?'

'Nope. He's an obstetrician, for God's sake. He's

probably dying to settle down, get married and deliver his own ten children. I don't think we'd suit.'

I gave up and we spent the remainder of our catch-up on our usual conversational topics of mutual friends and work. Our vocations were poles apart and we shared the sort of fascination with one another's work that you usually experienced when viewing an exotic animal at the zoo. Cate loved hearing about the art world and Cruella, who she firmly believed was missing her true vocation as a corporate raider. On the other hand, I was endlessly intrigued by Cate's job as a director for a huge consultancy firm. I still wasn't entirely sure exactly what it was she did at work but had a vague idea that it involved initiating and implementing strategies for the benefit of key stakeholders. Even after all these years, I had no clear picture of who exactly these stakeholders were, but I always pictured a mob of villagers setting forth, wooden stakes in hand, to kill the local vampire, which made me slightly envious of Cate's far more exciting job.

Despite her hectic work schedule, Cate still somehow managed to find a few hours each week to volunteer for a counselling telephone service that she had worked for since we were at university. Cate wasn't at liberty to discuss all of the conversations she had with callers but she did occasionally share the more unusual ones with me. Recent calls had included a dwarf-tosser who was trying to break the habit; Warren, who was forty-eight but liked dressing up in nappies; and an anonymous caller who I was convinced was Doug, as he had confessed to wanting to kill his hideous boss by hitting her over the head with Jake the Peg's extra leg.

It was only after I left the bar that I realised that, despite breaking the biggest news of my life to Cate, we had still ended up having a conversation that was mainly about her love life and work. Not that I minded. I had deliberately diverted the conversation so that I could prove that I was not going to be one of those women whose sole topic of conversation was babies and pregnancy. In a weird way I felt quite proud of myself. Perhaps it signalled that some things were going to stay the same.

10
Aunt Audie

Four years ago, my sister Audrey had married her long-suffering boyfriend, Henry. They had had a very stylish country-style wedding where all the stationery, decorations and bonbonnière had been designed and made by Audie. She hadn't had a honeymoon as much as a recuperative holiday following her nervous breakdown from the stress of organising every last detail of the event, but they were very happy together, as evinced by the emergence of my nephew Felix a year later, and then the twins, Noah and Margot, who were now eight months old.

Energy that Audie had previously poured into organising elaborate dinner parties for eight with a Tunisian theme or to ensuring that the space under the fridge was spotless, she now lavished on her children. The twins were still only little, but Felix was a normal, healthy toddler who I had christened the Boy in the Bubble. This was due to Audie's habit of only feeding Felix organic, locally grown produce and dressing him in natural fibres. A piece of white bread making its way towards Felix's mouth could send Audie diving across the room like a champion rugby player, in order to tackle the offending item and bring it to the ground before it could damage her darling child's digestive system. Felix also had books read to him in French and had already started to learn ballet. He was three years old. At this rate he'd have read Proust in the original before he started kindergarten and would no doubt be a member of the Australian Ballet before he was fully toilet-trained.

My sister Audrey and I had always been reasonably close, but since the advent of her children she had unfortunately developed a few conversational habits that made me want to dismember her with a chainsaw. As the proud mother of three sprogs, Audie was firmly of the opinion that childless women didn't know what they were missing. She was like a Mothercare missionary, and her constant hints to Jack and me about 'not leaving it too late' had driven me insane and imbued me with the desire to bite the head off Felix's teddy bear.

Knowing that I had to break the news to Audie, I was trying to explain the situation to Jack. 'She's the sort of person who believes that when a couple gets a dog they're practising for kids. That pets are only substitute children.'

'Well, we are having a kid after getting a dog a few years ago,' he said reasonably.

'That has nothing to do with it! I *like* dogs. I did not get a dog with a view to undertaking some bizarre inter-species Mummy-training. Besides which, having a baby is nothing like owning a dog.'

'They're kind of the same. You have to feed them and worm them and clean up their poo.'

'Dogs don't talk back. I didn't have to give birth to Rufus or breastfeed him. And, most importantly, his life expectancy at best is about fifteen years. Right about the time he'd start yelling that he never asked to be born, he'll probably cark it. It's perfect.' I paused and then admitted shamefully, 'I've occasionally had fantasies about never procreating just to spite Audie. She's the human equivalent of a "Baby on Board!" bumper sticker. She fills me with rage and makes me want to deliberately drive my car into her. Just when this topic comes up, you understand,' I clarified. 'The rest of the time I love her.'

'Remember what Bert told you about the earthquake,' Jack said anxiously. 'Earthquakes are no good for the house.'

'You see?' I moaned. 'And this is the effect that she has on me under *normal* circumstances. She's going to be *ecstatic* when she finds out that I'm pregnant. It'll confirm all her beliefs and I just know that she'll start treating me like some sort of initiated member of her Secret Mother's Sect.'

'What do you think their password is?' Jack asked, diverted by the idea of a Secret Mother's Sect.

'Mastitis,' I said gloomily.

'You know what I think, Belle?'

'What?'

'I think that in your usual Isabelle fashion you're blowing this up into something much bigger than it needs to be. Why don't we go round there this weekend and get it out of the way?'

I shook my head. 'If we have to do it, I want it to be on neutral ground. Audie loves weirdly timed meals like brunch and supper. I'll organise for all of us to go out for afternoon tea on Sunday.'

Jack consented to this plan but I still wasn't happy. This wasn't going to be good.

I had chosen to break the news to Audie in one of those Devonshire tea houses in the Dandenong Ranges that was cluttered with gingham curtains and patchwork cushions, and was run by the sort of people who collected china cats. Audie loved that kind of stuff, and

I hoped that, by telling her in an environment she would find pleasant, she might tone down the over-the-top 'Welcome to Mummydom' reaction that I feared.

But it was worse than I had anticipated. Audie didn't say a word. She didn't even smile. She just looked at me, her eyes welling with tears, and then she swept me into a hug. I repressed the urge to bite her neck and made eye contact with Jack over her shoulder while I stood limply, with her arms wrapped around me. Catching the dangerous look in my eye, he stared pleadingly at me and drew the shape of a house in the air, reminding me that I could no longer give in to earthquakes.

When Audie finally released me, she clasped my hands in hers and led me over to a corner armchair near the window. Fussing over me, she placed about thirty-six patchwork cushions around me so that I was more uncomfortable than I had been in the mosh pit at the last Big Day Out. Then she shooed Jack and Henry away.

'Go away, you two. Take the kids outside to feed the rosellas. We need some private girls' time.'

'No we don't,' I said desperately, shooting a look at Jack that said, 'If you move a single step from this room, this is the last child you'll have because I will personally remove your penis with a rusty hacksaw.'

But Henry handed Felix to Jack and steered the double pram containing the twins through the French doors. 'We'll leave the Mummies to it,' he said, with a wink.

'No! Please don't go!' It burst out of me but it was too late. The doors had already shut behind them.

Audie turned to smile at me and I was in agony. She was my sister and I loved her. She was such a good person. She really was. And in about ten minutes, barring divine intervention, I was probably going to grab the framed sampler hanging on the wall behind her that read 'Blood is thicker than water' and throw it at her head.

'Let's get comfortable and have a proper chat.' She squeezed my hand. 'Ah – here's the waiter. What would you like to drink?'

'An English Breakfast tea please.'

Wrong.

Audie's smile faded. 'You're not still drinking tea, are you?'

'Well, that is the customary way to consume it. Would you prefer that I ate it?'

'But what about *the baby*?' she remonstrated.

'Fine.' I turned to the waiter. 'One English Breakfast and a babycino. Audie, what are you having?'

She turned to the waiter and said with a steely smile, 'Can you give us a few minutes?' He was barely out of earshot when she hissed, 'Do you have any idea what caffeine can do to an unborn child?'

Luckily, I had had days to prepare myself for the onslaught. I took a deep breath and launched in. 'Audie, I don't take drugs, I don't smoke, but I do have a daily cup of tea and that is not going to change. I am also going to continue to watch 18-rated television shows and read books without pictures or barnyard noises. This is because I am an adult. I am not a three-year-old and I don't intend to be treated like one simply because I'm pregnant. Now, are you ready to order?'

Feeling very pleased with myself, I beckoned the waiter back and we ordered our drinks, Audie a trifle sulkily.

'So where are you having it?'

'The Royal Women's Hospital.'

'Not private?' she said, in the same tone that she might have said, 'Oh, so you're having it on the floor of a public ward in a third-world hospital surrounded by dysentery patients?'

'Jack and I are old-school Lefties. We believe in public hospitals and state schools.'

'Oh. Well I'm sure it will be just fine.' Her tone indicated the precise opposite.

The waiter returned with our drinks and she took a sip of her cappuccino. 'Do you know how you're going to give birth?'

'In a hospital,' I said blankly.

'No, I mean, have you explored the different options? There are a lot of things to consider, Belle. I can recommend the birthing pool – I used that for the twins.'

'I haven't really looked into it,' I confessed. 'The only one that I like the sound of is the one where they send you to a nice hotel after the birth because apparently hotel rooms are cheaper than hospital beds these days. But they only give those rooms to women who have given birth naturally and I'm thinking of having an elective caesarean.'

At the mention of the C-word, Audie blanched. She practically trembled. She put down her cup and was so agitated that she didn't even notice that she had a milk-froth moustache.

'A caesarean? Belle, you *can't*!'

'Yes, I can,' I said firmly. 'I hate the idea of natural childbirth. I always have. It completely freaks me out. I'm a total coward when it comes to physical pain, and I know a caesarean isn't a walk in the park but I'm much more comfortable with the idea of stitches in my stomach than in my . . . you know.' I couldn't even say it out loud. I had to re-cross my legs just thinking about it.

'But the endorphins . . .' she said hopelessly. 'You get a surge of natural happy feelings after the pain of the birth. You'll miss out on that.'

'Fine by me. I can buy half an ecstasy tablet for about forty bucks and get endorphins that way. Oh, for God's sake, stop looking at me like that,' I said irritably, for her face had collapsed in horror. 'I was *joking*.'

'Think about the natural benefits to your child,' she wailed.

Although I wasn't about to tell Audie this, the idea of an elective caesarean was really only floating around in the back of my mind. I wanted to find out a lot more about everything to do with childbirth before I came to any firm decision. But I'd had about enough of this.

'I have genital herpes,' I stated baldly.

She looked at me in consternation.

'It's an active case,' I said, dredging my memory for what the books had said about medical reasons for having a caesarean. 'So I can't have a vaginal birth.'

'Belle, I'm so sorry.' She did look sorry too. And grossed out.

'That's OK,' I said handsomely. 'You weren't to know. So do you want to order anything to eat?'

She fiddled with her cup, then took a deep breath and looked up at me. 'I had vaginal warts once,' she confessed.

Kill me. Kill me now.

At this opportune moment, the waiter returned. 'Are you ladies ready to order?' His pen was poised expectantly over his pad. 'I can recommend the meatballs. They're excellent.'

We both looked doubtfully over to the table next to ours, where a woman was about to tuck into a plate of meatballs. The meatballs were covered in a bright-red tomato sauce and had unsightly knobby growths all over them.

In unison, we both swallowed hard and shook our heads and the waiter disappeared.

Unfortunately, this intervention had given Audie

time to think about her next line of attack. 'Have you put its name down at any schools?'

'*School?* It's not even born yet!'

'Isabelle, it's very important. The best schools and childcare facilities book out immediately. People plan these things, you know.'

'How can I put its name down when we haven't even decided on a name?'

'What names do you like?'

A tremendous weariness overcame me. 'If it's a boy we're going to call it Darryl. If it's a girl we're calling it Mona. Will you excuse me? I need to throw up.'

'So that went well,' Jack commented, as we arrived home from our disastrous Devonshire-tea outing.

I flung my bag down on the couch. 'I'll ring her tomorrow and apologise for encouraging Felix to eat the jam and cream with his hands.'

'I've been a doctor for about ten years now and that was honestly the first time I've ever seen anyone turn purple.'

'She deserved it. She criticised every single bloody thing! She even told me off for not enrolling Fetid in school.'

'Well, she has had three kids. She does know what she's talking about.'

I wheeled around. 'And I don't?'

'Not really,' he said mildly. 'Neither do I.'

I sat down limply. 'Oh God. I'm sorry. She's my sister and I know she means well, it's just – well, what did you and Henry talk about?'

'Carlton's chances for a Premiership this century and the state election,' he admitted sheepishly.

'You see? You still get treated like a normal human being who can talk about things other than babies. I can't bear it.'

'OK then. What do you want to talk about?'

'You mean, right now?'

'Yep.'

I considered for a moment. 'Whether an Amish person would be allowed to wear roller-skates.'

'I think they're allowed wheels. It just can't be motorised. You're confusing the Amish with Luddites. A Luddite is anti-technology. An Amish person avoids modern conveniences for religious reasons.'

'I know what an Amish person is!'

'I'll bet you fifty bucks that the sum total of your knowledge of Amish people comes from that Harrison Ford movie *Witness*.'

He was right so I decided to change the subject. 'Jack?'

'Yes, sweetness?'

'I'm scared.'

'Of what?'

I tried to articulate my main concerns. 'Being in a world where Audie knows what's wrong and what's right and I have no idea. Having no control. Failing. Giving birth to a human–eel hybrid. Having to face scary clowns at children's birthday parties. Leaving our baby on the car roof and driving off. Not enrolling it in school on time so we'll have to home tutor it and it will grow up innumerate and not knowing where El Salvador is.'

'Isn't it near Mexico?'

'It's not,' I said tearfully. 'That's a very common misconception. It's actually bordered by Honduras and Guatemala. You see? We're totally unfit to be parents.'

There was silence for a long moment. Finally he said, 'Clowns aren't that scary, you know.'

'They are too. It's their big shoes.'

There was another silence until Jack tentatively asked, 'Why would you give birth to a human–eel hybrid?'

'Because things like that happen! And because I ate prawns that night we went out for dinner with Bert and Mona.'

'But why would it be a human–eel? Wouldn't it be a human–prawn hybrid?' he persisted.

I glared at him. '*Must* you be pedantic?'

'You're the one insisting on having El Salvador in its proper place!'

'Misplacing an entire country is *completely* different to mixing up sushi toppings,' I retorted.

'I really can't argue against that,' Jack said plaintively. 'Look, all of the stuff that you're worrying about is well into the future. There's not much point tying yourself in knots about it now. Is there anything that's really bothering you right now?'

I thought for a moment. 'Men are just *leering* at my breasts.' And no wonder. Over the past few months my breasts had expanded by about two cup sizes. As I was still wearing my normal bras and didn't have any maternity clothes as yet, the effect was distinctly Jordan-esque.

Jack gave a contented, self-satisfied chuckle that he quickly turned into a cough. 'Belle, you've always shown off your beautiful breasts.'

'You make it sound like I'm a stripper or a centrefold!'

'You know what I mean. You do have a preference for cleavage-enhancing tops and bras.'

This was true. I loved my breasts. My legs were shorter than I would have liked and I had a belly that could quickly go to pot, but my breasts had always been my favourite body part. Biggish but firm, and perky enough that I could occasionally go without a bra. Until now, of course. After breastfeeding they would probably end up looking like two potatoes hanging in a pair of stockings slung around my neck. Another score to settle between Fetid and me.

'This is different. I'm pregnant.'

'So why shouldn't men find you sexy while you're pregnant? That's very narrow-minded of you.'

'Because I can't help thinking that they're probably into dressing up in nappies like Warren.'

'Who's Warren?'

'One of Cate's counselees.'

'Cate has got to stop volunteering for that hotline,' Jack said firmly.

'She doesn't mind it. She says that most of the people who ring the counselling line are nice. Apparently it's just the dwarf-tossers that you have to watch out for. They're really mean.'

I thought for a moment and then opened my mouth but Jack got in first. 'Our child is not going to be a dwarf-tosser. Or into wearing nappies. Apart from the first few years, obviously. God, now *I* sound insane.' He paused and took a deep breath. 'Belle, you have to stop this. It's not like you to be so pessimistic.'

'I know,' I sighed. 'Don't worry about me. I'll probably be fine once we've finished telling everyone and things have settled down.'

'Who do you have left to tell?'

'I'll call Frannie now. And I'll take Doug out for a drink after work tomorrow and tell him then. Thank God I won't have to hide it from him any longer,' I added. 'He keeps coming back into the gallery, sniffing the air and saying that he can smell soy sauce and something deep-fried.'

'So you'll tell Cruella tomorrow too?'

I shook my head vigorously. 'No way. I need to plan how I'm going to tackle her without losing my life, my internal organs and my job, in that order. What are you grinning at?'

'I'm laughing because you're planning on telling Doug but not Cruella? Do you really think he's going to be able to keep it a secret?'

'Of course he will! Doug can keep a secret when he has to.'

'Belle, Doug is about as discreet as a Fleet Street tabloid newspaper with a scoop on Posh and Becks.'

I dismissed Jack's argument with an impatient shake of my head. 'You're being silly. Doug's my friend. I know he'll be discreet.'

11

The Mastitis that Barked

It took about ten minutes for Doug's high-pitched squeals to die down, and by that time practically everyone in the bar had either smiled at me or come over in person to congratulate me.

I shook hands with the last of my well-wishers and confirmed that, no, I didn't know the sex of the baby, and then turned back to Doug, who was already steaming full speed ahead.

'Right. Now who are we thinking of for your yummy-mummy role model? Angelina Jolie? Betty Rubble? As long as it's not that knickerless Spears woman, you have my blessing to go forth and procreate.' He stopped and then looked at the shapeless tunic that I was wearing. 'So all those horrible clothes you've been wearing – it's because you have a baby bump!'

'My clothes aren't horrible!' I protested, feeling pleased and proud at the same time. I did have the beginnings of a baby bump, even if it was just a tiny one that could be mistaken for the natural consequences of not doing three hundred abdominal crunches a day, or whatever it was that women like Posh Spice did when they weren't hosting parties for Elton John or having Botox injections.

'I thought you were putting on weight, but I figured

it was the natural result of all that crap you've been eating.'

'How did you know about that?'

Doug looked guilty. 'I may have nicked one or two Cheezels when you weren't looking.'

Before I could tell him off for his petty pilfering, he gestured with one hand. 'Show,' he demanded. 'Lift up your top and let me see.'

We were in a corner booth so I stood up and complied. Doug leaned back and looked at my bump in awe. 'Darling,' he said in a hushed tone, 'how do you do it? I mean, I can't even go out in public if I have a *pimple* ...'

A wave of relief washed over me. Bless him. There was no chance Doug would give me Audrey-like strictures or advice.

'Do you know what mastitis is?' I asked him tenderly.

He perked up. 'Is it one of those cute breeds of dog that you can pop into your handbag?'

'I love you. Don't ever change. Let's get a drink.'

'Shall we get the usual?' Without waiting for a response he called out, 'Oi! Bartender! A bottle of personality and two glasses.' As this sally failed to attract the bartender's attention, he slid out from the booth.

'One glass. I'll have a mineral water. With lemon,' I said daringly.

Doug, who was halfway to the bar, spun back around and looked at me in shock. 'No alcohol?'

'That's just the start of it,' I said, with a kind of grim satisfaction. 'I'm not allowed pâté either. Or sushi. Or—'

'But – but that's barbaric. What is there left to eat?'

'Muesli,' I said gloomily. 'And brown rice and red meat and the sort of stuff they make the contestants on *The Biggest Loser* eat.' I waited for him to come back from the bar with our drinks before continuing, 'Only I don't get the satisfaction of losing weight either. The average pregnant woman puts on between ten and twenty kilos.'

'*Ten kilos!*' Doug shrieked, his squeal of horror drowning out the final part of my sentence.

I decided not to repeat the twenty-kilo bit. He might faint, and then I'd have to waste my nice mineral water by throwing it in his face.

We chatted for a few minutes as Doug put all the pieces of the puzzle together and made exclamations along the lines of 'I *knew* the gallery smelled like something deep-fried!' but after a few minutes he looked at me with an expression that could only be described as sheepish.

'It's funny that this has happened now, Belladonna, because I have something I want to tell you too.' He took a deep breath and then looked at me, practically bursting with excitement. 'It's just – Zac and I are going to adopt a child.'

I looked at him in complete shock. 'You're kidding,' I finally managed.

He shook his head.

'But – but you have absolutely no idea what's involved,' I stammered. 'You thought mastitis was a type of toy dog.'

'What is it?'

'It's a nipple infection that comes from breastfeeding.'

His face screwed up. 'Well I don't really need to know about that, now do I?'

My mouth dropped open as it hit home. Doug and Zac were going to have a baby. Only they didn't have to deal with pregnancy. They would be handed a sweet, newborn bundle of innocence with absolutely no knowledge of morning sickness, constipation, tiredness, mood swings, bloating or farting.

'Goodbye,' I said, getting up and looking for my handbag. 'We can't be friends any more.'

Doug pulled me back down. 'Don't be silly. Just because we don't have to go through pregnancy doesn't mean we don't have to put up with poo and vomit and all the yucky stuff.'

He had a point but I refused to be mollified. 'Do you still have that white velour couch?'

'Yes.'

'I hope your baby poos all over it.'

There was a silence.

I looked at him more closely. 'Doug? What aren't you telling me?'

'We're not exactly thinking of adopting a newborn.'

'How old?' My voice trembled.

'A toddler. About three,' he admitted.

'So it might be toilet-trained?' I asked, in a very high-pitched voice.

'Possibly. Not definitely.'

'You're going to have my dream child!' I shrieked, jumping up again and clobbering him around the head with my handbag. 'I want to give birth to a three-year-old!'

'That would really hurt, love,' a nearby wit drawled, and then cowered as I spun around and aimed my handbag at him too.

Doug continued to duck for cover while he elaborated. 'We've been looking into it. Apparently, there's a high demand for newborns and babies – ow! – under one year. You can understand it. People want to know the child from as young an age as possible. And we talked about it – stop it! – and decided that that wasn't so important for us. So we're going to adopt a slightly older child.'

'You're a very good person,' I panted, in between blows.

'Stop hitting me! And no, I'm not,' he said with a rueful grin. 'How else could we possibly have a child?'

'Oh, Doug. I'm sorry. I didn't mean to be tactless.' I abandoned my physical assault on him and sank back down. 'Does it bother you? You know – that it's not yours genetically?'

'We could have gone down the sperm-donor route so that the child would have been genetically "one of ours". But we decided that it didn't really matter.' His eyes grew dreamy. 'We're just so excited about raising a child. Taking her to school. Teaching her how to ride a bike and how to recognise a real Sidney Nolan painting from a fake one. Helping her to discover all of those amazing childhood books and taking her shopping to buy a dress for her high-school dance.' He grew tearful. 'Maybe she'll even marry the future Danish Crown Prince.'

Bloody hell. Fetid was probably going to be home-schooled, given that I hadn't enrolled him/her in school yet. Meanwhile, Doug and Zac's child was already wedding Scandinavian royalty.

'How do you know it's going to be a girl?' I asked stupidly, without thinking it through.

Doug sighed heavily.

'Oh. Yeah. You're adopting. Sorry. Do you have any names picked out?' Help, I was turning into Audie.

'If she's three, she'll probably already have a name,' Doug pointed out gently.

'What if you don't like it?' I persisted desperately. This was not my experience of how breaking the news of one's intention to start a family went. It was freaking me out completely.

'Well, I think it's probably more to the point if the

child doesn't like it when she grows up.'

'You know how I always talk about my friend Fran and her baby, Sienna?' Sienna, who was just past her first birthday, had been named after Fran's favourite painting pigment.

'Of course.'

'They just changed her name to Flora.'

'Huh?'

'They changed her name by deed poll to Flora. Sienna is about as common as Mary used to be. Fran couldn't bear it because everyone thought that they'd named her after Sienna Miller. Can you imagine? Fran's spent her entire life being a bohemian artist and she kept getting mistaken for some mainstream Hollywood-aspirational type.'

'But what about Sienna? I mean Flora? She's a year old. Didn't she already know her name?'

I shrugged. 'Hard to tell. I wanted to ask Fran if kids are like dogs and just respond to tone and inflection, but I was worried she might get offended.' Something suddenly occurred to me and I turned a face full of remorse on Doug. 'I'm a wench. I haven't even said congratulations yet!'

Doug laughed and accepted my belated hug and kiss. 'That's all right, honey. I did spring it on you. But think! This is going to be so much fun! We'll be yummy mummies together!'

I screwed up my face. 'I'm not entirely sure about that term. Do you know what a mummy is? It's a creature from a horror film, swathed so tightly in bandages that it can't even move properly.'

'I can't think why Hallmark hasn't snapped you up to write greeting cards for memorable occasions. Your response to life-changing news is so appropriate,' Doug said drily.

'I'm sorry. It's just – I'm finding being pregnant difficult,' I confessed. 'And now you get to have a child without going through it. It doesn't seem fair.'

To my surprise, he countered, 'Well, have you had to fill in about a billion forms in triplicate?'

'I have, as a matter of fact,' I said, thinking of the hours of my life that I had lost at my first hospital appointment.

Doug ignored me and swept on. 'Have you had to sit through meetings where they make it quite clear that they think you're unfit to be a parent if you've ever once looked at a pornographic magazine? Nope. You just get to have a roll in the hay and that's it.'

'I don't care how many forms you've had to fill out to have your fitness as parents assessed,' I argued. An idea had just occurred to me. 'That's all theoretical. You should try being pregnant.'

'I'd love to, sweetums, but – oh, that's right. No womb. Shame, it wasn't a bad idea.'

'Forget the biology – there are tons of things you can do to simulate what it's like to be pregnant.' I paused and added cunningly, 'You really should try it, Doug. You're missing out on valuable preparation.'

I knew that I would hit home with the use of the word 'preparation'. Old boy scouts never die, they just grow up and acquire a more expensive taste in neck attire.

'What do you mean "valuable preparation"?' Doug asked suspiciously. 'Preparation for what?'

'The sacrifices involved with having a child, of course.'

'What would I have to do?'

'Well, your diet would have to change for starters. No alcohol—' I paused, waiting for the shrieks.

To my surprise he just nodded. 'Sure thing. No alcohol. Except Billecart champagne, of course.'

'No alcohol. Full stop. Least of all Billecart champagne.'

'Darling, nothing that expensive could possibly be bad for you,' he protested.

'We're not talking about *you*. We're talking about your hypothetical unborn child. And alcohol is very bad for it indeed. So no alcohol.'

'For how long?' he asked apprehensively.

'How long do you think?' I replied in exasperation. 'Nine months. Longer if you're breastfeeding, but as you're not we'll call it even at nine months.'

His face paled. 'No alcohol for *nine* months?'

'That's just the start of it,' I said grimly. I was aware of a vague sense of satisfaction that came from imparting maternal horror stories and had to swiftly push away the unwelcome thought that I was turning into Audie. 'No soft cheeses. No deep-sea fish. No pâté. No sushi.'

'I'm going to starve,' he said almost tearfully.

'No, you won't. You'll be replacing all those things with lots of spinach and brown rice and red meat. Oh yeah. No tea or coffee either.'

'*No coffee?*' His shriek pierced the gentle hum of the bar.

I shook my head but then relented. 'I'm still having one cup of tea a day, so you can have one cup of coffee in the morning.'

'*One* cup of coffee a day? I'll have to take up smoking.' He groaned as I shook my head.

'No wonder so many kids experiment with cigarettes and alcohol,' he muttered. 'It's a perfectly justifiable reaction to all the deprivation they suffered in the womb.' He drummed his fingers against the tabletop, his mouth set. 'And you're sticking to this diet?'

'Unfortunately, yes,' I sighed. 'And, even if you stick to it, be grateful that you won't get morning sickness.

Which, by the way, is completely misnamed. It can happen at any time of the day. And the only thing that gets rid of it is to eat something. I can't begin to tell you what a disgusting feeling it is to eat, not because you're hungry, but because you're trying not to vomit.'

'Eew.' Doug looked revolted but I could see that he was thinking of something else. 'Maybe I should still be allowed to have alcohol,' he suggested craftily. Seeing the look on my face, he hurried on. 'Think about it. If I wake up with a hangover, feeling like hell, it will be like my own version of morning sickness.'

'Nice try. But at least you had the fun of the night before.'

'Well, you must have had fun with the lovely Dr Jack to be getting morning sickness now.' He sniggered.

'*One* romp equals weeks of nausea? I don't think that's a fair trade at all.'

'Ooh. It's a Theoretical Equation. I love these. Let me solve it.'

Our system of Theoretical Equations had evolved from a drunken night out several months ago when Doug had brought up the thorny problem as to whether one night with George Clooney would be equivalent to six months of happiness.

It wasn't until several hours later, when I was on the tram home, that it occurred to me that Doug and I had only spent five minutes working out the Theoretical Equation while the next three hours had flown by as we discussed the ins and outs of pregnancy and becoming a parent.

And I hadn't been bored once.

12
Cruella's Coup

By the time I reached fifteen weeks, we'd told most of the important people in our lives and there remained only one person who I was really under an obligation to tell. That person was Cruella. And I was dreading it. Apart from her normal inclination not to humour her staff, Cruella was childless through choice. However, unlike Cate, she detested small children. It wasn't exactly personal, as she also reviled most of our clients, old people, animals and, for reasons known only to Cruella, anyone with freckles. While she wasn't legally permitted to ban infants and children from Durville Gallery, people who were unwise enough to bring their progeny in were left in no doubt that they had committed a cultural outrage equivalent to hosting a McDonald's birthday party in the Louvre. These people were also always the ones who were talked into buying the worst piece from the exhibition. Basically, if Cruella had had her way, she would have disposed of any child found in her gallery by means of a glass pipe, akin to the one that sucked up Augustus Gloop in *Charlie and the Chocolate Factory*.

'You're telling her today,' Doug informed me as I walked into the gallery, bearing some disgusting whole-bran fruit muffins for our newly instituted pregnant ladies' morning tea.

'Why today?' I asked, fear clutching at my heart at the mere thought of it.

'Because you're showing! And she's coming in. She rang just a moment ago to say that she'll be here in an hour. She has something she wants to tell us.'

'Did it sound like good or bad news?'

Doug raised one eyebrow. 'It's Cruella. She only gets her news from the dark side.'

I opened the bag containing the muffins and nervously started to eat one. 'Have you told her about your baby?' I demanded through a mouthful of crumbs.

'I don't need to yet,' Doug said smugly. 'Zac's taking paternity leave first so it won't affect my work for ages.'

Exactly sixty minutes later, the front door of the gallery swung open and Cruella stood framed in the doorway.

It made no difference that, when she entered, Doug was on the phone organising the delivery of a sold work or that I was discussing a painting with a client. We both jumped guiltily as though we had been sprung sitting with our feet up reading trashy magazines.

The client I was talking to, who'd had previous experience of Cruella, fled as soon as he was able. Without explanation, Cruella placed one bright-red talon on Doug's telephone and cut off his call.

Cruella wasn't much of a one for pleasantries such as 'Good morning' or 'Good heavens, you're on fire, do let me call an ambulance'. So it was unsurprising that, once she was sure she had our attention, without preamble, she announced, 'At the start of December, Durville Gallery will hold a show of new works by—' she paused for added melodrama before dropping her bombshell, '—Keedin.'

At least Doug could always be relied on to overreact. By the time he'd finished hyperventilating over

Cruella's admittedly impressive coup, I had managed to gather myself together to face the fact that we'd be staging a major exhibition at pretty much exactly the same time that I was scheduled to give birth.

'Keedin? *The* Keedin?'

Cruella nodded tautly but even she couldn't conceal the fact that she was quite pleased with herself. As she had every right to be.

Keedin was the current It Boy of contemporary Australian art. He was an installation artist whose signature style was his use of 'organic materials'. Otherwise known as raw meat, cow manure and pigs' blood. His major works, such as the *Intestines* series, could sell for hundreds of thousands of dollars, and he'd been chosen to represent Australia at the forthcoming Venice Biennale. He was every gallery owner's dream come true – a critically praised artist who was also spectacularly successful in commercial terms.

He was also undeniably one of the biggest twats the Australian art world had ever had the misfortune to throw up. His pretentious name was only the start of it. Keedin (he was too important to have a surname) had a habit of solemnly informing anyone within earshot that his name was Aboriginal for 'The Moon'. Exactly which one of the estimated two hundred Aboriginal languages his name had been taken from he didn't know, which was unsurprising given that he was an Anglo-Saxon private-school boy who'd grown up in the quiet suburb of Glen Waverley.

Another of Keedin's many affectations was to wear the same pair of horrible Thai fisherman's pants every single day. These pants were always tied so loosely that they were in constant danger of falling down. It was therefore common knowledge that Keedin didn't wear any underwear. Whenever we saw him at an art fair or gallery opening, Doug would always try to make me bet on whether today would be the day that we saw 'The Moon' moon.

I harboured the uncharitable suspicion that Keedin had been christened Kevin, and that his horrible fisherman's pants betrayed flasher tendencies. However, there was no denying that luring Keedin away from the gallery that currently represented him was the sort of sneaky yet brilliant manoeuvre that had earned Cruella her fearsome reputation.

Cruella basked in our admiration for a few more minutes before something caught her attention. 'Isabelle! When you're at work you represent this gallery! What the hell do you think you're wearing?'

While my bump was still small, it was definitely noticeable but I hadn't yet felt the need to go shopping for maternity clothes. I had been so fearful of Cruella sniffing out my secret, though, that I had taken to wearing excessively oversized clothes at the gallery. Today I had on a peculiar ensemble consisting of one of Jack's old shirts and a pair of harem-style pants that I had bought for a fancy-dress party.

'I, er ...' I tried to ignore Doug, who was nodding vigorously and egging me on behind Cruella's back, by means of various face-pulling exercises.

I took a deep breath. 'Cruella, I'm pregnant.'

Her head whipped around. '*What* did you call me?'

'Carmela,' I said in a panic. Shit, shit, shit. 'I said Carmela. Didn't I, Doug?' But Doug, who had a highly developed sense of self-preservation, had already disappeared into the stockroom.

She looked at me through narrowed eyes. 'Do you know who the father is?' she demanded.

'Yes,' I said, a little startled by this. And then, as she still seemed to doubt me, I added, 'My partner. Jack.'

'Is he the good-looking one?'

'I think you're thinking of Doug's partner, Zac.'

'I am not interested in your personal lives. It's better that you don't bring them to work.'

'Our partners?'

'Your personal lives!' she snapped.

'Oh. Of course. Except, well, I'll have to bring the baby in with me.' I faltered under her withering stare. 'Because of its being inside me and everything.'

'Kindly spare me the disgusting biological details. So I assume you'll be wanting time off then?'

'Yes. But not for ages,' I said hastily. 'If it's all right with you, I'm intending to keep working until about two weeks before the baby is due.'

'When is it due?'

Oh fuck. 'The first week of December,' I said in a small voice.

She had started to shake her head even before I finished the sentence. 'No, Isabelle. It's not possible. Were you not in this room just now? Did your little ears not hear what I said? We are having an exhibition of works by Keedin! *Keedin!* Do you know what I had to do to secure this exhibition?'

No, and quite frankly I didn't want to either know or imagine. Cruella would have stopped at nothing to pull off this feat. The path that she had trodden was probably littered with corpses, dirty money, odd sexual favours and the occasional traumatised Dalmatian puppy.

'But, Carmela, I didn't know about the exhibition until just now and I'm already fifteen weeks pregnant,' I protested.

'That's hardly my fault or my problem. You'll have to sort something out.'

I had no idea whether she was suggesting that I find a

replacement staff member or have an abortion. Possibly both.

'You have now wasted exactly five minutes of my time, Isabelle. Don't do it again.' She cast a contemptuous glance around the pristine gallery. 'I want the entire gallery re-hung by the time I return. Preferably not at a height intended for giants.'

She swept out.

Doug peered around the corner. 'Are you alive?' he asked in a stage whisper.

'No,' I said morosely.

He emerged from the stockroom and generously offered me the muffin that I had bought for him. 'Well, what did you go and tell her for?' he chided me affectionately.

I looked at him in outrage. 'You were the one carrying on behind her back, insisting that I tell her!'

'I was trying to tell you *not* to mention it right then! Any idiot would have known not to say anything after her big announcement. She was always going to feel as though you'd stolen her thunder.'

He was right. I should have known better.

'Well at least you've told her,' he consoled me. 'The worst is over now.'

'What are you talking about? I don't even know whether I'm going to be allowed to take time off to give birth!'

'So don't,' Doug suggested. 'Squeeze out a big gooey baby in the middle of the exhibition opening, right when the waiters are popping open the champagne and serving the canapés. That'll teach her.'

'Everyone will probably think I'm one of Keedin's installation pieces,' I said gloomily. 'Hey, speaking of Keedin, have you heard the rumours about him?'

'Dear sweet Isabelle, I don't just *hear* the rumours,

I'm in charge of starting them. Which ones are you referring to?'

'The ones about him being off his head on drugs more often than a group of Sydney stockbrokers.'

'What do you expect? He's a young, commercially successful contemporary artist, which is an anomaly for starters. He has to do something to ruin his health and prospects. Whoever heard of a happy, emotionally stable artist?'

'Aren't you worried that this might turn into another nightmare like the Chuck Egress show?' I said.

Chuck Egress was the artist responsible for one of the most memorable opening nights in Durville Gallery's history. Poor old Chuck had unfortunately allowed his euphoria at having an exhibition at the gallery to spill over into drunken hubris on the opening night. He had made a pass at Cruella (her dominatrix thing worked for some), which had so infuriated her that she had turned his moniker into a literal translation, booting him out of the door in front of the entire crowd and hurling a tray of sushi at his head for good measure.

Doug dismissed my concerns with a wave of his hand. 'Of course not. Chuck was overwhelmed by it all. Besides, from what I know of Keedin, he's on hallucinogens most of the time. They just make him vague and a bit nutty. There's no harm to him. He'll make the gallery look like a crime scene and smell like an abattoir of course, but that can't be helped. Anyway,' he concluded optimistically, 'Keedin only has one name. He's less trouble already.'

13

Pathological Peeing

I was running ten minutes late for my sixteen-week check-up. Actually, I had only been running two minutes late, but for the last eight minutes I'd been stuck in a queue at a hospital reception desk. I was also bursting to go to the toilet but I was so terrified of losing my place in the queue that I hadn't dared to make a quick trip to the bathroom.

When my turn finally came, I handed the hospital card with my identification number and details on it to the receptionist.

She typed my number into the computer and then handed the card back to me with a dismissive sniff. 'You're in the wrong place.'

'Oh. But this is where I came last time.'

She launched into a spiel that she had obviously delivered several thousand times before. 'All expectant mothers have their first visit on this level. But, for all appointments after the initial visit, you need to go to the midwife clinic, which is on the ground floor.' She paused, but couldn't resist adding, 'You would have been told that on your first visit.'

'Oh. Maybe I was. There was such a lot to take in,' I added, in a pathetic bid for sympathy.

My bid failed. She looked at me distinctly unsympathetically. 'You're now fifteen minutes late, and before you go to the midwife clinic you need to go to Pathology so that they can collect a sample. They're also on the ground floor. If you're more than twenty minutes late, your appointment will have to be rescheduled. Is there anything else?'

'What? No. I mean, thank you.' I was already panicking. I couldn't reschedule. It was hard enough getting time off work for all my appointments as it was. I started to leave and then turned back as it occurred to me that I didn't know where on the ground floor Pathology was located. But I was too late. The receptionist was already dealing with another nervous pregnant woman and, if I waited for her to finish, more precious minutes would have elapsed.

The lift always took too long so, casting a longing glance at the sign for the women's toilets, I bolted down the stairs and made my way back to the main entrance, where I was confronted with confusingly long signs indicating the way to exotic medical destinations such as Obstetro-Dentistry and Paediatric-Ornithology. No signs for Pathology.

Even without the added stresses of being late and lost, being sent to Pathology wasn't entirely reassuring. In my admittedly limited lexicon, the word pathological tends to be followed by either 'liar' or 'serial killer', and I was in no frame of mind to test positive to either of those. I was pregnant, and that was enough to be getting on with, thank you very much.

By the time that I worked out that the Pathology department was actually just a window in a corridor lined with people (tantalisingly opposite the toilets), they were calling out number 3488. I looked at my card. I was 3467. Bugger it. I was going to have an accident if I didn't relieve myself soon. I fled into the toilet. All of the people lining the corridor interestedly watched me emerge a few minutes later.

Excusing myself and plastering an ingratiating 'I'm not really queue-jumping, I have a very good reason to be barging in front of you' expression on my face, I managed to get to the window, although I did hear one heavily pregnant woman protest, 'Hey – that's not fair. She went to the toilet first.'

'My name is Isabelle Beckett,' I said breathlessly to the nurse at the window. 'I'm so sorry I'm running late but I was actually *here* – well, not here exactly, but in the hospital. I was waiting in the wrong place and then—'

The nurse glared at me. To say that she appeared hard-bitten would have been an understatement. The woman had been well and truly mauled. Possibly by a werewolf.

'Beckett? You're number 3467. We're up to 3494.'

'I know, but I was here. I went upstairs to the obstetrics department—'

'You only go there for your first appointment. They would have mentioned that at the time.'

A pox on you all.

I took a deep breath. 'Please. I know I'm late but I work and it's very hard for me to get time off. Couldn't I *please* just do whatever it is that I have to do? I'll be quick, I promise.' God, I was actually begging.

You couldn't have said that the nurse relented – that would have implied some sort of softening, and we were clearly in the middle of a full-moon cycle. But after weighing up her options and realising that the alternative course meant seeing me again sometime in the near future, she seemed to come to the decision that she might as well get me over and done with now.

She pressed a buzzer and the door next to the window

swung open. 'Come through. *Quickly.* I need to take your blood.'

I meekly followed her through into a curtained-off cubicle and lay down on the hospital bed, while she did mysterious things with medical equipment.

She swung around holding an evil-looking hypodermic needle and looked at me like I was an idiot. 'What are you lying down for? I'm only taking some blood! Sit in that chair and roll up your sleeve. And hurry up. There's a queue out there, in case you hadn't noticed.'

I was tempted to offer her my neck so that she could bite into it and draw blood in the manner to which she was clearly more accustomed, but, after receiving another glare and realising that I was mixing my monster metaphors, I meekly rolled up my sleeve.

It was over in about two minutes. I grabbed my bag and was preparing to depart when Nurse Fenrir Greyback handed me a small specimen jar, a plastic bag labelled with my details and some medicated wipes.

'Go to the toilet. Stop midstream, then catch the remainder in the jar. Use the wipes – front to back – and then bring it back to me. Don't queue up again – oh that's right – you didn't the first time.' She stopped and gave me a nasty sneer.

It was official. We hated each other. My only consolation was that I would shortly be giving her my waste product to examine, which clearly made me the winner in any contest.

I wanted to ask her to repeat the instructions that she had just rattled off, but I didn't dare. Without ceremony, I was shunted off in the direction of the loo, clutching my little bundle.

That I was expected to wee into the jar I understood. Unfortunately, I had just been to the toilet for the first time in three hours.

I sat on the toilet and strained. Nothing. I tried a few pelvic-floor exercises, which wasn't much help as I still wasn't entirely sure where my pelvic floor was. I was therefore probably just doing sit-ups while sitting upright, which definitely wasn't the highlight of my athletic career.

I thought about fountains and rivers and listened to the other loos flushing, but nothing worked. I still couldn't muster a wee. This from a woman who, until recently, had been getting up five times a night to pee. The one time I have a healthcare professional depending on my urine to perform her job, I get stagefright.

After about ten minutes of cursing the fickleness of my bladder, I finally managed a pathetic little trickle which I captured in the jar. Belatedly I remembered something about stopping midstream and catching what came after, but it was too bad. They'd barely have enough to test as it was.

I then looked helplessly at the sterile wipes. I had absolutely no idea what I was meant to do with them. I hadn't understood a word that the werewolf had said. Were they intended to be submitted for testing too? Was I meant to use them and put them inside the plastic bag? Or, horror of horrors, what if I wasn't meant to and I handed the nurse a bag filled with wee-smeared soggy tissues? She'd probably mark me down as pathological on my file, and they'd take my baby away from me as soon as it was born and it would be brought up as a little werewolf cub.

Then again, what did I know about medical procedures? Maybe it was like when they scraped cells from the inside of your cheek to perform tests under a microscope. I opened one of the sachets containing a wipe. The nurse had said something about back to front. Or front to back. I couldn't remember. I turned the wipe over. Both sides looked exactly the same to me. I had no idea which was the back and which was the front.

Desperate for help, I pulled out my mobile phone and rang Fran. 'Frannie, it's me,' I hissed.

'Hello? Hello?'

'It's Belle,' I said, a bit louder. 'They've taken my blood and now they want my wee.'

'Who has?' she asked, bewildered.

'The hospital of course. Who did you reckon?'

'I thought maybe you'd been kidnapped by one of those child-smuggling operations.'

'I'm only four months pregnant! They'd have to wait a while. You have to stop watching depressing documentaries.'

'Well, why are you whispering?'

'Because I'm in the toilet. Listen, when you were about sixteen weeks pregnant and you gave them a urine sample, did they give you some wipe things too?'

She sighed. 'I really don't remember, Belle.'

'Come on, Fran, *think*,' I said urgently. 'Surely you'd remember wiping your vagina and handing the wipes back to the nurse?'

'Belle, I don't remember half the things that happened to me when I was pregnant. I spent nine months finding packets of pasta in my knickers drawer and driving around roundabouts for half-an-hour because I'd forgotten which direction I was going.'

That actually sounded like fairly normal Frannie-type behaviour, but I wasn't about to go into that now.

'If you're not sure, why don't you just go out there and ask them?' she asked sensibly.

'Because the nurse is a vampire who's been bitten by a werewolf and she hates me. And I was late for my appointment and I had to jump the queue and there are about a thousand people out there waiting their turn and if I barge in again to ask a question they'll all hold me down while the nurse bites my neck. And I don't have time to stand in line just to ask a question because then I'll be so late getting back to the gallery that Cruella will kill me instead.'

Being Frannie, she honed in on the most pertinent part of my tale of woe. 'Can werewolves overpower vampires? I would have thought it would be the other way around, because—'

'*Fra-aan*!'

'OK, OK. Calm down. Have you been spending too much time surfing the internet or something? You're getting very paranoid, you know.'

'I'm not paranoid! I can't help it if everyone's out to get me.'

'Well, why don't you just use the wipes and then ask the nurse when you hand your wee in if she wants them?'

'The reception area is filled with people!' I said, scandalised. 'I can't go out there, clutching the equivalent of used toilet paper in my hand, and ask her if she wants it.'

'Then put them in your pocket and, when you hand in your wee, you can drop a few hints and see what happens,' Fran suggested helpfully.

'Drop a few hints? What sort of hints?'

Fran thought for a minute. 'You could hand over the wee and then say, "Do you need *anything else*?" And then you could wink.'

Oh dear God. I was going to be arrested for acting like Benny Hill. It was almost worth getting arrested just to get out of this situation, until I remembered that, when they asked me to turn out my pockets at the police station, I'd still have to explain the wee-wipes.

I told Fran that I'd give it a go, thanked her and hung up.

Fuck. I looked doubtfully at the wipes and then at the neatly labelled bottle of wee, and finally decided that a major hospital would surely find a better way of conducting tests than poking and prodding used toilet paper under a microscope.

I gave myself a quick once-over with the wipes and then resolutely flushed them away and marched back outside and up to the window. I handed over the bag containing the bottle with the dismally small amount of wee in it, and then I bolted for the midwife clinic, before I could be called to account for the missing wipes or for my inability to wee like a stallion on command.

14
Moving Away From Ug

'How did your appointment go?' asked Jack, as he entered the living room that evening.

I looked up from the chapter in the Hangman pregnancy book that had just been advising me, '*Should you have a vaginal discharge that is green or smells like cheese* . . .' Presumably the remainder of the sentence read, '. . . *run screaming to the nearest hospital and demand an irreversible intercourse bypass operation*'. I made a face. 'Fine, if you don't count the wee-wipe disaster.'

Jack had been about to bend over in order to give me a kiss, but he stopped short. 'Do I even want to ask?' he said with trepidation.

I sighed. 'No, you don't. Let's just say I was handed a specimen jar and some wee-wipes and I wasn't sure what I was meant to do with them, so I rang Fran.'

'Why didn't you call me?'

'Because you have one of the few jobs that actually entails dealing with full-blown emergencies, so I try never to call you at work unless it's a full-blown emergency. And I don't think not being able to work out the back and front of a wee-wipe constitutes an emergency.'

'What *are* you talking about?'

'They gave me sterile wipes to wipe myself with after I went to the toilet. The nurse said something about using them back to front or front to back, but both sides looked the same to me.'

Jack started to laugh. 'Belle, she meant you should wipe from the front of your *vagina* to the back of it.'

'Well, how was I meant to know?' I asked plaintively. 'She could have just said that.'

'Who did you have?'

'I don't know her name. The Bride of Frankenstein.'

Jack chuckled again. 'It sounds like you had Nurse Petunia. She's been at the hospital for decades. I don't know her personally but I know her reputation. She's quite a character.'

'Could you *please* not make her sound like a gruff but kindly matron?' I begged. 'She was rude and horrible and quite clearly would have preferred me to have been booked in for my autopsy.' I stopped as something he had said registered. '*Petunia?* Her name is really Petunia?'

'Yep.'

'Well, her parents stuffed that one up. Venus Flytrap is more like it.'

'If it's any consolation, you only have to visit Pathology once unless there's a problem and they need to do further tests, so you're unlikely to see her again. Now, Belle, I need to talk to you about something serious. We need to think about moving.'

I looked at him, completely startled. 'Huh? What? But why? I love this house.'

Jack had a determined expression on his face, which meant that he had already marshalled and rehearsed his arguments. 'We can't rent forever. And when the baby comes this house won't be big enough.'

'What on earth are you talking about? How big do you think this child is going to be?' Before he could respond, I added, 'We do have a spare room.'

'Right. So you'll be happy to throw out all those boxes of art magazines that you still haven't got around to unpacking, will you?' Without waiting for an answer, he continued, 'It's the perfect time for us to buy. We could get something with a bigger garden. Rufus would love it . . . what's wrong with you?'

I had started to shake my head violently. 'Nuh-uh. Stop right there.'

'Why?'

'Because I know what's coming. This is how the suburbs were invented. Once upon a time all the cave people were happy together, and then all of a sudden one couple got pregnant and decided that Ug was too hairy to be near their baby, so they moved to the outer precipice.'

'Who's Ug?'

'A hairy caveman.'

Jack sighed and assumed his embarking-on-tortuous-conversation-with-Isabelle expression. 'What does Ug have to do with us getting a bigger garden?'

'Because you know as well as I do that the bigger garden is a subterfuge to make me move, when what you *really* want is to live in a homogenous suburb simply because we're having a baby. This is how intolerance starts. I want my child to grow up surrounded by all different sorts of people.'

'Like all the drug addicts and sex workers in St Kilda?'

'Some of the drug addicts can be mean,' I admitted, 'but all the kids around here just think that the sex workers are gigantic live Bratz dolls.'

'Belle, I'm not being intolerant. I just really think we're going to have to move, and I'd rather house-hunt before the baby comes.'

'How long have you been thinking about this?' I

finally asked, more to buy time than anything else.

'Since we did that first pregnancy test at home,' he admitted. 'I've just been waiting for the right time to bring it up with you. I know how much you love this place.'

I fell silent. This was starting to feel very weird. Discovering that we were pregnant had thrown me into a world where the physical changes to my body, the hospital appointments and dealing with everyone else's reaction to the news had taken over most of my head space, leaving whatever was left of my brain to handle disgusting revelations about vaginal cheese. In contrast, impending fatherhood had resulted in Jack being consumed by the desire to live in a suburb where no one played bongo drums in the park, and the need to learn the significance of terms such as 'north-facing aspect'. Our respective parent-to-be priorities seemed to be wildly incongruent.

Jack had been watching me and now he said persuasively, 'How about we just go and look at some houses this weekend?'

'We'll just look?' I asked suspiciously.

'I promise.' He gave me a quick kiss. 'It'll be fun.'

On a list that includes the less enjoyable aspects of life, such as death, disease and natural disasters, I'd rank house-hunting somewhere around dating a serial killer or bungy-jumping into an active volcano. I don't just hate house-hunting, I want to send it death threats.

My predicament was not helped by the fact that Jack seemed to have contracted a disease of the mind which caused wild mood swings between euphoria (when he found a suitable house) to depression (when said house ended up selling for the equivalent of Oprah Winfrey's last pay cheque), and an inability to think logically.

Well, either he'd caught something or he was pregnant.

Thus it was that we looked at houses in the west in Yarraville, Williamstown, Seddon and Newport. We looked at houses on the beach in Port Melbourne, St Kilda and Albert Park. We looked at houses in the north, and I swear that one desperate day I found him on the internet checking out house prices in the industrial wastelands of Broadmeadows.

In rapid succession, Jack wanted to buy a five-bedroom, three-bathroom house in Northcote that was almost a complete ruin; his next favourite was a tiny cottage in Spotswood that was practically adjacent to the largest petrol refinery in the state. The asking price wasn't very high and Jack kept trying to impress upon me what fabulous value it was. When you factored in the hospital bills for the diseases that we would undoubtedly contract if we lived in it, it wasn't that cheap, but by this stage I was starting to lose heart.

'Look at that!' he said enthusiastically, gesturing towards a sorry patch of withered grass opposite the petrol-refinery house. 'Rufus could have his own park!'

I looked doubtfully at the black clouds belching on the horizon. 'Jack, you *are* a doctor, aren't you?'

'Last time I checked my CV.'

'Then why aren't you worried about the health risks of living here?'

'Very funny.'

'Jack, I'm serious! This place is horrible.'

'Belle, *we* have to get serious about finding somewhere soon.' He paused and added in his best grown-up tone of voice, 'You need to start accepting that we might not move into a beautiful renovated home in a trendy suburb.'

'Stop making me sound like a princess,' I said crossly. 'I've been camping. I know how to rough it.'

'When I met you, you were living in Woollahra,' he said pointedly.

Fine. So technically I had once lived in one of the wealthiest suburbs in Sydney, but it had been a two-bedroom apartment that I had shared with my flatmate Harriet, not the celebrity-style compound that Jack was making it out to be.

But, as much as I hated to admit it, Jack did have a point. I was resistant to the idea of moving miles away from everything that I knew simply for the sake of having a bigger house and more land. More land – that was the real-estate mantra that we heard on all our house-hunting expeditions. As though all the people trooping through the open for inspections were hunter-gatherer nomads who had just cottoned on to this newfangled farming idea.

But it was true that living in St Kilda was more than just a geographical decision. It was a lifestyle. And all of a sudden it seemed that I was morphing from a swingin' St Kilda girl with an arty job to a mum with a baby, living in a suburb where the main topic of conversation was probably interest-rate rises. And rather than basing our decision on where to live on sensible factors, such as whether there were decent cafés and bookshops near by, or whether the house was within walking distance from the city so that we could go out and get pissed on New Year's Eve and stumble home, all of a sudden Jack was prioritising things such as whether the local schools had a good reputation. And the number of bedrooms. This last one in particular made me feel exactly like choleric old Mr Bumble, who bellowed at Oliver Twist, '*MORE? You want MORE?*'

The longer we looked, the more depressed I became, and the more a creeping resentment started to build between Jack and me of the disparate ways we were envisioning our future.

'So how's the house-hunting going?' Doug asked, from where he was balanced on the top of a ladder.

We were changing the exhibition, which was always a depressing job, as Cruella would invariably walk in five minutes after we'd finished, cock her head to one side, purse her lips and say, 'No, no, no! That's not working *at all.*' We'd then have to re-hang the entire show another four times before Cruella would eventually decide that she wanted it how we'd had it to begin with, only with every picture moved six millimetres to the left.

'Don't ask.' I handed him a length of fishing wire. 'We're looking at five-bedroom houses now.'

'*Five bedrooms?*' Doug looked at me suspiciously.

'He's gone biblical. I think he wants to beget a tribe of Israel.' I stopped and then burst out, 'Doug, I don't *want* to live next to the petrol refinery!'

'Of course you don't, poppet,' he said soothingly, his attention focused on the painting that he was trying to hang. 'Now, remember we have to hang these lower than we usually do. The last time Cruella wanted to know whether we'd had a sudden surge of interest from contemporary-art-buying basketball players.'

I didn't have his full attention. I cleared my throat. 'I *said*, I don't want to live next to the petrol refinery in Spotswood.'

I only just managed to catch the painting. Doug had collapsed on the top rung of the ladder and was holding his chest and hyperventilating. '*Spotswood!*' he shrieked. 'You can't move to *Spotswood*!'

I was actually rather impressed that Doug had even heard of Spotswood until I remembered that there had been a movie of that name made with Anthony Hopkins.

'It's within walking distance of historic Williamstown,' I said unconvincingly.

'*It's over the bridge!*'

'Oh shut up, Doug, this isn't Sydney. The West Gate Bridge isn't the same as the Harbour Bridge.'

'Cruella will sack you,' he said simply.

'She can't sack me just because she's a snob!'

'Darling, don't be ridiculous. She'll sack you because you're *not* a snob. I'm pretty sure it's written into our contracts.'

He had a point. 'I don't know why I'm arguing with you,' I said, depressed. 'It's not like I want to live there. Jack's just gone . . . mad. I don't know what's wrong with him. He's obsessed with buying a house.'

Doug descended the ladder. He sat down and put an arm around me. 'He can't help it. It's his primitive instincts.'

'Well, that's what I said,' I replied, heartened that someone understood my reasoning. 'I told him that the only reason he wanted to move from the cave to the precipice was because Ug was too hairy.'

Doug blinked but continued, 'It's the male form of nesting. You have heard about nesting, haven't you?'

I nodded. 'Apparently while I'm pregnant I'll be overcome with the desperate desire to scrub floors and clean out the fridge in preparation for the baby's arrival. I can't for the life of me imagine why I'd want to pop the baby into the fridge, but none of the books explain that bit.'

'That's because the books are written for normal people. My point is, Jack is really being very sweet. He wants to provide for his family. Find them a safe nest. You're doing all the hard work during the pregnancy. This is one of the few things that he can do.'

'You really think that's what's behind it?'

Doug stood up and dusted off his jeans. 'I know it. Zac went through the same thing recently.' He added in a worried tone of voice, 'I think Zac has couvade.'

I assumed that was the name of some French designer label and couldn't think why Doug was changing the subject so abruptly, so it surprised me when Doug said, 'Has Jack had it?'

'Huh? Has Jack had what?'

'Couvade,' Doug repeated impatiently. 'It's derived from the French word meaning "to hatch".'

'I haven't a clue what you're talking about.'

'Couvade Syndrome happens to expectant fathers who suffer from pregnancy symptoms including morning sickness, weight gain, appetite changes, cravings and fatigue,' Doug reeled off. Clearly he had been Googling the subject. 'It's a form of empathetic pregnancy that often happens to the partners of pregnant women. Poor Zac has it quite severely.'

'Er, Doug?'

'Mmm?'

'I hate to break it to you, but you're *not* a pregnant woman.'

Doug looked affronted. 'You just *love* rubbing that in, don't you, Little Miss Haemorrhoids?'

'I do not have haemorrhoids!'

'Fine. Little Miss Stretch Marks then. Anyway, as *you* convinced *me*, being pregnant isn't just about growing a baby in a womb.'

'It kind of is, really,' I said apologetically.

Doug glared at me. 'It's about *sacrifice*, and, given that *you* were the one who talked me into sacrificing my diet for nine months, I think it's perfectly logical that Zac has a bad case of couvade.'

Now I felt guilty, so I gave in. 'What are his symptoms?'

'He's been throwing up in the morning. He gets really tired during the day and he keeps having a big fry-up and a can of Coke for breakfast,' Doug said, in a transparent bid for sympathy.

'Doug, that's not couvade, that's Le Hangover.'

Doug looked sulky. 'You just don't want to admit that anyone but you is suffering through these changes.'

And some people thought *I* was hard work. I gave in. 'OK – Zac probably *does* have couvade. Don't worry, it will wear off when you get over your morning sickness.' Doug looked happier so it was worthwhile engaging in the conversational equivalent of hypochondria. 'Doug?'

'Talk and work,' he instructed, climbing the ladder once more.

I handed him the painting. 'I feel like a bad person. For not wanting to move from somewhere I love, for the sake of our child.' I bit my lip. What I really wanted to ask was: was I being selfish, not wanting to sacrifice my lifestyle for the baby's sake? And, if I was, did that mean I wasn't ready to be a mother?

But Doug's attention was on the painting. 'You just need to find the right house. Now, come on,' he added. 'If we don't have this hung by the time Cruella blows in, the only place we'll be safe is Spotswood.'

Late that night when Jack got home from work, I led him into the spare room.

He looked around in disbelief at the newly clean and tidy space. 'What happened to all your junk?'

'It's not junk, they're art catalogues!' I said indignantly. 'But I'm sending them all to Fran in Sydney.'

Jack cottoned on in a flash. 'Belle, you know we can't stay here for ever—'

'Just hear me out,' I begged. 'Please. I know we can't stay here for ever. But I love living here. I like the neighbours and the people in the shops up the road, and the off-leash park for Rufus is only a minute's walk away. We're happy here. And there is enough room really. And—' I stopped, furious to discover that I was on the verge of tears.

Jack put his arms around me and then firmly lifted my chin up so that I had to meet his gaze. 'And what?'

'And I just really don't want to move,' I said, as the tears started to spill over. 'Everything in my life is about to change for ever. I want familiarity. I want the people and places that I know. I don't want to move to a suburb where I know no one and my friends are twenty minutes' drive away. I'm terrified of feeling isolated and alone with a baby while you're off at work.' I pulled away from him and took a deep breath. 'Jack, when the baby is born, how do you think your life is going to change?'

He looked at me uncertainly. 'Well, I imagine we'll be sleep deprived for a while, which will make things hard. We won't go out as much as we're used to.'

I couldn't believe it. He obviously hadn't even thought about this. I waited, my arms crossed in front of my chest, refusing to let him off the hook.

'I don't know – we'll have a baby! Of course things are going to change! What more do you want me to say?'

'I mean that, after the baby is born, for five days a week, eight hours a day – or, knowing you, six days a week, fourteen hours a day – your life will still be the same when you're at work,' I almost shouted. 'For me, this baby is going to change everything. It's already changing my body. It's going to change my work, my life, my *everything*.'

He looked at me helplessly. 'But, Belle, you knew that it would. And you wanted it as much as I did.'

'I know, I know! That's not what I'm trying to say.

I just want you to realise that my whole life is going to change and it's already started and . . . I'm scared.' I was on the verge of tears again, which seemed to be my default emotional state these days. I didn't really know why I was getting so angry with Jack. It wasn't as though any of it was his fault. It just seemed outrageously unfair that my life was being consumed by upheaval while his was remaining untouched to the point where he hadn't even thought about the same issues.

Seeing how upset I was, Jack pulled me in very close and we were silent for a few minutes.

'You really don't want to move?' he finally said.

'I really, really don't. Not right now, anyway.'

'OK then. As long as you realise that we can't go on renting here for ever.'

'Agreed.'

There was another silence, which was broken by Rufus, who padded into the room and began to sniff the bare corners with great interest.

Jack swung me around so that my back was against his chest. I snuggled into him and he folded his arms around me. We both watched Rufus for a few moments. 'You know, you might find that your fear of change is worse than the actual changes,' Jack said.

'I hope so,' I replied mournfully. 'Otherwise being a mummy is going to be scarier than *The Shining*.'

'You're the only person I know who would equate impending motherhood to Jack Nicholson going berserk with an axe.'

'Is that why you love me?'

'No, that's why you scare me. I love you because you've managed not to cry for three minutes.'

'It's not my fault that I'm hormonal.'

'Oh, that's right. I forgot. It's mine.'

'Exactly. See, now that's why *I* love *you*.'

Jack squeezed me tighter and then added quietly, 'There has to be more to life than coming home to Rufus.'

I looked over at Rufus, who had started to energetically scratch himself. I let out a half-sob, half-laugh. 'Poor Rufus. He has no idea what's about to hit him.'

Neither, for that matter, did I.

15
Work it, Baby

I knew that Audie had forgiven me for my 'Encouraging Felix to eat with his hands' revenge, when I returned home from work one night to discover that she had very kindly left a bag of her old maternity clothes on our doorstep. Which was lucky, as I was now nineteen weeks pregnant and my silhouette was most definitely starting to resemble Alfred Hitchcock's. I started to sort through the clothes, but it didn't take very long before I realised something had gone amiss.

I dialled Audie's number and heard her pick up while I was still holding a skirt out at arm's length and eyeing it with confusion.

'Audie, it's Belle.'

'Belle, I can't talk for very long. I'm making cassoulet and I'm at a very delicate stage in the procedure.'

'Oh. What are you doing?' Being the sort of cook who puts everything in the microwave or the jaffle iron, I was always intrigued to hear of the obscure things Audie did in the kitchen, and I don't just mean using her saucepans every day. She was the type of person who had filleting knives and a fish-scaler, and other bizarre kitchen equipment that no one apart from television chefs ever used.

She didn't disappoint. 'I'm salting pig skin.'

'Ugh. Does the pig mind?'

She wisely ignored my witticism. 'It's for the cassoulet that I'm making. I've already made the duck confit and stock,' she said, sounding smug.

'How many courses are you having for dinner?' I asked in bemusement.

She gave one of her oh-how-the-non-culinary-genius-half-lives laughs. 'All of those things are for the cassoulet. It takes about three days to make. I'm making my own sausage to go in it too.'

'It takes you *three* days to make a casserole?' I gasped.

'It's not a casserole, it's cassoulet,' she said sniffily.

'What exactly *is* cassoulet?'

There was a small silence. 'It's French for casserole,' she finally admitted, her tone daring me to say anything.

Luckily, I knew better. I could make fun of Audie's Martha Stewart brand of insanity to a certain extent, but if she was in the middle of a three-day recipe it was safer not to push it. I got to the point. 'I think you've given me the wrong bag of clothes.'

'Are you talking about the maternity clothes I left at your house?'

'Yes. Your note said that you made two piles that day. One full of maternity stuff for me and one of old clothes that you don't wear any more for the women's shelter.'

'Yes, but I know that I didn't mix them up.' Audie was sounding huffy, which was unsurprising as she prided herself on her organisational skills.

'You must have,' I insisted. 'The bag you've given me is full of normal-sized skirts and pants. None of it is specialised maternity wear.'

'That's right,' she said, sounding impatient and distracted. I could hear Felix demanding something in the background. Probably begging for some salted pig skin to go with his wholegrain toast and organic tofu, the poor deprived tot.

'What do you mean – "that's right"?'

'I didn't buy anything from the maternity shops.'

'Audie, some of the skirts are a size *eight.* I couldn't even fit into them under normal circumstances.'

'They have elasticised waists,' she said, as though that cleared everything up. 'Belle, I really have to go now.'

I hung up and eyed the bag of clothes malevolently. I should have bloody known. Thanks to her regular Pilates classes and her unnatural self-discipline, Audie had gone through both of her pregnancies looking like she had a small mango shoved up her top. Which therefore made me the first woman in history who was going to have to diet and lose weight in order to fit into maternity clothes.

Given that Diego was still singing his way through my local yoga classes, I decided that I needed some other form of exercise while I was pregnant.

I hated gyms. Or health clubs, I should say. They used to be called gyms but it was all meditative kickboxing and yogalates these days. There were many reasons why I disliked gyms with the sort of passion that I normally reserved for house-hunting, but high up the running order was the fact that they always had a bank of plasma screens playing horrible music videos at a volume that was guaranteed to penetrate your iPod, if not perforate your eardrums; they were invariably staffed by perky young things with improbable names who enjoyed eating fruit and competing in triathalons; and, last but not least, I could never work the bloody equipment. And I do mean *never*. Against my better judgement, I had sporadically taken out gym memberships over the course of a varied and inglorious non-athletic existence, and I must have undergone at least a dozen demonstrations of how to work the lateral crunch abdominal bedazzler and its evil ilk, and I still always ended up pointlessly flailing my limbs around for a few minutes before spending the next three days unable to move my neck.

Yet here I was again. Thanks to my cravings for junk food and the not-so-gentle reminder delivered by Audie's skinny-mini maternity clothes that some pregnant women managed to exercise both their bodies and self-restraint, I was once again filling in a form that asked me about my exercise habits as though it was perfectly reasonable to expect a busy, professional person to make time for dragon-boat racing in the middle of winter.

Then again, it was either this or resign myself to a wardrobe consisting entirely of duvet covers. So I answered as many of the questions as was humanly possible until I got stumped by: *Describe your diet*. I thought about answering, 'Mr Chocolate Cheesecake is approximately six foot wide, has several bite-sized chunks missing and is often seen in the company of Ms Potato Chip and Auntie Fried Dim Sim'. But I couldn't bear to sit through the lecture on nutrition that they always gave me, so instead I wrote 'Average', and hoped that would suffice.

A perky athlete in neon-bright gym-wear tossed her apple core into the bin, finished her conversation about the triathalon that she had competed in over the weekend, and then, much to my alarm, bounded over in my direction.

'Hi!' she exclaimed. 'I'm Brandy!'

It was too cruel. I had been in constant mourning over the absence of alcohol from my existence, and when it finally re-entered my life it was in the non-drinkable form of my gym instructor.

'Hi. I'm Isabelle.'

'Great! Let's get started!'

I quickly handed over my form before she could emit any more exclamation marks.

Brandy was clearly a multi-tasker, as she managed to scan my questionnaire while emitting a healthy glow. 'You've written that your diet is average. Could you be more specific?'

'I'm not sure what you mean. I just eat normal stuff. Average portions too,' I said, dredging up the word 'portions' from a conversation that I'd had with my old Sydney flatmate Hattie. Hattie belonged to the same tribe of exercise freaks as Brandy, and had settled down happily with an ultra-marathon runner named Brad, who she had met when we competed in the City to Surf fun run. That is to say, Hattie had competed and actually run. I had walked, carrying a handbag, and somehow still managed to sprain my ankle.

Brandy didn't seem to be a portions girl. 'No, I mean what kind of diet are you on? No carbs? Low GI? The tuna and water diet?'

Obviously I couldn't say that I wasn't on any sort of diet. I knew full well that, if I did, Brandy would gaze at me blankly and then repeat the question more slowly and in a louder tone of voice.

'I'm on a special pregnancy diet,' I compromised.

'What's it called?'

'The K.D. Lang diet,' I improvised, thinking longingly of foodstuffs fried, fatty and flavoured. 'It, um, focuses a lot on cravings.'

Brandy clearly didn't want to admit that she'd never heard of the K.D. Lang diet so thankfully she moved on to her next question. 'So, what exercise do you do?'

'I was doing yoga but I haven't done it for a while. I walk the dog every day.'

'Walking doesn't count!'

'Walking is an Olympic sport!' I said, nettled, entering the duel of the exclamation marks.

'So is table tennis,' she replied, unmoved. 'OK. I guess the most important thing we need to know is what your goals are.' She looked at me, pen poised expectantly over the sheet.

To not end up with an arse the size and texture of a duvet, I thought. To not use waddling as my primary means of locomotion a second longer than would be necessary.

'Um, I'm eating a lot more than I usually do. I just want to balance that out with some gentle exercise. I was thinking maybe I'd do the Tai Chi class.'

'Tai Chi is great for relaxation, but it's not really going to help you manage your weight or fitness. I think what we need to do is make up a programme for you. You can't run, of course, but you can still ride the exercise bike and do some light weights. And you can still use most of the gym equipment.'

'I'm *pregnant*, you know.' I enunciated very clearly, just in case she thought that my bump was a spectacularly bad case of spare-tyre-itis.

'Yes, of course. But there's still tons of things you can do. Pregnancy really doesn't have to limit you that much.'

Bugger. I had been hoping it would provide the perfect excuse to limit me. Especially when it came to incomprehensible gym machinery.

'One of my regular clients just gave birth a few weeks ago,' Brandy said. 'She was doing three sessions a week right up until she went into labour.'

'Let me guess,' I said sourly, 'she gave birth naturally, without any pain relief.'

'And not a single stitch!' Brandy said merrily. 'Which is amazing when you consider she had triplets!'

'Yay for her,' I said unenthusiastically, as a response was clearly required.

'She's not back at the gym yet, but I made up a programme she can do at home for the next few weeks. Wanna see?'

To my considerable alarm, Brandy dropped to the floor, in a *Mission Impossible* prone position, and proceeded to whip off a couple of push-ups, complete with intermittent hand-claps.

'You see?' she beamed up at me between push-ups. 'Even a simple exercise like this can be turned into a game that you can do with baby.' She raised herself up. 'And kiss the baby!' She dropped down into the push-up. 'And up again! And down to kiss the baby!'

Oh dear God. She was actually puckering up. It was horrible.

Brandy sprang up into a lunge position. 'These are great for tightening your butt—'

Bum, Brandy, *bum*. We are not American. Although it wasn't entirely Brandy's fault that she spoke Americanese, given that she was besieged with third-rate American hip-hop music via the plasma screens every day.

'And if you do it while holding your baby out at arm's length you can work your shoulders at the same time. Kids love it. You can tell them a story while you work out!'

One thing I knew with utter certainty: in whatever freaky world mothers were reciting stories to their newborns while performing bum-clenching lunges, I would not be joining them. I had my suspicions that these were the same mothers who shot triplets out of their birth canals with the nonchalant ease with which the stripper in *The Adventures of Priscilla, Queen of the Desert* had dispensed ping-pong balls from her vagina.

Brandy gave me a thumbs up. 'Okeydoke! Let's go!'

I spent the following half an hour trailing Brandy around the gym and nodding my head as she pulled levers and twiddled with knobs and did all those mysterious things that the gods of the gym equipment require you to do before they accept you as a sacrifice. And then Brandy left me on an exercise bike, with the strict instruction to watch my heart-rate and not to get off until I'd cycled a distance that was roughly equivalent to participating in Melbourne's famous 'Around the Bay in a Day' bicycle race.

After about fifteen minutes, I realised something very strange. If I ignored the hideously sexist hip-hop videos, for the first time ever in my life I was enjoying being in a gym. My tummy gave a clear indication that I was a pregnant lady, undertaking moderate exercise. I was not here to be ogled by bodybuilders with no necks and the alarming tendency to think fitted mesh a suitable medium for a sweat-soaked codpiece. I no longer felt the need to be competitive with the woman on the bicycle next to mine who was clearly training for the Tour de France. Instead, I switched my iPod on, and sang along while I cycled at a sedate pace.

On the way home from the gym, filled with the virtuous feeling of having done something beneficial for my health, I patted Fetid affectionately.

I was growing rather fond of my tummy.

16
Do the Maths

'So how pregnant are you exactly?' Cate asked. We were sitting on the couch in her stylish flat in Prahran, having just replayed, for the fourth time, the scene from *Alien* where the alien bursts out of John Hurt's stomach. Cate had very kindly agreed to yet another at-home catch-up for my benefit. I hadn't realised until getting pregnant how much of my social life had revolved around alcohol. Given the ban on alcohol and the fact that the smell of cigarette smoke made me want to throw up, my idea of a perfect night out was now a night in, so sitting at home watching DVDs with Cate suited me just fine.

'Six and a half months. Are you *sure* this is a good idea for me to keep watching this?' I asked, stroking Shnoodle who was asleep on my lap.

'Yup. It's therapy. There's no way actual childbirth could be as scary as that scene.' Cate's brow furrowed as she tried to figure something out. 'Are you really six and a half months pregnant? Bloody hell, it seems like just yesterday you were in the first trimester.'

'Nice use of trimester.'

'I thought so. So really? Six and a half months?'

'Yep.'

'That means your baby is due in November.'

'No, it's due in December,' I said patiently.

'Well, that can't be right.'

I smiled kindly at her confused expression. 'Of course it is. My baby is due on the fourth of December. We're now in the middle of August.'

'Exactly. That means you're five and a half months pregnant.'

'No, I'm not. Look—' I spread my fingers out and began to count the months off. 'We had sex in March—'

'Eew. Can't you say "conceived"?'

'And this level of refinement is coming from a woman who just relived *in detail* her recent encounter with a Spanish backpacker whose name was definitely either Pedro, Pablo or Craig.'

'Yes, but you're pregnant.'

'Your point?'

She screwed up her face. 'Sex and pregnancy don't mix.'

'*Sex and pregnancy don't mix?* Not including allegations involving Boris Becker and a turkey baster, how the hell do you think most people conceive?'

'Oh you know what I mean. Anyway, you're using the word "conceive" now so it doesn't matter.'

I was irritated beyond belief that Cate thought pregnant women ranked somewhere around Ronald McDonald for shagability, but I couldn't be bothered arguing the point so I started to count again. 'March, April, May, June, July, August – wait a minute.'

'I told you,' she said smugly. 'You're only five and a half months pregnant.'

'But that *can't* be right. I'm in my sixth month.'

'Yes, but that doesn't mean you're six months pregnant.'

'Nine months from March gets us to November.' I counted it out on my fingers once again, just to be sure.

'You're forgetting to include the ninth month as an

entire month,' Cate said, honing in on where the problem lay.

'But March to December is *ten* months,' I wailed, holding up two outstretched, completely counted hands.

'Oh dear God, this really can't be that hard. Look, forget about counting on your fingers. You're five and a half months pregnant. That's all you need to know.'

'I can't believe that I've been going around telling everyone that I'm six and a half months pregnant when I'm a whole month behind.'

'Oh well. It's not that big a deal.'

'It bloody well is!' I said indignantly. 'I thought I was in my third trimester and it turns out I'm still in the second.'

'What's the difference?'

'Psychological mainly. Third trimester is the home straight. The last bit of the tunnel before the light. The fast-flowing slippery-dip before the big splash.'

'That's enough vaginal metaphors, thank you very much.'

'I wasn't actually doing that on purpose,' I said apologetically.

'It doesn't matter if it was intentional or not, now I need a drink.'

'You can't have one.'

'Yes I can. Just because Doug wants to do your insane empathetic pregnancy thing, it doesn't mean that I have to.'

As Cate poured herself a gin and tonic, her mobile phone beeped, indicating that she'd received a text message. She checked it as she took a sip of her drink. 'Sorry about this, Belle, but I'm going to have to throw you out.'

'Why?'

She positively smirked. 'I just got a text. A . . . friend is coming over.'

'What, now? It's ten thirty at night!' Even before Cate's pitying look landed on me, I realised how tragic I'd become. Maybe Jack was right. Maybe it *was* time to move to the suburbs and make friends with couples called Bert and Mona, so that we'd have someone to discuss the fascinating topics of nappy contents and teething with before we all went to bed at eight p.m.

'Do you want me to call a taxi for you?' Cate asked. 'You can't catch the tram home, it's freezing outside.'

'No need. I've got Jack's car. There was no way I was going to wait at the tram stop when it's about three degrees.' I pushed an indignant Shnoodle off my lap and then heaved my considerable bulk up off the couch. 'Are you going to tell me who it is?'

'Nope. If it turns into anything serious you'll be the first to know.'

'Is it Dr Bert?' I asked excitedly.

She looked at me in exasperation. 'Why on *earth* would you think that?'

'Wishful thinking, I guess. I still think you two would be fantastic together. He's broken up with Mona, you know.'

'I didn't know, but *you* know that I don't want kids, so dating an obstetrician is hardly going to be a match made in heaven! Now stop trying to set me up – unless you happen to know what Charlie's up to these days.'

'Charlie?' I repeated, startled. '*My* Charlie?'

She laughed. 'Yes, your Charlie. Oh, don't look like that. You know that I would never go out with your ex-boyfriend. I was just joking. Even though he *is* cute and he's about the only guy I've ever known who didn't seem to want kids either.'

'What makes you think Charlie didn't want kids?' I asked curiously. 'Did he ever say anything to you?'

She looked taken aback. 'I can't remember his exact

words. I don't know – it was just the impression that I got from him once when we had a long conversation that time I came and stayed with you in Sydney. He seemed to agree with my way of thinking about how impossible it would be to balance a family and our sort of careers.' She watched my face for a moment. 'Why are you looking like that? You and Charlie must have discussed having kids. Everyone I know who dates for longer than six months discusses it at some point. And these days I feel like I have to point out that I don't want kids on the first date or else I'll get sued for misleading conduct,' she added glumly.

She was wrong. Charlie and I had never discussed the issue of children. He had never brought it up, probably assuming from my indifference to other people's children that I wasn't the maternal type. Which I wasn't. Or at least I hadn't been until now. But it had only just occurred to me that, during all those years with Charlie, I had avoided the topic too. Cate was watching me, so I gave a small shrug, and then, for some reason, I did something that I never did: I lied to Cate. 'Of course we discussed it. It just wasn't really a big deal for either of us.'

'Does Charlie know that you're pregnant?' Cate asked suddenly.

I shook my head. 'We lost contact. We used to email each other occasionally but then he got a job overseas and moved to London and I moved to Melbourne. I could probably get in touch with him through his family but it's a bit weird to contact him just to tell him that I'm having a baby, don't you think? Remember that time your ex rang you to tell you he was engaged?'

'I didn't know whether to congratulate him or offer my condolences to her,' Cate reflected. 'Is Charlie still with Sleazel?'

'I think so but why are we even talking about him?'

'Calm down,' Cate said, surprised by my heated reaction. 'And there's no reason in particular that I brought him up. It's probably just because I drove past a guy on Fitzroy Street the other day who looked a bit like him.'

'Cate, I know you and Charlie got along really well, but you like Jack, don't you?'

'I liked Charlie but I *adore* Jack, and he's much better for you,' she said firmly. 'Now, I'm sorry but I really need you to bugger off before my guest arrives. You're a bit of a walking statement against purely recreational sex.'

I picked up my bag. 'Considering that I'm about to go home to bed, can't you give me something? *Anything?*'

Cate blushed. 'He's twenty-four, he's studying politics and he's got a thing for older women. So if you don't mind I need to get ready.'

'Twenty-four? You go, girl.'

'Thanks. Now *goodbye*, Belle.'

She bundled me out of the front door, and as she kissed me goodbye – I knew she couldn't help it – she threw me a smug look that had quite a bit to do with her still being a size eight, me being a size twenty-eight and the fact that she was heading for a wild night in bed while I was heading for a mild night in bed.

'Just tell me this – is his name Pablo?' I called out as I headed to my car.

She grinned. 'Maybe. Or Craig.'

She closed the door firmly to get ready for her passionate toy-boy but as I drove home I didn't envy her in the least. Funnily enough, we were both pretty happy with our lot.

17

You Must Suffer For Your Art

Refreshed by a wholesome night's sleep (while Cate had, no doubt, been doing her best Mrs Robinson impression into the early hours of the morning), my working day got off to a sterling start when I approached a client who was admiring an enormous Pop Art-style portrait. Intending to impress the client with my personable demeanour and wealth of art historical knowledge, I instead got as far as saying hello before stridently farting. The client beat a hurried retreat, while Doug collapsed into hysterics and proceeded to make comments along the lines of 'You put the F into art' for the entire morning.

'It's not my fault,' I said, with as much dignity as I could muster. 'It's the baby.'

Doug stopped laughing and gave me a severe look instead. 'That's about as bad as blaming it on the dog.'

I glared at him. 'You know what I mean. I can't help being . . . gassy. It's the baby causing it.'

'Are you giving birth to a child or a can of baked beans?'

Before I could respond, the gallery door swung open and Doug's amusement at my uncontrollable flatulence was halted by the terrifying entrance of Cruella, with Keedin trailing in her wake, hitching up his fisherman's pants.

We all stood around awkwardly for a moment, except for Cruella, who was gloating while she displayed Keedin as though she were Salome showing off the head of John the Baptist.

Finally, Doug held out his hand and introduced himself to Keedin. Cruella looked at Doug askance, as though it had just occurred to her that we had names.

'What? Oh, yes. That's Douglas.' She jerked her thumb at me. 'And she's pregnant.'

Hating Cruella, I held out my hand. 'I'm Isabelle,' I said.

To my surprise, Keedin held on to my hand and gazed at me intently. 'The miracle of life,' he breathed reverentially.

Cruella looked around in surprise. 'What?'

'The fecund goddess. Hathor. Aphrodite. The Venus of Willendorf,' he intoned.

Great. Keedin was off his head on drugs. As usual. And, while it made a nice change to be likened to mythical fertility goddesses, I wasn't too happy with the comparison to the Venus of Willendorf, a tiny Paleolithic limestone sculpture of a squat pregnant woman with pendulous breasts and what appeared to be an upturned colander on her head. Suffice it to say that the concept of a yummy mummy had not been invented in 24,000 BC.

'Douglas, get us coffees,' Cruella commanded.

Doug looked distinctly sulky and I couldn't blame him. I was usually the one relegated to the status of coffee-fetcher, but, as Keedin's bizarre interest in me had clearly pushed me up the hierarchy, he meekly departed.

I tried to free my hand from Keedin's sweaty grasp but he was having none of it. He collapsed on the floor in a cross-legged position and proceeded to stare up at my stomach. 'I must worship at the altar of your fertility,' he breathed.

Ugh. I tugged my hand away again and desperately tried to summon a fart. I then thought about disgusting pregnancy facts in the hope that it would make me vomit. I would have done anything to get away from Keedin but, sadly, my body betrayed me and nothing foul-smelling emerged from any of my various orifices in answer to my silent plea for help. That's the problem with bodily waste these days. No sense of chivalry.

'Nothing to worship here,' I said briskly, finally managing to free myself. 'This baby's an atheist. Complete waste of time.'

'What is it, Keedin?' Cruella asked urgently, as though Keedin was having a vision of something that she was incapable of seeing. Which was true to some extent, as Cruella had a tendency to look right through me.

Such a long silence ensued that I started to wonder whether I should do some work instead of just standing there acting as the equivalent of a stoner's television test pattern. But if I broke Keedin's concentration Cruella would probably kick me with the extremely pointy toe of her black thigh-high boot, so I stayed put.

Finally Keedin pronounced, 'You are inspiring me.' His habitually dazed look gave way to a more intent expression. 'Yes,' he murmured. 'Yes. Your child. No. Not the child. The birth perhaps ...' His mutterings grew increasingly incoherent. Cruella and I were both watching him with bated breath: Cruella because she was hoping to make money out of whatever idea he was hatching, and me because I was still trying to push out a fart to get rid of them both. And then Keedin triumphantly announced, 'I must make art from your placenta!'

I choked but it went unnoticed as Cruella celebrated

this idea as though Keedin had just invented Impressionism.

'No.' Keedin frowned, and waved off Cruella's effusions. 'It is not an original idea. Many others have made placenta art. There is a long tradition of laying the placenta in paint and making a print. I will not be the first but I will be the best,' he added modestly. 'So I must be at the birth,' he finished, in a reasonable tone of voice. 'It is very important to me that the placenta is fresh.'

No. No, no, no, no, no. This was not happening.

Keedin misinterpreted the look on my face. 'Naturally I will give you a print to keep,' he said kindly. 'It will make a wonderful present for your child.'

Great. I could hang the placenta print on the wall next to the framed plastic wee stick and our Fetid painting. That should ensure that Jack and I never had guests around to dinner again.

'You'll still have to pay the gallery commission,' Cruella snapped, furious at the thought that Keedin would give away an artwork to me of all people.

I cleared my throat, but, sensing that I was about to voice an objection, Cruella interjected, 'If you were planning on eating your placenta, it's too bad. Keedin's art must come first.'

Trust Cruella's sole fragment of baby-related knowledge to be about the eating of raw organs.

'I had no intention of eating my placenta—' I began with dignity, but that was as far as I got.

'Excellent. Then you couldn't possibly have any objections. Right then. We must sit down and plan this. Over lunch?' Cruella cocked her head invitingly.

Enough was enough. 'Look, I really don't think—'

'I didn't mean *you*, Isabelle. You must stay and mind the gallery.'

I considered my options. I could headbutt Cruella, pull Keedin's pants down and make a run for it. Or I could kill myself, which wasn't very fair to Fetid.

Before I had the chance to put plan A into action, Cruella clapped her hands. 'Come, Keedin! We have so much to discuss!'

With one last possessive glance at my belly, Keedin was towed from the gallery by Cruella, passing Doug, who was holding a disposable tray filled with hot drinks, in the doorway.

I clutched the edge of the desk limply after they'd gone.

'What did I miss?' Doug asked avidly, knowing that Keedin always put on a good show.

'Not much,' I said weakly. 'They've gone out for lunch to discuss the birth of my child.'

'Why?' he asked, taking the lid off one of the coffees and inhaling the scent of the forbidden elixir with regret.

'Keedin wants to be present at the birth of my baby so that he can take the placenta and make a series of prints,' I informed him in a hollow tone.

'You're kidding?'

'Sadly, I'm not. And believe me, Doug, the thought of having Keedin and his horrible fisherman's pants present at the birth of my child is not one that fills me with joy.'

'And Cruella,' Doug added, starting to sip his hot chocolate.

I paused in the act of removing the lid from my drink. 'What do you mean?'

'I mean, Cruella will probably insist upon being there too. You know what she's like with her star artists. She stuck to Chuck like glue when he went on that painting trip to Lake Eyre.'

And that was when I felt it. A small but firm little kick.

Holding my breath, I put down my hot chocolate and then placed my hand on my stomach and waited. Nothing.

'Doug? Say that again.'

'Say what again?' he asked in confusion.

'That thing about Cruella.'

'Cruella wouldn't leave Chuck's side when they went to Lake Eyre,' he said obediently.

'No, you idiot. The bit about Cruella wanting to be present at the birth of Fetid.'

Kick.

'Oh my God.' I sat down abruptly on my chair.

'Belle? What is it? Are you OK?' Doug asked in alarm.

I was fine. I was more than fine. I was grinning like an idiot. 'There's nothing wrong, Doug. I'm just going outside for a minute to make a call, OK?'

With my phone in hand, I raced out of the gallery for some privacy (if that term can apply to standing on the footpath of Toorak Road). I was about to madly dial Jack's pager when I suddenly hesitated. Given that Jack's work often involved emergencies, ironically I was only meant to interrupt Jack at work in an emergency. I chewed my lip and then I felt Fetid kick me again. Filled with joy, I pressed the call button.

A bare minute later Jack called me back.

'It's me.'

'I know it's you. You paged me so I'm calling you back. What's up?'

I tried not to feel hurt by his abrupt manner and reminded myself that he loved me, he just didn't have time to engage in chit-chat while he was at work. I took a deep breath. 'I felt it. Fetid kicked me.'

There was a silence and a horrible feeling descended upon me. Jack was about to chastise me for paging him for something unimportant. I just knew it. And then—

'You felt it? Really?'

Happiness flooded over me. 'Really. And I think it's going to be really smart too.'

'Oh yeah? Why is that?'

'Because the first two times it kicked me were when it heard that Cruella wants to be at the birth. I think it was protesting.'

'*Cruella* wants to be at the birth?'

Oops. Kick.

'Look, don't worry about it. It's definitely not going to happen.'

'You can bet anything you like it's not going to happen! Why the hell would she even want to be there?'

'Because Keedin's going to be there.'

'He bloody well is not!'

'I know, I know,' I said soothingly. 'He just had the idea that he'd like to be there to take away my placenta so that he can use it in his next series of work.'

'Belle, I am warning you, I am not having your nutcase employer or any of her even more insane artists anywhere near during our child's birth.'

'You don't have to warn me, I don't want it either!' I said, starting to get irritated. 'Look, forget about it. Keedin has enthusiasms all the time. He'll have forgotten about it by next week, or whenever he comes down from his high. Whichever happens first. Now say it again.'

'Hold the phone to your tummy,' Jack instructed, but I could hear the excitement in his voice.

I pressed the speakerphone button and then held my mobile to my belly. Jack's voice came faintly through the tiny speakers. 'Cruella is *not* going to be at your birth!'

And this time it didn't feel like a kick. It felt as though Fetid had just turned a joyous somersault inside me.

18
Pick a Number

'What about Ella?'

Jack and I were trying to think of names for our baby as we lay snuggled together in bed. Well, as much as you can snuggle up when you have the equivalent of a fit ball strapped to your tummy. Jack had his hand on my stomach, in hopeful anticipation of feeling Fetid kick, but, no matter how many times we threatened to make Cruella its godmother, Fetid was staying stubbornly still. Either it was asleep or it had gone to visit my pelvic floor in Patagonia.

Feeling Fetid kick for the first time that morning had added a sense of urgency to our task of choosing a name. We had decided not to find out the baby's gender until it was born, which meant we had to decide on a girl's and boy's name. But it was proving to be more fraught than we had anticipated. There were currently two dominant schools of thought when it came to naming your child. The first school advocated traditional, no-nonsense names. So popular Australian baby names included James, William, Isabella and Olivia. (How things changed: when I was at school I had been the sole Isabelle in a sea of Kates and Sarahs.) The other school of thought believed in giving your child a unique and original name, such as Harmony, Patchouli or Juniper, which sounded like a shelf of aromatherapy oils to me.

I didn't like either of these trends. I most certainly did not want my child to have the same name as ten of his or her classmates, but I couldn't help thinking that the 'unique' names that people tended to choose weren't really that unusual at all. You *really* want your child to have an original name? Christen it Falco or Helmut or Fanny and I can guarantee the little tyke will have those personalised licence plates all to themselves.

Jack was waiting for my answer so I shook my head. 'We can't. If Cate gets a female puppy as company for Shnoodle she wants to call her either Mia or Ella.'

He looked at me in disbelief. 'But – that's absurd. Why should Cate's potential dog get preference over our child? And anyway, you can't just *reserve* names.'

'Well, *you* try telling her that. She's having a hard enough time as it is, with everyone settling down around her and popping out babies like we used to burst out champagne corks. The very least that I can do is to not use her favourite names.'

'All right then, what girls' names do you like?'

There was a prolonged silence.

'Belle? Are you asleep?'

'Of course I'm not. I was trying to think of a name that I liked. I can't think of any.'

'Not *one*?'

'There are lots that I like but they all have a problem with them,' I amended. 'I like the name Phoebe, but I went to primary school with a Phoebe and she picked her nose. And Sadie is cute, but there's that song about Sadie the cleaning lady. And one of your ex-girlfriends was called Celeste and—'

Jack put a pillow over my face to silence me. I let out a squawk, which he took as surrender. He removed the pillow and I looked up at him.

'I've just realised that this must be the reason why celebrities choose such outlandish names for their children,' I said thoughtfully. 'They know more people than the average person and they have enormous entourages. So, by the time they've eliminated their chauffeur's cousin's daughter's name, the only options left would have to be Shiloh or Bluebell.'

Jack seemed to be enduring my pop-culture theories rather than enjoying them, and it looked like he was about to pick up the pillow again, so I switched back to defensive ground. 'It's not very nice to smother your pregnant partner.'

'It was either you or me,' he retorted. 'If I'd let you go through the entire list of names that we *can't* use I would have had to throw myself out of the window.'

'This is a single-storey house.'

'It still would have hurt,' he said with great dignity.

'For a doctor, you're a terrible coward when it comes to physical pain,' I remarked. 'But anyway, maybe making a list of the names we definitely *don't* want to use is a good way to start. You know, like a process of elimination. What are you doing?'

Jack had taken the pillow that he had recently removed from my face and clamped it firmly over his own. 'Smothering myself,' he said in a muffled voice, through the pillow. 'It's easier than trying to reason with you.'

I pulled the pillow off him and he lay on his back, staring mournfully at the ceiling. 'Most people – no, let me correct myself – everyone in the entire world makes a shortlist of their favourite names before their baby is born. Not you. Oh no – you want to compile a list of approximately fifty thousand names that you *don't* intend to use.'

'One of our clients at the gallery has a son called Rover and a dog called Ian,' I responded cheerfully.

Jack propped himself up on one elbow. 'Was there a point to that comment?'

'I'm just saying: it's a mixed-up, crazy world. It's a wonder people haven't abandoned names altogether and started using numbers instead. OK, forget girls' names. What boys' names do you like?'

'What about Leroy?' he responded immediately.

'Ha ha. Come on, we really need to take this seriously.'

There was silence as a hurt expression crossed Jack's face. And then it hit me.

'Oh.' I gulped. 'You weren't joking.'

He shook his head.

'*Leroy?* You really like the name Leroy?'

'It's a bit different. Every second kid these days is named Harry or Max.'

'Yes but – *Leroy*?' The only Leroy I could think of was the male ballerina on *Fame*. 'Aren't there any other names that you like? What about the names of our favourite writers or musicians or something?'

Jack brightened. 'Marvin. After Marvin Gaye of course,' he added helpfully.

I blinked, took a deep breath and decided to clarify his position, just in case I had misheard or had fallen asleep and into a nightmare. 'You want to call our child Leroy or Marvin?'

'They're great names. All right then,' he said a bit crossly, 'what boys' names do *you* like?'

'I can't think of any right now. Look, what about footballers?' Jesus, I must be desperate. 'Who's the best Carlton player?'

'Historically or playing now?'

'Historically,' I chose hysterically. What difference did it make when the future of little Leroy Marvin was at stake?

'That would be Jezza, I guess. Jesaulenko.'

'Is that a first or last name?' I asked cautiously.

He sighed. '*Alex* Jesaulenko.'

'Alex is a nice name,' I encouraged. I didn't love it, but it was sure as hell better than Leroy or Marvin. Marvin. Starvin' Marvin from *South Park*. Marvin the Martian.

Jack shook his head. 'When I was studying medicine my cadaver's nickname was Alex. Where are you going?'

I had pushed back the duvet and started to climb out of bed. 'To throw myself out the window,' I retorted. 'So far we've come up with names associated with a nose-picker, a martian and now a corpse. Fetid's doomed. It's best that I end it for both of us.'

Jack pulled me back into bed. 'Maybe there's something to be said for your process of elimination after all. I didn't think it would be so hard to come up with two names.'

'Three,' I corrected him. 'We need three names. A first name, a middle name and a name for the placenta.'

Jack sighed. 'Prepare to hear a phrase that will be repeated endlessly throughout our long, long life together: What the hell are you talking about, Belle?'

'The third stage of labour is when I give birth to the placenta,' I said smugly, thrilled to show off what I had learned from all my reading. 'If I'm going to give birth to something, I think we should at least have a name for it.'

'We're having so much trouble naming the baby that I don't think we can ever have a second child, let alone give our firstborn a middle name, and you want to name the placenta?' Jack protested.

'This from a man who had a pet name for a dead body that he experimented on,' I sniffed.

'Fine. Let's call the placenta Luigi.'

'*Luigi?* What on earth is wrong with you? Why do you have such horrible taste in names?'

Jack sat up in bed. 'Because it's a placenta! Who cares what we call it?'

'You'd care if you were giving birth to it,' I said, a note of bitterness creeping into my voice. I struggled to sit upright so that I wasn't at a disadvantage.

Jack looked at me. 'Is there a problem that I don't know about?' he asked, all of the laughter gone from his voice.

I felt like saying yes. The problem was that Jack didn't have to get time off work to go to boring hospital appointments. He wasn't frightened of losing his career. He wasn't terrified that he'd never recognise his own body again.

But I was tired and I knew that rationally I couldn't resent him for these things. So I shook my head and instead said, 'OK. Let's call the placenta Luigi.'

Jack shot me a look that showed I hadn't fooled him by glossing over whatever it was that was bothering me, but merely said, 'Good girl. You know, come to think of it, Luigi's not a bad name for our—'

'Don't even think it,' I warned him. I patted my tummy. 'Fetid, meet Luigi. Be nice to him because he's the one who brings you your dinner.'

Feeling as though we had accomplished something by naming the placenta, we turned off our bedside lamps and settled back down. Jack fell asleep quickly, as he usually did, but I lay awake for a long time, feeling Fetid moving inside me.

It felt strange not to tell Jack exactly what I was thinking and feeling, especially when those thoughts and feelings were about our baby. But I couldn't. Because lately it seemed that I was constantly annoyed with him for not even considering issues that I couldn't stop turning over in my mind. The simple fact was that, for Jack, the reality of having a baby would probably start to kick in around about the time the baby's head emerged from my – ow, I didn't even want to think about it. For me, the baby was already real. I could feel it moving (unless I was bonding with my dinner), and its presence was going to disrupt every single aspect of my life. Jack's carefree optimism was directly related to the fact that the baby wasn't inside *his* body and he wouldn't be its primary carer once it was out.

I knew that it was unfair, but I couldn't help it – I resented him for it. And, if we couldn't even agree on a name, what hope did we have when it came to all the really big issues, like education and moral guidance and teaching Fetid that it would be wrong to date the future Danish Crown Prince because Doug's child had first dibs?

So I lay in the dark, worrying, while Jack slept, until he rolled over in his sleep, on to his side. Wanting comfort, I tried to snuggle up to him and put my arm around him, but my stomach was too big for me to get very near.

I had thought that having a child would bring Jack and me even closer together, but right now it felt as though it was doing the exact opposite.

19

Birthing Brazilians and Epi-Ladies

'Don't forget our childbirth classes start tonight,' I warned Jack the following morning, as he prepared to race out the front door to go to work.

'Oh shit. What time is it again?'

Not exactly the response I would have liked, but at least he was planning on being there.

'Seven o'clock.'

'I'll have to meet you there. The classes are at the hospital so there's no point me coming home first.'

'OK. But please, *please* try not to be late.'

I wasn't sure if he'd heard because the door had already slammed behind him.

I had been looking forward to the childbirth classes for a long time now because, despite my extensive reading on the subject of pregnancy and childbirth, a lot of it still didn't make sense.

From what I could tell, there seemed to be a hierarchy to giving birth that was even stricter than the high-school pecking order, where Madeline Chan (fashionable, popular and smart) had trickled all the way down to Eugene Radish (dorky cry-baby who smelled like wee). Only the birthing hierarchy made no sense to me at all. For starters, it seemed to be closely modelled on the most popular styles and systems of hair removal.

The reigning queens of childbirth were undoubtedly those opting for natural labour, who I liked to call the Brazilians (after the waxing procedure). Forget elective caesareans or pain relief, if you wanted R-E-S-P-E-C-T these days, it was all about giving birth 'naturally'. As in drug-free.

There was nothing bloody well natural about it if you asked me. In no other situation, barring an actual Brazilian wax, a visit to an S&M club or watching an episode of *Big Brother*, does anyone willingly give themselves up to extreme physical pain. Whenever I encountered a Brazilian birther gushing about how she had wanted to really *know* what childbirth felt like, it utterly baffled me. If I had asked her if she'd like to swallow an entire watermelon and excrete it whole, she would probably have politely declined. And yet, that's basically how the physics of childbirth works.

Why the Brazilians didn't give birth in a dominatrix club fitted with a large plasma screen tuned to *Big Brother* just to really ramp up the pain factor was beyond me, as surely their zenith of happiness would have been giving birth while having hot wax dripped on to their bare flesh as they watched Sheree and Skylar sit in the hot tub and complain about how Jayson didn't respect their opinions on pole-dancing.

Then there were the devotees of stupid pain-relief methods, known amongst pregnant women as the 'Epi-Ladies'. Epilady is the company behind many electric, hair-removal devices, which, as we all know, can hurt a teeny weeny bit. The Epi-Ladies' preferred pain-relief options included, but were not restricted to, self-hypnosis, hypno-birthing and acupuncture. These weren't pain-relief options, but a smorgasbord of mental-health issues.

I wasn't really sure of the difference between self-hypnosis and hypno-birthing, apart from the fact that the hypno-birthing kit came with a CD. Suffice it to say that both doctrines involved meditating while something the weight of a medicine ball *only with limbs* was coming out of your vagina. Yeah, right. And maybe I could learn to levitate while I was at it.

Acupuncture was outright insanity. Anyone who opted to have needles inserted into them at the exact moment that they were thrashing around in the worst pain of their life was clearly not just flying over the cuckoo's nest but had taken up residence inside Michael Jackson's head.

When it came to determining which category I fitted into on the birthing method/hair removal table of preferences, I was favouring elective caesareans/depilatory cream. Admittedly, I had never enquired deeply into exactly *how* the chemical properties of Nair made hair melt away, but then again I didn't really want to know. I was sure that, somewhere in Nair HQ, someone knew what they were doing. An elective caesarean appealed to me for the same reason. It was a surgical procedure conducted by professionals who had done it countless times before. Having them, not me, in charge of proceedings seemed eminently sensible.

The only thing that had given me pause was a quote from Britney Spears that I had seen in an old magazine. Britney had been discussing the birth of her second child, who, it was breathlessly reported, had been delivered by caesarean (or C-section, as they called it in the USA). According to the star, it had been 'a piece of cake!!'

I had stared at the quote for a very long time. A caesarean was, by any measure, *not* a piece of cake. The doctors had to cut through layers of fat and muscle, as well as cutting open the uterus, to pull the baby out.

There would be seven layers of stitches and a long, slow recovery. One of the books I had read stated that recovering from the major abdominal surgery that was a caesarean was comparable to recovering from a serious car accident.

I remembered visiting Audie in the hospital a day after the birth of the twins. She had given birth naturally and had been up and dressed, smiling and seemingly fit and well. With a caesarean, the recovery time was a minimum of six weeks. I imagined that, if, like Britney Spears, you had a full time staff including a chef, a nanny, several maids to do the housework and laundry, a chauffeur and your own doctor, then, yes, a caesarean probably would be a piece of cake. But for most women it would mean pain and immobility, right at the time when they were also suffering from sleep deprivation, trying to learn how to breastfeed and having to deal with a small helpless creature with inexplicable demands.

And, if I was really honest with myself (and I might as well be in the privacy of my own head), there was a whiff of unnecessary consumerism about an elective caesarean. My argument with myself went something like this:

ME: So what? Why shouldn't I avail myself of every available advance in medical practice? What's the point of living in a developed country in the twenty-first century if I don't?

ME: I'm not saying that you ought to deny yourself good medical care and pain relief if you want it. But having an elective caesarean is as extreme as an unassisted home-birth. Why do you have faith in doctors but not in yourself?

ME: Because they know what they're doing and I don't! I can't believe you would even ask me that. You know me as well as I do.

ME: Are you sure you haven't been a bit sucked in by the 'fashionable' aspect of a caesarean?

ME (sulkily): No. Yes. Maybe. Probably.

ME: And you're worried about your vagina stretching to the size of a soccer net, aren't you?

ME: Eew. But yes. I am.

ME: You know that's silly, don't you?

ME: Of course I know. But I don't think it's a completely silly and vain thing to think about. I love Jack and we've always had amazing sex. What if I'm not sexy any more?

ME: That was far too much information.

ME: I think you're taking this dialogue thing a bit too far now.

ME: A part of you knows that this is a cop-out. It's because you're the product of an affluent society, so you've always been able to buy your way out of anything difficult.

ME: That part of me would be you. *My* part of me thinks that I'm fortunate to have choices and that choosing to have an elective caesarean isn't shameful.

ME: Ooh, that was a bit deep, Britney. Can you sing it to the tune of 'My Prerogative'?

ME: Shut up, hippy.

I have never broken a bone. Never had an operation. The worst injury I'd ever had was the time I sprained my ankle during the City to Surf fun run in Sydney and I wasn't even running at the time. The upshot is: I don't understand physical pain. I've never really experienced it and, quite frankly, I don't want to.

Which was why I was looking forward to the class that night. Maybe there was a secret to giving birth that no one let you in on until you were past the halfway mark of your pregnancy. Maybe tonight it would finally all make sense.

'Want to go for a drink?' Doug asked, as we turned the Open sign around to read Closed, switched on the alarm and locked the gallery door behind us.

I gestured for him to be quiet as I listened to the message that Jack had just left on my mobile.

Hi, Belle, it's me. Don't be mad but I'm not going to be able to make it to the class tonight. Something's come up at work and I have no idea what time I'm going to get out of here but it's not looking good. So don't wait up for me. Love you.

'Belle? I asked if you wanted to come for a drink?'

'What?' I tried to concentrate on Doug, even as I wondered what my foremost emotional reaction to Jack's message was. Sympathy that he was so overworked? Anger that he was missing out on something so important? I realised that Doug was looking at me impatiently.

'A drink?' I repeated, my mind still on Jack's message. 'Hey, wait a minute. We're pregnant. We're not meant to be drinking.'

'Mineral water was still a drink the last time I checked. Don't be so bolshie.'

'Oh. Well I can't anyway. I have to go to my childbirth class.' I paused and then added bitterly, '*Alone*.' Right. So it was a victory for anger then.

'Is the divine Dr Jack busy saving lives again?'

'Do you have to put it like that when I'm trying to stay mad with him?'

There was a pause and then Doug offered, 'Would you like me to come with you?'

'You'd do that for me?'

'Well, yes. But to be honest I want to come for my own benefit too. You know that I don't like to do things by halves, and if this is part of being pregnant then count me in. Anything you can do, I can do, and all that. Where is this gig?'

'It starts in forty-five minutes in the basement of the Royal Women's Hospital.'

'OK, I'll meet you there.'

'But I'm going straight there! Why don't you just come with me now?'

He gave me a look filled with horror. 'Like *this*?' he said, indicating his immaculate Paul Smith suit, Harrolds' shirt, Ted Baker tie and antique cufflinks.

'You look very nice.'

He cast me a withering look. 'I don't look "very nice", I look *fabulous*. "Very nice" only applies to ensembles under a thousand dollars. And that's not the point. I'm not dressed appropriately.'

'But it really doesn't matter what you wear,' I said, suddenly wondering in alarm whether Doug was planning on attending the class with a cushion shoved up his top. I wouldn't put it past him. Doug had embraced his empathetic pregnancy a little more whole-heartedly than I had intended.

'What I wear *always* matters,' Doug replied severely. 'And, if I'm standing in for Jack, I need to look fatherly.'

I breathed a sigh of relief.

'The problem is how to interpret fatherly,' he went on. 'Are we thinking Mike Brady or David Beckham?'

'Well, Mike Brady was gay, so maybe use him as a role model.'

Doug shot me a pitying glance. 'And you think David Beckham isn't?'

'Oh for Pete's sake. The man is happily married, he has a brood of kids, and the only whiff of a sex scandal around him involved another *woman*. Let the dream go. Now, we'd better hurry up or we'll both get stuck in traffic. Call me if you get lost.' I started to walk away and then I turned back. 'Doug?'

But Doug was already striding in the opposite direction and he didn't turn around. Instead he waved one hand in the air and called over his shoulder, 'It's OK, Belladonna. You're very welcome.'

20

Childbirth 101

Unprepossessingly, the childbirth education classes were held in the basement of the hospital. As I wandered around the dimly lit corridors, seeking the right room, I couldn't help reflecting that the last time I had taken a night class was after the break-up of my relationship with Charlie. My experience of night classes was that they were filled with bitter, single people who were all hoping to meet the love of their life while salsa dancing or learning to play the lute.

Childbirth education classes were apparently where you went once you had paired up with your lute-playing, salsa-dancing fantasy and decided to procreate. The hilarious thing was that all of the couples in my class looked *exactly* as though they were born for each other, with the exception of one couple who looked disturbingly like they had been born of the same mother.

There was a dorky couple, who were overly friendly in the desperate way of people who are aware of their own dagginess and realise that everyone is disinclined to make friends with them. Their names were Gareth and Nancy. I knew this because they were wearing nametags. We all had to wear nametags that had been prepared for us.

There was a trendy couple there too; even though

they had their backs to me and were standing in the far corner of the room perusing a fascinating poster dedicated to (surprise, surprise) the pelvic floor (Use It or Lose It!), I could tell that she was wearing very expensive maternity garments, while her partner was wearing a designer jacket that was similar to one that Charlie had once owned.

The sibling couple, Joan and Evan, were so quiet and non-descript that I almost tripped over them as I tried to find a spare chair to sit on.

And finally there was Nadia, whose husband had run off with a Crown Casino croupier only a month ago. Nadia was a very angry woman, as she had every right to be. We all sat there in stunned silence as she gave us her considered opinion on her husband, croupiers, the den of iniquity that was Crown Casino, and Billy Crudup, the actor who had run off with Claire Danes when his partner was seven months pregnant. For Billy Crudup's sake, I hoped that he never decided to go to Crown Casino, unless he was prepared to play Russian roulette with Nadia.

By the time that Nadia's vitriolic tirade finally ran out of puff, Doug still hadn't arrived. The instructor clapped her hands to get our attention and the trendy couple in the corner finally turned around.

And that was when my heart stopped beating.

It was Charlie and Sleazel.

The good news was that Sleazel was quite obviously pregnant, which meant that they had a good reason to be there, so I hadn't accidentally dipped into Keedin's stash and started to hallucinate. The bad news was that she was pregnant. To *my* ex-boyfriend. Who, according to Cate, had never wanted children. Unless he had just never wanted children with *me*. Good grief. Charlie had only been back in my life for thirty seconds and the bellboy had already dumped an entire range of Louis Vuitton-encased emotional baggage at my feet. The aforementioned ex-boyfriend, it had to be said, was looking as stunned as I felt, as he was currently doing his best 'goldfish with extra goggly eyes' routine.

I made a valiant attempt to speak, but only succeeded in whimpering. However, the small noise was enough to draw the instructor's attention to me. Seemingly unaware of the drama unfolding in her classroom, she squinted at my nametag and then asked, 'And will your partner be joining us tonight, Isabelle? His name is Jack, isn't it?'

I nodded, trying to drag my gaze away from Charlie, who was now opening and shutting his mouth, which only added to the goldfish impression. Sleazel and I had never met in person before, but she must have recognised me from old photographs or something as she had instinctively placed her hand on Charlie's arm in a possessive 'keep your hands off my goldfish' gesture. Although I had never met Sleazel, I had immediately known it was her for two reasons. Firstly, I had heard through the grapevine that Charlie was still with her and, secondly, Charlie had told me ages ago how tiny she was and that she was an oboist. It was hard to explain, but she just *looked* like an oboist. There was a little telltale pucker around her mouth.

I gathered my wits and was about to respond, but at that moment everyone's head swivelled to the door as Doug made his entrance.

He wasn't just Mike Brady; he was Jim Robinson from *Neighbours*, Alf Stewart from *Home and Away* and a walking tribute to bad taste, all in one.

Doug was wearing a truly hideous cardigan (*cardigan!*) that appeared to have shoulder pads. Underneath the cardigan was a T-shirt bearing the slogan 'Warning – Dad Jokes Ahead'. Cream-coloured chinos with a perfectly ironed crease up the middle of each leg, grey zip-up Hush Puppies and what I was reasonably certain from this distance were novelty socks completed his outfit. Never one to forget accessories, Doug was clutching a brown vinyl man-bag.

Before Doug could introduce himself, the instructor bustled up to him, slapped the only remaining nametag – which was Jack's, naturally – on Doug's cardigan and told him to take the seat next to mine. She then strode to the front of the room and launched into her introduction.

'Good evening, everyone. My name is Angela and I'm your childbirth educator. There are three classes to attend. Tonight we're going to cover the different stages of labour and childbirth. In the second class, we'll watch a video on childbirth and discuss pain relief, and the final class will be about basic newborn care. The midwife clinic will also be running an optional breastfeeding class in a few months' time that I strongly recommend you sign up for. Now, we're running a little behind time, so I'm going to push straight on and you can all have a chance to chat further when we break after an hour.'

Angela made us rearrange our chairs so that we were all in a circle facing one another. Charlie dragged his gaze away from Doug's ensemble, caught my eye and smiled weakly. I tried to smile back in a 'My, hasn't it been a long time since we lived together, broke up acrimoniously and moved on with our lives' kind of way, but caught Sleazel's expression instead. She was staring at Doug with a smug look on her face. As you would, if the father of your child was wearing a Prada jacket rather than a cardigan in a virulent shade of puce. She caught me looking at her, gave me a nasty glare and tucked her arm more firmly into Charlie's. Meanwhile, Doug had registered that Sleazel was giving us dirty looks and was now looking at me as he tried to figure out what was going on. Honestly. It felt like we were all auditioning for an episode of *Days of Our Lives.*

'Have I got something weird on my face?' Doug muttered under his breath.

'Your face is about the only part of you that *hasn't* got something weird on it,' I whispered back.

'Then why is that woman over there staring at me?'

I desperately wanted to tell him, but Angela had already started to talk and I knew that Doug would freak out – and probably at considerable volume – if I revealed Charlie's identity. So I shushed him, tried not to focus on Charlie and how well he was looking, and forced myself to gather up a modicum of equilibrium and pay attention to Angela instead.

'Let's begin with some basic pelvic floor exercises. As I'm sure all you ladies know by this stage of your pregnancy, looking after your pelvic floor is *extremely* important. So I want you all to sit up straight and then lean forward slightly. Right. Good. Now clench your buttocks.'

I looked over at Doug. He was leaning forward with an intense look of concentration on his face. I nudged him. 'Not you!' I hissed.

'Huh?'

'*You're* not meant to be doing it! It's just the mothers.'

'Oh.' He sat back, not at all abashed. 'Shame. I'm quite good at that one.'

I sneaked a peek over at Sleazel. Of course she had been watching.

'Everyone clenching their buttocks? Good. Now that,

ladies, is *not* your pelvic floor,' Angela boomed. '*That* is your rectum.'

'Good grief, *I* could have told you that,' Doug muttered in disgust. 'Honestly, if you heterosexuals don't even know the difference between your bum and your vagina, the miracle of birth is that you manage to get pregnant in the first place.'

'Now, I want you to try again, but this time clench your vaginal muscles,' Angela instructed.

'Like you're trying to stop a wee,' Nancy interjected, clearly vying for the role of teacher's pet.

Unfortunately for Nancy, it backfired. Angela, who obviously liked to run a tight ship, turned on her and said icily, 'I prefer to tell my ladies to imagine that they're trying to hold a rolled-up hundred-dollar bill in their vagina.'

Nancy choked; Nadia muttered something about how that was probably what her husband's croupier was doing at this very moment; and Doug looked appalled.

'This is a childbirth class!' he said under his breath.

'So?' I whispered back.

'So I was expecting Mary Poppins!' he hissed. 'Not the ruddy Mayflower Madam.'

Angela was glaring at us, so I hastily snapped back to attention and tried to do the exercise. We sat there for a few very long minutes, with strained looks on our faces. The men all stared at their feet, with the notable exception of Doug, who had got bored rapidly and had started to practise his buttock clenches again. I had no idea whether the other women were actually exercising their pelvic floor, but I was reasonably certain that I was conducting the world's first combined buttocks, abs and Manipura chakra workout. I was also now firmly of the opinion that my pelvic floor was like the secret floor 7½ in *Being John Malkovich*. Which potentially wasn't all bad. If my pelvic floor had a secret portal into John Malkovich's head, maybe the baby could exit that way. God, that new haircut really suited Charlie. I shook myself, tried to focus and re-clenched.

After we'd finished, Angela gave a talk about the stages of labour. At first I found it hard to concentrate, what with Charlie sitting opposite me and Doug's headache-inducing cardigan in close proximity, but then it got interesting. The first stage was waiting for the cervix to dilate to about four centimetres. Apparently, this could take anywhere between a few hours and several days, and would involve contractions that would be around five to twenty minutes apart and last for about twenty to forty seconds. According to the handout Angela gave us, I would have a smiley face, despite the fact that I might also be experiencing diarrhoea, backache and period-like pain. Of course I would be smiling at this juncture. Because I was only pregnant and about to give birth: IT WASN'T LIKE I WAS SICK OR ANYTHING.

Next came the active phase of the first stage when the contractions would last about a minute and come three to seven minutes apart. The smiley face on the handout now had a straight line where the smile used to be. I could expect to have a horizontal line for a mouth for approximately three to five hours.

Then there was something called transition, when the cervix dilated to the magic ten centimetres. This could take a couple of hours and contractions might last for over a minute and come every couple of minutes. The smiley face was now represented by a frowny face, which was unsurprising as the side effects of transition can include vomiting, anal pressure and feelings of panic. I was already panicking and wanting to vomit just thinking about anal pressure. Angela's chief suggestion for dealing with these horrible symptoms was 'a cool washcloth on the face and neck'. In my humble opinion, this would be about as helpful as aromatherapy, unless the washcloth was dipped in chloroform first.

I could hardly bear to even look at the illustration for the second stage of labour. Suffice it to say the smiley face looked like it had served as the model for Edvard Munch's *The Scream*. The second stage comprised pushing, crowning (I perked up for a moment until I discovered that this did not involve me and a tiara but was the part where the dreaded episiotomy reared its, er, head) and the all-important birth. The second stage could last for a couple of hours unless it was a really fast birth, which sounded preferable until Angela cheerily informed us that a fast birth could send our bodies into shock. We could also expect to poo in the last stages of labour. Excellent. Then there was the third stage, when I'd give birth to Luigi the placenta. There was no smiley face for this stage, as presumably by the time we got to this bit, the smiley face had been carted off for electroconvulsive shock therapy.

The only part that I really understood was Luigi's bit. The rest was a complete mass of contradictions. Some women didn't notice the first stage, others suffered intense pain and 'back labour'. Contractions could be regular or irregular. We were advised not to call the hospital until contractions were two minutes apart, but were helpfully reminded that for some women contractions never had a consistent pattern.

The waters breaking, which I had always thought was an irrevocable part of giving birth, apparently didn't happen to everyone either. And then there was the bloody show. This was not a reference to a poorly performed Broadway musical, rather it was the discharge of the mucus plug (Doug went pale at this point) that had been blocking the cervix, and acted as a sign that labour was about to commence. Unless, of course, it didn't happen. Quite frankly, the 'may or may not happen' basket was starting to resemble my overflowing in-tray.

It seemed to me that with six billion people on the planet, we really ought to have sorted out a better system for this birthing business by now. No one seemed to have any bloody idea of what was really likely to happen. When it came to things like space exploration and international finance, serious organisations like NASA and the World Bank had been set up to oversee the smooth running of their operations. Childbirth, on the other hand, had apparently been left in the sole care of a schizophrenic smiley face and a clairvoyant.

'Are there any questions?' Angela asked.

Doug had been busily taking notes (in between occasional emulations of the final smiley face's look of horror), but now his hand shot up into the air. 'Are there special birthing measuring tapes or can we just use normal ones for measuring the cervix?' he asked politely.

Angela looked at him askance. 'What on earth are you talking about?'

'Measuring the cervix,' Doug repeated, with a look of surprise. 'That's how you tell what stage of labour you're up to, isn't it?'

Sleazel sniggered.

'Yes, but we don't use a *measuring tape*,' Angela said severely. 'You insert two fingers into—'

She broke off, mainly because Doug had put one hand over his face and was holding the other up to forestall any further information.

'Please make her stop,' he whispered faintly to me. 'I just heard the words "mucus" and "plug" used in conjunction for the first time a few minutes ago, and now this.'

'Stop over-reacting Doug,' I hissed back.

'I *ate* before I came tonight, you know,' he ended plaintively.

'*You* don't measure the cervix anyway, the midwife does,' Nancy informed him superciliously.

Doug glared at her, but, before he could retaliate, Angela clapped her hands. 'We'll have a short break now. You can help yourselves to a drink and a biscuit from the kitchen next door, and then please be back here in fifteen minutes' time to continue with the class.'

As everyone rose, I had a split-second decision to make. I could try to explain to Charlie and Sleazel why Doug was my partner for the childbirth class and why he was wearing that insane outfit and Jack's nametag. But I didn't want to. Charlie had always been embarrassed by my propensity for falling into unlikely situations. But, more importantly, this was the first time that Charlie and I had seen each other since we had broken up all those years ago. I wanted to be radiating happiness at the way my Charlie-free life had turned out. I wanted to be poised and friendly but emotionally distant. Above all else, I desperately wanted Jack by my side, the way that Charlie had Sleazel by his.

I grabbed Doug by his cardigan and pulled him back down. Charlie and Sleazel were already bearing down on us. There was no time to waste. 'The guy in the Prada jacket is my ex-boyfriend Charlie,' I whispered.

Doug started to emit a high-pitched noise. I clamped down so hard on his arm that his squeal turned into a whimper instead. 'He's the pilot who left me in Sydney to move to Adelaide and then started seeing Sleazel. She plays the oboe,' I gabbled, trying to relay all the pertinent information that Jack would obviously have known.

I remembered the most important thing: 'Don't forget you're Jack.'

And then they were right in front of us.

21
Frisson-ing

Sleazel and I looked nothing alike. Instead of my long brown curls and green eyes, she had a honey-coloured bob and big brown eyes, which was a little disappointing. When it comes to your own ex, I think everyone secretly hopes that the girl who comes after you will resemble you. That way you can convince yourself that your ex is making a pathetic attempt to replace you with a poorer, paler imitation of yourself, and that he will never really get over you but will always maintain a candlelit shrine to your memory, although not in a serial-killer kind of way, with pictures of you plastered all over the walls, because that's a bit too spooky. But Charlie dating someone who resembled me for the rest of his natural life would have been perfectly acceptable.

I had last seen Charlie five years ago when we had bade each other a passionate farewell, as he left me behind in Sydney to move to Adelaide to take up a new job. Several months later, our relationship had fallen apart in spectacular fashion. Then he had met Sleazel and I had met Jack. And now here we all were, face to face for the first time. Well, with Doug standing in for Jack, of course.

Doug, bless him, gamely took it upon himself to break the ice. 'I'm Jack,' he introduced himself, holding his hand out to Charlie. He continued in a tone of admiration, 'I have to tell you, I absolutely *love* your jacket. It's from quite a few seasons ago if I'm not mistaken, but it has those classic Prada lines—' He broke off as I viciously elbowed him in the ribs.

As he turned to look at me in outrage, I discreetly mouthed the words '*Too gay*,' which then made Doug say 'Whoops-a-daisy!', cover his mouth and giggle nervously, which didn't exactly rectify the impression. Looking contrite, Doug tried to remedy matters by launching into his blokiest voice and booming, 'So, Chuck, you used to date Belle. She's a regular little firecracker in the sack, isn't she?' He finished by pinching my bum, which shocked both of us so much that we simultaneously squealed.

I glared Doug into silence, and, although he did subside, he cast me an injured look that clearly said, 'What more do you want from me?'

Charlie was looking at Doug as though he was utterly unfathomable, while Sleazel was sizing me up in a way that I didn't like one little bit.

'Izzy,' Charlie finally said, with a forced smile. 'How are you?'

I met his gaze, and then something truly awful happened. Perhaps it was hearing his old pet name for me, the one that no one else had ever used. Maybe it was because we hadn't broken up face-to-face all those years ago. Whatever the reason, at that moment, a tiny, Charlie-shaped piece of my heart, which I hadn't even known was still there, melted, causing an emotion in me that I had thought was reserved for Jack.

'Fine,' I managed to respond, unable to tear my gaze away from his. 'What – what are you doing in Melbourne?'

'We moved back a few months ago.' He gave an

embarrassed laugh and gestured towards Sleazel. 'For the baby's sake. You know, to be with our families.'

I nodded, even though I didn't know, because the Charlie I had known had always put his career first and everything else, including me, had always come a distant second. But right now I didn't care, given the way he was looking at me.

It was at this point that Sleazel cleared her throat at a volume that was only warranted if you'd swallowed a hairball.

'Oh God, sorry.' I made a belated attempt to gather my wits. 'Er – Jack, this is Sleazel. Sleazel, this is Doug. I mean Jack. Doug's the hairball. I mean the cat.'

For reasons that I couldn't comprehend, Sleazel shot me a look that ought to have slain me on the spot. She ignored Doug's outstretched hand and instead said icily, 'My name is *Liesel*.'

Oops.

Charlie tried to smooth the situation over by saying, 'Oh well, you used to call her Isa-smell . . .' but faltered as his beloved turned her slayer gaze on him. I had to hand it to her. The woman could give good Gorgon.

'So how many months are you?' asked Sleazel, somehow managing to make the question sound like verbal abuse.

'Six. I think.' I tried to focus. 'I might be five. Or seven. Actually, I'm not too sure. Only my friend Cate seems to know the exact number.'

'How is Cate?' Charlie asked warmly.

I smiled. I had always liked it that Charlie and Cate had got along so well. 'She's great. She's doing amazingly at work. She'll be running the country soon.'

'*We're* twenty-six weeks,' Sleazel informed me, even though I hadn't asked. 'My goodness, look at the heels on your boots.' That was all she said, so how she managed to imply that I was endangering my child's life for the sake of looking fashionable I had absolutely no idea. But the onslaught didn't stop there. 'How many centimetres are you?'

Doug shuddered. 'If this has anything to with that cervix thing, I'd prefer it if we changed the subject.' Catching my admonitory 'don't-be-gay' look he lamely added, 'Your boobs look great in that top, Belle.'

'I wasn't talking about your cervix, I was talking about your bump.'

'You measure your bump?' I said blankly.

Sleazel nodded. 'Of course. Well, *I* don't, but our obstetrician does.'

'Oh. Well that would explain it. I don't have my own obstetrician. I just see the midwife on duty.'

Sleazel looked delighted. 'Don't tell me you're going public? Oh, you brave thing.'

I looked at her in confusion. 'Of course I'm having it at a public hospital. I'm having it in *this* public hospital. If you're not having your baby at the Royal Women's, what are you doing in this class?'

'We're at Frances Perry, of course,' she said, naming the posh, private maternity hospital that was attached to the Royal Women's Hospital. 'But unfortunately because we just moved back to Melbourne all their classes were full, so we have to attend these ones.' She looked around the tired room with disdain. 'The Frances Perry classes are held at the Sofitel hotel,' she finished with a sigh of regret.

Now it was Doug's turn to nudge me. 'Why are *we* slumming it?'

I gritted my teeth. 'Because *we* believe in supporting the public hospital system,' I said. 'The public hospital system that *you* work in, remember?'

Charlie was still looking at Doug as though he was

trying to make sense of him. Which I could understand. In the same way that you don't want your ex to trade up too much, discovering that you have been replaced in their affections by a Hush Puppies-shod, man-bag-toting, novelty-sock-wearer doesn't do much for the self-esteem either.

'You're a doctor, aren't you?' Charlie asked Doug.

I shot Charlie a shrewd look. Guess the grapevine worked both ways.

'Yes. Yes, I am,' Doug responded nervously.

'What do you specialise in?'

Doug had started to sweat, although whether this was as a result of nervousness or of being clad entirely in man-made fibres I had no idea. 'Bruises,' he attempted gamely.

Charlie laughed, but Sleazel looked suspicious. 'No, really, what do you specialise in?'

Doug looked at Sleazel with dislike. 'Hydrocarbon pneumonitis. Shall we go and get a drink before the break is over?'

Vanquished by Doug's display of medical terminology, Charlie and Sleazel meekly headed off towards the kitchen.

Doug started to follow them but I caught his sleeve and held him back.

'What the hell is hydrocarbon pneumonia, or whatever it was that you said?'

Doug grinned. 'Hydrocarbon pneumonitis. It's a real condition,' he continued in a superior tone, 'but you're unlikely to contract it unless you're a fire-eater, in which case I suppose it's only one of many occupational hazards.' He caught my look of awe and shrugged. 'What can I say? I surf the web.'

We exited the classroom in Sleazel and Charlie's wake and joined the others in the kitchen, where they were headily indulging in cordial from plastic cups and stale biscuits. I was itching to drag Charlie off and talk to him in private but I couldn't see how. Nadia had clearly just been letting off another head of steam about her no-good husband because Gareth and Nancy were both staring at her with their mouths open, while Joan and Evan looked terrified and as though they were trying to hide behind the coffee urn.

Perhaps to avoid further awkward questions from Sleazel or Charlie, Doug launched, slightly maniacally, into conversation. 'Whatever happened to the womb, that's what I want to know,' he began nostalgically. 'These days it's all uterus this and uterus that. Womb just sounds so much *cosier*, don't you think?'

We all watched in silence as this conversational gambit fell to its death. Sensing that there was someone potentially more unpopular than them in the group, Gareth and Nancy leaped at the chance to talk about themselves.

'We're having a boy,' Gareth said, beaming.

'I want to name him Gareth,' Nancy said, then added unnecessarily, 'after his dad.'

'Luckily, I'm having a girl,' Nadia said viciously, knocking back lemon cordial like it was pure bourbon, 'or I'd have to name mine Unfaithful Bastard. I hope his penis falls off.'

Correctly discerning that this final comment was aimed at Nadia's husband rather than their offspring, Nancy determinedly swung the conversation back in their direction. 'Whenever Gareth puts his hand on my stomach, Gareth Junior kicks me like you wouldn't believe! He's going to be a real daddy's boy, I can just tell.'

'That's probably a good thing,' Doug remarked. 'Because if he was a mummy's boy he'd be a Nancy boy.'

There was a dead silence.

'Are you insinuating that our son is going to be gay?' Gareth asked, in an 'I-may-be-dorky-but-I-can-take-you-Cardigan-Boy' kind of a voice.

'Of course not,' Doug said hastily. 'Not that there's anything wrong with that. If he is.'

'I play in an orchestra and many of my best friends are gay,' Sleazel said coldly. 'I don't find gay jokes amusing.'

Doug looked at her with disdain. 'That's a shame, because I know a great one about an Englishman, an Irishman and a frozen hot dog—'

I dragged Doug off to a corner of the kitchen, under the lame pretence of wanting another stale biscuit. 'What is wrong with you?' I scolded, when we were a safe distance away. 'You can't make comments like that!'

'I *always* make comments like that!'

'Yes, but that's when you're being *you*. You're not gay tonight, remember? You're the father of my child.'

Doug had the good grace to look ashamed. 'I forgot,' he admitted. 'But that Sleazel. If she has a single gay friend I'll measure your cervix the midwife way. I know her type, all PC views while the closest she's probably ever come to a gay person is watching *Little Britain*.'

'Just please try to remember that you're Jack, *not* you.'

He grinned but merely said impishly, 'Your ex is cute.'

'Stop perving on Charlie,' I growled. 'You're a taken, pregnant man, remember?'

Rejoining the group, we discovered that Sleazel was holding forth on nicknames. 'We call ours Bambino,' she said fondly, patting her stomach and directing a mawkish look at Charlie. 'But usually we shorten it to Bambi.'

'I hope you've written your will!' I said merrily. Everyone stared at me and I collapsed into incoherent muttering. 'Because of the hunter shooting . . . honestly, has *anyone* apart from me ever seen that movie?'

'What are you calling yours?' Charlie asked, in a not very pleasant tone of voice.

Shit. 'F- er, we call it Fergus,' I compromised wildly. I had a hunch that a detailed explanation of the origins of Fetid's name would not leave me looking poised.

'We do fucking well *not*,' Doug said indignantly. '*Fergus?* What the hell kind of a name for a baby is that?'

'It's a damn sight better than *Leroy*,' I flared up.

Doug looked at me for a long moment and then finally shook his head. 'No,' he said simply. 'No, I just didn't understand that riposte at all.'

And then, for the first time, Joan spoke up. 'I've been rubbing my nipples with steel wool.'

As one, everyone's heads swivelled around, our eyes riveted to her bust.

'Someone told me that it helps toughen them up in preparation for breastfeeding,' she added.

Doug was looking at Joan, absolutely aghast. '*You rub your nipples with steel wool?* For the love of God, woman, do you think you'll be giving birth to Jaws?'

'Freak,' Sleazel said audibly, and this time she wasn't directing it at Doug.

'What Jack meant is, um, do you think maybe that it's a case of the cure being worse than the cause?' I said hastily.

'It does hurt,' Joan agreed mournfully.

Evan nodded and then they both went back to sipping their cordial.

As one, all of the other women crossed our arms in

front of our chests, surreptitiously rubbing our nipples as we did so, to reassure ourselves that they were still in working, non-abrasive-scarred order.

'Have you thought about whether you'd prefer to be cut or tear naturally?' Nancy asked chattily.

'Cut or tear what?' Doug said, through a mouthful of biscuit.

Everyone looked at him.

'What?' he mumbled again.

'You know.' I attempted to laugh off his ignorance in a playful 'Men!' kind of way. 'My vagina.'

Everyone ducked as crumbs sprayed forth in a horrified torrent. '*Cut your—*' Fortunately, the rest of it was muffled as I hastily bundled Doug out of the room.

'I'm just saying, it's not like I'm an innocent straight off the train from Katoomba,' Doug said, when he'd finally stopped choking on his biscuit and had regained an element of composure. 'I went through a period where I visited certain *establishments* – purely for interest's sake, you understand, – that catered to the sado-masochistic crowd.'

'What's your point, Doug?' I asked wearily.

'My point,' he said, his voice now practically squeaking in indignation, 'is that not even in the furthest reaches of fetish freakdom would you find people who openly discuss scrubbing their nipples with steel wool and cutting their you-know-whats!'

'You're so gay,' I said, unmoved. 'It's the fact that these people are straighter than a ruler that really upsets you the most, isn't it? You think your lot has a monopoly on shock.'

'I think it's *shocking* manners to bring up a subject like that amongst strangers over a cup of lemon cordial,' he said haughtily. 'There's a time and a place for everything, and the time and the place for *that* particular subject is past midnight in a gay fetish club in King's Cross. I mean, really.

You people are going to be *parents*. It's perverted.'

'If it's any consolation, I have absolutely no intention of using steel wool on my nipples,' I offered.

He shuddered, and as he stalked back to the classroom, in answer to Angela's summons, I heard him mutter, 'Icky. You're. All. Just. Icky.'

I was about to follow him when I felt a presence behind me. I turned around. It was Charlie.

'Hey, Iz.'

'Hey,' I answered breathlessly, wondering where my breath had disappeared to. 'Where's Sle – Liesel?'

'She's in the bathroom. Um, look, this might sound strange, but I just wondered if maybe we could catch up sometime? Just you and me?'

I ought to have been looking at him in bewilderment, wondering what he wanted after all these years. But I wasn't, for the very simple reason that I knew exactly what he wanted because I wanted it too. We wanted to talk to each other. Alone.

Charlie pulled off his nametag and hastily scrawled his mobile phone number on the back of it. I held out my hand to accept it. As he pressed it into my palm, a sudden shock of remembered physical familiarity passed between us.

Thankfully, Doug chose this moment to stick his head out of the classroom. He looked at us suspiciously but contented himself with saying, 'Hurry up, Belle. We're about to discuss the man's role during labour and I need you to know it all in case I faint.'

Without another word, Charlie slipped away to find Sleazel.

I took my seat next to Doug, who instantly hissed, 'What the hell is going on between you and Maverick over there?'

'What are you talking about?'

'You know *exactly* what I'm talking about. You and he have been exchanging long, intense looks and frissoning all over the place from the moment you first saw each other. It's positively indecent.'

I attempted to laugh it off while trying not to think about my aberrant little melting moment and the phone number that was now tucked safely into my jeans pocket. 'You're being silly. Charlie and I haven't seen each other since we broke up. It's just a bit of a … shock.'

Doug shot me a sharp glance. 'He's the one you broke up with over the phone, right?'

I nodded and Doug heaved an enormous sigh. 'Oh dear god of unresolved issues. I forsee a lot of soggy tissues in your future.'

'Doug!' I said, starting to get seriously annoyed. 'Stop it! I'm in love with Jack. Charlie is my ex-boyfriend. For God's sake, we're both having children with other people.'

'So you didn't feel a … twinge when you saw him?'

I shook my head and lied. 'Nope.'

'Liar,' he stated baldly. 'I don't know what's going on between you two, but there's *something* going on, as sure as my name's Jack.' And with that he crossed his arms, settled back in his chair and directed a furious glance across the room at Charlie and Sleazel.

22
The Date

I was planning on telling Jack about my unexpected meeting with Charlie and Sleazel. Of course I was. But, when I returned home from the childbirth class, the house was dark and the only being there to greet me was Rufus.

I fell asleep before Jack got back, and, when I woke up on Saturday morning, my head heavy from disturbed dreams about Sleazel chasing me with her oboe, there was a note on the kitchen table.

Belle

Sorry I didn't make it to the class last night. Work is crazy. I'm at a weekend seminar in the city today so my phone will be switched off. But give my love to little Fetid and I'll see you both tonight.

Love

Your secret admirer

I scrunched up the note and balanced it in one palm. The feel of the paper against my skin reminded me of the previous night and of Charlie, pressing his phone number into my hand. Putting Jack's note to one side, I went in search of Charlie's number.

Smoothing the creases out of it, I gazed at Charlie's

familiar handwriting. It was so strange. I had seen that handwriting so many times before – in birthday cards, professing words of love to me in impassioned letters and in tender domestic notes exactly like the one Jack had left for me this morning. Seeing Charlie again and now holding a note with his phone number on it was like having a memory suddenly come to life. Just thinking about calling him felt as though I was returning to my past.

Then I gave myself a little shake. For God's sake, I was six months pregnant, give or take a month, as was Sleazel. Charlie and I were hardly about to elope. I paused for a moment, as I wondered whether Charlie and Sleazel were married. I tried to imagine their wedding day. No doubt Sleazel had played the oboe while Charlie did fly-overs in a white ribbon-bedecked Cessna.

Exes sometimes caught up. It was no big deal. In fact, it was a sign of maturity. It would be silly *not* to call him. I thought about ringing Cate for advice, but then decided that I was old enough to make these decisions for myself. Taking a deep breath, I rang the number.

'Er, Charlie? It's Belle.'

'Iz! Great to hear from you.' He sounded far more relaxed and warm than he had done last night. I didn't have to wait long to discover why. 'Liesel's visiting her mum. I don't suppose you're free today?'

'Um, I guess so,' I managed, rather taken aback.

It was just a bit too sudden. For a long while after Charlie and I had broken up, I had fantasised about the next time that we would meet. In most of these fantasies I looked remarkably similar to Catherine Zeta-Jones, but had spiritually and emotionally evolved to the level of a Buddhist monk. I had not foreseen that we would be catching up when I was pregnant and prone to flatulence.

We made a plan to meet at Federation Square in two hours' time. It was only once I hung up that I realised why I was feeling so guilty.

I had that same feeling of excitement in my stomach that you get when you have a date.

Charlie was waiting for me at an outside table at a Federation Square café. Despite having lived interstate and overseas for the past few years, he evidently hadn't lost that Melburnian streak of defiance which dictated that one must always choose to sit outside, even if it's mid-winter and you have to put up with being frozen by the wind while the top of your head is scorched by a towering gas lamp. I thought briefly about suggesting that we move inside, decided that that would look too much like I was trying to hide, had a mini-panic as I wondered whether I *was* trying to hide and ended up wishing, not for the first time, that there was a treatment facility for people like me who flung themselves into mini moral crises on an hourly basis.

It felt so weird to be walking towards Charlie, even though I had done this a thousand times in another lifetime. He smiled as he saw me and got up to give me a kiss on the cheek. This time it wasn't his proximity that unnerved me. It was the fact that he smelled the same.

I gathered myself together and we sat down at the table, close to the throngs of passers-by.

'I ordered you a cup of tea,' he said. 'White with one, right?'

'Right.' There was a pause during which we both remembered the numerous cups of tea that he had made for me when we lived together.

'You look exactly the same,' I finally said awkwardly.

He looked at my belly and grinned. 'You don't.'

We laughed, and then all of a sudden it was easy to talk again. We spent about half an hour asking after family and mutual friends and reminiscing about our life together in Sydney all those years ago. Then Charlie filled me in on the past few years of his life. He and Sleazel weren't married, which made me feel oddly relieved. They had moved back to Melbourne two months ago. He hadn't wanted to, but she had insisted, so he'd requested a transfer.

'At least it's flying the international routes, which is what I've always wanted, so it made up a bit for leaving London.'

'Doesn't that mean you'll be away an awful lot?' I asked. I had been with Charlie long enough to know what being an international pilot involved, and it certainly wasn't the ideal career for a new father.

He shrugged. 'Of course. But that comes with the job. Liesel understands. So what about you?'

'I'm working at Durville Gallery, which specialises in contemporary artists. I have a crazy boss but I'm great friends with Doug, the other gallerina – I stopped abruptly. I was about to launch into an explanation of how the Jack that Charlie had met was really Doug, but I didn't get the chance.

Charlie had clearly had something on his mind ever since we sat down, and now, when I paused, he came out with it.

'Iz, do you remember, way back after we'd broken up, I sent you a text message?'

I furrowed my brow as I pretended to try to recall. I remembered the message exactly. He had written: *Hi Iz. I miss u & thnk bout u. Do u miss me 2? Call me. Luv Charlie.*

At the time, this message had irritated me no end for

several reasons. The first was that I hated text message shorthand almost as much as I hated emoticons, which was quite a bit. ☹ The second reason was that Charlie had known this. The third was that he had bothered to spell his own name correctly, when I knew perfectly well who he was, but he had skimped on crucial words such as 'love'. The fourth was that I had spent *months* waiting for a message like that from Charlie, *dying* to hear that he was thinking about me. But by the time it finally arrived I had met Jack and discovered that Charlie was no longer the sun around which my world revolved.

'You never replied,' he said, sounding injured. 'How come?'

I thought about relaying reasons one to four but decided it was safer to switch the subject. 'Charlie, that was *ages* ago. I don't really remember. What does it matter now?' I paused and then continued, 'Do you remember how my dad always says things happen for a reason?'

He nodded.

'Well, I think he's right. Things worked out how they were meant to. If we hadn't broken up I would never have met Jack and you wouldn't have been with—' I made a heroic effort and got it right '—Liesel. And now here we all are. About to be parents. It's exciting, isn't it?' I asked, trying to change the topic to a more positive one.

Charlie was still frowning. 'You really love that guy, Iz?'

I focused on the Jack that I adored rather than the unreliable Jack who had been driving me mad lately. 'I love him to bits,' I said firmly. 'And we're much better suited than you and I ever were.' I didn't really know why I was launching into this discussion. I wasn't entirely sure whether I was trying to convince him or myself.

'Oh yeah? Why is that?'

'Because I drove you crazy,' I answered bluntly. 'You loved me, but I think we both know that you used to get . . . embarrassed by me.'

He looked defensive. 'Well, stuff always happened to you that never happens to normal people.'

'I know. I can't help it though. But, anyway, Jack loves that about me.'

'He does?' Charlie asked, in a sceptical tone of voice.

I nodded. 'He always says that he fell in love with me the day that I sent him a cat wearing a bandanna,' I said fondly.

'Why was the cat—' Charlie began, but then shook his head. 'Doesn't matter. We don't have that much time. So that's why you love him?'

I was about to add, 'And because he's there when I need him.' But I couldn't. Because Jack *wasn't* there for me. Not lately, anyway. 'You must be happily in love too if you're starting a family?' It came out as a question rather than a statement.

'Yeah, I guess.' He ran a distracted hand through his dark hair, in a gesture that was so achingly familiar it wreaked havoc on my concentration. 'She's just so caught up with this pregnancy, though. Sometimes I wonder if she even knows that I'm there.'

'I'm sure she knows that you're there,' I retorted crisply, suddenly remembering from days long gone Charlie's tendency to sulk when he wasn't the centre of attention. 'But being pregnant does tend to take over body *and* mind, you know.'

He grimaced. 'Believe me, I know. Liesel can hardly talk about anything else.'

'What about you?' I asked, even as I wondered

whether I really wanted to hear the answer. 'How do *you* feel about becoming a parent?'

'Freaked out,' he replied instantly, with a disarming grin. 'You?'

'So freaked out I'm practically an honorary member of Sister Sledge,' I answered fervently. 'Which bits freak you out the most?'

Charlie thought for a moment. 'Wondering how much having a child is going to affect my career. Feeling like a bad person because we moved back to Melbourne for the sake of the baby but I really, really didn't want to move and I'd much rather still be overseas.'

This was both very peculiar and strangely comforting. Charlie had just articulated two of my main anxieties. I had assumed that they were exclusive to the female experience of becoming a parent, but clearly this was not the case.

'So what are you freaking out about? No, wait – let me guess.' He sat back and considered me and then clicked his fingers in triumph. 'You can't decide on a name, can you?'

I wasn't sure whether or not I liked it that Charlie's uncanny intuition when it came to me was still intact. 'How did you know that?'

'Oh, I don't know. Maybe it had something to do with that goldfish that I bought you when we moved to Sydney. I seem to remember it threw itself out of the bowl about three weeks later and you were still trying to decide on a name for it when we gave it the funereal flush.'

I remembered. I had wanted a dog but we couldn't get one because Charlie was away so much. So he had bought me a goldfish instead. I hadn't really liked it very much and had been secretly relieved when it had committed fishy suicide.

'We have a dog called Rufus,' I informed Charlie.

'That's a good name for a dog,' he said, impressed. 'Did you choose it?'

'Not exactly. We adopted him from a shelter so he already had a name,' I confessed.

Charlie started to laugh but I didn't pay him any attention because, at that moment, one of the figures in the crowd passing through the square before us suddenly sprang into focus. It was Jack. For one wild moment I thought that perhaps he had followed me, until I remembered that he was attending a seminar in the city. He must be on his lunch break.

I wasn't sure that he had seen me, but nevertheless I panicked. 'Charlie, I have to go to the toilet,' I said, standing up and almost spilling my cup of tea.

He managed to look simultaneously amused and annoyed, but merely commented, 'You're as bad as Liesel. She needs to go every ten minutes.'

I thought about retorting that maybe that was because we both had babies bouncing up and down on our bladders, but I didn't have time. I wasn't entirely sure why I felt the need to hide from Jack at that moment but I did.

I fled.

23
The Horror Movie

If Jack had seen me at Federation Square with Charlie, he didn't mention it. So maybe it was just my guilty conscience, but I couldn't shake the feeling that something had come between us, only neither Jack nor I wanted to initiate a discussion about it.

A week later, when the next childbirth class rolled around, I was tempted not to remind Jack about it. Doug would come with me, and it was probably easier that way anyway, given that the entire class, including Charlie and Sleazel, still thought Doug was Jack. Moreover, if I turned up with the real Jack, complicated explanations would ensue which would no doubt leave me looking foolish and Sleazel delighted. I only had to get through another two classes and then I probably wouldn't see Charlie again, assuming that the god of small things didn't decide to put Sleazel and I in the same mothers' group for its own petty amusement.

On the other hand, these were *our* childbirth classes that Jack was missing out on. It was beside the point that, as a doctor, he was better prepared than most new fathers for what took place in the delivery room, so didn't need to attend for the informative aspect. What mattered was that the classes were another milestone in our pregnancy and Jack was missing out.

Having tied myself in knots, I finally came to the heroic decision that it was better to throw myself on the pyre of humiliation in front of the entire class and my ex-boyfriend if it meant that Jack could be there. However, my heroism proved pointless when, the night before the class, I reminded Jack about it and a look of trepidation immediately descended upon his face.

'Oh God. I forgot to tell you. Belle, I'm really, *really* sorry but I can't make it.'

I looked at him in disbelief. 'Why? What could possibly be more important?'

'Mrs Chung's coronary angioplasty,' he said apologetically. 'We've had to move her surgery up due to complications. My schedule is so tightly packed that tomorrow night was the only time I had free.'

'But it wasn't free,' I protested. 'You already had something scheduled. You were meant to be with *us*.'

'Belle, please don't do this to me. I hate this as much as you do. Where do you think I would rather be? But I can hardly ask Mrs Chung to put her heart disease on hold to suit our convenience.'

This was why I sometimes hated being in a relationship with a doctor. If Jack said a work matter was a case of life or death, he meant it literally. Which also meant that, compared with poor Mrs Chung's heart disease, everything, including our childbirth classes, dwindled into insignificance. Unless I wanted to appear impossibly petty and selfish, I couldn't get angry with Jack. I couldn't blame him, I couldn't even show him how hurt I felt that once again he was sidelining Fetid and me. I had no choice but to swallow very hard and tell him that it was OK; that of course I understood. And then I waited until I was sure he was asleep before I cried myself to sleep.

*

The following evening Doug and I entered the class late in order to avoid any further awkward conversations. As we found seats at the back, I couldn't help scanning the room until I'd found Charlie. With a jolt of surprise, I met his gaze; he had twisted around in his seat to look at me. I gave him a small smile and he reciprocated before Sleazel elbowed him and Doug dragged me down into my seat.

We had missed the pelvic floor exercises but we were in time for the infamous horror movie. Given that the film from my Year Eight science class was still seared into my memory, I had been dreading watching the birthing video from the time Angela had first mentioned it. Thankfully, the start of it wasn't so bad. There was a montage of black and white still shots of mothers and babies, while an earnest voice gave us a bit of historical background to childbirth and pain relief. Apparently, back in the early days, when they used to clamp a chloroform-soaked wad over your mouth, so that you weren't entirely sure whether you were giving birth or being kidnapped, a huge debate raged over the morality of pain relief. Many Christian types (presumably men) thought that it was immoral for the pain of childbirth to be dulled because it was a woman's duty to experience the pain in order to atone for Eve's sin in tempting Adam with the apple.

Doug snorted and nudged me furiously. 'The bloody Church!' he muttered. 'They always need someone to persecute, don't they? If it's not the gays and women, it's the poor old farmers found guilty of planting two different crops in the same field.'

'Huh?'

'Leviticus 19:19,' he whispered. As I stared at him, he blushed. 'I went to Sunday school for ten years. Quite a bit of it stuck. Except for the part about homosexuality being an abomination against God, of course. That was just silly.'

I turned back to the video, which was featuring some lovely scenic shots of a heavily pregnant woman wandering through sunlit glades wearing only a boob tube and an ankle-length skirt, which had Doug furiously elbowing me again in a vain attempt to express his outrage at this crime against fashion. Then the music started up as the woman on the film went into labour.

Apparently, during the first stage of labour, I would be magically transported from a forest to a beach. Once there I would wander the foreshore, looking a bit grumpy, while 'All I Want to Do is Make Love to You' by Heart played in the background. It seemed a bit cruel to increase the woman's distress by forcing her to listen to one of the all-time crappiest songs ever recorded, but then again maybe she was a Brazilian birther and had requested the song in order to intensify her pain quota.

Doug was unable to contain himself. 'Isn't this song about a woman having a one night stand with a stranger in order to get pregnant?'

I nodded and paraphrased the unforgettable lyrics that would for ever rival the finest of Shakespeare's odes. 'She was the flower. He was the seed. They walked in the garden and planted a tree.'

Doug pursed his lips in disapproval. 'It's a bit of an *off* choice, isn't it? Couldn't they have chosen something a bit more tasteful and conventional?'

I shot Doug a severe look. 'Let's see if I have this right: the gay man who's adopting a child with his partner is complaining about the lack of convention while pretending to be a straight man and the father of my child. Doug, the Scissor Sisters couldn't write the song for your situation.'

Doug was about to retaliate, but then Angela told us off for talking, so we tried to concentrate again. This video was turning out to be quite an ordeal, and we hadn't even reached the scary part.

Only then, all of a sudden, we did.

Within seconds, Doug had turned an ashen colour and was moaning and rocking from side to side with his arms clasped protectively around his drawn-up knees.

As for me, I couldn't look. I just couldn't. The brief glimpse that I had caught was *worse* than the meat-tray porno film I'd seen. Come to think of it, there were quite a few similarities between the two films, mainly involving close-ups of genitalia and a soundtrack consisting of grunts and crap music. That was it. I'd made my mind up. Cowardly or not, I was going to have an elective caesarean. I just wasn't the type who could give birth the natural way.

Finally it ended, and Angela snapped the lights back on and turned to survey us with a look on her face that was oddly reminiscent of my science teacher, Mr Perkins. I was hunting around for a paper bag to hyperventilate into so I didn't see the door to the classroom opening.

'Can we help you?' Angela asked.

'I'm here for the class.'

There was a silence as everyone looked around the room and then looked blankly at the new arrival.

'I'm Jack,' he said helpfully. He spotted me and gave a hesitant smile. 'I'm the father of her child.'

'I just don't understand how you can do something as innocuous as attend a childbirth class and end up convincing everyone that our child has two fathers, one of whom is a homophobic gay man,' Jack said, for what I thought was an unnecessary *fourth* time, as we drove home.

'You weren't at the first class,' I replied spitefully. 'If you were, it would all make sense. But, more to the point, if you had been there, then it never would have happened.' Continuing on this train of thought, I added, 'But why were you there tonight? What happened to Mrs Chung's surgery?'

'They brought some car-crash victims in so all available theatres were being used. I've had to reschedule her again.' Jack was sounding frustrated. 'First you're angry with me because I'm never around. Then I do the wrong thing by turning up. I can't win, can I?'

There was really no answer to this so I didn't even try.

Jack heaved a sigh. 'OK, Belle. Out with it.'

'Out with what?'

'You know what I'm talking about. You're pissed off with my job again.'

'I'm not pissed off with your job, I'm pissed off with *you*.'

'It's the same thing.'

'Maybe that's the problem. You can't seem to draw a distinction between your life and your work.'

'Belle, you know long hours go with my job.'

I stared out of the window. I *did* know. It had just never bothered me this much before.

Then, in a very measured tone, Jack asked, 'Why haven't you mentioned Charlie?'

I winced. Following the revelation of the real Jack, Sleazel had wasted no time in bustling up, with Charlie in tow, to introduce themselves to him. Her delight at my humiliation had been palpable. As for me, I had practically broken the land-speed record while pushing Doug and Jack out of the classroom, before everyone else could surround us and start asking embarrassing questions like: '*Now* whose surname will the baby take?' or 'Why isn't the real father dressed more like a dad?'

'I don't know. It never came up,' I muttered.

'Your *ex-boyfriend* is in the same childbirth class and you didn't think to mention it to me?' he asked, in an incredulous tone.

'No, Jack, I didn't. Mentioning things requires being in the same room at the same time, and that doesn't seem to happen to us so often any more.' Terrified that he was going to say that he had seen me with Charlie in Federation Square, I took a deep breath and tried to speak more calmly. 'Look, I know you're very busy doing amazing and important work that you love. But I also know that we're only a few months away from having a baby and I feel like you're never around.'

'You know that my work—'

I snapped. 'I know, I know, I know! I know that a heart-surgery patient is more important than us. I know that your job isn't nine to five. I've known all that since we first met. What I *don't* know is if you'll be able to find time in your schedule to turn up for the birth of our child.'

Jack's grip on the steering wheel tightened until his knuckles turned white. 'Of course I'll be there.'

'Can you promise? Can you *swear* it? What if there's an emergency with a patient? What then? You were the one who said you can't ask your patients to put their conditions on hold to suit our convenience.' With a sudden flash of insight, I demanded, 'Have any of your colleagues missed the births of their children because of work?'

Jack was silent.

'Jack?' My tone was icy.

He cleared his throat. 'Sanjeev didn't make it to the birth of his second child. He was in surgery and the labour was so quick it was over by the time he got there.'

He took his eyes off the road briefly to ascertain my

reaction and so was able to see exactly how aghast I was looking. 'Belle, Sanjeev's son was his *second* child,' Jack tried to placate me. 'The labour for a second child is usually much shorter than for a first child.'

'Well, that's OK then. As long as you show up halfway through the labour, I suppose I should be grateful.' Great. I had now sunk to using sarcasm. A sudden wave of weariness swept over me. I was so *tired* of fighting with Jack all the time. Abandoning my sarcastic tone, I made a declaration. 'That does it. I want to have an elective caesarean. I'm terrified of childbirth anyway and at least this way I won't have to worry about going into labour and not having you there. I assume you'll be able to find time for the birth if we know the date in advance and you remember to put it on your schedule?'

To my surprise, Jack slowed the car down, then pulled over and put the hazard lights on. The tightness around his mouth that had been visible when he mentioned Charlie had disappeared, but now he was looking at me with an expression that I didn't like at all.

'What are you talking about? You can't have an elective caesarean.'

'What do you mean? Why can't I?' Panic was gripping my heart.

'Belle, it's a public hospital! They only do elective caesars in private hospitals. And the waiting lists are huge these days. You won't get in at this stage.'

'Well then, maybe we should have a home birth and you can do it!' I said wildly. 'You're a surgeon! It's perfect!'

Jack was looking at me as though seeing me for the first time. 'Don't be ridiculous. You know that's out of the question. Why didn't you say something before this? Why didn't you tell me – or Bert – that this was what you wanted?'

'Because I didn't know!' I started to bawl. 'It never came up, and I wanted to think about it and make an informed choice after attending the classes. So I did all the reading, but after that video tonight I don't think I can do it and I know that I *really* can't do it if I'm not one hundred per cent sure that you'll be there with me. Only now you're telling me this.' I looked at him distraught. 'Jack, *I didn't know* and no one told me and I just assumed that I had the choice—' The remainder of what I had to say was drowned in tears.

Very sensibly, Jack did the only thing that he could. He put his arms around me and let me sob as the full horror hit home. I was going to have to go through childbirth. Possibly alone. There was no way out.

And I was terrified.

I hardly slept the entire night, and what little sleep I did manage to get was disturbed by nightmares. The following morning, Jack came into our bedroom and sat on the bed next to me. I thought he was going to bring up the subject of Charlie or his work again or give me some words of wisdom regarding managing my irrational fear of childbirth, but to my surprise he said, 'Why don't we organise a trip somewhere? Maybe we could go to Queensland or somewhere warm.' He gave me a sheepish grin. 'It must be my Sydney genes. I still haven't learned how to cope with winter in Melbourne.'

I propped myself up on a pillow and regarded him. 'How can you get time off when you're overworked as it is?' I asked suspiciously.

'I'll sort something out,' he promised. 'I've certainly got enough leave owing. Think about where you'd like to go and we'll book some flights.'

'What about Rufus?'

'I'll ask Bert to look after him.'

'A holiday still doesn't make up for you not being around when I need you.'

'I know. But at least we can spend some time together before the baby comes – just the two of us. I think we need it.' He paused. 'Are you OK after last night?'

I shook my head. 'No. But I don't want to talk about it.'

Jack looked at me. It seemed as though he was about to say something else, but then he changed his mind. He pulled me into his arms. 'So will this count as our first family holiday?'

The prospect of a holiday with Jack had already brought back some of my optimism. 'I'm not sure. What about Fetid's other daddy?' I teased. 'Shouldn't Doug come too?'

'I'm starting to worry about you and Doug. You're positive he's gay?'

'He has the collector's edition of *Brokeback Mountain* to prove it. You've got nothing to worry about there. I'm nowhere near as good-looking as Zac.'

'I don't know about that. You look pretty good to me,' he murmured, and started to kiss me.

'You'll be late for work,' I warned him, despite myself.

'Don't care.' Which was completely the right answer.

For the next forty-five minutes, neither Jack nor I thought about work or Fetid, or pregnancy, or childbirth. For the first time, in such a long time, we were concentrating on each other.

24
Frannie and Flora

Two weeks later, standing amidst the chaos of the domestic terminal at Tullamarine Airport, I looked at Jack in bewilderment. 'Why are we joining the queue for the flight to Sydney?'

He grinned. 'Little side-trip on the way to Queensland.' He paused for extra drama and then disclosed, 'I've organised it with Fran. We're staying with them for two nights before we head to Port Douglas.'

'We're going to see Fran?' I repeated, still confused.

He nodded, watching me intently. 'You haven't met Flora yet, and I know you miss Fran, so . . . oh, God, did I do the right thing?'

I looked up at him, my eyes brimming with tears. 'Yes. You did. *Thank you.*' I flung my arms around him, a feeling of happiness flooding over me. Fran, with her kooky way of looking at the world, her warm heart and her experience of childbirth and being a mother, was exactly who I needed most right now. I couldn't wait to see her.

'Frannie!'

'Belle!'

For the next few minutes, there was general shrieking

and rejoicing as we hugged each other while Jack and the fake botanist smiled awkwardly and shook hands, and then, by mutual embarrassed consensus, they carried our luggage into the spare bedroom of Fran's house in Bronte while Frannie and I carried on for a few more minutes.

After we'd calmed down and exchanged tummy pleasantries, which were directly the inverse of one another – 'Look at the size of your belly!' 'You look skinnier than before you had Flora!' – we all tiptoed into Flora's room to admire her as she lay sleeping in her cot.

Flora was the perfect picture of a one-year-old baby. She had the same dark-red hair as Fran and her long eyelashes lay on rosy cheeks, while one little fist was curled up near her face. She was very cute.

But, as we gazed at the little bundle that was Flora, Jack caught my hand and squeezed it. And all at once I felt as though there was something terribly wrong with me.

Nestled inside me was a little baby, exactly like Flora, only ours. And yet I was feeling nothing except general goodwill towards Flora because she was Frannie's daughter. I certainly wasn't experiencing the sort of hand-squeezing emotion that Jack was.

Jack caught my eye and I managed to smile. Thankfully, Fran gestured that it was time for us to tiptoe out again, so we did, closing the door gently behind us.

'She's gorgeous,' I said sincerely.

Frannie laughed. 'When she's sleeping,' she agreed. 'You should see her when it's time to change her nappy. She wriggles all over the place. It's like trying to put underwear on a cat.'

'Maybe you should be in charge of nappy-changing while you're here,' the fake botanist suggested hopefully. 'It would be good practice for you both.'

Jack shook his head firmly. 'That's a very kind offer, but Belle and I are taking the bungy-jumping approach to nappy-changing. Practice would take away the thrill of doing it for the first time.'

They gave us a quick tour of their lovely house, and it was then decided that Jack and the fake botanist would go for a swim, while Frannie and I caught up.

Fran brewed a pot of herbal tea and we carried it out to the little courtyard that was catching the late-afternoon sun. It was so gloriously balmy. I'd forgotten how warm Sydney could be, even while Melbourne was still shivering through the last days of winter.

I cast off my cardigan and luxuriated in the sunshine while we talked.

'I still can't believe that you and Jack organised all of this without me knowing!'

Fran smiled. 'Initially, he was going to bring you up here for longer. I said that was fine with us but that I thought it would be a good idea for the two of you to go on a babymoon as well.'

'A what?'

'A babymoon. It's like a honeymoon, except it's the holiday you take when you're pregnant with your first child. Your last holiday as a couple.'

'There's a name for it?'

'Of course there's a name for it. There's a name for everything these days.'

'With the notable exception of our child,' I sighed.

'Jack still wants to call it Marvin?'

'Yep.'

'What if it's a girl?'

'If it's a girl we have a long list of names that we're definitely *not* going to call her.'

'That's progress,' Fran said encouragingly.

'You think?'

'Not really, no. I was trying to be optimistic.' She took a sip of tea, looked at me and, when she spoke again, her tone had changed. 'There's another reason why Jack wanted you to see me, Belle. He's worried about you.'

'Did he tell you about Charlie?' I asked resignedly.

She looked startled. '*Charlie?* What does Charlie have to do with anything?'

I took a deep breath and then filled her in on the fiasco of the childbirth classes with the ex, followed by a rudimentary outline of our catch-up at Federation Square. I left out the frisson-ing and heart-melting bits.

Why I bothered, I don't know. That's the problem with good girlfriends. You say 'I love your shoes' and they hear 'Please, please tell me where you bought them so that I can buy myself a pair.' Subtext is their speciality.

Fran brushed past my would-be nonchalance and launched straight in. 'How did you feel when you saw Charlie?'

I shrugged. 'I don't know. It was . . . weird. He hasn't really changed that much.'

'He must have changed if he's about to become a father,' Fran retorted. 'I never knew Charlie that well but I thought he didn't want kids.'

'Why does everyone think that? Charlie and I just never got around to discussing it, that's all.'

She looked at me, surprised by my aggrieved tone. '*I* think that because once at a party Charlie said to me that he couldn't think of anything worse for his career than having kids.'

'Oh.' I tried not to look too taken aback as I processed this. First Cate and now Fran. Why hadn't Charlie ever discussed this with me? And, if it was true, why had he been so vehemently opposed to having children with *me* when he was now about to have a child with Sleazel?

'So what's Sleazel like?' Frannie asked, unconsciously picking up on my train of thought.

I considered her question for a moment. 'Competitive.'

Fran looked surprised. 'Why would she be competitive? You're not competing for anything!'

I wasn't so sure but I simply said, 'She's competitive about our babies. She wanted to know how big my bump was and all that kind of crap.' I had no desire for the discussion about Charlie to continue so I quickly changed the subject. 'Anyway, if Jack didn't tell you about Charlie, what *is* he worried about?'

'He said that you've been having nightmares in your sleep.'

I jumped. I had had no idea that I'd been waking Jack up at night.

'It's not nightmares,' I prevaricated, but, under Frannie's penetrating stare, I admitted, 'It's the same nightmare, over and over.' For the past two weeks, since Jack had told me that an elective caesarean wasn't an option, I had woken up in a cold sweat every night.

'So what's the nightmare about?' Fran pressed. 'Is it scary?'

I played down my fear. 'A bit. It's confusing more than anything.'

'Well, tell me about it and I can try to interpret it. Actually, wait a minute and I'll go and get my dream symbols book.'

As I waited for Fran to return with the book I mused upon the fact that this was one of many things that I loved about my female friends. No male would ever voluntarily say, 'Hey! How about we spend the next half-hour interpreting your dreams?'

Fran settled back on the bench with her book and nodded at me to start.

'I walk into a room and all of my relations and friends are gathered there, including you,' I began.

Fran interrupted me. 'What am I wearing?'

I screwed up my face as I tried to remember. 'A green dress, I think.'

'Oh good. I hate it when I'm wearing jeans in other people's dreams. It just seems too casual.'

I ignored this quintessential Frannie-ism and continued, 'Everyone looks at me expectantly as I come in and then I see that they're gathered around a baby in a basket. I don't want to hold it but I know that's what everyone is waiting for me to do. So I pick it up. It's kind of cute but it has lots of hair. It actually looks more like a two-year-old than a newborn. And it's very articulate.'

'It can talk?'

I nodded.

'What does it say?'

'"Pleased to meet you." And then it asks me what its name is.'

Fran's brow furrowed and she started to leaf through her dream symbols book.

The feeling of helplessness that I remembered from my nightmare swelled up within me. 'I can't answer because I have no idea what its name is. Everyone, including the baby, is looking at me, waiting for me to say something. But I don't know the answer. The baby only wants this one thing from me and I can't provide it. I have no idea what I'm meant to say or do.'

'What happens next?'

I gulped. This was the worst part. 'It always ends the same way. I'm staring in complete terror at the baby in my arms, wondering what the hell I'm going to do with it. And then I realise that this time I can't hand it back to its parents.' I finished in a small voice, 'Because this time it's mine.'

Frannie heard the distress in my voice and she patted my hand.

'What do you think it means?' I asked anxiously. 'Is it bad that in the dream I'm not even at the birth of my baby?'

'I wouldn't worry too much about that,' Fran said reassuringly. 'I think that's probably just a classic case of a dream as wish-fulfilment, as is the bit about it being older and able to talk. You're more comfortable with older children and you'd also prefer to have the baby without going through childbirth. Completely understandable.'

I took a sip of tea and decided to confess. 'I wanted to have an elective caesarean, Fran. The thought of natural childbirth completely freaks me out.'

I sat back and waited for Fran's reaction. There was every possibility that she wouldn't comprehend how terrified I was. Fran was the hippy, earth-mother type whose absolute faith in her body's abilities had resulted in Flora's drug-free water birth.

To my relief, however, Fran nodded understandingly. 'You should talk to your mother about your own birth. You'll probably find that you had a very traumatic birth, which is still causing you psychological repercussions.'

'I read that theory in one of the pregnancy books,' I said glumly. 'And I've already asked Mum.'

'And?'

'And nothing. Mum started laughing and said that, after Audrey's birth, mine was a breeze. I believe her exact words were that I popped out like I'd been blown out of a greased pea-shooter. Apparently, it was sheer luck that the doctor was an amateur cricketer who was used to fielding in the slips, or like as not I would have shot straight out and landed on the floor.'

'Oh.'

'Audrey's birth, on the other hand, was terrifying,' I continued. 'According to Mum, they practically needed forceps, a diesel engine and a steel towing cable to extract her from the womb. And guess what? Audrey has given birth three times with absolutely no pain relief whatsoever.'

Fran was silent for a moment. 'I still like that theory,' she confessed. 'It makes sense to me because of what happened when I was born. Mum thinks that's why I became an artist.'

'What are you talking about?'

'When I was born I was yellow. I had jaundice of course. We know that *now*. But Mum didn't know that then. She assumed I had an unusual sense of colour, so she did all she could to encourage me in art.'

Before I could respond to this, we heard a cry from inside as Flora woke up. Frannie went off to rescue Flora while I sat in the sunshine by myself. She returned a few minutes later, holding Flora, who was looking most indignant at finding herself awake.

'I want to show you something.' With one hand, Frannie handed me a photo and I looked curiously down at it.

One second later I had flung it back at her and shot halfway across the courtyard in order to put even more distance between me and the horror.

'Belle, come down from that birdbath. It's really not that bad.'

'I can't *believe* you would do that to me! I thought you were my friend.'

'I *am* your friend, which is why I'm trying to help you.

Now come down from there before you break it and get your bum back over here.'

I looked over at Flora, who I swear gave me a look that said, 'You'd better do what you're told.' In silence, I got down from the birdbath and sat mutely back down on the bench.

'Right. Now look at the photo again. Properly.'

'I don't want to! No offence, but it's horrible.'

'It's a photo of me and I can tell you that it wasn't horrible at all,' she said, smiling mysteriously, as she handed Flora a rusk to chew on. 'Tell me what you saw.'

I took a deep breath. 'It's a photo of you screaming your head off while Flora's doing a backwards somersault out of your vagina and into the birthing pool.'

'Correct. Now look at the expression on my face in the photo. Oh, for God's sake, if you're that squeamish, cover up the lower part.'

I placed my hand over the scary bit and then obediently opened half an eye to peer again at the image.

'Now, describe to me what you see.'

'Pain,' I said immediately.

'Naturally. What else?'

I opened one eye up more fully and considered. 'All I see is pain. Lots and lots of pain.'

'You're not *looking*. You're projecting. Forget that this is a photo of me in childbirth and treat it like an artwork that you have to write a catalogue entry on. Tell me what else you see.'

Reluctantly, I opened both eyes and finally looked properly at the photo. After a few minutes, I picked it up in both hands and stared intently. Fran's face and body were contorted and the expression on her face was primal. She looked like the statue of the Laocoön in the Vatican Museum, only without the beard and writhing serpents.

I thrust the photo back at her. 'Power,' I said. 'You look powerful.'

She smiled and held Flora a little closer.

'Frannie, I appreciate what you're trying to do, really I do, but the fact remains that I'm not like you. I know that I should think of it as good pain and have faith in my body and all those things, but to me it just sounds like a bunch of hippy crap and the sort of thing that people who buy healing crystals would advocate.'

Fran sighed. 'If you're honestly that terrified of childbirth, why don't you just book in for an elective caesarean?'

'Because I *can't*. They have waiting lists these days.'

'But, for God's sake, Jack is a doctor! Can't he pull strings somehow?'

'You know what Jack's like. The hospital has some stupid code of ethics, which I'm positive every other doctor knows is strictly for show, but of course Jack would never consider bending the rules in order to bump me up the waiting list. He couldn't even figure out how to get me an appointment with an obstetrician that wasn't Bert.'

'Belle, you're still not making sense to me. I hated the thought of a caesarean because I didn't like the idea of handing control over to a doctor. And you're the biggest control freak that I know.'

'I know I am, but the way I see it, a caesarean lets me stay in control. It's a surgical procedure that I can understand. This—' I held out the photo of Fran's primal self '—this *terrifies* me.'

She refused to take the photo. 'Look at it again and tell me one thing,' she said softly. 'Do *I* look terrified?'

I didn't even bother to look. 'No. But that's you. I'm not like you.'

Fran considered me for a moment and then shifted Flora into a more comfortable position. 'Well, you need to do something about your state of mind, Belle, because, whether you like it or not, in a couple of months' time, you're going to be exactly like me.'

25
The Test

The following day, Frannie and I left Flora with the boys while we went swimsuit shopping at Bondi. To begin with I was buoyed by a sense of optimism. Perhaps shopping for a maternity swimsuit would be like going to the gym while pregnant. Maybe the pregnant version would be more enjoyable than the regular experience.

Sadly it was not to be. Shopping for bathers is, at the best of times, a demoralising experience. Shopping for bathers when your profile resembles Homer Simpson's is infinitely worse.

Fran, who was enjoying her post-baby body, sashayed forth from a dressing-room cubicle in Bikini Island, wearing a nifty little striped bandeau top with matching boy shorts.

'That looks great,' I said sincerely. 'You should get it.'

'I think I will.'

Our pleasure faded as we both grimly surveyed my ensemble. In an attempt to break free from the black mu-mu style that dominated maternity swimwear, I was trying on a bright watermelon-coloured halter-top with a matching skirt. The result, unsurprisingly, was that I looked like an enormous frilled watermelon.

'Maybe try it on in black,' Fran suggested.

I did, but I still looked terrible. Worse than terrible. In a futile effort to camouflage the pregnant belly, maternity swimsuits were big on ruching, drapery, pleating and other design elements that were more commonly found in the construction of curtains. It was all doomed to failure and merely trying the different suits on made me feel like the proverbial ostrich who believed that no one could see it if it stuck its head in the sand. Actually, maybe that wasn't a bad idea. Maybe I should just buy some bikini bottoms, stick them over my head and go skinny dipping. The horror and revulsion that I would evoke in other holidaymakers would be their problem, not mine.

This excellent notion was promptly quashed by Fran, who cleared her throat and said, 'Er, Belle? We haven't got anything planned for this afternoon. Do you want me to see if my beautician has a free waxing appointment?'

I looked in the mirror at my admittedly hirsute legs. It was odd. In my former non-pregnant life, my pre-holiday routine involved buying a plane ticket to somewhere warm, followed by the immediate booking of a waxing appointment. In pregnancy mode, my grooming standards had dipped so severely that I was surprised I was still bothering to bathe rather than just giving myself a cursory lick, à la Rufus.

'I suppose I should do something about my legs and underarms,' I conceded.

'And maybe a bikini wax,' Fran suggested delicately.

I looked down and, realising that was futile as all I could see was a ruching-swathed stomach, peered in the mirror instead. Hmm. Either the stitching on the swimsuit briefs was faulty and had started to unravel, or my bikini line was mounting an expedition to my knees.

Fran hadn't even waited for my acquiescence. She had already pulled out her mobile and was making an appointment for me that afternoon.

I sighed and lumbered back over to the racks to search through them once more, trying to ignore the gaggle of lanky teenage supermodels who were trying on crocheted triangle bikinis in the cubicle next to us.

Ten minutes later, I was paying an exorbitant amount of money for a swimsuit that contained more square metres of fabric than the Melbourne Cricket Ground covers. And, courtesy of Fran, I now had a waxing appointment to look forward to.

Fran sat next to me in the beauty therapist's waiting room, as we flicked through old copies of *Marie Claire*. She put one hand on my nervously jigging leg to still it.

'Belle, it's just a wax! What's wrong with you?'

What was wrong with me was that my tried and true pre-waxing procedure was to wash a couple of Aspirin down with a glass of wine. Hell, they could have waxed my head after that and I would probably have only emitted a mild 'ouch'.

Only this time, of course, I couldn't have either of those things. I went through my list of pregnancy-related ailment alleviations but none of them seemed to really cut it. Hot ginger tea wasn't going to help me get through a bikini wax unless I threw it over a different part of my body in order to distract myself from the original source of pain.

'I'm not very good with pain,' I finally answered. 'Usually I take a couple of Aspirin before I have a bikini wax.'

Fran put her magazine aside and looked at me sternly. 'You need to retrain your mind. Instead of being so frightened of pain all the time, you need to learn strategies to cope with it.'

'Frannie, if you even *think* about telling me to embrace the pain of a bikini wax, then I'm sorry but we can't be friends any more.'

'Well, that's too bad because that's exactly what you should do. It's the perfect opportunity for you to practise for labour.'

Maybe she was right. 'Is having an unmedicated wax really comparable to the pain of labour?' I asked suspiciously.

'Mmm. Yep. Sort of.'

'Could you *please* learn how to lie? You're pathetic.'

'It is. Definitely. Almost.'

'Rate getting waxed on a pain scale of one to ten,' I challenged her.

'What's one equivalent to?'

'That feeling you get when you rip a nail and have to cut off the rest of the nail really short and your fingertip feels all weird.'

'Belle, that's not *painful*! That's just . . . tingly.'

'Speak for yourself, Shaolin monk. But, anyway, I'm not saying it's terrible pain. That's why it's number one.'

'Good grief. OK then, what's ten?'

'Childbirth,' I answered immediately.

She gave me one of those looks. 'What about medieval torture? The Iron Maiden or the rack?'

'Number nine,' I said inflexibly.

'Why on *earth* didn't you adopt?' Fran muttered. 'Look, forget the pain comparisons. Just go for your wax and try to think of it as preparation for the pain of childbirth. There will be something unpleasant happening in the general area. Deal with it. You might even surprise yourself.'

Fran's beautician popped her head around the door and beckoned me in with one perfectly manicured finger.

I groaned, but remembering the horrid sight in the bikini-shop mirror I heaved myself out of the chair and followed her in. I could do this. I could do this. I was Woman, Hear me Roar. I could . . . FUUUUUUUUU-UUCKKKKK!!!!!!!!!!!!!!!!!!!!!!!!!!!!!!!!!!!!

That night we had a farewell dinner with Fran and the fake botanist. I was feeling considerably lighter thanks to my waxing ordeal, which had ripped out at least two kilos of hair. Happy that it was over and that Jack and I were flying out to Port Douglas the following morning, I was stirring the pasta sauce for dinner when Fran re-entered the kitchen carrying Flora.

Jack and the fake botanist immediately went all gooey over her. I looked over and smiled. Flora had just had her bath and was going to bed. She looked very sleepy and adorable in her tiny pyjamas.

Fran caught my smile and came up to me. 'Do you want to hold her?'

I shook my head. 'No, I'd better not. Babies always start screaming when I hold them.'

Fran laughed but didn't push it. 'It's not *you*. Babies scream for all sorts of reasons.'

Unfortunately, Jack decided to push it. 'Why don't you hold her?' he coaxed. He held out his arms and Fran handed Flora over to him. I watched as Jack rocked her gently. She looked very comfortable in his arms. He looked up and smiled at me. 'See? Nothing to it.'

He came towards me, intending to put Flora into my arms, and I felt a sense of panic. I didn't want to hold her. It was as though I was being given some sort of test.

And I couldn't bear to think what it would mean if I failed it.

I backed up against the kitchen bench, crossed my arms in front of me and shook my head. 'No, Jack. I mean it.'

Jack stood very still. I didn't look at his face. I didn't want to.

An uncomfortable silence fell, until the fake botanist came to my rescue.

'How's that sauce going, Belle?' He came up beside me and, to my utter surprise, he put an arm around my waist and squeezed me. 'Don't worry. You're going to be just fine,' he whispered.

I had always thought that he didn't like me very much. And I think it was because his kindness was so unexpected that it completely unnerved me. To my utter shame, I fled out into the back garden, terrified that I was about to cry.

Fran, the fake botanist and Flora discreetly withdrew to the front of the house while Jack came and sat next to me on the bench. I couldn't help noticing that he didn't put an arm around me or attempt to comfort me; he merely sat beside me while he waited for me to regain my composure.

'We need to talk, Belle,' he finally said, softly. 'I think we have a real problem.'

'We?' I shot back. 'Don't you mean *me*?'

'*We* have the problem because *we're* having a baby,' he said firmly. 'What's the matter with you? Why couldn't you hold Flora, just for a moment?'

'Look, I didn't want to hold her. Why is that such a crime?'

'Why is it such a big deal?' he countered. 'She's just a baby. And that's what people do – they ask you to hold them for a few minutes and sometimes the babies cry. It's not a reflection on you personally.'

'I've never been one of those maternal sort of girls. I don't see why you should expect that to change just because I'm pregnant!'

'Belle, *we're* going to have a baby. You're going to have to hold it.'

'Is that what this is about? You think I'm going to be a bad mother?'

'Oh, for God's sake. What I think is that you're terrified whenever you go near a baby, and one of your best friends can't even ask you to hold her daughter without you almost bursting into tears.' He paused and then continued, 'We're going to be parents soon. Don't you think it would be a good idea to practise a bit?'

'You're the one who said you didn't see any need to change nappies for practice!'

When Jack spoke, it was in a strained voice. 'Belle, *please*. Help me understand. Explain it to me.'

I took a deep breath and started to pick my way through the jumble of emotions. 'I know this might sound weird, but I don't feel as though I'm going to be a bad mother or afraid of picking up *our* baby. If I don't think about the childbirth bit, I'm happy being pregnant and I'm excited about Fetid. You know that I am. But other parts of me haven't changed. I still don't want to cuddle other people's babies, and I resent being made to feel that I *should* want to.' I looked at him pleadingly. 'Jack, I'm not like Audie. I'm never going to be. She's amazing – she oozes maternal warmth and instinct. I don't. But I don't see why I can't be equally as loving towards our baby in my own way.'

'I understand that but that's not what's worrying me. My worry is that right now you can't even hold a baby – you recoil from the suggestion. I just feel like there's a deeper problem and, if we can work on it now, maybe it won't be as confronting for you when we have our own.'

'There is no deeper problem!' My frustration surged up, turning into anger. 'Unless you consider my personality a problem, in which case I think we probably are in trouble.'

I went into our bedroom and rang Cate. I would have spoken to Frannie but she was putting Flora to bed. Cate was also more direct than Fran, and if I was being an idiot she would set me straight. I desperately wanted Cate's reasoned and logical perspective on my fight with Jack. But, before I had the chance to tell her why I was calling, she had launched into a story of her own.

'I had dinner with Eva and Tania the other night,' she said, in a tone of voice that suggested she had inadvertently dined at an offal restaurant. 'It was horrible.'

Eva and Tania were two of Cate's closest friends from work, so my prompt was clearly: 'What was horrible about it?'

'Babies!' Cate declared dramatically. 'They wouldn't stop talking about their babies. I completely understand that becoming a mother is a major part of their lives, and that it's exactly the same as me going on about my love life, but *all night*? It was awful. I just sat there nodding and got drunk by myself and ended up going home with one of the waiters.'

'You picked up a waiter?' I asked, startled. That wasn't like Cate.

She giggled. 'Yep. I started flirting with him out of sheer boredom.'

'Why didn't you try to change the subject?' I asked diplomatically.

'I did! But they just kept bringing the topic back to their kids again. I swear that you could say to a new mother, "What do you think of North Korea's missile tests?" and she'd probably start banging on about how Junior's favourite toy is his rocket ship.' She took a deep breath. 'Promise me that you won't ever be like that.'

'Cate, I've already told you about a million times that I won't,' I said wearily. 'And anyway, I would hope that we're good enough friends that, if I did turn into a mummy robot, you would snap me out of it.'

'I shouldn't ever have to do that,' she replied immediately. 'You just shouldn't ever get like that.'

Inside, I was aware of a miserable, sinking feeling. Cate and I were about to have an argument. Strangely, this was worse than having a fight with Jack. Cate and I had been friends for longer than I cared to remember, and during that entire time we'd only ever had two proper arguments.

'Cate, I am having a baby. I'm probably going to talk about it some of the time, in the same way that you talk about your love life.'

'I understand that,' she said, in an icy tone that made my heart plummet into my shoes. 'But, considering that *you've* always railed against women who can't talk about anything except their children, I would have thought that you'd agree with me. Or is it different now that you're going to be one of them?'

'I agree with you! I'm not arguing! I don't want my whole world to consist of nothing but my child. But things aren't going to stay the same for ever, either.'

'Oh, I'm sorry. I didn't realise that I was boring you just because I still go out and have a good time and I'm not settled down and . . . and *breeding*.'

It was her use of the deliberately insulting term 'breeding' that hit me like a slap in the face. And that's when I realised that Cate, my wise and calm friend, was trying to pick a fight with me. She was angry, pissed off with me for deserting her and moving on somewhere she didn't want to go. But, coming on top of my argument with Jack, it was too much. I snapped back.

'Yeah, well, I'm sorry that I'm no fun any more. It's just I stopped flirting with waiters about ten years ago.'

I'm not sure which one of us banged down the phone first, but after I hung up I was in no mood to leave our room and face Jack.

There remained one person who I was sure would understand what I was feeling at this moment. Hating myself, knowing that in some fundamental way I was betraying Jack, I texted Charlie.

He responded almost immediately. I opened up the message and read: *U thnk u have problems? L wants help choosing theme for baby's room. Baby doesn't even know WTF a jungle or farm IS.*

I choked back a giggle and texted back: *Suggest battery hen farm theme. Guarantee she will stop asking for your input.*

I sent it and then immediately felt remorseful. Why had I turned to Charlie, instead of Jack? And, as much as I hated to admit it, I didn't like feeling that I had undermined Sleazel's attempts to involve Charlie in the preparations for their baby. If anyone knew what it was like to feel as though you were doing it all by yourself, it was me. The misery I had felt when I hung up on Cate came back again, stronger than ever, as it was now backed up by a hearty dose of guilt.

When I finally made my way into the hall, I could hear the sound of conversation and music coming from the kitchen. I wasn't ready to go back in yet. I hesitated outside the door to Flora's room, and then I pushed it open and went in.

Flora was tucked up but wide awake, her gaze intent on the dog mobile that was strung over her cot. She turned her head towards me as I crept in. Holding my breath, I waited to see what she was going to do. She looked at me. But she didn't start to cry.

My heart hammering, I picked her up, carefully, as though I might break her. She was warm and so very small. She nestled into my arms and I held her cheek against mine and listened to her breathing. After a few moments, her eyes closed. I held her until I was sure she was asleep and then gently settled her back into the cot. Tip-toeing from the room, I closed the door behind me.

I ought to have been feeling jubilant that I had held Flora and she hadn't cried. But holding a real, live baby had only made me even more conscious of my inexperience. With my back to Flora's bedroom door, I slid down awkwardly until I was sitting on the floor.

It felt as though half of the people in my world felt that I wasn't maternal enough, while the other half were furiously warning me against becoming *too* maternal. And the only person who seemed to understand me was my ex-boyfriend.

Burying my face in my hands, I fought against the lump in my throat, as I wondered what had happened to my life.

26
The Babymoon

Far North Queensland is really very beautiful, but the overwhelming gratitude I felt towards the people of Queensland was not primarily for their kind hospitality or for sharing their amazing, albeit crocodile-infested, beaches with me. Nope, it was for maintaining a really rather fabulous standard of cleanliness in all their public toilets.

Because when you're almost seven months pregnant, you're basically a walking bladder. In fact, a very inefficient bladder, that isn't so much walking as crawling between bathrooms, looking for a telegraph pole to pee on between stops. Never before had I felt such empathy with Rufus's desire to stop and pee on every single bush. It was really quite surprising that I wasn't running up to complete strangers and sniffing their bottoms.

In the non-pregnant universe, holidays were probably still considered a marvellous way to relax. Unfortunately, I was still in the pregnant universe. What with the painful waxing, the super-sized helping of swimsuit-shopping humiliation, my arguments with Jack and Cate, my clandestine texting with Charlie, and now the never-ending toilet stops, our babymoon was proving to be less sight-seeing and more fights-and-peeing. Furthermore, I kept catching sight of my reflection in shop windows on Macrossan Street and wondering who the fat, frumpy woman stalking Jack and me was.

We had hardly spoken for the rest of that final night in Sydney, but, on the plane trip to Port Douglas, Jack had gently taken my hand.

'Are you OK?'

I shook my head mutely. I didn't want to tell Jack that I'd had my nightmare about our nameless baby again. It would only freak him out more.

'Belle, I'm sorry about last night. We'll work it out.'

There's nothing to work out, I felt like saying. Unless you include my deformed, inadequate maternal instincts. But I didn't say that. Instead, we kissed and made up, even though we both knew that our differences hadn't really been resolved.

Then again, if you're going to be unhappy anywhere, Port Douglas is a fabulous place to be. Four Mile Beach was utterly beautiful, with its broad sweep of white sand flanked by the waters of the Coral Sea on one side and lush tropical rainforest on the other. We bathed in waterfalls amongst the quiet greenery of Mossman Gorge and hired a car to explore the Daintree Rainforest. I was a bit nervous about this last expedition, as I didn't expect toilet facilities in a rainforest, but my fears proved unfounded, and swimming at Cape Tribulation (feeling weightless again!) was heavenly. We joined a chartered tour boat out to the Great Barrier Reef where we saw a whale, which cheered me up enormously because it was the first time in months that I'd seen something bigger than me. Best of all, Jack and I were able to spend time together and, gradually, our makeshift peace became the real thing.

To see Jack relaxed had become so unusual that I was disappointed, but unsurprised, when it started to wear off on our final night in Queensland.

'Do you mind if I have something to drink?' he asked, after a bout of uncharacteristic fidgeting.

For our last night, we had decided to splash out on one of the most beautiful restaurants in Port Douglas. We were sitting on enormous throne-like seats in an open-air restaurant, surrounded by palm trees, while flames from bamboo torches flickered around us.

'Of course not. Are you OK?' I asked curiously.

'Yep. Absolutely.' He then ordered a Long Island Iced Tea, which has about five shots of alcohol in it. When it arrived he gulped it down and promptly ordered another one. 'Is this table OK? We can sit over there if you prefer.'

'Jack, it's fine. It's more than fine, it's lovely. You're being very peculiar, you know.'

He looked sheepish. 'I think I may have got a bit too much sun,' he said lamely.

As a diagnosis from a qualified medical practitioner, 'a touch of the sun' was right up there with 'bile and humours' as an explanation for his odd behaviour, but I decided not to push it.

'Do you know what you're going to order?'

'I'm going to have the crab,' I decided. I wasn't meant to eat it and I knew that I'd regret it, as whenever I ordered shellfish I ended up eating about two teaspoonfuls of seafood while the rest remained stubbornly tucked away inside its carapace. But I couldn't resist. Those two teaspoonfuls were worth the three hours of messy wrangling with crab crackers – a gadget that seemed to have been invented for the sole purpose of making otherwise intelligent people look stupid in restaurants.

Over the next twenty minutes, Jack went to the toilet almost as many times as I did, and I eventually gave up trying to make conversation with him. Whatever was bothering him, I was sure he would tell me when he was ready.

And he did, moments later. As I tucked a napkin into the neck of my dress and brandished my crab crackers gleefully, it is not entirely improbable that I smacked my lips in anticipation. But I can't quite remember because of what happened next.

'Belle, before our meals arrive and you get stuck in and have crab meat all over your hands, there's something I want to ask you.'

Before I knew what was happening, Jack was on bended knee on the floor and was pulling something out of his pocket.

Something that looked like a ring box.

He opened the box and my mouth fell open.

'Isabelle Beckett, will you marry me?'

'You're *proposing*?' I gasped. 'But – but *why*?'

'Because I feel that I ought to make an honest woman of you,' he said nobly.

I knew that he was joking but I was too startled to respond.

Seeing that I was at a loss for words, his tone altered. 'Because I love you. Because I want you to be my wife. Because calling you my partner or my girlfriend doesn't convey what you are to me. Because we're going to be a family and I want to marry you in front of all of our friends and our family. Because you're wearing an enormous bib around your neck and I still think you're the most beautiful thing that I've ever seen.'

I sat there, stunned. Inside, Fetid kicked me as if to hurry me up.

Even though I had never placed a particular emphasis on getting married, when I had imagined this moment (if I'm honest, it didn't always feature Jack popping the question, sometimes it was Josh from *The West Wing*, and occasionally, if I'd had too much to drink, it would be Toby from *The West Wing*) never once had I envisioned it taking place while I was heavily pregnant, wearing a bib around my neck and brandishing crab crackers.

I looked into Jack's beloved face and my throat constricted.

'I . . . can't.'

After a moment, he got up from his kneeling position. He sat back down in his chair. I prepared myself for sorrow, disappointment, God knows what, but when he spoke it was in an almost conversational voice. 'Is this anything to do with Charlie?' Despite his quiet tone, there was a taut anger below the surface.

'Charlie?' I repeated weakly.

This proposal scene was now featuring an ex-boyfriend as well as crab crackers. It had definitely *not* been scripted by the good folk at Mills & Boon. Knowing my luck, Toby from *The West Wing* would shortly be making an appearance.

'I know you met up with him at Federation Square that day,' Jack informed me grimly. 'I saw you. You saw me too, I know you did. And yet you ducked off to hide and you never mentioned it.'

'I wasn't hiding, I had to go to the toilet,' I said lamely. 'And you can't get angry with me for not mentioning it when you never brought it up either.'

'I didn't know who you were with! It was only after I met him at our childbirth class that I realised.'

'*Our* class? You only showed up for the last five minutes! And, if it bothered you so much that I'd met up with Charlie, then why haven't you brought it up till now?'

'Because you freaked out completely that night about giving birth and you've been a complete mess ever since!' Jack's tone of voice was no longer quiet, and the other diners, who had been looking over at us and smiling since Jack had gone down on one knee, were now starting to look away. 'I've been walking on eggshells around you, trying not to upset you. You're meant to stay calm for the baby's sake and you're anything but calm! You cry in your sleep, did you know that?'

I looked down.

Jack took a deep breath. If I hadn't been in such turmoil I would have paid more attention to the fear in his voice. 'Belle, do you still have feelings for Charlie?'

'*No!* I don't know. That is, I felt something when I saw him again. I didn't want to but I did.'

Oh, God, why had I told him that? He didn't need to know that. But I'd said it and now I couldn't take it back. What I should have said was that this did have quite a bit to do with Charlie, but not in the way Jack thought. I desperately wanted to tell Jack that a happy ending to my own love story was the one thing that I had always longed for but that I couldn't accept his proposal because, the day that Charlie had left me behind in Sydney, all those years ago, he had shattered my faith in fairytale endings. But if I said those things I would be saying that I didn't believe in us. So instead I tumbled into incoherent speech, in a desperate attempt to shift the focus away from Charlie.

'Jack, this isn't about Charlie, it's about *everything*. It's about how I didn't want to pick up Flora in front of everyone and I am terrified – *terrified*, do you understand? – of the pain of childbirth and that I don't know how to be a mother, and Cate hates me, and I feel like you and I barely have a relationship any more because you're never around and when you are we always seem to be on completely different wavelengths and we can't even agree on a name for our baby and now you want to get *married*?'

Jack looked down at the table for a very long moment, while I fought back tears.

When he finally spoke, his words took me by surprise. 'Fran told me about the nightmare you've been having,' he said. 'Can I ask you something?' He paused, and then, in a constricted tone, continued, 'Am I amongst the crowd of people who are in your dream?'

I looked at him, aghast that, despite the number of times I had had the nightmare, this had never occurred to me. I thought about lying, but what would be the use?

'No,' I choked. 'You're never there.' And then I stopped fighting against the inevitable and burst into tears.

It was at this auspicious moment that our waiter appeared, bearing two steaming plates. 'Now then,' he beamed, 'who's having the crab?'

Third Trimester

27
Scorpio Rising

After our return to Melbourne from Port Douglas, to say that things were strained between Jack and me was something of an understatement. We still slept side by side and spoke civilly to one another, but spats kept erupting between us over the most trivial things. Somewhere in our house, an unwanted diamond engagement ring was hidden away, and the knowledge of it was having a corrosive effect on both of our hearts. I ached to make things right with Jack, to take away the hurt and sadness etched into his features – but I didn't know how. The only way to do it was to say that I would marry him, and that was the one thing that I couldn't do.

We had both agreed that we wouldn't tell anyone about the proposal. This was made easier for me as Cate, the person I usually went straight to with any relationship problems, wasn't talking to me. Post-natal depression I had heard of. But *pre*-natal depression, brought on by my ex-boyfriend, my best friend, my unborn child and the father of the aforementioned child, was in a whole other diagnostic basket.

Having to return to work after a holiday wasn't exactly a blues buster either, although I was looking forward to seeing Doug, who could usually cheer me up. Starting back at work on a Sunday morning made it infinitely more depressing, but I had no choice. The catalogue for Keedin's exhibition had to go to the printer, and preparing catalogues while the gallery was open was impossible. The trade-off for taking a holiday had been that I would be back in time for the Sunday cataloguing session, so there was no escape.

After bidding Jack a dismal farewell as he set off for work, I lay in bed, staring at my enormous stomach. I had to get dressed for work, which meant that I had a choice of about three boring maternity outfits, all of which I had worn on alternate days for what felt like the past ten years.

I heaved myself out of bed, opened my cupboard and looked longingly at my normal clothes, which hung in an enticing array of colours and designs from the clothes rail. Turning my back on them, I pulled on my black skirt with the ruched waist and then sought out the maternity tops that I had bought in three different colours. With a sense of masochism, I reached for the black one. Teamed with the black skirt, it matched my mood exactly.

Staring at my Goth alter-ego in the mirror, I felt even more depressed until I suddenly remembered something that I had read in one of the pregnancy books about accessories being a pregnant woman's best friend. Instead of indulging my melancholy, perhaps I should try to lift my mood instead. With that in mind, I yanked off my black top and started to rummage in the back of my cupboard.

As I entered the gallery, in silence Doug took in my hoop earrings, flat cap, hot-pink Converse sneakers, electric-blue fishnet tights, African wooden bangles and the neon-coloured studded belt that I had last worn in the 1980s, which was belted around an oversized fluorescent ‘Choose Life!’ T-shirt.

‘No legwarmers?’ Doug finally managed, in a pained tone.

‘Is it too much?’ I asked, crestfallen.

He looked me up and down once again and shuddered. ‘Not if you’re Missy Elliot.’

‘Oh.’

‘I mean, really. You spend one week in Queensland and look what happens to your dress sense.’ He paused in his lecture and then added, ‘And, er, Belle? What’s with the T-shirt slogan?’

‘It’s a vintage Wham! T-shirt from their 1985 “Choose Life!” tour,’ I said indignantly.

‘Thank heavens for that. I thought you were making a Pro-Life statement.’

‘You thought I was anti-abortion?’

‘Well, you are pregnant and you’re walking around with “Choose Life!” written in gigantic fluorescent capital letters on your belly.’

‘Oh my God.’ I sat down abruptly and my bangles clanked. ‘I wore this all the way down Chapel Street. No wonder that girl hissed at me.’

‘Don’t worry about it. She was probably too young to remember Wham!’

‘What’s your excuse? We’re the same age.’

‘I was cool. I didn’t listen to Wham! I liked The Cure.’

‘Oh fuck off. I liked The Cure too.’

‘Bet you only liked “Love Cats”.’

‘Shut up. I was cool.’

‘Belle, I’ve seen your iPod. You liked Wham!, Spandau Ballet and Duran Duran. You were Queen of the Dags.’

‘I was thirteen!’

‘Yes, and back then you had them on vinyl, and last

year you went out and downloaded them on to your iPod. Which means that you're still a dag, only now you're an even bigger one.'

For lack of a rejoinder, I stuck my tongue out at him. 'I can't be bothered arguing with you too,' I said wearily.

'Who else have you been arguing with?' Doug asked with concern.

'Jack,' I said. Oops. It had only been five minutes and I was already in danger of spilling everything.

'You had *another* fight? Didn't you just finish arguing about houses? What's wrong with you two? Don't you know that holidays are meant to be all about romance?' Doug sighed and propped his elbows on the desk, adopting his 'listening' pose. 'Come on, then. Out with it. What was it about this time?'

I decided to relate our latest argument, rather than tell him about the more significant happenings that had taken place in Port Douglas. 'We had a fight over what music we should play in the hospital room while the baby is being born. Jack wanted Mozart because he read somewhere that Mozart's music makes you smarter so it's good to play it to young children to stimulate their intellect.'

'Jeez, no pressure on the kid then, the instant it draws its first breath.'

'Exactly. So I said we should be thinking about what music *we* like, because the baby couldn't possibly have a preference.'

'So you said you wanted Wham!, Spandau Ballet and Duran Duran,' Doug said understandingly.

'I did not! I'm *much* cooler these days. I said that I wanted Britney Spears.'

'Remind me to give you a rundown on the correct meaning of "cool".'

'There's a reason I chose her,' I said with dignity. 'I associate her with having a birth that's a piece of cake.

Even though she had a caesarean and I'm not, and ... anyway, it made sense to me at the time. But then Jack said that Britney was an awful choice—'

'She is,' Doug interjected, nodding his head vigorously.

'And so I said I didn't care, so why didn't he choose. Then he chose a Marvin Gaye CD—'

'That's better,' Doug said encouragingly.

I glared at him. 'It is *not*! He didn't choose it because he wanted to listen to the music, he chose it as a way of putting extra pressure on me to name our baby Marvin.'

'That's most definitely not better.'

'Exactly. So I said, "Over my dead body", and then Jack shouted that it didn't make any bloody difference anyway and that I could pick the duet between Huey Lewis and Gwyneth Paltrow for all he cared.'

'Oh dear.'

'So I did,' I concluded in a small voice.

Doug blinked. 'Pardon?'

'I said fine. So during the birth of our child we're going to have "Cruisin'" by Huey Lewis and Gwyneth Paltrow on in the background.'

There was a stunned silence.

'But ... but that's *horrible*.'

'I know,' I wailed.

'Why don't you just apologise to Jack and make up and then choose that Israel Kamakawiwo'ole CD that you both love?'

'Why should *I* apologise to *him*?' I asked, bristling.

Doug eyed me suspiciously. 'Don't tell me you two spent your whole holiday arguing?'

'Of course not,' I said shakily, then quickly changed the subject before I started to cry.

Luckily, Doug had oodles to tell me about their progress on the adoption front. By the time that he had recounted in detail his administrative battles with the adoption agency and I'd heard all of the gossip from Zac's latest project (a reality-television series called *Dancing Under the Stars!* in which eight C-grade celebrities were dropped in to the Simpson Desert and forced to ballroom dance their way back to civilisation), I had got my emotions back under control and it was time to tackle my emails, which had mounted up alarmingly in my absence.

The first one was from Audie and was titled: *Kids say the darndest things!* Examples included:

> HOW WOULD YOU MAKE A MARRIAGE WORK?
> Tell your wife that she looks pretty, even if she looks like a truck.
> Sam, age 12
>
> WHAT DO YOU THINK YOUR MUM AND DAD HAVE IN COMMON?
> Both don't want any more kids.
> Caroline, age 7

It continued in this vein for about the equivalent of three A4 pages. I sighed. Why did people assume that because you were having a baby you would suddenly find crap like this endearing? Laughing at emails like this was only a short step away from buying calendars featuring photographs of infants sprouting out of plant pots. And, in my humble opinion, the complete oeuvre of Anne Geddes is the visible manifestation of Satan in our midst. Thanks to her, there was a multitude of babies and toddlers growing up who would forever be fighting the urge to climb into the refrigerator crisper in order to curl up around a pumpkin or to put a cabbage leaf on their head. God only knows what impact it had had on their developing psyche. One could only presume that, in years to come, difficulties in their adult relationships would be dealt with by donning a costume and imploring, 'But how can you break up with me? I'm thirty-four years old and I'm dressed like a woodland sprite and sitting on a courgette. I'm adorable!'

I deleted the email and read the title of the next one, which was from Cate. For one brief, happy moment I thought she had emailed me in an attempt to make up, but then I checked the date and realised that she had sent it before our argument. I was already missing Cate, but the contents of her email didn't make me inclined to bury the hatchet. She had sent me a list of animals and insects that ate their young. As I cursorily glanced at the email before deleting it, it occurred to me that, for different reasons, I didn't find Cate's email funny either.

As I dealt with work emails, something about Cate's email continued to nag at me. Tigers. Praying Mantids. Scorpions. *Scorpions* ... Wait a minute. My baby was due on the fourth of December, but there was every chance it might come early. And if it came early ...

'It might be a Scorpio!' I shrieked for the fortieth time, as Doug tried to console me.

'They're not that bad,' he said, unconvincingly.

He didn't fool me for a minute. Both Doug and I owned well-thumbed copies of the astrology classic *Sun Signs.*

'They're horrible! Every single Scorpio that I've ever met in my entire life has been awful. They're named after an insect that *eats its own kind.*'

'Lots of amazing people are Scorpios,' Doug said.

'Like who?'

He thought for a moment and then said triumphantly, 'Picasso.'

It was Charlie's star sign too, I suddenly remembered, momentarily thrown off by this recollection. And *he* wasn't awful. 'OK, maybe there are a few exceptions. But they only prove the rule.' Determined to prove my theory, I landed the knockout blow. 'Cruella is a Scorpio.'

There was a silence and then Doug said waspishly, 'Well, you're just going to have to cross your legs and sit tight then, aren't you?' He paused and muttered underneath his breath, 'Maybe if you'd kept your legs crossed in the first place . . .'

I banged my head on my desk and moaned. 'I'm going to give birth to a Scorpio called Marvin. I know it. I just know it.'

'You don't *know* that,' Doug reprimanded me. 'It might be a girl Scorpio.'

I refused to be mollified. 'She'll still be called Marvin. We can't come up with any other names.'

'Well, too bad,' Doug said unexpectedly.

I lifted my head from the desk and looked at him in surprise.

'Zac and I are going to take the child we're given, and I can tell you right now, we're going to be eternally grateful for her,' he continued. 'And it's the same for every other parent on the planet. So I don't see why you should be any different.'

He was right. He was absolutely and utterly right. So many aspects of little Fetid were completely out of my control, and I was going to have to start accepting that. For a control freak like me, that wasn't the easiest thing in the world, but, if Doug could do it, then so could I.

I took a deep breath, and in the resolute tone of an AA member declaring their addiction at a meeting, I announced, 'My name is Isabelle and I'm going to be proud of my little Scorpio daughter called Marvin, even if she does try to eat her baby brothers and sisters. Because that's what being a parent is all about.'

'Being a parent is about accepting cannibalism within the family?' Doug asked with interest.

'Exactly,' I said. 'And loving your child, regardless of their unspeakable star sign.'

'Good girl!' Doug applauded.

I beamed. 'It's nothing,' I said modestly. 'As you so rightly pointed out, that's what *all* parents do.'

Something occurred to Doug. 'Do you think Cruella's parents love her?' he asked, awestruck at the idea of anyone feeling a warm emotion towards Cruella.

I contemplated the image of a young Cruella striding around the playground in tiny black leather boots, using a miniature whip to flick her peers off the monkey bars.

'Do you think she even has parents?' I whispered, even though Cruella, to the best of our knowledge, was nowhere near the gallery.

'She couldn't possibly have,' Doug whispered back. 'The only possible explanation for Cruella is that she was hatched.'

We both shivered, looked over our shoulders and then went back to work. The mere mention of Cruella tended to have that effect on us.

A few moments later, I looked up. 'Doug?'

'Mmm?'

I felt strangely shy. 'Would you be my birthing partner back-up?'

His head snapped up. 'What did you just say?'

'I said, would you like to be there at the birth? Or, what's more likely, at the start – when I go into labour?' I hurried on, feeling self-conscious. 'Jack's impossible to reach half the time and, even when I can get a message through to him, he can't always drop what he's doing and come running. And I'm scared of being in labour alone. So I just thought maybe—'

The rest of my sentence was cut off as Doug jumped up from behind his desk and barrelled towards me, shrieking and hugging me.

'But are you sure?' he asked again, several minutes later, when both of us had calmed down. 'Why not your sister? Or Cate?'

My face fell at the mention of Cate, but I quickly regained my composure. 'I'm not sure that Audie would cope with the mess. And being a birthing partner isn't really Cate's thing.'

Doug wiped a tear away from his eye and then drew himself up proudly. 'It would be an honour and a privilege.' He paused and opened his mouth to say something else but, knowing what was on his mind, I got in first.

'A hospital gown,' I said with a smile. 'You'll have to wear a hospital gown.'

28
The Perfect Mum

I was now about thirty-one weeks pregnant, and all of the books were very insistent about how good walking was for me at this stage. Taking advantage of being at home midweek on a lovely spring day (even though I had recently taken holidays, Doug had given me a day off without telling Cruella, as compensation for having to work that Sunday), I grabbed the leash, whistled for Rufus, and we headed out into the sunshine to the nearby park.

As Rufus ran ahead, I sauntered along, hoping that we wouldn't bump into anyone I knew. I was in no mood for a conversation about how elephantine I looked. But we didn't. Instead, we happened upon a mothers' group.

They were occupying several picnic rugs on a patch of grass in the sunshine. I shot them a brief glance, enough to see that there were several newborn babies. I honed in on one baby and looked at it a little bit longer to see if it evoked any response in me. Nope. Nothing. I *still* couldn't connect the idea of Fetid who was in my tummy with the actual baby that would come out.

I looked away briefly and then looked again, this time at the mothers. That's when something inside me started to intone, 'I am not like you. I am not the sort of woman who can be found in a park in the middle of the day. I have a stimulating and interesting job. I am *not* like you.'

Of course, the only problem was, despite my terribly intriguing job, I was *exactly* the sort of woman who could be found in a park in the middle of a working day, considering that's where I was. But I was on a day off. I was walking the dog. That was different.

As I neared them, I saw one of them register my belly and smile. Hating myself, I avoided eye contact and strode on, assuming my 'I am thinking about VERY important matters which are crucial to the continued economic prosperity of this country' expression.

A sense of panic filled me as I contemplated a future spent passing my days in the park, cut off from my job and the world, with only other mothers and babies and daytime television for company.

I wouldn't let it happen.

I was busy. I had a life of my own.

I was *not* like them.

'I haven't seen you in ages.' A sense of relief flooded me as Audie picked up the phone. A chat with Audie was exactly what I needed after my little freak out in the park.

'It must be ESP. I just rang the gallery to speak to you and Doug told me you had the day off. Listen, the twins are with Henry's parents so I'm taking Felix to the Collingwood Children's Farm this afternoon. Why don't you come and we can chat there instead of over the phone?'

I instantly deflated. 'Oh. I, er . . .' Bloody hell. I was seven or so months pregnant and the thought of spending time doing kiddy things still utterly appalled me.

Audie was waiting.

I took a deep breath and decided to start facing my fears. 'Sure,' I said firmly. 'Shall we meet at the entrance in an hour?'

The Collingwood Children's Farm was unexpectedly lovely. Despite having lived in Melbourne for most of my life, I had never been there before, which probably had quite a bit to do with the fact that it had no liquor licence and it had the words 'Children's Farm' in its title. Nestled in the shelter of the Abbotsford Convent, it was reached by a winding path with old-fashioned wooden stiles that made me feel as though I had fallen into an Enid Blyton book. It was hard to believe that near by the traffic was still raging along Hoddle Street. Here it was all peace and sunshine, with ducks wandering around and pre-school kids gathered in the barn, learning how to milk a cow.

Having given permission to Felix to go and pat the horse, Audie and I were seated under the shade of an umbrella at a table at the outdoor café, sipping on cool fruit juice and waiting for our lunch order to arrive. After we'd caught up on each other's news, a companionable silence fell, while a warm breeze played around us.

'Audie?'

'Mmm?'

'What's it like being a mum?'

She looked fondly over to where Felix appeared to be discussing with the farrier the best way to shoe a horse. In Italian.

I waited breathlessly for her wise revelations.

'Cleaning,' she finally disclosed. 'There's lots of cleaning. By the time I finish washing and sterilising the kids' clothes and toys and the furniture and the floors and, well, basically everything, the day's over and it's time to do it all again.'

'You sterilise *everything* every day?'

She nodded. 'Twice a day, actually.'

'Did you get the nesting instinct before you gave birth?' I asked, awed by the thought of Audie in the grip of an even more uncontrollable cleaning instinct than the one that ruled her daily life.

'Of course.'

'Er – how did you know?'

She looked sheepish. 'I didn't really. But Henry suspected it when he caught me vacuuming the washing machine.' Registering my look, she snapped, 'There was *lint*.'

I decided it was safer not to pursue this tangent and tried again. 'OK. Forget that you're you for a moment and try to pretend that you're normal. Apart from the cleaning, what's motherhood like?'

Audie furrowed her brow while she concentrated very hard on thinking what else her life comprised apart from cleaning. 'It's wonderful,' she said simply.

'You don't get . . . bored?'

She shook her head. 'Never.' She looked at me and then said bluntly, 'But you probably will.' Registering the expression on my face, she tried to elaborate. 'It's entirely likely that you will be bored. You hate domestic chores and responsibilities, you always have. And you've never been very maternal either. Remember Molly Dolly?'

'Oh for fuck's sake. She was a doll. I'm hardly going to rip the head off my baby.'

Audie held out her hand. 'Swear jar.'

'You don't have a jar and I'm an adult. I'm allowed to swear.'

'Not in the presence of my child you're not. Gold coin donation.'

'Felix couldn't possibly have heard. He's over with the cows now and he's too busy teaching the other kids an improved milking method or something.'

'Fine. You're buying me lunch. But to return to the original topic, you buried Molly's head in the back garden.'

'Audie, it was a *doll* and it happened about fifty years ago.'

'She was *my* doll, and it happened exactly twenty-six years ago.'

'You're a bit spooky sometimes, you know?' Before she could respond, I continued, 'If I promise never to rip Felix's head off and bury it in the back garden, will you please keep helping me with my unresolved maternal issues?'

She took a meditative sip of her juice. 'At least you're finally asking for help,' she said begrudgingly.

'What does that mean?'

'It means that I *hate* how you never ask for advice even when it's obvious to everyone that you're completely in over your head.'

I looked at her in wonder. 'But *I* hate how you always give advice, especially when I haven't asked for it!'

'Huh.'

'How about that.'

We sat in silence for a few moments as we digested this.

'So all that time you were driving me crazy, I was driving you crazy?' I asked, just to be sure.

'Yep.' Audie looked around to check on Felix and then relaxed, once she had reassured herself that he was happily occupied discussing organic farming procedures with the farm's overseer. 'All right then, seeing as you've asked for my advice, this is what I think.' She took a deep breath and launched in. 'Don't put unrealistic expectations on yourself, Belle. Nobody expects you to be a perfect mother. For starters, there's no such thing.'

'Yeah, right. I'm looking at one.'

Audie looked at me and then said, very slowly, 'I don't like to let Felix get dirty.'

'What?'

'I said, I don't like it when Felix gets dirt all over his clothes. It drives me mad. I'm practically sitting on my hands right now to stop myself from hauling him away from that filthy barn.'

I looked at her incredulously. She looked the picture of serenity.

'A perfect mother would probably encourage her children to explore the natural world,' she continued.

'But – but that's exactly what you're doing,' I said, bewildered.

She gave a sudden laugh. 'I wouldn't say that I'm encouraging him. *Tolerating* is probably a more accurate description. And I'm hating every minute of it. I'm *itching* to go over there and give his face and hands a wipe.' She saw my confusion and added kindly, 'The point I'm trying to make is that as a mother you find yourself doing things for your kids that you might not choose to do under any other circumstances. I hate farms and animals and dirt and, well, basically the entire natural world. But Felix likes farms and animals, so here I am.'

I looked over at Felix and then back at Audie. She grinned. 'Belle, you won't know what kind of a mother you are until you *are* one. So try to stop worrying about it and just enjoy being pregnant. I know it might not seem like it at the moment, but it really doesn't last very long.'

'I've only got two months to go,' I said, trying to take in everything Audie had said.

She looked confused. 'I thought it was more like three months?'

I groaned. 'Somewhere in the near future I'll be

giving birth, OK? If you want the exact date, you'll have to ring Cate.'

She gave up and instead said, 'When I rang the gallery before and spoke to Doug, he mentioned that you've asked him to be with you when you go into labour.'

'That's the plan,' I sighed. 'Providing I don't go into labour during gallery hours. There's no way Cruella would let him close the gallery in order to be with me. I'm so scared of being alone when it starts.'

Audie looked at me searchingly. 'Where will Jack be?'

I avoided her gaze. 'Working probably. You know how impossible his job is.'

There was a silence and then Audie exhaled in frustration. 'There you go again!'

'What?' I asked, startled. 'What did I do?'

'It's what you *didn't* do. You've hardly mentioned Jack. Obviously something is wrong, but you still refuse to talk about it or ask for help.'

'Maybe that's because you *can't* help.'

Sensing that I wasn't to be budged, Audie decided to come at the problem from a different angle. 'If it's any consolation, Henry and I disagreed all the time when I was pregnant.'

I suppressed a smile. It was so like Audrey and Henry to *disagree*. Disagreeing sounded so much more genteel than fighting like cat and dog as Jack and I had been doing. 'What about?'

'All sorts of things.' She stopped and thought for a moment. 'Actually, most of it was to do with the decoration of the nursery, now that I think about it. Henry had his heart set on some ghastly Disney bed linen.' Audie had won that battle, I knew, as I had had the pleasure of tucking in Felix's French white cotton sheets, which had been hand embroidered with storybook motifs. 'The theme for the nursery caused all sorts of arguments too,' she reminisced.

This uncomfortably reminded me of Charlie. We had continued to text each other sporadically, usually lamenting the changes to our lives that impending parenthood was bringing. But we hadn't seen each other again, and we had stopped short of actually calling. I think we were both aware of a line that ought not to be crossed.

Now, as though to prove to myself that my relationship with Charlie was entirely above reproach, I airily commented, 'Charlie was saying the exact same thing to me the other day. He and Sleazel can't decide on a theme for the nursery.'

Audie didn't exactly spit out her mouthful of juice in shock, but she did sputter a bit. I then had to backtrack and fill her in on the Charlie saga, once again giving her the edited version that I had given Fran, without the frisson-ing or texting details.

I finished and waited for the barrage of questions and probing, but to my surprise she relaxed back into her seat, took a sip of her juice and then said, 'Isn't it odd? If you hadn't broken up with Charlie, we wouldn't be here now, having this conversation. There's no way you'd be pregnant.'

'I don't see why not,' I retorted, irritated. 'After all, Charlie got Sleazel pregnant, didn't he? The same thing could have happened to us if we'd stayed together.'

Audie shook her head. Her certainty was really starting to infuriate me now. 'Not a chance,' she said calmly. 'Charlie always walked all over you and he never wanted kids. If you'd stayed with him, he would have got his own way, like he always did.'

'What on *earth* are you talking about? Charlie never walked all over me!'

'What would you call applying for a job in another

state without telling you?' Audie politely enquired. 'Not to mention accepting the job and leaving you in Sydney, all within the space of about a month?'

I couldn't believe what I was hearing. I had *never* seen myself as the downtrodden-girlfriend type. That Audie could have seen me this way came as a complete and utter shock. Had other people also thought this of me?

'It wasn't like that,' I attempted.

Audie didn't ask me to explain and I didn't try to. She waited while I gathered my thoughts.

'Anyway, how do you know Charlie didn't want kids?' I challenged, but without much conviction. Already, I knew the answer.

'Because he told me so,' she replied, without hesitation.

Of course he had. Apparently, Charlie had spent our entire relationship telling *everyone*, bar me, that he would rather eat his own head than become a father. But why hadn't he said anything to *me*?

Obviously wanting to give me some more time to absorb all this, Audie called out to Felix and smiled as he waved impatiently and then turned back to what he was doing.

The waitress placed our sandwiches in front of us and, after she'd gone, I met Audie's gaze hesitantly.

'You know you can always ring me to come over when you go into labour,' she said, switching back to our original subject. Her tone was so kind that I instantly knew how shocked I must still be looking.

I mustered up a smile. 'That's very sweet of you, but that won't work either. What would you do with Felix and the twins?'

'Then why don't you get a doula?' Audie suggested.

'A what?'

Audrey looked surprised. 'Haven't you heard of

them? They're professionally trained birth assistants.'

'You mean like a midwife?'

'Kind of. A doula supports you during the labour and birth and helps you with breathing and massage and making a birth plan. That kind of thing.'

I had no idea what a birth plan was, but the idea of hiring a professional who would *definitely* be there when I went into labour, and who would know what was going on, was very appealing.

'How do you find a doula?' I asked, imagining a *Lord of the Rings* type of epic journey to entice the wise woman from her mountain lair.

'They're probably in the telephone book,' Audrey said prosaically. 'But you should just ask Jack. I'm sure the hospital must have doulas through all the time.'

I spent the next few hours feeding the goats, which was strangely comforting, and watching Felix collapse into giggles at the pig rolling in the mud. Felix's laughter was contagious, and, when I finally left Audie, Felix and the Collingwood Children's Farm, despite still grappling with Audie's unwelcome perspective on my relationship with Charlie, I was feeling much happier, not least because I had another potential source of support, apart from Doug.

Why had no one told me about doulas before? A doula was *exactly* what I needed.

Now I just had to find one.

29
Hula Doula

'Don't we have more childbirth classes to attend?' Jack asked me, as we lay in bed that night.

I shook my head. 'We missed the last one because we were in Queensland, and I'm not going to the breast-feeding class.'

He sat up and looked at me. 'Why not?'

'*Why not?* There's no way I can walk back into that room after what happened with Doug and you both showing up to the last class. It was humiliating. Since then I've had emails from Nancy and Nadia. Nancy said that she and Gareth understand our situation because one of their relatives married a Mormon polygamist and settled in Utah. Nadia wrote that the statistics for single mothers are bad enough as it is without people like me having two partners.'

My arguments didn't appear to have carried much weight with Jack. 'Belle, you're freaked out enough as it is about giving birth. I really think you need to do all of the classes. Can't you join another group, just for the final class, so that you'll have done them all? The more information you have, the better prepared you'll be.'

'They're my thoughts exactly!' I said triumphantly. 'But we don't have to get the information from the classes.'

Jack groaned. 'Not more books? Please don't tell me you've bought more pregnancy books. You end up several degrees more insane every time you read one of those.'

I was tempted to point out that I had read approximately eight pregnancy books from cover to cover, while he had read a total of none, but I was loath to get into another argument. So I compromised by saying, 'No, I don't. But I'm not talking about books anyway. Jack, I want to get a doula.'

He looked at me in surprise. 'Where did this come from?'

'Audie suggested it. And I think it's a fabulous idea. She'll be our very own midwife.'

'A doula isn't exactly like a midwife,' Jack warned. 'She doesn't play a clinical role like the obstetrician or the midwives.'

'I know, but she'll come to our house and be here during the labour until I go to hospital, won't she? And that's the bit I'm freaking out about.'

'I thought you were freaking out about giving birth?'

'I freak out about giving birth after I've finished freaking out about the first bit,' I explained.

'Oh.'

'I know it's another expense, but, given there's a chance you won't be with me when I go into labour, it would make me feel a lot better,' I beseeched him.

An expression that I couldn't fathom crossed Jack's face. It was strange, because if I'd had to name it I would have said it was sadness. But what on earth had I said to make him sad? Before I could question him, he asked, 'Are you sure you want a stranger, even if they're a professional? And, anyway, haven't you asked Doug to be with you?'

'Yes, but who knows if Doug will be able to be there either? Please?' I begged.

Jack gave in. 'All right. I'll make some enquiries at the hospital and see if there's someone they recommend.' He switched off his bedside lamp and rolled over.

For a minute or two there was silence.

'Jack?'

'Trying to sleep,' he murmured.

'We could call her the Hula Doula.'

'*Goodnight*, Belle.'

I snuggled down next to him as much as my tummy would allow, absurdly relieved that we had made it through this conversation without arguing.

A doula was the very thing that I needed. A calm, kind, wise older woman who would bathe my forehead and be gentle but firm with me throughout the contractions. Exactly like Jack, in fact, only definitely there.

One week later, Doug dropped around in the evening while Jack was at work, to tell me the exciting news that the adoption agency had called and said that they had a child for him and Zac. They would be told within the next few weeks when they could meet her and take her home. He had also brought with him a beautiful white wooden rocking chair, with an enormous hot-pink ribbon tied around it.

'Do you like it?' he asked eagerly, having deposited it smack bang in the middle of the hallway.

I flung my arms around him. 'I love it. Thank you!'

'Technically, it's your present from the gallery,' Doug admitted. 'Cruella signed the cheque, but I chose it.'

'I'm surprised she signed the cheque.'

'Yes, well, there's no need to go thanking her for it,' Doug said hastily. 'I'm not saying she knew what the cheque was *for*. But as you're owed about triple what the chair cost in unpaid overtime I thought you deserved a present from us. I brought this to celebrate too.' He waved a bottle of non-alcoholic sparkling cider in the air and I clapped my hands in glee.

We had just opened it and poured out two glasses when the doorbell rang.

'I'll get it,' Doug offered, as I groaned and started to heave myself to my feet.

I waved him off. 'Stay there. The more walking I do the better, even if it's just down the hallway.'

I opened the front door and looked curiously at the youngish man standing on our doorstep.

'Hi!' the man said cheerily. 'I'm Randolph.'

'Hello, Randolph,' I said cautiously.

We eyed each other for a bit longer.

'Can I come in?' he finally asked.

'Thank you, but whatever it is that you're selling I'm not interested. Unless—' I eyed his satchel optimistically. 'You're not doing a chocolate fundraiser, by any chance, are you?'

He laughed. 'I'm not a door-to-door salesperson. I'm your doula.'

I looked at him blankly. 'You can't be. There must be some mistake.'

'There's no mistake,' he replied. 'Your husband set this appointment up. I thought you were expecting me?'

'We're not married,' I said, trying not to wince at the distressing memory of Jack's ill-fated proposal. 'And I do want a doula, but I want a kindly, older, *female* doula.'

Randolph sighed. 'This happens all the time. Could I at least come in while we discuss it?'

'It's nothing personal,' I said, as I led the way down the hall, manoeuvring around the rocking chair. 'It's just that this is my first child and I want someone who's been through it themselves to look after me.'

'What an extraordinary thought,' Randolph mused. 'Thank heavens hospitals don't follow your philosophy. Otherwise, in order to attend to the patients, all the nursing staff would need to have had a hip replacement, a heart condition and a dog bite. They'd be no good to anyone at all.'

'Very funny.'

We entered the kitchen and I introduced him to Doug. 'That's not champagne,' I said hastily, before I made a bad first impression. 'It's non-alcoholic cider. We were celebrating because Doug's adopting a child.'

Randolph offered his congratulations and then Doug asked curiously, 'What exactly is a doula?'

'They're birthing assistants. They stay with you during labour and the birth,' I answered.

I swung around to Randolph. 'Are you still called a doula if you're male?'

'Strictly speaking, it's a Greek word for a woman who attends another woman, so probably not,' he replied. 'But I don't think there's a male form of the word so I just stick with doula.'

'Technically, you're probably a doule,' I decided, adding glumly, 'It doesn't even rhyme with hula.'

It was at this point that Doug cleared his throat loudly. 'Isabelle? May I have a *word*?'

I looked at him enquiringly. 'Sure.'

He glared at me. 'In *private*.'

Wondering what was going on, I asked Randolph to excuse us and told him to help himself to some cider. Randolph watched as we made our way into the living room. Aware of his gaze, Doug pulled the door firmly shut behind us and then jabbed his thumb over his shoulder in indignation. 'Who the hell is *he*?' he demanded furiously.

'He's Randolph, the male doula,' I replied. As the words left my lips, I couldn't help thinking that that had to be one of the most preposterous sentences I had ever uttered in my life.

'I *know* that! What's he doing here? What do you need *him* for?'

Oh.

'Doug, don't be like that,' I cajoled. 'I still want you there when I go into labour, it's just – well, he's a professional.'

'Is he a midwife? Or a doctor?'

'Er, no. Not exactly.'

Doug regarded me with his arms crossed.

'Has it occurred to you that I might go into labour while you're at work? What's going to happen then?'

Doug sniffed but didn't say anything. He had no answer for that dilemma, I knew, so I pressed home my advantage. 'And you and Zac are going to be parents yourselves very soon. You might not be able to leave your little girl to come and be with me.'

'I hadn't thought of that,' Doug admitted. 'OK, fine, but I wish you'd told me.'

'I had no idea he was coming tonight. Jack organised it.'

'I hope you don't mind me saying so, Belle, but Jack has some very peculiar notions. I mean, really. A *male* doula! Where's it all going to end?'

'I know,' I murmured. 'Society's going to hell in a handbasket. Shall we go back in?'

Doug agreed to accompany me back into the kitchen, but he subjected Randolph to a very hard look as he pulled out his chair and sat down.

'OK, Randolph – can I call you Randy?'

'No.'

'Shame,' I said regretfully. 'My gym instructor is named Brandy so it would have had a nice symmetry.

Anyway, Doug and I were just wondering what it is you're qualified to do for me?'

'For starters, I'm trained in lymphatic drainage massage, which I can tell you right now, you could use on your feet. If they get any more swollen you're going to end up in hospital. Here, kick your shoes off and put your feet up here.'

It felt a bit odd to put my bare feet into the lap of a stranger, but the instant that Randolph started to massage my feet, I sighed with pleasure. Ooh, he was good.

I reached for my glass of cider, but Randolph shook his head and pushed a steaming cup towards me instead. 'I brewed this while you were in the other room. From now on I want you to drink this whenever possible.'

I sniffed the concoction suspiciously. 'What is it?'

'Raspberry leaf tea. I've mixed it with peppermint so that it tastes better. It's bloody horrible by itself,' he confided to Doug, who gave a nod that somehow conveyed the impression that there was nothing Randolph could tell *him* about raspberry leaf tea.

'Why am I drinking it?'

'It's very good for softening the cervix.'

'What does the cervix do again?' I asked cautiously.

'It's the bit that you need to be soft in order for the baby to come out,' Randolph answered.

This was a perfect answer as far as I was concerned. Simple, to the point, and no use of nasty phrases like 'mucus plug'.

'Research has also shown that using a doula can help to reduce the caesarean rate, the need for forceps, the length of labour and even the need for pain medication,' Randolph continued, in his calm, soothing voice.

'Really?' I liked the idea of him cutting my labouring time but I felt that I ought to set him straight. 'But that's not exactly why I wanted a doula. I quite like the idea of pain relief, you see.'

'So you've thought about pain relief?'

Only three hundred times a day. 'Yes. A bit.'

'Tell me what you're thinking of having.'

I took a deep breath. 'Chloroform, Aspirin, heat bag, massage, acupuncture, a warm bath, aromatherapy, self-hypnosis, pethidine, gas, epidural, healing crystals, several bottles of wine, a TENS machine, cups of tea, hypnotherapy, a hot water bottle, reflexology and whale music.'

To my disappointment, Randolph had stopped massaging my feet midway through my recitation and was now staring at me instead. 'Is that all?' he asked faintly.

I nodded. 'Oops, no. I forgot chocolate.'

Randolph regained his composure. 'You want *all* of those things?'

'Please.'

'Any particular order?'

'I'd prefer simultaneously.'

Randolph seemed to think I was going a bit overboard, but, quite frankly, I was planning on sending Jack out on to the streets to buy crack cocaine if that would help.

'Isabelle, have you done anything at all to prepare for the pain of labour and childbirth?'

'I had a bikini wax without first taking an Aspirin with a glass of wine,' I said proudly.

Doug nodded approvingly, while Randolph continued to look from me to Doug and back again, as though we were both mad.

'If you're planning on having all the pain relief, what do you want me for?'

'I need you as back-up,' I said anxiously, nudging my foot closer to his hand again. 'I don't think my right foot's lymphs are completely drained yet.'

Randolph didn't hear the last part because Doug had interjected in an outraged voice, '*I'm* your back-up!'

'Sorry, Doug. He's right,' I said apologetically to Randolph. 'Although actually Jack is ostensibly my main support person, but he might not be able to get there in time because he's a doctor and he's never around. So Doug's my back-up which would make you the back-up's back-up.'

'I'm the back-up's back-up?' Randolph repeated, sounding dazed. He gathered his thoughts and then said tentatively, 'I'm not sure if I'm the right person to take you on. I think we have different philosophies about childbirth.'

I couldn't believe this. I was getting dumped by my doula. Already. If he went through with it, Randolph would hold the record for my all-time briefest relationship, even including the time I started going out with David MacKenzie at break in grade three, only to have him break up with me at lunchtime because I wouldn't swap my Vegemite sandwiches for his horrible egg ones.

'No,' I said in alarm. 'Wait a minute. Let me make you a Vegemite sandwich and we'll talk it over.'

'I don't want a Vegemite sandwich. Isabelle, most of my clients embrace the idea of natural childbirth.'

'Exactly!' I said triumphantly. 'I'm not like your other clients. Randolph, how long have you been a doula?'

'Three years.'

'You need me,' I said firmly. 'If you take me on, I guarantee that you will never in your professional life face a bigger challenge than dealing with me.'

Doug nodded. 'She's right. We love her but she's completely cracked. Drives me out of my mind most days. And, between you and me, sometimes she forgets that she's not the only one around here who's pregnant.' He patted his stomach fondly. 'Pass the raspberry leaf tea please, Belle.'

Randolph opened his mouth to clarify what Doug had just said, then decided against it. Mechanically, he started to massage my feet again, as he thought through what we'd both said. I watched him anxiously. I didn't want my lovely foot masseur going anywhere.

He looked up at me with a determined expression. 'If I take you on, you have to do *exactly* what I say, understood?'

I nodded. Anything. Just keep rubbing my feet.

Randolph nodded decisively and then snapped back into bossy-boots doula mode. 'OK then. From now on, I want you to drink lots of water and try to stay off your feet. Keep them up whenever possible. Are you intending to breastfeed?'

'I'm going to try.'

'Good for you. Breastfeeding helps to contract the uterus, you know.'

Doug emitted a snort as though to say *that* was common knowledge around every Australian kindergarten.

Wisely, Randolph ignored him and continued, 'One strategy that can be very effective during labour is for your partner to pull on your nipples.'

'I beg your pardon?'

'Nipple stimulation helps the uterus to contract, which in turn helps the contractions. He could always suck them,' Randolph said cheerily. 'That works too.'

'You want Jack to suck my nipples while I'm in labour?' I repeated, drawing my feet away from Randolph's grasp.

He nodded.

Before I could respond, Doug stalked from the room muttering dark imprecations about the unnaturalness of pregnant women.

'Is he all right?' Randolph asked with concern.

'He's fine. He's just very squeamish about certain things. You're not going to suggest that I use steel wool on my nipples, are you?'

'Certainly not.'

'Oh good. Doug hasn't had really clean saucepans since the first childbirth education class. He can't bring himself to use steel wool any more.' I paused and then smiled at Randolph. 'So you'll be my doula?'

He handed me a business card with his contact details on it. 'Yes.' He talked over the top of me as I clapped my hands with delight. 'We'll need to have at least one more meeting, preferably next week.'

'OK. Should we discuss doula moula?'

'Because that's only the seventy-fifth time I've heard that joke,' he said drily. 'And no, there's no need. Your partner has sorted all that out.'

It was only after both Doug and Randolph had departed that I looked down at Randolph's business card and discovered his last name.

As if my recurring nightmare about my nameless baby wasn't enough, the god of baby names had sent yet another sign that Jack and I had better start thinking long and hard about what baby names we wanted on our shortlist.

For, while I might be deprived of having a Hula Doula, helping to bring my baby into the world would be Randolph Reindeer.

30
Plan B

When Randolph Reindeer showed up the following week, I tried very hard not to stare at his nose. Too hard.

He sighed. 'OK. Let's get it over with.'

'What?'

'The discussion about my name. You're trying *not* to stare at my nose. It's been happening to me since I was five. Why people find it so difficult to understand that my name is *Randolph*, not Rudolph, I will never understand.' Thankfully, he sounded resigned rather than annoyed.

'Sorry,' I muttered. 'I'm just a bit obsessed with choosing a name for our baby right now, and—' What I wanted to say was 'What in the hell were your parents thinking?' but that wouldn't be very polite. And I needed Randolph. So I changed the subject instead. 'Shall I lie down on the couch?'

'Only if you want to.'

'I'm thirty-three weeks pregnant. I *always* want to lie down on the couch. Are we going to practise breathing or something?'

He shook his head and poured me a cup of raspberry leaf tea. 'Not today. Today I want to do some work on your state of mind.'

'My mind's fine,' I said firmly. 'I want to concentrate

on my cervix and my pelvis and all of the bits that are going to be doing the hard work.'

'Your bits are in perfect working order, but they won't work properly unless we sort your head out. And your mind *isn't* fine.' He waited a beat. 'I've hardly spent any time with you and it's clear to me that you're very frightened of the pain of labour and childbirth.'

Well, that was no big insight. I practically had it tattooed on my forehead.

Randolph continued, 'And I have a suspicion that you've been so consumed by this pregnancy that you haven't given any thought to your child.'

'What does that mean?'

'It means that I know you have no answer to the following basic question.'

'Which is?' I prompted.

Randolph looked at me, a little smile playing around his lips. 'Do you think you're having a boy or a girl?'

Oh, for Pete's sake. 'How could I possibly know?'

'What does your gut feeling tell you?'

I thought hard. 'Girl. No – wait. Boy. Definitely a boy.'

Randolph beamed. 'You see? That wasn't very hard. You just needed to tune into your instincts.'

I chewed my lip. 'It might be a girl, you know.'

'Isabelle!'

'I can't help it,' I wailed. 'I just don't know.'

'All right, forget the gender. Try this one instead – what do you want for your child?'

'I'd prefer that it was human and didn't vote Conservative,' I answered confidently. 'Actually, as long as it doesn't vote Conservative, I'm flexible on the species.'

Randolph stared at me. 'Why do you think your baby might not be human?'

'Have you read *Woah Baby!*?' I asked darkly. 'Strange things happen, you know.'

Randolph scribbled furiously in his notebook for a moment and then tried again. 'OK, Isabelle, imagine this: if you could be fairy godmother to your own child, what gifts would you give it?'

I thought for a moment. 'Do I have a wand?'

'What does that have to do with anything?'

'It has everything to do with your question,' I said indignantly. 'If I don't have a wand, it has to be something that I can buy.'

'Fine. You have a wand. I meant non-material things.'

'Oh. Well, then, I suppose I'd like our baby to have a sense of humour.'

Randolph heaved a sigh of relief. 'Excellent. Now we're getting somewhere.'

'A good sense of humour,' I added anxiously. 'Not the sort that finds *Australia's Funniest Home Videos* amusing. Because really, that's not the same as having a sense of humour at all. That's more like being a sadistic moron.'

'Isabelle, I want you to come up with *one* thing that you hope for your child. A firm, solid hope, with no clarifications or qualifications.'

I thought hard. 'I'd quite like it if my child wasn't a sadistic moron.'

'That's it? *That's* the extent of the hopes and dreams that you have for your unborn child?'

'That and I'd prefer that it wasn't a Scorpio.'

Randolph decided to try a different tack. 'You work in the art world. Would you like it if your child was artistic?'

'Good grief, no. We're all a pack of lunatics. That would be condemning the poor thing to a life of insanity *and* poverty.' I followed this line of reasoning. Feeling pleased with myself, I produced another example. 'I feel quite sure in saying that I'd prefer my child not to be poor and insane.'

Randolph grimaced and rubbed his eyes. It made me feel quite affectionate towards him as, funnily enough, Jack often employed the same gesture when we had long conversations together.

'I suppose it wouldn't matter so much if it was one or the other,' I added thoughtfully. 'But the combination of both of them is a bit much. What have we got so far?'

He read aloud from his notes. 'You'd prefer your child not to be a sadistic, moronic Scorpio artist who ends up poor and insane.' He got up and paced the living room for a few moments, absent-mindedly poured me another cup of raspberry leaf tea, and then said, with a tinge of desperation, 'OK, this isn't working. I want you to have a read of this and then write your own. You have half an hour.'

'What is it?' I looked curiously at the neatly typed A4 page he had handed me.

'It's a birth plan. Using that one as an example, I want you to write your own, covering all the same major points.'

Randolph disappeared into the kitchen in order to give me some private thinking time, and I started reading through the handout.

The birth plan he had given me had been written by a couple called Valerie and Jim. Right from the get-go, I was pretty sure that Valerie and Jim and I were not going to get along. Everything was written out methodically using bullet points and sub-headings such as 'First Stage, Transition, Second Stage and Complications'.

Valerie was clearly the Brazilian type of birther.

There was lots of repetition of the phrase 'Valerie would prefer no intervention or anaesthesia'. Oddly, however, Valerie was happy to suck down the gas.

The list of preparations continued. Apparently, I needed to think about what to wear during labour. For fuck's sake. My initial preference was to wear the peach taffeta dress I had worn to my high-school dance. If I was going to be on my hands and knees, screaming and pooing in front of a bunch of strangers, I may as well roll all my embarrassing moments into one, so that they were in a tidy package for the therapist who would no doubt play a formative role in my future.

And then I reached the final paragraph of Valerie and Jim's birth plan. This covered the contingency if the baby was critically ill or stillborn.

Unknowingly, my hand moved to my belly. No, I thought fiercely. It's OK, little Fetid. I won't let that happen to you.

Picking up my pen, I set to work.

Half an hour later, I handed my completed birth plan back to Randolph. He gave it a cursory read-through and then looked at me with a pained expression on his face.

'Isabelle? Under Preferred Method of Birth you've written "parthenogenesis".'

'That was how the Greek goddess Athena was born. I have it from a very reliable source that she sprang fully formed from her father's forehead,' I informed him.

'Nice try, but I know that myth and I'm pretty sure that Zeus had his head cleaved open with an axe,' Randolph said drily. 'And, if I recall correctly, Zeus also ate Athena's mother. But by all means we can give that a go if you have your heart set on it.'

'Apart from the bit about me being eaten, I would like to try it, as it seems to be the only birthing method that involves Jack experiencing all the pain,' I responded, with dignity.

'You're paying me by the hour you know,' he sighed. 'OK, on the off chance that the hospital doesn't offer elective parthenogenesis-ians, or whatever the plural noun is, how about we have a Plan B?'

I thought hard for a moment. 'I suppose you wouldn't approve of using the portal in my pelvic floor that leads to John Malkovich's head?'

There was a silence and then Randolph spoke up. 'Are you on any form of medication that I need to know about?'

'No,' I said mournfully. 'Don't worry about it. It was just a thought, but any plan that involves the co-operation of my pelvic floor is doomed anyway. We'd have to find it first, and that thing puts the Yeti, Jason Bourne and the lost city of Atlantis to shame.'

Randolph fixed me with a penetrating stare and then demanded shrewdly, 'Have you heard the theory that some people make jokes as a defensive tactic to avoid discussing uncomfortable issues?'

I shifted under his unblinking gaze and cast wildly about in my mind for a Knock-Knock joke to break the unnerving silence before I realised what a tragic head-case I was. Randolph was absolutely right. For some reason, the final part of Valerie and Jim's birth plan, which had dealt with the prospect of a stillbirth, sprang into my mind. No wonder I didn't want to board the spaceship and leave Planet Tangent. It was much more fun there than back in the real world.

Randolph was refusing to let me off the hook. 'Can I ask you something, Isabelle? Given that you're so utterly terrified of childbirth, why on earth did you get pregnant in the first place?'

Fair question. Luckily, I had my answer all worked out, because I had been wondering the same thing myself since about ten minutes after Jack and I had conceived. 'Because the childbirth bit is only temporary, of course. And – and I do want to have a baby with Jack. I do. I know it might not seem like it but . . . it's not the baby that I'm scared of.' As the words tumbled out, I realised they were true. 'It's me.'

Randolph waited, refusing to help me out by prompting me.

'I'm scared of failing. I'm scared that I'll never be alone again. I'm scared of losing my life – I *love* my life – of not knowing what to do when it cries, or that I'll hate being a mother and it will be a terrible mistake. Most mistakes you can undo. But this one . . .'

Randolph gently interrupted, before I became overwrought. 'You must have made mistakes in the past, though.'

'Yes, of course,' I said, instantly thinking of my one night stand that had led to the break-up of my relationship with Charlie.

'And, although you probably wish you hadn't made them, did anything good ever come out of your mistakes?'

'I met Jack.'

'Well, that's a very good thing,' Randolph said, smiling. 'And it proves that, even though you don't always know it at the time, perhaps things happen for a reason.'

'That's what my dad always says,' I said, surprised. 'But the problem with hindsight is that it only lets you *see* the past in a different way. You can't actually go back and fix or undo things.'

Randolph looked at me thoughtfully. 'If there's anything in your past that's bothering you, Isabelle, now could be a good time to address it. It's much easier to face your future when you've dealt with your past.'

'Is that a fridge magnet or an internet quote?' I asked archly, trying not to think of Charlie and why he hadn't wanted to have children with me.

Randolph laughed. 'Both, probably. But true, nonetheless. So that's the first part of the homework that I'm setting you. Now, before I tell you the second part, I want you to answer me this: what do you think a mother is?'

'Someone like my sister Audie,' I replied instantly. 'She lives for her kids. She sews their clothes and cooks them nutritious food and, despite the fact that she also has twins, she spends her entire life shuttling Felix around to playgroup and dancing lessons and something called Gymbaroo.'

'If you consider yourself a twenty-first-century feminist, you certainly have some very peculiar and outdated notions. That's one way to be a mother, certainly. But there are others. Hillary Rodham Clinton is a mother. Naomi James, the first woman to sail solo around the world, is a mother. Anita Roddick, the founder of The Body Shop, and a phenomenally successful businesswoman, was a mother. Shall I continue?'

I nodded.

'OK then. How about modelling – an industry that revolves around body image? Heidi Klum and Elle Macpherson, who have several kids between them, are still amongst modelling's highest earners. Political leaders like Catherine the Great, Indira Ghandi and Margaret Thatcher were all mothers.'

'That's enough! You can stop now. I'm starting to feel like an underachiever for not running an empire or being a supermodel.'

'As long as you realise that this idea you have that in order to be a mother you have to fit a certain mould is completely false.'

'I can't help it,' I said despairingly. 'I walked past a mothers' group in the park the other week and I freaked out. I couldn't even look them in the eye. I just don't want to end up like them.'

'How do you know that those women aren't doctors or lawyers or chefs or computer technicians?' Randolph challenged me.

He waited but I didn't respond. There wasn't really anything that I *could* say.

'The answer is, you don't know anything about them. You see them with their kids and you can't see past the fact that they're mums. And worse than that – you judge them negatively because of that one facet of their identity.'

I was scarlet with embarrassment. He was absolutely right about all of it. I was horrible.

I hung my head in shame and waited for the lecture to continue. But, to my surprise, when he spoke, his voice was incredibly gentle. 'Isabelle, you're not the first woman to panic about losing her identity as you become a mother, and you certainly won't be the last. It's completely natural. And I know this seems out of the question right now, when you're doubting everything about yourself and your body's abilities, but there is one possibility that you don't seem to have considered at all.'

I lifted my head and looked at him. Finally, here was the mummy secret that I had been longing to discover. Randolph was about to initiate me into the secret society, I just knew it.

'What is it?' I asked breathlessly.

Randolph smiled. 'You might be a good mother. And you might love every minute of it.'

31
The Pregnant Pause

I decided to deal with the first part of Randolph's homework the following day, but in truth I hadn't needed much convincing. Ever since my conversation with Audie at the farm, I had been itching to see Charlie again, and now I had an excuse.

Charlie sounded surprised when he answered his mobile phone, and I didn't blame him. Texting one another was one thing, actually calling felt like crossing the invisible ethical line. 'Iz, you just caught me. What's up? Don't tell me you've finally decided on a name for your baby?'

'That would warrant more than a phone call, I can tell you. I'm thinking of hiring skywriters and billboards to break the news of our baby's name.' I took a deep breath. 'I was wondering whether we could catch up sometime in the next few days.'

There was a silence. Oh, God, this was excruciating. I felt like a pregnant ex-girlfriend stalker, which was right up there in the undesirable combo stakes, next to 'bunny-boiling ex-mistress' and '*Neighbours* star turned pop singer'.

'Sure. But it will have to be this afternoon. I'm flying to Jo-burg tonight.'

I had forgotten how much I hated the nicknames and

abbreviations that Charlie and his pilot friends used for various cities. Thus, Johannesburg became Jo-burg and the sophisticated cities of Hong Kong and New York turned into Honkers and Yonkers, which sounded like a circus act.

'Are you at work?' Charlie continued. 'Shall I come to you?'

'Um, sure.' We made a hasty plan to meet at a nearby coffee shop.

I hung up and turned around to see Doug glaring at me.

'Stop looking at me like that or I'll demonstrate how to perform perineal massage,' I said defensively. 'It's my homework. Blame Randolph.'

'Blame the reindeer all you like, Belle,' Doug retorted. 'I just hope for the sake of the three of you that this is about closure, not reopening a wound that ought to have closed over years ago.'

He walked away, but it took me a few minutes to realise that, when Doug had referred to 'the three of you', he hadn't been including Charlie.

I was waiting for Charlie in the back corner of the café, at a table that was surrounded by walls, not windows. Even though I knew Jack was at work, I was determined not to take any chances this time.

'I've found the perfect birth plan for you,' Charlie said by way of greeting, as he bent over and kissed me on the cheek. 'It's no use this time around, unfortunately, but, in the unlikely event that you have another child, it's perfect.'

'What is it?' I asked, glossing over the fact that he thought Jack and I were only going to have one child. Were we? I had no idea. Apart from Jack's emphasis on buying a house with numerous bedrooms, it was something we hadn't really discussed.

'Have sex with a seahorse,' Charlie informed me, ordering a coffee from the waiter. 'The male seahorse is the one who gets pregnant and gives birth. I've already decided to stock up on good karma during this life so I don't come back as one.'

'So basically a fate worse than death is to be a seahorse or female?' I asked sardonically.

Charlie laughed. 'We can argue if you want, Iz, but I take it you didn't invite me here to discuss seahorses or my chauvinist-pig tendencies. So what's up? Have you had a fight with Jack?'

I looked at him, horrified. Why on earth would he think that I would run to him if Jack and I were having problems? Oh, God. Because I *had*.

'No,' I said curtly. 'I want to talk about us.'

Charlie raised an eyebrow. 'Us? There hasn't been an "us" for years. Or is this a new "us"?'

I ignored his flirtatious tone. 'I want to talk about the old "us". Specifically the old "you", who I've recently discovered used to galumph around the countryside telling all and sundry that you never wanted to have a family with me.'

Charlie looked genuinely puzzled, which only made it worse. 'So what?'

'*So what?* So you're about to become a father, that's what! What happened to you?'

'What happened to *me*? What the hell happened to *you*? You were always the least maternal woman I knew, apart from Cate.'

'No I wasn't,' I said defensively.

Charlie looked at me.

'All right,' I said crossly, 'so I wasn't a pin-up girl for *Pre School*.'

'You mean *Play School*.'

'Whatever. Anyway, I don't know why you're looking at me like I've grown another head. You were never exactly Father of the Year material either.'

'Doesn't it freak you out that you really *are* growing another head in there?' Charlie said, momentarily diverted, nodding at my stomach.

I closed my eyes. 'I can't begin to tell you how much,' I said faintly. 'Please don't mention the eyelids. They're the worst for some reason.'

We both shuddered and then Charlie responded to my earlier comment. 'I doubt that I'll ever be Father of the Year. Liesel understands, though, because it's not like we planned it or anything. You know what I mean.'

'You didn't mean to get pregnant?' I repeated in confusion.

He looked at me in equal bewilderment. 'Of course not. Wait a minute. Are you telling me that you *did*?'

I nodded.

'You *planned* it?' He was staring at me in disbelief. 'You *wanted* a baby?'

'Of course we wanted it,' I said, starting to get irritated. 'Why is that such a big deal? People change. *I've* changed.'

'Yeah, but I mean, Iz, come on. *You?* Changing nappies and wiping up vomit and walking the floorboards for hours holding a crying baby?' He shook his head as the waiter set his coffee down in front of him. Tearing open a packet of sugar, he added, 'I just don't see it.'

I couldn't see it either, which was why the future seemed so scary. But it wasn't exactly reassuring to have Charlie hiring a marching band to draw attention to my maternal deficiencies either.

'I might be a good mother,' I said, trying hard to recall exactly what Randolph had said and to sound convincing. 'And there's every chance I might love every minute of it.'

'I'll remind you of that when you text me at three in the morning, complaining that your baby has projectile-vomited all over you and you haven't slept in eight months,' Charlie said dismissively. Clearly I hadn't been as impressive as Randolph. 'I *know* you, Iz. Your store of patience is the size of a tic-tac and you've got more in common with an Egyptian mummy than the other sort. The first day you're left at home by yourself with the baby, you'll be bored out of your mind in the first three minutes and you'll be on the phone to Audie, begging her to come and rescue you.'

The strange part was that it wasn't as though anything that Charlie was saying was revelatory. He wasn't even trying to be intentionally cruel. From Charlie's perspective, a dearth of maternal inclinations was something to be admired. But it's one thing to be aware of your *own* shortcomings and failures. It's entirely another to have someone who knows you well catalogue them out loud, citing them as an irrevocable part of your makeup, right when you're trying to change.

And then something struck me. 'Is that why you never wanted babies with me? Because you thought that I'd be a bad mother?'

Charlie rolled his eyes. 'Oh, for God's sake, Iz. Is this why you dragged me here? To go over ancient history?'

'Number one, I didn't drag you here. Number two, I'll have you know that it's very important to deal with ancient history in order to face your future history.'

'I don't think future history is a real term.'

'Shut up. You know what I mean. Answer my question.'

Charlie looked me straight in the eye with an expression that for some reason made me nervous. 'You really want to know?'

I nodded.

'OK then. I still think that we could have been good together for several reasons, but one of them is because neither of us ever really wanted children. I love my career and you've always loved swanning around the art world, a glass of champers in one hand, air-kissing everyone in sight. And a smelly, crying baby just doesn't factor into either of those lifestyles.' He stopped and took a sip of his coffee. 'You asked for my honest opinion so here it is. You might have planned this baby, but that was probably because you fell in love with some fleeting notion of being a fashionable yummy mummy. In the real world, I think you don't have the first clue of what to do with a baby. And, before you go berserk, neither do I.' He paused, for what felt like for ever, and then leaned in closer. 'Considering that we're both about to become parents, our dirty little secret is that neither of us really wants to know, either. Face it, Iz, we're just not mummy and daddy material.'

He sat back and I looked down, as all of the confidence and optimism that Randolph had inspired in me slowly trickled away to be replaced by a torrent of despair and horror.

The despair was because everything he'd said was true. The horror was caused by the realisation that, out of everyone who made up my world, it seemed that Charlie was still the only one who knew the real me.

32

Bonnets, Bloomers and Bibs

Seeing that the first part of my homework had gone so swimmingly (Raise past issues with ex: Check. Deal with past issues: Ongoing. Raise new issues by trying to deal with past issues: Check.), I decided that I may as well ruin my evening as well and tackle the second part of my homework. I needed something to do anyway, in order to make the time pass, as Jack was working late – again – so I was on my own with only Rufus and my confused thoughts for company.

Randolph had been very insistent that the task he was setting me would be seminal in helping me to mentally prepare for the baby. This sounded very grand and impressive until I had discovered that the second half of my homework was to sort out the baby's room. (Otherwise known as the nursery, which made me feel like I would shortly be giving birth to a pot plant.)

I hadn't really been into the spare room since I'd cleared it out, all those months ago. Now, walking into it, its emptiness seemed somehow charged. It was waiting for an occupant, and, I suddenly realised, it was also waiting for furniture and nappy-changing equipment and the hundred and one necessary items that I hadn't even thought of till now. Trying not to feel overwhelmed by the list of things that I needed to organise,

I unrolled a farmyard rug that Audie had given us, in a vain attempt to *do* something. Someone had given the rug to Felix when he was born but she had never used it. I smiled, knowing now that that was probably because even the mere thought of a farmyard made her break out in hives. I spent a few minutes fussing over the placement of the rug until Rufus padded softly into the room and promptly curled up on it.

My old childhood books lay stacked in one corner and there were also several toys that had either belonged to Jack or me or which had been given to us as early gifts. Apart from Doug's rocking chair, the only other items in the room were a child's car seat that Jack's parents had bought for us and bags of hand-me-down clothes passed on to us from friends and family, which made me feel thrifty in a very housewifely way.

I decided to begin with the clothes but there were so many to sort out that I needed some sort of surface. Taking the bags into our bedroom, I emptied them on our bed. A few minutes later, the size of the task that I had set myself started to dawn on me.

The problem was that baby clothes are exactly like grown-up clothes. Different brands make different sizes. Different countries have different sizing labels. And I was staring at a jumble of miniature clothing from different brands and different countries.

There was only one thing to do. Taking a deep breath, I began to sort through the muddle and make piles. The clothes started at triple zero and went through to size two. I picked up a pair of size-two leggings and stared at them. They looked gigantic. Then again, anything in size triple 000 also looked enormous when I imagined a baby that size having to come out of me. But then I picked up a jumpsuit whose label only read 'Suitable for 68 cms'.

What the hell did that mean? I measured it against a size 00 and it seemed roughly the same so I threw it in that pile. But the next pair of pants that I picked up were size 000. They looked big enough to fit Felix. I held them against a size 00 and they were twice the size. My system wasn't working.

I started from scratch, this time ignoring labels and putting together piles of clothing that seemed approximately the same size. That's when I realised that the problem was further compounded by the fact that these clothes had belonged to an assortment of different babies who had all been born at different times of the year. So now that I had my size piles I had to do a seasonal sort. Our baby was due in summer so there wasn't much point even putting the woolly jumpsuits suitable for a newborn in the drawers. Fetid probably wouldn't get to wear them.

The task ended up taking me four hours. This may have been because I found the repetitive nature of sorting and folding oddly soothing in my emotional state, but it was probably also because I was side-tracked by the – how shall I put this? – pathologically freaky nature of infants' clothing. One hat, for example, seemed fond of non-sequiturs. Glove, it solemnly proclaimed. Kitten. Skipping. Kitten I could understand. Animals were big in the world of children's clothing. But glove was mystifying. Why only one? And skipping had to be the most useless form of locomotion since the hot air balloon.

A cream-coloured jumpsuit had a long, embroidered poem on its front about a toy elephant named Humphrey whose teddy bear liked to whistle. Why a soft toy needed a soft toy was beyond me but it seemed to be carrying the chain of emotional dependence too far. Furthermore, bears cannot whistle. It is an anatomical impossibility. Show me a bear that can pucker up and I'll show you another book deal for the author of *Whoa Baby!*

Babies also apparently wear outfits that have been put together with little thought of co-ordination or fashion sense. Shoes didn't seem to be a necessity but singlets were. The fastening of choice was press-studs, located on the shoulders or in the crotch. Last but not least, bibs, an item of apparel that is perfectly acceptable when one is being proposed to but which otherwise conjures up images of uncontrollable drool (and which you would therefore think would be made in discreet shades of baby-vomit colour), were brightly coloured and gaily festooned with slogans proclaiming the wearer's adorability.

The slogans plastered over everything were another problem. If you believed everything written on their T-shirts, it would be fair to assume that babies were, quite frankly, up themselves. 'World's Cutest Kid, Daddy's Little Angel, Princess In Training . . .' Why they didn't make baby T-shirts that simply say 'Ego is not a dirty word', I really didn't know.

And then there was the new, cool stuff. Chic, ironic baby wear. You could tell that it was ironic because for starters it was black. It topped this by having a screen-printed image of Jim Morrison from The Doors or The Rolling Stones tongue on it, or else a slogan that read something like 'I cry therefore I am.'

In my humble opinion, a baby has absolutely no business being ironic. Anyone that can't control their own bowel movements doesn't get to practise irony. Furthermore, having The Doors or The Rolling Stones on your jumpsuit is advertising the fact that you like your grandparents' taste in music. Or it would have done if my parents had been cool. As it was, we really ought to have been stocking up on jumpsuits bearing the beaming visages of Neil Diamond or Cliff Richard, even though this would no doubt ensure that a considerable portion of Fetid's early years would be spent having his or her head buried in the playground sandpit by the cool babies wearing black Jimi Hendrix romper suits.

Assuming that your baby wasn't into chic irony, its standard outfit seemed to comprise a long-sleeved bodysuit with crotch fasteners, socks, a hat and mittens. If fashion is a statement, presumably babies were trying to say, 'I may need assistance getting out of this bodysuit as I'm wearing mittens, which makes it difficult to undo my crotch snaps.'

I mean, let's be honest. If a baby sat down next to you on a bus, you'd move seats. What with the anti-social behaviour, the smell and the weird dress sense, you'd probably prefer to take your chances sitting next to the guy wearing the White Pride T-shirt.

When I finally finished, piles of tiny clothes were stored neatly in the drawers and shelves of the built-in robes. Previously bare shelves were now bright with my old childhood books and early gifts of wooden toys, while Rufus still lay, gently snoring, on the farmyard rug.

I sank down into the soft cushioned seat of the white wooden rocking chair and looked around, pleased with my efforts. The baby's room was still very empty, but the bright splashes of colour from the toys and books created a sense of promise and joy.

Unbidden, the memory of Charlie and the certainty in his eyes when he had looked at me and told me that I wasn't cut out to be a mother, cut sharply into my mind. In an effort to banish it, I pulled the string on a musical puppy dog that my cousin had sent me, and the tinkling sounds of 'Over the Rainbow' filled the room.

I had always loved this song, but now its lyrics filled me with despair. How could I wish upon a star when I no longer even knew what to wish for? I wanted this baby but I was terrified of the changes it would bring. I loved Jack yet I couldn't bring myself to marry him. Cate, my best friend, wasn't around, but Charlie, who had been absent from my life for so many years, was back, playing a starring role. Nothing made sense any more.

As I sat there, feeling more lost and alone than I could remember feeling for a very long time, I placed my hands on my belly, in what had become an unconscious habit. Closing my eyes, I gently began to rock back and forth, waiting for the kicks inside me that I knew would come.

It was only when they did that I realised the tangible presence of my baby inside me somehow had the power to comfort me and take away the sting of Charlie's words, in a way that nothing anyone else might say or do ever could.

33
The Tram Seat

One of my main fears with regard to falling pregnant had been the thought of giving up work. But I was now thirty-five weeks pregnant and, although I only had another three weeks to go before I would be on maternity leave, those three weeks were beginning to feel like an eternity, as hauling myself out of bed each morning became more and more difficult. As much as I hated to admit it, as the weeks progressed and I became heavier and heavier, the idea of staying home was growing far more appealing. Accentuating this change in attitude was the fact that one of the main reasons that I had accepted the job at Durville Gallery had been my excitement at the prospect of working more closely with contemporary artists. Once again, however, the idealism of my daydreams was being brutally struck down by the reality. Or, to be more exact, the unreality that was Keedin.

'Yesterday I arranged for Keedin to use a rental car,' Cruella announced, without preamble, striding into the gallery with Keedin in tow, and scaring the hell out of Doug and I. 'And he's lost it. One of you needs to go and look for it.'

'You lost a car?' Doug asked in disbelief. 'How do you lose a *car*?'

Cruella immediately bristled. 'Keedin is an *artist*! He is above mundane considerations! Anyway, it's easily resolved. He's simply parked it somewhere but he can't remember where, so one of you must go and look for it.'

'Send Isabelle,' Doug said immediately.

'Me? Why me?'

He turned to look at me in surprise. 'You were just saying the other day how walking is good for you.'

Crap. So I had. I sighed and accepted the car key and the remote locking device from Keedin. 'Where did you leave it?'

'He doesn't know,' Cruella said impatiently. 'That's why we need you to look for it.'

'Yes, I know, but *roughly* where did you leave it?'

Keedin stared at me as though I was speaking Swahili.

I tried again, enunciating very slowly and clearly, 'Did you leave it in this suburb?'

He nodded. That was a start at least.

'Yes.' He tried vainly to focus his gaze on me. 'It is definitely somewhere in Fitzroy.'

'Keedin, we're in Toorak!'

He looked around in surprise. 'What am I doing here?'

I groaned inwardly and tried again. 'What sort of car is it? What colour and make is it?'

Keedin concentrated very hard. 'Black. There was black.'

'He's referring to the tyres,' Doug said, before I could get my hopes up, and Keedin nodded again.

Resisting the urge to strangle Keedin, I took a deep breath, but Cruella cut across me impatiently. 'Isabelle, stop wasting Keedin's time with these inane questions and get going! He's obviously here, so the car must be parked near the gallery somewhere. We have more important things to discuss. Douglas, we need to reprint the catalogues and invitations.'

Doug turned white. 'But we just had five hundred of each printed!'

Cruella waved her hand, dismissing this as a minor objection. 'Keedin has just finished an amazing new work.'

Keedin tried to look modest as he hitched up his pants.

'I want it on the front cover of the catalogue and on the invitation. And we're pushing the date of the opening forward by ten days. A very important collector is going to be in Melbourne and I want her to attend the opening.'

'But . . . but . . .'

Even though I was about to set off on foot in search of a car that was quite possibly several suburbs away, my heart went out to Doug. Trying to explain tedious matters like printing deadlines to Cruella was nigh on impossible. She simply refused to believe that her commands could not immediately be translated into action.

Luckily, Doug had the sort of spirit that comes with not having to rely on his day job to survive financially. He now said heatedly, 'Carmela, we have to book the printing presses and they require at least three weeks' notice—'

'Do I look like an administrative assistant to you, Douglas?'

As the pitched battle between them started, only Keedin noticed that I was making an exit. As the door closed behind me, I heard him say in a tone of faint alarm, 'Hey – where's she going with my placenta?'

Two hours later, my mobile rang.

'Douglas,' I answered wearily.

'Where are you?'

'Where do you think? I'm looking for a car. Make unknown, colour unknown, last-known whereabouts – oh that's right – unknown. But luckily I know that it has black tyres.'

He sighed. 'I'd gladly swap with you. I've just spent an hour and a half on the phone explaining to the printers why we need a rush job that's almost exactly the same as the job that they just completed for us. And Cruella's refusing to pay them a cent extra. I haven't had this much fun since I had to take the calls from Chuck Egress's lawyer. So, where are you *exactly*?'

'In a car park in South Yarra. I've just been randomly pressing the remote locking device and hoping that something flashes or an alarm goes off.'

'You mean you're *actually* looking for it?'

'Of course I'm looking for it! Wouldn't you?'

'God, no. I would have found a nice little café to sit in and settled down with a herbal tea and the newspaper for a couple of hours. You're so conscientious.'

'And, if I'd done that, how exactly would that have helped me when I had to walk back into the gallery in a few hours' time and I still hadn't found the car?'

'Darling, you haven't the faintest chance of finding it. You're doomed either way.'

'Then why did you insist on me being the one to go look for it?' I asked, exasperated. 'What was all that stuff about it being good for me to go walking?'

'I thought you could use the time to go shopping for bunny rugs or something. It never crossed my mind that you'd actually waste time looking for it.'

A wave of exhaustion swept over me. He was right. I was an idiot.

'Have you had lunch yet?' Doug asked sympathetically.

'No.'

'All right, this is an order. I want you to find somewhere to sit down. Eat something and I'll call you back when I have more information on the car.'

'How are you going to get that?'

'I'm going to swipe Cruella's mobile when she's not looking and make a list of all the calls she made yesterday. The number of the rental company must be on it, and I'll call them and get some more details.'

'You're a genius,' I said with relief.

'I know. It still might mean the car is anywhere between here and Darwin, but at least we'll have something to go on. If we get desperate we can always report it stolen and have the police look for it, so don't stress. Now go and get some lunch.'

Like all the other cafés in South Yarra, this one was packed to the rafters with everyone in the lunchtime rush just dying to pay fifteen dollars for a ham and cheese sandwich. Only they didn't call it that in South Yarra, of course. If you tried to order a ham and cheese sandwich in South Yarra, you'd be met with a blank look. You had to request a ciabatta from Brown's with Jamón Ibérico and King Island brie.

Even though I was longing to sit down and ease the pressure on my back and legs, I was waiting my turn patiently when suddenly I caught sight of someone familiar in the crowd in front of me. It was Sleazel.

Sleazel had been an abstract concept to me for so long that it felt unutterably strange to have her transmute into a living, breathing human being who I could casually run into around town. And having her right in front of me made me feel horribly awkward about the text messages that Charlie and I had been exchanging and our clandestine meetings.

I tried to slowly back out, but given my size this started to cause so much disruption that I decided to stay put and just keep my head down.

Sleazel was right up the front anyway; she would be leaving soon. Sure enough, a moment later she started to order, but abruptly the counter hand turned his attention to a gaggle of office girls behind her.

'Excuse me,' Sleazel interjected. 'I think I was next.'

The girls looked embarrassed for cutting in, but the counter hand, while not exactly rolling his eyes, did manage a look that suggested Sleazel had barged through the crowd yelling, 'Lady with a baby! Coming through!'

'You don't mind waiting, do you, love?' he asked, patronisingly.

'Actually, I do. I was before them and I'm in a bit of a hurry—'

When he spoke, his tone was the sort that you'd use to address a three-year-old. A slow-witted three-year old. 'Yes, but they're in a bigger hurry. They're on their lunch breaks from *work*.'

He had already turned his attention away from Sleazel. I was pretty sure that Sleazel must have been looking as furious as I was feeling on her behalf. Apparently, the idea that she too might be on her lunch break from work was too absurd to contemplate. She was pregnant, ergo she couldn't possibly be working in a paid capacity as well.

I considered coming to Sleazel's rescue and arguing with the counter hand but I am not the sort of person who is good with confrontations. I'm the sort of person who thinks up witty repartee and composes stirring speeches to prick my opponent's conscience three days after the confrontation has actually happened.

Perhaps Sleazel and I had more in common than just

Charlie, because she didn't force a confrontation either. Instead, she continued to stand there, and I just knew that, by the time she was served, her back and legs must have been aching, the way mine were. I was close enough to hear her order and, despite the fact that the counter hand skimped on the mayonnaise, forgot to toast her sandwich and practically hurled her change at her in his anxiety to be rid of her and return to nourishing the worker bees, we all knew that it was her duty to be grateful for her overpriced lunch and to make a quiet exit. Which she did.

And never in all my life could I have imagined any scenario in which I would find myself fighting the urge to run out into the street after Sleazel, in order to offer her sympathy and tell her that I knew exactly how she felt.

Waiting at the tram stop after a day spent looking for a car that, come to think of it, was probably parked in Keedin's driveway, I felt the sort of draining tiredness that I had previously associated with the creation of Luigi the placenta, way back in the first trimester.

Normally I hated catching peak-hour trams; everyone was always jammed in and there was invariably a perilous moment when the doors almost closed on some poor sod wedged in the stairwell who refused to face the fact that the laws of physics would not allow them to occupy space that was already taken up. Being at the shorter end of the supermodel scale also meant that I was usually perfectly positioned to have my nose stuck into the sweaty armpit of the unhygienic man who seemed to stalk my public-transport outings and always clung on to the strap nearest me.

So it was understandable that, for possibly the first time in my life, I was looking forward to catching a peak-hour tram. Given that I had been enormous throughout my entire pregnancy, caring bystanders would surely assume that I was close to eleven months pregnant. I was assured of obtaining a seat. And I couldn't wait. My feet were throbbing, my back hurt and I was already dreaming about crawling into bed.

I coughed as the young man next to me exhaled a cloud of cigarette smoke. He gave me a look which clearly said that I was the sort of whiny pregnant woman who probably kicked up a fuss about people breathing near her and his eyes practically dared me to ask him to butt out his cigarette. The really stupid part about this was that, as he exhaled once more, I needed to cough again, but I didn't dare after his hostile display so I ended up semi-choking but trying not to make a big deal out of it.

Thankfully, the tram arrived, and as I boarded I could even see a spare seat. I made my way towards it but was shoved aside as smoking boy pushed past me, as quickly as he could, to claim it. He promptly pulled his iPod out of his inner coat pocket and switched it on.

I ended up standing in the aisle, clasping on to a hand strap. The tram was so crowded I could barely move. My stomach was protruding right into smoking boy's face but he simply pretended not to see me.

An elderly woman sitting across from smoking boy, who had seen him nip in front of me to take the seat, caught my gaze. 'Here, love,' she said, taking the opportunity to start getting up while the tram was still stationary. 'You sit down.'

I watched as she struggled painfully to her feet. She had to be in her seventies, at least. For some reason, I thought of the look of humiliation on Sleazel's face as she had pushed past me on her way out of the sandwich shop. And that's when something inside me snapped.

I put out one hand to stop her. 'Thank you,' I said. 'But I'm OK.'

She looked at my enormous belly doubtfully. 'Are you sure?'

I smiled. 'Very.'

She sat back down and, as the tram lurched into motion once more, so did I. I didn't so much intrude upon smoking boy's space as mount an immediate invasion. Taking advantage of every rocking movement of the tram, I shmooshed my enormous belly into his face. My protruding belly button mounted exploratory expeditions into his ear and up one of his nostrils. Still nothing. He stared stonily down at his feet.

I considered turning 180 degrees so that, in the famous words of Monty Python, I could fart in his general direction, but I didn't think it fair that the nice lady should be caught in friendly fire.

It didn't seem to be working. It was time for something more direct.

I tapped smoking boy on the shoulder and gestured for him to remove one headphone. Rather to my surprise, he obeyed, possibly because he was in such complete shock that anyone would break the first of the public transport sacred commandments: Thou Shalt Not Make Conversation.

'Hello,' I said cheerily. 'I'm Isabelle. What's your name?'

He muttered something that I didn't quite catch but that I was pretty sure was 'Fuck off' and put his headphone back in.

'Oh well, it doesn't really matter what your name is,' I said, raising my voice in order to penetrate the sound of his iPod. 'Because I want to talk about *me*.'

Already, most of the passengers on the tram were listening in.

'You see, I'm almost eight months pregnant. I'm carrying an extra fifteen kilos. By the end of every day I have severe backache. I don't sleep much either. That's partly because of the leg cramps, which can be very painful, but mostly because I have to get up to go to the toilet approximately nine hundred times a night. I also have swollen ankles, headaches and occasional pain in my sciatic nerve. Did I mention the leg cramps?'

A woman standing in the aisle next to me nodded, practically hypnotised. By now the whole tram was definitely listening. Smoking boy had turned a little pale. One could only hope that it heralded the early onset of emphysema.

I continued, practically shouting. 'So you see, when someone gives up their seat to a pregnant woman, they're not just being well mannered or courteous. In that instant, they're pretty much an honorary member of Médecins Sans Frontières.'

About fifteen seated people jumped to their feet, but I ignored them. I wanted the seat that was rightfully mine.

Smoking boy sat, frozen. I leaned in close and hissed, 'Don't make me mention the vaginal discharges.'

Wordlessly, he got up from the seat and pushed his way towards the doors. When they opened at the next stop, he practically leaped from the tram. As he did so, several women, who I rather suspected must have been mothers, cheered.

I slid into the seat with relief and the elderly woman looked at me and grinned. 'Well done, duck.'

I grinned back. 'Thanks. Can I ask a favour? I think I might fall asleep. If I do, would you mind waking me up when we reach the Alma Road stop?'

I did fall asleep, but, as the elderly lady kindly woke me up in time, I disembarked without further incident.

And, as the tram trundled off into the night, I felt something inside me stir. Only this time it wasn't Fetid.

I smiled. Unless I was very much mistaken, for the first time in my life, my inner mummy lioness had just flexed her claws and was now purring with contentment.

34
Cate

Snorting yourself awake is not the most ladylike of ways to greet the new day. I was therefore immeasurably glad that Jack had already left for work by the time I roused myself with a good old twitch and a grunt. Good grief. What with having to sit with my legs apart, the tendency to unconsciously scratch my belly, and the relentless burping and farting, at this most feminine time of my life, I was apparently turning into a bloke. And not just any bloke either; at this rate I seemed destined to end up as Sir Les Patterson.

It was six-thirty in the morning and, although I had gone to bed at eight o'clock the previous night, worn out from the Great Tram Seat Victory, I still felt tired. I was finding it harder and harder to get comfortable at night, even though I had taken to sleeping with one leg slung over a pillow in order to take some of the weight of my enormous tummy. One thing that I was definitely looking forward to, post-childbirth, was being able to sleep on my tummy again.

As I hadn't gone to the toilet for at least, ooh, let's see, two and a half hours, I hauled myself out of bed and made my way to the bathroom. I didn't have to be up for work for another hour yet, so as I returned from the bathroom I switched my mobile phone on and then snuggled back into bed. I was about to shut my eyes, when, to my surprise, my phone beeped twice in quick succession.

The first message was a text from Charlie, sent late last night: *Hormone alert #65: L in tears tonite. Over a sandwich!!*

This was getting truly weird. Now I felt like I was being disloyal to *Sleazel.* I deleted Charlie's message as soon as I had read it and then checked my other message. It was a voicemail that had been received twenty minutes ago.

From Cate.

Sitting up in bed, I replayed it but still couldn't make head nor tail of it. This was the first time that I'd heard from Cate since our fight over the phone. Without stopping to think, I dialled her number.

'Belle? Is that you?'

'Cate? Why are you whispering?'

'IS THIS BETTER?' she yelled.

I dropped the phone in shock, and by the time I had it the right way up again, Cate was halfway through a paranoid ramble about a taxi driver who had refused to take her as a passenger because he feared she was going to throw up. Cate was, I quickly realised, extremely drunk.

'Cate, where are you?'

She giggled. 'In the city.'

'Bloody hell. You've been out all night?'

'Yep,' she said proudly.

'And you're plastered.' It was a statement, not a question, and I was starting to make sense of why Cate had decided to call me now.

'Nope. Not plastered exactly.'

'Rubbish. I can hear it in your voice.'

'I'm not drunk!' she said indignantly. 'I took drugs.

Not the same thing.'

'What did you take?'

'I don't know,' she said vaguely. 'Stuff.'

'Cate, listen to me. Do you think you're beautiful?'

She laughed. 'Don't be silly.' She hadn't taken cocaine then. 'I'm *gorgeous*.'

Right. So she'd had coke. 'Did you take pills too?'

'Mmm. Hey, I can see a street-sweeper. Maybe he'll give me a lift home.'

'Forget the street-sweeper and concentrate on me. Tell me what you feel like doing right now.'

There was a pause.

'Cate? Are you there?'

'Have you ever noticed how beautiful litter can be, Belle?' she asked earnestly. 'I mean, really, really beautiful? Really?'

I groaned and, with difficulty, swung my legs out of bed. 'OK. Listen to me. I want you to go to Degraves Street, OK?'

'Are we going to have breakfast?' she asked with interest.

'Exactly. Sit down at one of the tables in the middle of the lane and order a coffee, OK? And keep your phone switched on.'

'Sure,' she said agreeably. 'What are you going to do?'

'I'm going to meet you there. Now promise me, Cate. No talking to the street-sweeper. Just go straight to Degraves Street.'

'And order a coffee,' she repeated obediently.

I found her seated at one of the laneway tables, peering intently at a menu as though she was trying to decipher the Rosetta Stone.

'This is really trippy stuff,' she said by way of greeting.

'Did you have a coffee?' I asked, doing a quick scan of

Cate's appearance and taking in her dishevelled hair and dilated pupils.

Cate shrugged. 'Didn't want one. I tried to order a vodka but the waiter wouldn't serve me for some reason.'

I caught the waiter's eye, mouthed the words, 'Thank you' and grabbed Cate by the arm, steering her towards the nearest taxi-rank.

Once I had Cate safely home, I rang Doug to explain the situation and told him that I'd be in after lunch. He promised to cover for me, so then I rang Cate's work and told them that she was sick and wouldn't be coming in.

With our careers taken care of, I pushed open Cate's bedroom door to deal with the more difficult problem.

I'd instructed Cate to have a shower and drink an entire jug of water. She had meekly obeyed and was now tucked up in bed, wearing her pyjamas. She looked about twelve years old.

Cate saw me standing in the doorway and gave me a tremulous smile. I scooped up Shnoodle, who was dancing anxiously at my heels, and went and sat on the bed. Cate's eyes still looked enormous from whatever it was she had taken, but the shower had obviously had a sobering effect.

'Thanks for coming to get me, even though you hate me,' she said, with a slight catch in her voice.

'Oh, Catie,' I sighed. 'Of course I don't hate you. But what on earth is going on?'

Her eyes filled with tears and I sat there, holding her hand, utterly bewildered. What *was* she doing? Cate had always been my wisest and most level-headed friend. She *never* had wild nights on weeknights. And Cate was most definitely not the sort of person to take drugs or skip work because she was wasted. It suddenly occurred to me that Cate was also not the sort of person who slept with toy boys or waiters either. A wave of remorse hit me as I suddenly realised exactly how lost Cate had become over the past few months. And I had been so caught up with being pregnant that I hadn't even noticed.

I waited for her tears to subside and then I handed her a tissue. 'Was his name Pablo or Craig?' I asked gently.

She let out a half-sob, half-laugh and pushed Shnoodle aside as he tried to lick at her tears. 'No idea. But he left me alone in the city, off my head. What a jerk.'

I took a deep breath. 'Sweetheart, maybe that's your problem, right there.'

'What do you mean?'

'I mean you keep saying that you want to be in a relationship, but then you keep choosing to spend time with guys you don't even care enough about to discover their real names.'

She shredded the tissue angrily. 'You have no idea what it's like! There are no decent guys out there.'

'That's complete crap and you know it, and if you ever say that again I'm going to clobber you. Hard. That's the kind of thing bitter women say, and you are *not* a bitter woman.'

'Not yet,' she said ruefully. 'But I'm turning into one. I'm going to be the old spinster aunt who smells like kitty litter before I know it. And anyway, it's easy for you to say. You're with Jack and you're having a baby. You've left me way behind.'

'Cate, this isn't a race! It's not like we're all running towards some imaginary finishing line where partners and babies – *if* we want them – are waiting for us. It's just . . . life. It unfolds at a different pace for everyone.'

She didn't look convinced.

I tried a different tack. 'Given the divorce rate in

Australia, statistically, about one-third of the couples who are happy now are going to be very unhappy in the future.'

She cheered up a little. 'That's true.'

'Maybe you should hold off on the Pablos and Craigs for a while,' I suggested. 'It's not like you, and I don't think they're doing you any good.'

'I know,' she sighed. 'Thanks again for coming to get me. God, look at you! I haven't seen you for so long. And you've got so huge.' She looked at me earnestly. 'I'm really sorry to drag you out of bed when you're this enormous.'

'No problem,' I said, trying to pretend that when she had said 'huge' and 'enormous' she'd really meant 'curvaceous' and 'glowing'.

Cate rolled over and picked up a plastic bag that was lying on the floor. 'I almost forgot. I bought your baby a present while I was waiting for you.'

I turned the bag upside down on the bed. A tube of nappy-rash cream, an assortment of Chupa Chups and a bottle of glittery nail polish fell out.

I tried not to look confused. 'They're, um, lovely. Thanks darling.'

'The only place open at that hour of the morning was the 7-Eleven,' she said defensively. 'And I know you might have a boy, but that's no reason he can't wear nail polish. Kurt Cobain wore nail polish.'

'So did our Year Eight science teacher,' I reminded her.

She thought for a moment and then grabbed the bottle of nail polish and stuffed it back into the bag. 'I'll swap it for something else. You don't want your kid ending up like Mr Perkins.'

'OK. And maybe we'll eat the lollies. But the nappy-rash cream is excellent. I didn't have any of that.'

Cate's eyes suddenly welled with tears again. 'I just wanted to get you something to show you that I *am* happy for you. I'm sorry about our fight and I know that I haven't really been there for you during your pregnancy, Belle, but—'

Oddly enough, as soon as Cate said this, the little part of my heart that had been hurting since our fight immediately healed. 'I know.' I smiled at her. 'But I haven't exactly been there for you either. It's OK, Catie, we'll figure it out. This baby won't be like Shnoodle and Rufus, I promise.'

She smiled back at me. 'So what's been going on with you since we last talked properly?'

I settled myself more comfortably against a pillow and allowed Shnoodle to curl up beside me. 'Just the usual. Working. Getting fatter.' I was tempted to tell her about Jack's proposal but decided against it. Jack and I had agreed not to tell anyone. I had hurt him badly; the very least I could do was to honour our pact. But I could tell Cate about Charlie. I suddenly realised that Cate didn't even know that Charlie was back in Melbourne.

'I thought I saw him that day on Fitzroy Street!' she gasped, after I'd given her a hasty précis. 'Oh my God! And what are the odds of them being in your childbirth class?'

'I know,' I said, cheered up by her very satisfying reaction. 'And that's not all.' I filled her in on everything, right down to my last meeting with Charlie.

As my story progressed, Cate's initial excitement gave way to thoughtful and quiet attention.

'And he's right,' I finished miserably. 'He's right about all of it. I'm going to be a hopeless mother. I have no idea what I'm doing, and I never *wanted* to know about any of this stuff either.'

There was a silence.

'The one thing I never could understand about you and Charlie was how he always had the power to turn you into such an enormous wimp,' Cate finally pronounced.

I stared at her, appalled. 'That's what Audie said.'

She nodded. 'We all thought it. You were just so broken down after your relationship ended that we didn't see the point of rubbing it in. We really shouldn't go for this long without talking ever again,' she mused, almost to herself. 'You get too confused without me. Now, shut up and listen carefully. Belle, you're just scared! That doesn't make Charlie right.'

'But he *is* right! I don't have the first clue how to handle a baby. I've never even changed a nappy in my life.'

'So you'll learn. I can teach you. I've changed tons of nappies for my nieces and nephews. It's actually pretty hard to mess it up. Now, correct me if I'm wrong, but you are having this baby with Jack, not Charlie, aren't you?'

I glared at her and refused to answer.

She grinned. 'Well, then, I don't see your problem.' As she watched me, her brisk tone changed into something softer. 'You and Charlie *would* be hopeless parents if you were doing it together. You're too much alike, and you reinforce all those negative qualities in each other that Charlie was talking about. But you're not doing this with Charlie. You're doing it with Jack. And that's why Charlie's opinion of your mothering skills doesn't matter. Because he doesn't know what you're like with Jack. Charlie is making assumptions based on the Isabelle that he was with. He's never seen how Jack supports you and makes you more confident and how much he loves you.'

I concentrated on stroking Shnoodle as the import of

Cate's words sank in. Cate wasn't the only one who I had lost sight of during the last few months. Somewhere along the line I had entirely forgotten that Jack and I used to be a partnership. I had believed everything that Charlie had said, without hesitation, because I was so entrenched in my belief that I was doing this all alone.

Cate must have been able to tell by the expression on my face that I didn't want to pursue the topic further. So instead she said, 'I haven't even asked you what it's like.'

I swallowed hard and then answered, 'Being pregnant you mean?'

She nodded.

I managed to get my emotions under control and was able to answer in an almost normal tone of voice. 'It's bizarre, mainly. Especially at the start, when I kept thinking that all the bits were growing separately.'

'What?'

'I couldn't help thinking that there was a pair of eyebrows hanging out next to a lung,' I explained. 'Or a knee colliding with a spleen whenever I turned on my side in bed.'

'You're very weird, Belle.'

I hadn't finished yet. 'Then I couldn't get it out of my head that it would start to assemble itself, only it would have inherited my genes when it comes to putting furniture from Ikea together, so naturally it would get it all wrong and end up looking like a Picasso painting with three eyes on the side of its head or something.'

'If your kid has three eyes in the first place, that's probably enough to be getting on with, let alone having them all on the same side,' Cate pointed out.

I made a face at her but I didn't mean it. It was very comforting to be talking properly to Cate again, after such a long time.

'What else happens while it's inside you?' she asked eagerly.

I thought for a moment. 'Did you know that it's entirely covered with hair?'

'You're making that up,' she accused me, looking a bit green.

'I'm not. And from twenty-three weeks it's covered by a cheese-like substance.' I added with ghoulish relish, 'Imagine a little piece of brie in need of a shave.'

Cate turned pale and took a sip of water.

'And that's not all,' I continued relentlessly. 'There's something called a mucus plug, and—' I stopped as I started to gag myself, disgusting pregnancy facts apparently still having the power to physically nauseate me.

In quick succession, I pushed Shnoodle off my lap and Cate leaped up from the bed. As one, we both ran for the bathroom. I was more practised so I claimed the toilet, while Cate hung over the bathroom sink. When our nausea had subsided, we both sat on the bathroom floor while we recovered.

'Is that what morning sickness feels like?' Cate asked contemplatively.

'Pretty much.'

There was another silence.

'Can you eat hot chips when you're pregnant?' she asked.

I nodded.

She got up and then held out a hand to haul me up.

'You know,' she said happily, twenty minutes later, as we tucked into a large serve of hot chips doused in vinegar and salt at the nearby 24-hour fast-food joint on Chapel Street, 'this is just like the old days after we'd had a big night.'

I smiled at her. Perhaps that was the answer. If Cate

and I could find new ways of doing the old things together, then maybe not everything had to change, after all.

35
Baby World

While making up with Cate had made me feel about a thousand Lindor balls of joy (happiness was measured in units of chocolate in my world), Jack and I were still in the midst of our uneasy stand-off. I had told Cate about the problems that Jack and I were having, although I still left out the bit about the rejected marriage proposal. Her only advice had been to keep trying to talk to Jack. I didn't know how to tell Cate that somehow simply talking to the father of my child and the man that I loved had become one of the hardest things in the world to do.

It was frightening to realise how far from one another we had drifted. Spending time apart had become so normal for Jack and me that it felt peculiar to finally be doing something together. It was Sunday morning and, according to Cate, I was thirty-six weeks pregnant, so, while I was in Baby World, a baby shop roughly the size of Lichtenstein, Jack was circling the car park waiting for someone to either die or go into labour so that we could have their car parking space.

Since sorting out the baby's clothes, I had been consumed by the fact that we would very shortly be bringing a baby home from the hospital and, unless we did something about buying it a bed, we'd be popping young Marvin down for a nap in Rufus's dog bed. I was also hoping that shopping for the baby's things might be the joyful, anticipatory sort of activity that Jack and I needed to share in order to spark our relationship back to normal.

I had therefore come shopping armed with a sense of optimism and a vague idea that we needed to purchase a cot, a pram and bootees. (I didn't know why but I had it in my head that bootees were an essential item for babies in the same way in which kitties needed litter.) But, within ten minutes of setting foot in this baby mega-mart, I was all but convinced that we simply could *not* have this baby unless we purchased a nightlight that doubled as a classical lullaby player, a nursery humidifier, a specialised baby seat for the shopping trolley and a plaster-casting kit so that I could make a plaster-cast of my pregnant belly. Luckily, I would be spared the expense of buying the placenta printmaking set, as I had my very own contemporary artist on standby for that important milestone.

I had furtively darted into the baby section of department stores before this, but I'd always left after a few minutes, feeling overwhelmed by my ignorance, the way that I did in hardware stores. I didn't understand the sizing of the clothes or why so many people took their babies camping (baby sleeping bags seemed to be very popular), or what the difference was between a crib, a bassinette and a cot. On my lunch breaks I had also ventured into some of the upmarket baby stores near the gallery. The Toorak boutiques carried outrageously expensive and impractical items such as fake mink pram blankets, pure cashmere bodysuits and hand-carved ivory rattles. For reasons not explicitly stated, the Toorak stores were also always staffed by childless people, dressed in black, who were intense disciples of European design.

I had paused to contemplate a cradle sheet set embroidered with giraffes when a sales assistant, who had been lurking near by, suddenly sprang up beside me.

'My name is Norma. May I help you?'

'Um, no. I'm fine. Thank you.'

Norma caught sight of the sheet set in my hands. 'Lots of giraffes,' she said meaningfully. 'Lots and lots of giraffes.'

Hurrah. It must be time for my weekly dose of psychotic sales assistant.

'Yes. There does appear to be,' I said firmly, as I shoved the sheet set back on to its shelf and looked around for the quickest escape route.

Norma checked over her shoulder and then looked back at me. 'Do you want to know why?' she whispered.

'I'm sorry – why what?' I asked, my calm and firm manner deserting me, as I wondered whether Norma was completely unhinged.

'Why there are so many giraffes.'

'Oh.' I gave in to the inevitable. 'Sure.'

She checked the store again surreptitiously and then leaned in. 'Disney!' she hissed. 'You can't be sued for a giraffe.'

'Right then,' I said brightly. 'That's excellent news.'

Norma looked at me pityingly. 'They own the copyright on all the animals, you see,' she divulged. 'All the good ones, anyway. Lions and bears and mice and ducks. About the only thing they don't own is giraffes. You produce something with a bear on it, and the lawyers for Winnie-the-Pooh will slap you with a trademark infringement so hard and fast you won't know what's hit you.'

Why me? Why did this sort of thing only ever happen to me? All around, normal, happy people were shopping for their baby's layette. Close by, a well-informed, motherly looking sales assistant called Maureen was demonstrating how to put up a portable cot, to the delight of a happy couple who looked like they'd just strolled off the set of a television commercial for 'the model expectant parents whom others aspire to be like'. I looked closer and my day got worse. Not only was I stuck with Norma the paranoid shop assistant, but it turned out the happy couple was none other than Charlie and Sleazel.

I swiftly ducked down behind a shelf filled with mattress protectors. Anyone else would probably have thought my furtive behaviour peculiar, but it won the approval of Norma. She nodded grimly and then joined me in lurking. For now that she had broken the code of silence, Norma was singing like a canary. 'The only one they can't touch is the rabbit.'

'The rabbit?'

'Peter,' she said, tapping the side of her nose.

A shadow fell across us and we both looked up in fright. I was half-expecting to see either Charlie and Sleazel or a belligerent Disney lawyer so I was considerably relieved to discover that Jack had found my hiding place.

'Do I want to know why you're crouching on the floor?' Jack asked, without a hint of surprise in his tone.

I shook my head and he helped me up. He waited impassively as I thanked Norma warmly for my initiation into the cut-throat world of Beatrix Potter and Disney. But, as we made a hasty retreat, he didn't ask what I was talking about and I didn't offer to explain. I walked beside him quietly, feeling like I was about to cry. Jack had always loved the fact that I was the only person he had ever known who could find themselves embroiled in an imbroglio simply by leaving the house.

Now, when I was imbroglio-ing my little heart out right in front of him, he didn't even ask what was going on.

'Are you sure you want to do this right now?' I asked nervously, wondering where Charlie and Sleazel were. 'It's pretty busy. Maybe we should come back another time.'

He looked at me in disbelief. 'Belle, I just spent twenty minutes trying to find a car park. We are *not* coming back.' He looked around the mega-mart with distaste. 'God, this place is horrible. Let's get what we need and get out of here. Have you chosen the pram?'

I had, actually, but not while I had been waiting for him to park the car. Unbeknownst to Jack, I had decided on the pram that I wanted several months ago. For reasons that had absolutely nothing to do with anything except shallow consumerism, I had set my heart on having a Bugaboo. It cost more than the first car I had owned. It was an outrageous rip-off – whereas all the other prams came with everything included, with the Bugaboo, despite the fact that it already cost double the amount of the other prams, you had to pay extra for the sunshade and other necessities.

Perhaps I had been seduced by a viewing of the 'instructional' DVD in one of the upmarket baby stores. (The DVD was actually more like an MTV clip, with virtually no practical information but some rather groovy footage of an empty pram propelling itself across the wilderness, while ambient house music played in the background.) Whatever the reason, I had come to the conclusion that the Bugaboo was the only pram that wasn't obscenely ugly and gadget-y. I wanted it. Although this was probably a natural consequence of having recently spent too much time around sales assistants who had impressed upon me the importance of European design.

Keeping a sharp lookout for Charlie and Sleazel, I led Jack over to where the Bugaboo stood in all its glory, on a raised plinth.

'So this is the one I thought we'd get,' I said nonchalantly, hoping that Jack would smile, acquiesce and sweep me up into a kiss.

Unfortunately he went straight for the price tag instead. 'This is double the price of the other prams.'

I was prepared. 'Yes, but that's because it has a scientifically engineered mattress, and you pay a bit more for the chassis, of course, because it's aluminium, which makes it extremely lightweight.'

'You've been studying the properties of aluminium?' he asked in disbelief. 'And are you honestly telling me that you want this pram because of its scientifically engineered mattress?'

Damn it. That's the problem with having a child with someone who knows you really well.

'It comes in pretty colours,' I admitted in a small voice.

'How about we buy a five-hundred-dollar pram and get a colourful blanket to throw over it? You could buy a range of blankets with the money we'd save.'

Time to move into justification mode. 'Look, we're getting so many hand-me-downs from Audrey that we'll hardly have to buy anything. We really only need to buy a pram, a cot and a change table.' And some of those cute bunny rugs and the darling little monkey with the patchwork ears, and we most definitely could not do without a hardback illustrated edition of *The Wind in the Willows*. But probably best not to mention all that at this stage.

Jack was still looking unconvinced. Right. Value for money argument. 'It is our first. If we have—' I paused and smiled coyly '—*more* children, we won't have to go and buy all of this stuff again. Provided that we buy good-quality things the first time around, of course.'

He had definitely softened when I mentioned more children. Sensing victorv at hand, I pulled out my trump card: emotional blackmail. 'After all, I'm the one who's going to be pushing the pram around every day while you're at work, so I think it's fair that I get to choose the one that's best suited to me.'

For one brief moment I thought that I had him. And then, 'How do you know this one suits you best?'

'What?'

'Have you actually tried it out?'

'No. But Fran has one and she loves it.'

'Well, why don't you give it a go?'

'Oh. OK.'

Jack lifted the pram down from its pedestal and I tentatively pushed it forward. As if by magic, Norma materialised by our side as soon as I touched the precious Dutch-designed, height-adjustable, reversible handlebar.

'This is a wonderful pram,' she gushed.

'What's wonderful about it?' Jack asked in a discouraging tone.

Norma beamed. 'It comes in a fabulous array of colours.'

Jack was most definitely not beaming. If I was to have any chance at all, I had to get rid of Norma and co-opt Maureen.

'Take it for a proper walk,' Norma encouraged, before adding darkly, 'be careful near the Disney display.'

Feeling like a complete dickhead, I half-heartedly trundled the empty pram around the shop, banging into racks of clothing and the Disney display, and somehow screwing up every single time I tried to turn a corner.

'Whoops-a-daisy! Looks like someone's on their learner plates!' Norma chuckled.

Unsurprisingly, Jack was unconvinced by my pram prowess. 'What about collapsing it to put it in the car? How does that work?' he demanded.

Norma smiled. 'It's simple. You just press this lever forward and push these side buttons in. Then you can remove the bassinette.' She demonstrated. 'Then to collapse the undercarriage you simply press these buttons on either side, while pulling this lever, here, up.'

My head was already hurting and the undercarriage was most definitely not looking like it was about to collapse. Despite Norma's ongoing struggles, the pram refused to fold up into a size suitable to fit into a car boot, unless you happened to drive a Hummer.

After a few more minutes of under-the-breath mutterings, Norma triumphantly showed us the collapsed pram.

'See,' I said. 'Easy.'

Jack remained unimpressed. 'Nice try.' He turned back to Norma. 'Could you put it back together please? And then we'll have a go at putting it up and down.'

Eager to please, Norma started to demonstrate the reassembly technique. 'So now what you have to do is press the same buttons in and pull the lever up again, but this time you have to kick out this bar here—' She kicked. The undercarriage stayed folded. She tugged. Still nothing. She smiled apologetically. 'It's really quite simple once you know how.' She continued to push and tug and kick while I fought the urge to kick her. Jack now had his arms folded, which was not a good sign.

I looked wistfully over to where Maureen was single-handedly assembling a three-storey cubby-house for the benefit of an admiring couple who were already pulling out their credit cards and playfully arguing: 'Let me pay for it!' 'No – let *me*!'

Bugger. Maureen wasn't helping Charlie and Sleazel any more, which meant that they were on the loose in the store somewhere.

That thought made me determined to speed things up and get out of there. 'Can I have a go?'

Bad move. Several minutes of tugging and kicking later, the bloody undercarriage was still folded and Norma had gone off in search of another sales assistant to help.

Jack was wearing an infuriating expression on his face that somehow managed to mix moral superiority with pleasure at my downfall.

'Ready to give up?' he enquired.

'I know it's easy,' I panted, between kicks. 'Frannie has this pram and she told me it's simple. There's just a trick to it that you have to master.'

'Try saying "Abracadabra",' he suggested.

'You could try helping your heavily pregnant partner,' I retorted.

'Belle, it's a stupidly overpriced pram that you can't even work. Let's look at the one that your sister recommended.'

With a sinking heart, I just knew which one Audie had recommended from the line-up of shiny new prams on the shop floor.

It was the ugliest.

Everything about it screamed Practicality by K-Mart. It was covered in ugly navy and green tartan (two of my least favourite colours) and had a foul bright-orange insignia plastered on the hood. The design was fussy, with straps and Velcro hanging off everywhere, the tyres were out of proportion, and – I'm still not sure how to explain this – viewed from the side, the pram bore an uncanny resemblance to Keith Richards. I'm just saying: *that's* how ugly it was.

From a distance of ten metres away, I had already made up my mind that, even if the Lord Almighty were to rent the heavens and command me in a voice of thunder to buy it or risk death by locust attack, I was *not* going to purchase this pram. But, in a spirit of faked co-operation, I followed Jack over to where the ugly practical pram stood in all its tartan hideousness.

'Shouldn't we wait for Norma?' I asked, as Jack started to fumble with various levers.

'No need.' He looked smug as the pram instantly collapsed into a lightweight bundle that could be picked up one-handed and merrily slung over your shoulder.

We looked at the tartan bundle and then, as one, we looked over to where Norma, who had now been joined by two other sales assistants, was still kicking the Bugaboo to bits. It kind of looked like a Baby World gang-bashing. I was torn between wanting to call the police and hoping that the Bugaboo would suddenly spring up and start laying into Norma.

'You try,' Jack said implacably.

Hating the pram, Jack, Audie and Norma from the depths of my heart, I feebly attempted to put the tartan horror back up. Despite doing my best to stuff it up, the bloody thing sprang together as though I'd waved a magic wand.

'So let's see – this pram is cheaper, easier to use by a factor of about ten thousand and it comes with everything included,' Jack said, in a patronising tone of voice that made me want to kick him, as he inspected the pram's swing tag.

'And you can add a toddler seat to it,' Norma said

helpfully. Evidently having sensed a lost cause with the Bugaboo, she had materialised once again, just in time to ruin my life.

I fought the urge to throw a potty at her head. 'Jack, it's hideous.'

'So your only objection to it is aesthetic?'

'I work in the art world. Aesthetics matter to me.'

'Belle, you're really not making sense. It's a pram. It's meant to be used for a specific, practical purpose. Applying the same criteria to the purchase of a pram as a painting is entirely illogical.'

'OK, let me put it this way. You can buy that pram but I am *never* going to use it. I don't just dislike that pram, I think it's an aesthetic crime against humanity that is worse – I repeat, *worse*, and I don't say this lightly – than Keedin's Offal Series.'

'That was offal,' he agreed.

Ignoring his pathetic pun, I swept on. 'And if you think that an aesthetic sensibility can be dispensed with simply because something also has a utilitarian purpose, then let me warn you, that's one step away from philistinism. What's the point of living if we only care about the practicalities? Why cook and eat gourmet food when we can survive on bread and cheese?'

'You *do* survive on bread and cheese and you never cook gourmet food,' Jack interjected.

I glared at him. 'Apart from completely invalidating my profession, would you really want a culture without art and beauty? You're exactly like those people who ring up talkback radio to complain that government money spent on art that they don't understand is a waste. That's not the point and it makes me furious.'

Jack turned to Norma. 'Could you give us a minute please? Somehow we've gone from objectionable tartan to the downfall of civilisation as we know it.'

Norma departed to join her colleagues for another round of Bugaboo bashing and Jack and I faced off.

'*I'll* pay for the pram,' I said icily. 'And I'll get Fran to teach me how to use it the next time she comes to Melbourne for a visit.'

'Stop being so self-righteous. If you really want it that much, *we'll* pay for it, and I'll even throw in extra if you let me watch Fran show you how to work it. That ought to be hilarious.'

'You think because we both work in the arts that we're complete flakes!'

'Your careers have nothing to do with it. I think you're both complete flakes because you *are* both complete flakes.'

'Why are you being so horrible?' I demanded.

'Oh, and you think you're Miss Sunshine and Light lately?'

Someone standing behind me cleared their throat.

'Hi, Iz.'

I could have wept. In a fair and just world, my ex-boyfriend and his new girlfriend would have happened upon us as Jack and I were exchanging tender glances while we playfully rocked a cot together. I mean a cradle. Bassinette. Whichever the fuck was the one that rocked. Instead, Charlie and Sleazel had interrupted us in the middle of a loud and acrimonious barney.

I swung around. 'Charlie,' I said dispiritedly. 'Hi.'

Sleazel thrust herself forward, which isn't that hard to do when you're heavily pregnant because pretty much all of you is forward all of the time. 'We meet again,' she said, looking intently at Jack. She gave a little laugh. 'Where's your impostor today?'

Oh ha. Ha ha ha FUCK OFF.

Jack was looking both unamused and displeased, which was quite a lot of negativity to display simultaneously. The worst part was that, although I didn't really like Sleazel, I still wanted Jack to charm her. I wanted him to be the loving, warm person that I adored so that she would walk away realising that I couldn't possibly be jealous of her relationship with Charlie, as I had scored the relationship equivalent of Willy Wonka's Golden Ticket. Instead of which, my beloved was glowering all over the place, which was something that I had thought only cross glow-worms did.

'Hi,' Jack said curtly. And then, even more abruptly, he nodded in Charlie's direction. 'Charlie.'

Charlie held out his hand so Jack had no option but to shake it, while I had a mini freakout (*My worlds are colliding! My worlds are colliding*!) and Sleazel inspected me for further flaws.

'How are things at the hospital?' Charlie said conversationally.

I couldn't believe that I was feeling gratitude to Charlie for making an effort while I wanted to hit Jack for being so rude.

'You specialise in hydrocarbon something or other, don't you?' Charlie asked.

Jack stared at him. 'I have no idea what you're talking about.'

Sleazel nudged Charlie. 'That's not him,' she said helpfully. 'That was the other Jack.'

'Oh yeah. Right. So, um, Jack, what do you do?' Charlie floundered.

'I'm a surgeon,' Jack said, enunciating very clearly, as though speaking to an imbecile. And then – I couldn't believe how awful he was being – he turned away from them, towards me. 'We'll decide on the pram later. Do we need anything else while we're here?'

'*Jack*,' I whispered, mortified.

'Isabelle, I am tired and I have to go in to the hospital in about an hour. Hurry up.'

'Hey, don't talk to her like that, mate,' Charlie intervened.

Jack looked at him levelly. 'I'm not your mate. And I'm pretty sure I don't need to take advice from you on how to treat Isabelle. Or have I got it wrong? Are you not the jerk who applied for a job interstate without telling her?'

Now it was Charlie's turn to look like an angry glow-worm. 'My relationship with Iz has nothing to do with you,' he snapped.

'You don't *have* a relationship with Isabelle any more,' Jack said coolly. 'Unless you're trying to start one up again. Is that why you met up with her in the city?'

Sleazel suddenly looked unsure of herself. 'Charlie?' she asked, with a quiver in her voice. 'What's he talking about?'

Oh God.

'It was nothing,' I said hastily. 'We met up just to, you know—' Oh crap, why had we met up? 'Clear the air,' I managed. 'We broke up over the phone, and then running into each other again like that . . .' I trailed off. Sleazel was paying absolutely no attention to me anyway. Neither was Jack or Charlie.

'I'm sorry you're feeling insecure,' Charlie began. I groaned inwardly. 'But Iz and I were together for a long time and you can't ever change that.'

'Thanks for the lesson in space–time physics,' Jack drawled. 'But I'm never going to feel particularly insecure around someone who Belle didn't care enough about to even be faithful to.'

'Oi!' I protested. It was the best that I could come up with under the circumstances, given that I wasn't sure whether Jack was trying to champion me or malign me.

'Oh yeah?' Sleazel said pugnaciously. 'Well, *he* didn't

care about *her* that much either, considering he was sleeping with me.'

I looked at her curiously. 'Yes, but that was after we broke up.'

There was a dead silence. And then …

I swung around to Charlie. 'You cheated on me?' I gasped. His hangdog look said it all. I felt as though all the wind had been punched out of me. 'You made me feel like *hell* all that time … even though you had done *exactly* the same thing to me?' I clutched at the shelf behind me for support as I tried to take it in.

'Belle, are you all right?' Jack asked urgently.

I shook my head. I felt sick. I couldn't believe it. How could he have lied to me like that?

'We were over anyway,' I heard Charlie say, from what seemed like a long distance away. 'What would have been the point in telling you?'

'You—' I didn't quite catch whatever expletive Jack shot at Charlie but it didn't matter. Because it was followed by a punch, and then all of a sudden there were two grown men crashing into prams and sending small, pastel-coloured fluffy toys flying as they tried to biff each other.

On my list of romantic events sadly unlikely to occur in the twenty-first century, having two men fight over me was definitely in the top ten. If I was going to be picky, I would have preferred them to have been clad in hose and wielding swords, while precariously balanced on a castle parapet. So maybe it was because they were trying to thump each other while surrounded by jumbo boxes of nappies, but regardless, the reality of having two men trading punches over me wasn't as romantic as I had previously envisioned. I wasn't even really sure that they were fighting over *me* anyway. Jack had seemed pretty keen to pick a fight with Charlie for his own personal satisfaction from the get-go.

Sleazel was having hysterics and was clearly going to be of no help whatsoever. I looked around in despair and then grabbed a nearby bunny shaped night-light. I waited for my chance, and then, with a certain amount of vindication, brought it down on Charlie's head. About a second after it made contact, he dropped to the floor.

Sleazel shrieked, 'You've killed him!'

'Of course she hasn't killed him,' Jack snapped. He was still breathing heavily, but had gone from trying to punch Charlie's lights out to checking his vital signs in about two seconds flat. 'He's not even unconscious.'

Jack and I looked at each other for a long moment. And then we both looked away.

A crowd had gathered around us and, now deeming it safe, one figure detached from the throng and sidled up beside me. 'Told you so,' Norma said knowingly, gesturing towards the fragments of blue and brown china in my hand.

I looked at her uncomprehendingly.

'That was a Peter Rabbit lamp,' she pronounced. 'And no one messes with the rabbit.'

36
The Bad Old Days

While breaking a ceramic Peter Rabbit night-light over the head of your no-good, cheating ex-boyfriend sounds like a wonderfully therapeutic thing to do, in actual fact the whole encounter with Charlie and Sleazel in Baby World left me so shaken that I cried all the way home in the car. When we finally reached home, Jack tried to talk to me, but I shook him off, went into the bedroom and continued to howl.

Only a very minor part of me was upset over the discovery of Charlie's betrayal. After the initial shock, in retrospect, it made complete sense. He *had* moved on to a relationship with Sleazel in record time, but back then I had been so consumed by my own guilt over my infidelity that it had never occurred to me to be suspicious.

The real reason that I couldn't stop sobbing was Jack. I was tired of the coldness between us and the constant arguments. I had so badly wanted this shopping expedition to be a catalyst for change in our relationship, and instead it had ended in disaster. I was even considering belatedly accepting his proposal – but agreeing to get married in order to fix a damaged relationship didn't seem like the right thing to do either. And underlying everything was the constant pressure to get it all sorted out, to have everything in perfect order by the time the baby was born.

After about ten minutes, just as my tears were abating, there was a knock on the bedroom door and Jack came in, bearing a cup of raspberry leaf tea for me. He set it down on my bedside table and then sat down on the bed next to me.

'You have to try to calm down for the baby's sake, Belle,' he finally said softly. 'You're meant to be the house, remember?'

I nodded and hiccupped as I tried to get my breathing back under control.

'I'm sorry about Charlie,' he added.

Whether he was sorry that Charlie had cheated on me or that he had had an all-in brawl with him, I had no idea, and I didn't ask.

'How about we go back to the store tomorrow and buy that pram you liked?'

It was a peace offering but I was in no mood for it. 'They probably won't let us back in the store,' I said pointedly. 'Considering that we had a security guard escort us out. What got into you anyway? Isn't it against your Hippocratic oath to inflict grievous bodily harm?'

Jack looked shamefaced. 'I'm not sure what happened. You just looked so ... and the guy irritates me, so I—'

'Sent him flying headfirst into a box of Wiggles Pull-Up Underpants,' I finished. It had actually been kind of impressive but I wasn't about to tell him that.

Jack's lips twitched. 'It's a shame we weren't in a pub,' he said regretfully. 'That fight was about the most macho thing I've ever done, if you don't count the fact that we had to pay for damages done to a nappy display and a bunny night-light.' The brief flash of amusement faded from his face and he rubbed his neck. 'I know you were looking forward to buying things for Fetid's room and I'm sorry this happened to spoil it. But we shouldn't let it ruin our excitement.' He looked at me pleadingly. 'Belle, I can't wait for us to be a family. And I know that you're doing all the hard work right now, but I promise, I *promise*, that, as soon as this baby is on the outside, we're going to share the load. OK?'

'How?' I asked uncompromisingly. 'How is that going to work, given that you can hardly find time to come home to sleep these days?'

Jack looked at me, the weariness etched deeply into his face. 'I've been putting in as many overtime hours as I can now, in the hope that I can get a bit of latitude once the baby's born,' he said in an expressionless voice. 'I keep trying to do the right thing – finding us a house, organising a holiday –' He paused and the taboo word '*proposing*' hovered unspoken between us. 'But even the baby names that I like—' he broke off and then finished helplessly, 'Nothing I do is ever going to be right, is it?'

There was a silence. I didn't know what to say. I knew that Doug would say that it was Jack's provider instinct kicking in and that this was the way he was demonstrating his love for us. But this wasn't what I wanted. I wanted him to be around. I thought we had well and truly left behind the bad old days of the man going out to work and only seeing his family briefly at night and on the weekends. Our baby wasn't even born yet, and I felt as though Jack had already missed out on so much.

'Look, I'm sorry about today, OK?'

I was about to say that I was sorry too when he abruptly got up to leave.

'Where are you going?'

He looked at me in surprise. 'To the hospital. Remember I said I had to go in to work?'

It was mean but I couldn't help it. 'Surprise, surprise.'

He gave me a sharp look. 'What's that supposed to mean?'

'It was sarcasm,' I said nastily.

'Belle, I *told* you I had to go in to work today. What do you expect?'

'Not a lot these days, obviously.'

Oh God, now I couldn't stop myself. And that's when I realised that I didn't *want* to stop myself. Jack was *exactly* like Charlie, putting his career first and everything else a distant second. And I had just been letting him, like the doormat that everyone thought I was. All of the hurt that I had felt all those years ago in Sydney, when Charlie had left me behind, swelled up and became a tidal wave of angry words that broke and started to come crashing down. On Jack.

'Let's see,' I began, in a vicious tone, 'I don't expect you to turn up on time for the hospital appointments or turn up *at all* for the childbirth classes. And I know you don't have time for anything other than work. You have no idea what it's like—'

And then, to my complete and utter horror, Jack started to yell at me. 'Oh, here we go. I'm the man and I don't understand anything because I'M NOT THE ONE WHO'S PREGNANT.'

I was so shocked I couldn't respond. Just about the only time that Jack ever shouted was when Rufus was disobedient.

Seeing the alarm on my face, Jack lowered his tone but I could tell that he was still furious. 'Do you have any idea of how hard this is for *me*? To see you sick and miserable and anxious all the time and to feel like it's my fault, and yet secretly I'm glad because I want this baby more than anything?'

'Well, try actually *being* sick and anxious all the time! AND YOU'RE NEVER BLOODY AROUND! If you don't have time for us now, what are we going to do with this child when it's born? Send it to boarding school when it's three?'

'*You're* having a go at *me* for not being around? You don't even want me around!'

I looked at him in shock. 'Why on earth would you say that?'

'Come off it, Belle. You asked Doug to go with you to the classes and you want him there when you go into labour. You'd even rather hire a doula than have me there. You've got an entire conga line of people that you'd prefer to have with you when our baby is born. Anyone but me.'

'That's crap and you know it. Doug only came to the classes with me because *you* couldn't. And the only reason *we* hired Randolph was because I don't want to be alone when I'm in labour, and, knowing you, you'll either show up when it's all over or have to leave halfway through. You said yourself that you knew a doctor who had missed his own baby's birth. What have you done to make me think you'll be any different?'

'What have you done to make me think you'd even want me there?' he retaliated. 'You've been shutting me out of everything for months now. You didn't tell me about Charlie. You didn't tell me that you were thinking of having an elective caesarean. You couldn't even tell me about your nightmare, for God's sake. I had to find out from Fran what was upsetting you so much.' He laughed bitterly. 'You don't even want me in your *dreams*. And now you're sitting in here crying over Charlie, like a heartbroken schoolgirl.'

'*Charlie?* I wasn't crying over Charlie! I was crying over *us*!'

'Why should I believe that? You just found out that he cheated on you and you told me yourself that you felt something when you saw him again for the first time.'

Why, oh why, had I told Jack about that? That heart-melting moment that I had briefly experienced seemed so ludicrous now. But I knew that, if I tried to explain, it would just sound like a hollow excuse.

The sound of Rufus whimpering made both of us swing around. Poor Rufus, who associated loud, angry voices with past miseries, had slunk into the bedroom and was now cowering down in a corner, looking terrified. I lumbered over and sat down awkwardly on the floor next to him and stroked his head. His tail started to wag again, slowly.

'There's one other thing that's been bothering me for a long time,' Jack finally said, when it became clear that I wasn't going to respond. 'That day that I saw you with Charlie at Federation Square. Do you mind telling me what you talked about?'

'We just caught up,' I said miserably. 'We talked about family and people we both know and all that kind of thing. It really wasn't anything more than that.'

'But you must have talked about the fact that you're both about to become parents?' he pressed. 'Did you ask Charlie how he feels about becoming a father?'

I thought back and then nodded.

For a very long moment, Jack was silent. When he finally spoke, the grief in his voice broke my heart. 'See, that's the funny thing, Belle,' he said softly, 'because you've never once asked *me* that question.'

And with that Jack turned to leave, but not before I had caught the expression of tremendous sadness on his beloved face.

37

My Cups Runneth Over

Cruella had granted me maternity leave beginning two weeks before my due date on the proviso that when my firstborn turned twelve I would give my child to her to turn into a gallery slave and act as chief puppy-skinner. Or something like that. To be honest, once she had uttered the words 'You may have time off, providing . . .' I hadn't paid all that much attention to what had followed, which had no doubt earned Cruella the admiration and respect of Rumpelstiltskin.

I soon discovered that being on maternity leave is like taking holidays in order to hang around at home, grunting whenever I needed to move, still trying to find my pelvic floor and wondering what was the point of living in a high-crime, inner-urban area when none of the local drug dealers dealt in epidurals. Ibiza, it ain't.

I was meant to pack a suitcase for the hospital but I couldn't quite bring myself to do it yet. Packing meant having to think about the birth and, despite Randolph's best efforts, I still hadn't jumped that particular mental hurdle. This was unsurprising, as I was now thirty-eight weeks pregnant and so ginormous that jumping anything, even mentally, was entirely beyond the realm of possibility.

Doug called me every day to check on my cervix

measurements and to discuss his outfit changes for the labour. (He had decided to have four T-shirts printed with the different smiley faces from the childbirth-class handout so that I could tell, just by looking at him, what stage I was up to and which smiley face I was meant to be emulating.)

Chez Jack and Isabelle, we were getting on each other's nerves, even more than usual. I was walking Rufus so much that he had started to hide whenever I came looking for him with his leash in my hand. Jack was keen for me to avoid artificial inducement, which meant that he was putting his faith in all the so-called natural remedies (I called them old wives' tales). The natural remedies basically comprised walking a lot, eating curries, drinking copious amounts of raspberry leaf tea and having sex. The first three options pretty much cancelled the last one out, as, by the end of a day spent eating curry, drinking tea and waddling around the neighbourhood, all I wanted to do was throw up and fall asleep. Furthermore, a prerequisite for sex is feeling attraction and warmth towards one another, and after our last huge fight Jack and I still hadn't made it much past polite but cool, necessary communication. It was also getting to the stage where if Jack tried to force one more cup of raspberry leaf tea down my throat I was going to throw the teapot at his head. And throwing a teapot at someone's head is far from a universally acknowledged aphrodisiac.

Given our disastrous shopping attempt at Baby World, we had ended up ordering all of the nursery things online. Once they had been delivered and I had sorted out Fetid's room, all of a sudden there didn't seem to be anything to do other than to finalise our short-list of names. By the third day of my maternity leave, I was bored stiff, as you would be if the highlight of your day was checking your underpants to see if your mucus plug had dropped out. In fact, I was getting so desperate for something to do, other than reading tremendously tedious baby-name books, that I had decided to attend the breastfeeding class at the hospital.

Randolph's cheery advice to ask Jack to suck on my nipples during labour in order to contract my uterus had refused to budge from my mind. I had never heard of such a thing, which meant either a) I had a doula whose freakiness was not confined to the fact that he was named Randolph Reindeer, or b) the limits to my ignorance knew no bounds. As I was pretty sure it was the latter, I rang up and enrolled in the class.

On the day the class was to be held, I was tempted not to attend, as I was feeling sick in my stomach, no doubt due to all of the horrible tea and curries that I had consumed. But the class was scheduled to take place directly before the opening of Keedin's exhibition, (which I had sworn an oath to attend), so I couldn't stay home in any event. I decided I might as well go and take my mind off my various aches and discomfort. After hauling myself up, I got dressed and headed for the hospital.

Due to the amount of pro-breastfeeding literature strewn around, and the posters they had plastered everywhere of happy mothers serenely breastfeeding their babies, I had already cottoned on to the fact that the hospital powers-that-be were more than a little keen for new mothers to breastfeed.

Basically, once you moved past the natural childbirth/too posh to push hurdle, the next politically charged brawl was breastfeeding versus bottle-feeding. This was the sort of spectacular fight usually reserved for a WrestleMania smackdown in a full-capacity arena.

I didn't have particularly strong feelings about the

issue either way. If breastfeeding didn't work for me for whatever reason, I doubted that I'd feel like a failure and cry for weeks, as some of the women featured in my pregnancy books had apparently done.

In fact, my strongest feelings of trepidation were reserved for returning to the scene of my crime. After the whole 'I brought a fake father of my unborn child to class' episode, I didn't particularly want to see everyone again. And I *really* didn't want to see Charlie and Sleazel again after the unbelievably embarrassing Baby World incident. Sleazel had been a bit further on than me, though, so, with a bit of luck, she might have given birth already and they wouldn't be there.

I compromised by loitering in the bathroom until the class had started, intending to sneak in the back. Thankfully, the room had already been darkened in preparation for the inevitable video. I started to slink into the back row, but was foiled by the midwife in charge of the class, who pointed out a seat at the front.

'There's a spare seat here.'

Oh, God. It was Nurse Petunia. She either hadn't looked at me properly or hadn't recognised me. I hoped it was the latter.

Despite Jack's claim that I had been shutting him out of things, I still hadn't asked him to come with me to this class. It was during his work hours, and I had reasoned that there wasn't a whole lot he could contribute to this topic anyway. I was therefore thrilled to discover that all of the other mums-to-be were accompanied by their partners, which naturally meant that the spare seat was next to Nadia, the world's angriest woman. To cap things off, in the semi-darkness I could just make out that Charlie and Sleazel were also in attendance. Great. A quick glance around confirmed that the whole gang was here.

There was something on my seat, so I grabbed it, chucked it on the floor and then settled in to watch the movie.

The video featured another inappropriate soundtrack (this time it was 'When the Rivers Run Dry' by the Hunters & Collectors), but it was actually quite informative. For starters, I learned that breastmilk is actually three different types of milk: the colostrum, which was like full-cream milk and came out in the first few days; the fore milk, which sounded like it showed up after a round of golf; and the hind milk, which made me wonder if I was going to develop udders on my backside.

Although the film's narrator kept going on about how miraculous breastmilk was due to its wonderful immunity-building properties, I couldn't help feeling cheated. These were my *breasts* that we were talking about, goddammit. If they were going to express anything, I wanted it to be a beverage that was a damn sight sexier than milk. At the very least, I wanted my cups to runneth over with Dom Pérignon.

The film ended and, as the lights came back on, I blinked, not so much as an adjustment to the change in lighting conditions but more as a startled response. All of the women in the class were nursing dolls on their laps. Horrible, ancient, plastic dolls, with a skin tone that was similar to the colour that I had ended up with the first time I experimented with foundation.

'Before the class I placed dolls on your chairs,' Nurse Petunia informed us. 'Interestingly, one of you is cradling the doll protectively.' Nancy smirked, like the know-it-all she was. 'Most of you have the dolls sitting on your lap, and *one* of you—' here she paused just so everyone had time to whip out their mobile phones and call Children's Protective Services '—threw their doll on the floor.' The malice was back in her tone. Excellent. So she had definitely recognised me now.

My cheeks burning, I leaned over as far as my enormous tummy would allow and managed to scoop the doll up by one ankle.

Nurse Petunia swooped. 'You have a habit of keeping everyone waiting, don't you? What was your name again?'

'Isabelle.'

'Well then, everyone, Isabelle has just given us all a perfect demonstration of how *not* to pick up your baby.'

Nadia tittered, which, to be fair, was an appropriate laugh for a breastfeeding class. I glared at her and tried to rearrange my doll so that it looked more like Nancy's. Naturally, its head fell off and rolled sadly under my chair.

Without a word, Nurse Petunia retrieved my doll's errant head, no doubt using a Children's Protective Services' approved method for picking up a baby's dislodged head, and handed it back to me.

I thanked her politely and wedged the head back on. I would not allow myself to be bullied simply because I had failed to bond with a plastic doll with decapitation issues. I could only be grateful that Audie wasn't here to witness it, as, no doubt, she would have brought up Molly Dolly. Honestly, two headless dolls in my life and everyone starts looking at me as though I'm a *tricoteuse*, sitting in the front row, blithely knitting a beanie while the guillotine cuts off Marie Antoinette's head.

'Right. Now, I want all of you to have a go at imitating what you just saw in the video. Assume the cradle position!'

For one brief, horrifying moment, I thought Nancy was about to whip out her breast and pop her nipple into the doll's mouth for extra credit. As soon as this thought occurred to me, my head swivelled in the direction of Joan, as some car-crash voyeuristic instinct impelled me to try to catch a glimpse of her steel-wool-rubbed nipples. And I wasn't the only one. Everyone who had been in our childbirth class was craning over in her direction, but we were destined for disappointment. Joan was holding an empty baby's bottle to the lips of her doll.

Nurse Petunia was also staring at Joan. 'Why on earth have you brought a bottle in? This is a *breastfeeding* class.'

'Yes, I know,' Joan said mournfully. 'I just wanted to know what it would have felt like.'

Even Fetid shuddered.

Over the next fifteen minutes, as I tried to ignore the malevolent glances that Sleazel was shooting in my direction, we practised the different breastfeeding positions, which included the cradle hold, the underarm hold and the lying-down hold. Feeling confident, I experimented with an over-the-shoulder hold, until my doll's head fell off again and everyone glared at me.

Even though I was concentrating hard on what Nurse Petunia was saying, I couldn't help noticing that Charlie and Sleazel didn't seem very happy. While Nurse Petunia illustrated the different types of breastmilk by pouring cow's milk into differently shaped and sized liquor glasses (I made a mental note to request a snifter of fore milk the next time I wanted to be interesting at a dinner party), I was sneaking glances at Charlie and Sleazel and noting that their body language was cold and they weren't making eye contact with one another. I recognised the symptoms easily because Jack and I were suffering from the same disease.

As much as I disliked Nurse Petunia, she did give us a lot of useful information that I hadn't known before, such as newborns need to feed roughly every three hours. At this point, a woman who was expecting twins burst into tears and had to be led out of the class by her partner. As she was led away down the corridor, the last we heard of her was a wail that sounded like: 'Fuck off! *You* did this to me! I was happy with the dog!'

We also learned about cheery things like mastitis (the breastfeeding infection, not Doug's imaginary breed of dog), how our nipples would in all likelihood get cracked and sore, and inappropriate leaks, which, sadly, did not involve the media getting hold of juicy political secrets but was similar to sweat marks on your breasts. But from milk. Ugh. I quite liked the sound of some of the breastfeeding accessories such as nipple shields though. Maybe they made little nipple swords too and my breasts could re-enact the fight scene between Eric Bana and Brad Pitt from *Troy*.

There were also a very weird and uncomfortable few minutes when Nurse Petunia discussed (in a matter-of-fact tone that was at complete variance with her subject matter) what to do if your elder children or partner wanted to taste your breastmilk. I think my mouth dropped open because it never would have occurred to me in a hundred years to offer Jack a squirt of breastmilk on his cornflakes. But everyone else seemed to take it in their stride.

Nadia put up her hand and asked whether it was safe to offer her cat some of her breastmilk, as she didn't have any other children or a husband and the cat was the only one left who still loved her. Emboldened by Nadia's query, Evan, the husband of Steel Wool Joan, then put up his hand and asked if he could taste *someone else's* breastmilk, at which point even Nurse Petunia freaked out. She hurriedly called a break and all the women made a stampede for the bathroom, as the men started to drift in an unwilling way towards the kitchen, where the inevitable cordial and stale biscuits awaited.

I'd spent so much time in the toilet before the class, I was the only woman who didn't need to go to the bathroom. So when Charlie cornered me there was no one else around.

'Iz, I need to talk to you,' he said urgently.

I looked at him coldly. 'About what?'

'Not here. Can we meet up? Maybe tomorrow?'

'No, we cannot!' Now I was seriously annoyed. 'Look, Charlie, catching up once for old times' sake was one thing, and the second time you were my homework, but I think we should stop meeting up with each other now, don't you? Besides which, I don't particularly *want* to meet up with you, unless you're planning on apologising for cheating on me and not telling me about it. And if you want to do that, you can do it now.' I waited, but clearly an apology had not been on Charlie's mind as he just looked confused by the very mention of it. I was about to walk away when he took me by surprise.

'I want to talk to you about Jack.'

'What about him?' I asked, my eyes narrowing.

'You're not in love with him, Iz. I know you're not.'

I felt my cheeks start to burn. 'My relationship with Jack hasn't got anything to do with you.'

'Your relationship with Jack is in the toilet,' Charlie said bluntly.

I opened my mouth to refute this, but no words came out.

Taking my silence for acquiescence, he ploughed ruthlessly on. 'It's obvious, Iz. He's never around. You had to get a friend to pretend to be him. And, when he saw you with me that day in the city, he didn't even care enough to come over.'

'He cared enough to beat you up in Baby World,' I

said, making a valiant attempt to defend Jack.

'I only have hazy memories of what happened, but I'm pretty sure *you* inflicted most of the damage on me,' Charlie said with a wry grin. 'And, even though I ought to be furious with you for the headache that you gave me, I know why you did it.'

'Because you're a lying worm who cheated on me and never had the guts to tell me.' I stated the obvious.

But Charlie shook his head. 'I think the real reason you hit me over the head with that lamp was because you still have strong feelings for me.'

I'd had enough of this. I picked up my bag, in preparation for leaving the room. 'You're right, Charlie, I do. Those feelings are called anger, resentment and disgust.'

'Iz, listen to me.' His tone was urgent and to my surprise he grabbed my wrist. 'I know this seems crazy but we understand each other. We always have. Are you sure you're with the right person? *Completely* sure?'

'Charlie, I'm having Jack's baby!' I tried to tug my hand away. I was utterly aghast by the turn this conversation had taken. 'And, for God's sake, you and Sleazel are having a baby. What the hell are you suggesting?'

He let go of my wrist and ran his hand through his hair in frustration. 'Nothing. I don't know.' He paused, looked around the room to make sure that we were still alone, and then he dropped his bombshell. 'I'm thinking of leaving Liesel.'

I let my bag fall in shock. '*You're what?*'

His mouth was set in a stubborn line. 'You heard me. It's just not working any more. We hardly talk to one another. And when we do it's always about the baby.'

'Charlie, she's nine months pregnant with your child,' I said, horrified. 'God – what is wrong with you? You can't do this. You *can't*.'

'And leaving her after the baby is born would be less callous?' he demanded.

I regarded him properly for the first time. He looked miserable. I tried a different tack. 'What does Liesel say?'

He didn't answer and the truth slowly dawned on me. '*You haven't told her?*' I wanted to hit him. 'Then why in the name of God are you telling *me*?' I was shouting at him now. 'I'm your *ex*-girlfriend, for heaven's sake! We've hardly seen each other for the past five years. If you're thinking of leaving your pregnant partner, then I suggest you go home and start talking to her, and leave me the hell out of it!'

Charlie looked at me mutinously. 'I thought you'd understand.'

'Why on earth would you think that?'

'Because you want out of this baby thing as much as I do.'

His words jolted me right back to the beginning: to the three lines on the pregnancy test, the excitement as my tummy had started to visibly swell, the misery of morning sickness and the joy of hearing Fetid's heartbeat for the first time. And lastly I remembered the sense of peace that had enveloped me, as I sat in the rocking chair in the nursery, feeling Fetid's comforting little kicks. For the very first time since I'd fallen pregnant, suddenly the idea of never having experienced any of this seemed much more frightening than all of my other pregnancy-related fears combined. I was scared, I was clueless, I was hopelessly unprepared to be a mother, but one thing I knew for sure. I *didn't* want out.

'You're wrong, Charlie,' I said simply.

'Am I? What about all the text messages that you sent me?'

I flushed but I held my head up. 'Fear,' I said

steadily. 'I've been terrified the whole way through. But that doesn't make you right.' Gaining in confidence, my voice grew stronger. 'You don't know the first thing about me any more. You don't know that there were three stripes on my pregnancy test or that my placenta's name is Luigi, and if *you* had wanted to move house we bloody well would have moved because you always got your way.' Something occurred to me and I continued, 'But Liesel made you move even though you didn't want to. That fact alone makes me think that she's a *much* better match for you than I ever would have been.'

'I don't know what you're talking about.'

'No, I don't suppose you do,' I said thoughtfully. 'I didn't know that I was a doormat in our relationship either, until everyone pointed it out to me. Speaking of which, why *did* you tell everyone, except me, that you never wanted to have children?'

He shifted uncomfortably. 'What does it matter? It's not like you wanted kids back then anyway.'

'That's not an answer and you know it. Do you want to know what I think? I think you told all my friends and family your feelings on the subject, as a way of insuring yourself against the topic ever coming up, without having to say it to my face. Because Audie was right. Once I knew how you felt, I wouldn't have asked you to change your mind for me. And, for the record, Jack didn't change *my* mind about having a baby. We changed it together.'

Charlie was looking both defensive and contemptuous. 'Forget that I ever bothered to try to make you see sense. It's your life, Iz, so go ahead and ruin it if you want. I think Jack's a complete jerk and he's clearly not serious about you.'

The memory of Jack, down on one knee, holding the

open ring box, suddenly flashed into my mind, sending a stabbing ache through my heart.

I shook my head slowly. 'Wrong again, Charlie.' I mustered up a shaky smile. 'If anything, it's the other way around. Jack thinks I'm not that serious about him.'

'You're pregnant with his child. How much more serious can you get?' Charlie turned bright red as the import of what he'd said hit home.

'Exactly,' I retorted crisply.

But you *can* get more serious, I thought. You can get married.

Not wanting to discuss my rejection of Jack's proposal with Charlie, I sidestepped. 'It's all your fault,' I added. 'I haven't wanted to trust Jack the way that I trusted you all those years ago in case he up and left me like you did.'

It was amazing. I could actually feel the grey clouds that had been clustered around me for so long, lifting and dissolving. Although the last thing that I wanted was for Charlie to leave Sleazel, it was *wonderful* to realise that Charlie had left me because going when the going got tough was what he did. It *hadn't* been my fault, which meant that my long-held fear of it happening again was groundless.

'Stop throwing that in my face! *You* cheated on *me*, remember!' Charlie said in outrage.

'I only cheated on you because you ruddy well left me and moved to another state! We were living together, Charlie! I thought we were going to be together for ever, and you went and applied for a job in Adelaide and didn't even tell me until you got it! And anyway, in case you've forgotten, YOU CHEATED ON ME TOO, YOU SELFISH, MORONIC—' I cast around in my mind for a suitably scathing insult, '—*SCORPIO*!'

If you're going to clear the air over a past relationship that has ended badly, then do it with an audience, I say.

Which, unwittingly, is exactly what we had done. I caught the expression on Charlie's face and swung around.

Gathered in the doorway, clutching their plastic, cordial-filled cups and half-eaten biscuits, were Gareth, Nancy, Evan, Joan and Nadia, their mouths agape. Taking advantage of the break in hostilities, Nancy nudged Gareth and muttered, 'Do you reckon she's got any *more*?'

Gareth was looking at me with an expression that was a cross between respect and disbelief. 'She couldn't possibly have. No one has that much time or energy.'

'It's better than *The Bold and the Beautiful*,' Joan breathed. 'Who do you think the real father is?'

'My money's on the first bloke with the nice cardigan,' Evan said knowledgeably. 'He just *looked* like a dad, don't you think? Oh, by the way, Charlie, we came in to tell you that we think Liesel has gone into labour in the bathroom.'

This was it. If Liesel was in labour, the eleventh hour had arrived. I needed to call in the big guns to set Charlie straight.

I beckoned to Nadia, and as she stepped forward I saw Charlie pale.

'Nadia, Charlie is thinking of leaving Liesel,' I said baldly. As Nadia turned puce and drew breath, I turned to Charlie. 'I'm assuming that Nadia is going to kill you and if there's any justice in the world you'll be reincarnated as a seahorse. Preferably a male, married seahorse, whose Catholic seahorse wife believes in the rhythm method. With a bit of luck you'll have to give birth at least thirteen times.' I issued my parting shot. 'And by the way, I *hate* being called Iz. Bye-bye, everyone. See you in the labour wards!'

As I exited the classroom, I had a slight pang that I

wouldn't get to hear Nadia's harangue in its entirety.

I didn't care. I had dealt with my past and it felt good to be walking away from it. Now I needed to tackle my future.

I needed to find Jack.

38
True Grit

Which, as it turned out, was easier said than done. I couldn't get in touch with Jack. I rang the hospital but they said he was in surgery and wasn't expected out for hours yet. I considered asking them to pass on a message saying that I'd been an idiot and I loved him, and that I knew now that leaving at inappropriate times was a trait of Charlie's and had nothing to do with me or him, but I ended up just muttering that I wasn't in labour and it could wait and not to bother telling him that I'd rung. I wanted to go home and wait for him there but I couldn't. It was half past seven, Keedin's exhibition opening had already started and that was now where I had to be. Reluctantly, I headed off to the gallery.

When you're almost nine months pregnant and roughly the size of the Michelin Man, the last place you want to be is at a crowded gallery opening. Least of all a gallery that is artfully strewn with raw meat on a hot summer's night. The smell was awful and my stomach was like some rampaging Godzilla-type creature from a horror movie. I kept knocking champagne glasses out of people's hands and sending people ducking for cover. All of our clients continually asked when I was due, and when I answered, 'In two weeks', they'd back away in horror, worried that my waters were about to break all over their expensive, imported shoes.

The exhibition was a sell-out before opening night, as we'd all known it would be, so why Cruella needed me there was incomprehensible. Until I found myself in Keedin's clutches and it all made sense. Cruella's star artist was still obsessed with my placenta, and my presence was obviously required to reassure him that I hadn't done a runner with it.

'Such magnificent bosoms,' Keedin said by way of greeting as he cornered me. 'Containing mother's milk – the elixir of life!'

'Well, yes, but did you know that it's quite OK to give some to the cat to drink if you want?' I responded, trying to back away from him.

I made up my mind that, if he sat down cross-legged in front of me in his worshipping position again, I was going to sit on him and suffocate him. It was self-defence really, and I wouldn't even get into trouble with Cruella as her favourite maxim was 'The only good artist is a dead artist'.

Keedin nodded. 'Perhaps, but you must never give the cat LSD,' he said earnestly. 'The cat doesn't like it.'

'Did you find your car?' I asked, deciding that the topic of what cats could ingest had run its course.

'I don't have a car,' he said blankly.

'I'm talking about the one in your driveway,' I said, acting on my previous suspicion.

A faint light dawned in Keedin's eyes. 'Ah, yes. The police came and asked me about that. They said it had been stolen.'

I contemplated squirting him in the eye with some breastmilk, in order to extract a measure of revenge for the day that I'd spent traipsing around looking for his bloody car, but, before I could do so, Keedin added mournfully, 'I wish I knew how to drive.'

I would have killed him then and there but at that moment I saw Doug and Zac making their way towards me through the crowd. I managed to escape from Keedin by saying that I had to go and take drugs. He nodded understandingly and immediately stepped aside to let me pass. I smiled at Zac, who I hadn't seen in ages, but then I looked down and saw that walking between Doug and Zac was a little girl in a red dress.

Doug's voice was bursting with pride and excitement. 'Isabelle, this is Rose. Rose, this is my friend Isabelle.'

Rose was holding Doug and Zac's hands. She looked up at me shyly and then smiled. With difficulty, I crouched down to her level, holding on to Doug's trouser leg for balance.

'Hi Rose,' I said. 'How old are you?'

She looked at me uncertainly and then glanced up at Doug for reassurance. He nodded and smiled. She gathered up her courage. 'I'm three.'

I looked impressed. 'That's very big.'

Doug came down to our level. 'She is a big girl,' he agreed. 'We were just thinking about what colour to paint her room, weren't we, sweetheart? She's going to decide tomorrow. It's definitely going to be either yellow or purple,' he finished with a confiding wink at Rose, and her entire face lit up.

There was something different about Doug's tone of voice, and I struggled to work out what it was. Then I realised. Doug habitually spoke with a faintly sarcastic drawl, as though the thing he dreaded most was being taken seriously. But when he spoke to Rose it disappeared. Doug was taking the wishes and dreams of this little girl very seriously indeed.

'It was very nice to meet you, Rose,' I said. 'You'll be

seeing a lot of me I expect. And I'm having a baby, so when it's a bit older you can play together.' I smiled at Doug. 'Can you help me up? I think I'm stuck.'

Doug heaved me to my feet, which was terrifying, as I immediately came face to face with Zac's beautiful visage. Zac was entirely too good-looking to be viewed at such close quarters. He was like Michelangelo's *David*; you needed to stand back a bit from that much perfection. Zac gathered Rose up, and she put her arms around his neck and nestled into his shoulder.

'I don't mean to run off on you, Isabelle, but I'd better get her home,' Zac said apologetically. 'She wanted to see where Doug worked, but she really ought to be in bed now.'

We bade Zac and Rose farewell and watched as they exited. Doug shook his head. 'Can you believe it? Zac leaving a party at *eight o'clock*! He usually gets home at that time, the following morning. Our social lives are over,' he concluded happily.

'She's gorgeous,' I said to Doug, putting my arm around his waist and giving him a squeeze. 'I'm so happy for the three of you.'

His eyes grew misty and, unable to speak, he simply patted my stomach instead. When he had regained his composure he asked, 'Where's my favourite doctor?'

'Saving someone's life, I think.'

'Oh, well. He can't help being excessively important. Now, how are you feeling?'

'Not too good,' I confessed. 'I have a horrible stomach ache. It's not surprising, really, considering the amount of raspberry leaf tea and curry that Jack has been forcing down my throat.' I stopped as I registered the look on Doug's face. 'What? What is it?'

'You have a *stomach ache*?' he repeated incredulously.

'You idiot! Don't you remember that lower abdominal pain is one of the early signs of labour?'

'The only thing I remember clearly from the childbirth classes is that cardigan you were wearing,' I retorted. 'Which reminds me, where *did* you get it from?'

'Never mind my cardigan! Belle, I mean it. I think you might be starting labour. When did your stomach ache begin?'

'Last night,' I said, starting to feel simultaneously excited and scared. But then reason asserted itself. 'Don't be silly, Doug. I'm only thirty-eight weeks. I've got another two weeks to go, and even then most first babies are overdue. It's just a stomach ache, that's all.'

Doug didn't appear to have listened to a word I'd said. 'How dilated do you think your cervix is?' he asked, with concern. 'Do you want me to—'

'You stay away from my cervix,' I said, backing away. 'And *you* stay away from my placenta,' I added, directing this last comment at Keedin, who had reappeared at my elbow. 'Honestly, I'm fine. I'm just a bit achy. It really doesn't hurt at . . . ooooh.'

'Belle! Are you OK?' Doug asked in alarm, as I suddenly went very pale.

'I'm fine. Something just really hurt.'

'It wasn't the placenta, was it?' Keedin asked anxiously. 'You didn't break it, did you?'

'Of course I didn't break it,' I said crossly. 'Primarily because there's no known way of breaking a placenta.'

Keedin didn't appear to place much store in my medical knowledge. 'I must find Carmela,' he announced. 'You must not be allowed to thwart my art.'

'I blame Hitler,' Doug said dispassionately, watching Keedin disappear into the crowd, hitching up his horrible pants as he went. 'Ever since young Adolf failed to become an artist, everyone's been too scared not to encourage every bloody idiot who picks up a paintbrush. More artists ought to be thwarted if you ask me.'

'Er-uhhhhh!' I said, by way of response, as another spasm of pain rocked my body.

Doug immediately snapped back to attention, as the people standing near us started to look concerned. 'I do love to say I told you so, and I did tell you. You're definitely in labour. Now what do you need me to do?'

'Get me out of here,' I said shakily. 'I need to call Jack. And Randolph. And I need to go home and pack my hospital bag and—'

'You haven't packed your bag yet?'

'I haven't had five minutes to do anything, what with all the raspberry leaf tea I've had to drink, and walking Rufus and eating curries and dealing with my past,' I said indignantly. 'If you must give me a lecture, can you please give it to me on the way home? Just get me out of here before Cruella and Keedin come back.'

Sensing that I was on the edge, Doug started to push his way through the crush, attempting to shield me at the same time. But we were too late. Cruella and Keedin were bearing down on us.

Cruella grabbed my elbow. 'Keedin tells me you're about to have the baby. Have you *no* consideration?'

I looked at her uncomprehendingly. 'Carmela, I can't help it.'

'Of course you can help it!' she snapped. 'Just try for a little backbone. That's what's wrong with the world. No one has grit any more.'

For some reason, it was the word 'grit' that pushed me over the edge. Grit was exactly the quality I was going to need in the coming hours, and here was Cruella accusing me of having none.

I swung around to face her. 'Grit?' I said viciously,

my voice beginning to rise. 'You want me to demonstrate *grit*? For your information, I'm about to push this baby through an opening that is laughingly called a birth canal, but which I can assure you is closer to a birth rivulet, and *you* think I don't have grit?'

'You're very gritty,' Doug intervened nervously, trying to head off an explosion from Cruella. 'You're John Wayne and Ken Loach rolled into one, Belle.'

Both Cruella and I ignored him. We were facing off, as though it were high noon in a Western and the lives of one hundred and one Dalmatian puppies were at stake.

'Keedin wants to accompany you, which naturally means that I must go with him,' she hissed, still trying to keep the altercation hidden from the clients. 'We are celebrating his most brilliant and successful show and *you* want to drag us off to some godforsaken hospital?'

'I don't want to drag either of you anywhere,' I retorted. 'I'd be much happier if you didn't come anywhere near me.' Another contraction erupted and I stopped arguing as the pain hurtled through me.

'Just sit in a corner and smile,' Cruella commanded. 'Douglas, prop her up somewhere. Don't let the clients see her. For God's sake, Isabelle, stop carrying on. Millions of women have babies every day. Don't make such a fuss. It's not like you're sick.'

'I KNOW I'M NOT SICK – I'M PREGNANT!' I bellowed.

I was beyond caring about repercussions from Cruella. But I already knew that nothing I could ever say would put her in her place. Which was why I would be eternally grateful that, for once, my body found its sense of chivalry and came to my rescue with the perfect retaliation.

As Cruella prepared to flay me to bits, my waters

broke, all over the expensive carpet in the gallery. Cruella's face collapsed in horror but there was worse in store. At almost exactly the same moment, something far more momentous happened. To the considerable horror of the fashionable Toorak crowd, the worn-out ties on Keedin's horrible fisherman's pants finally gave way and, at last, we saw the Moon moon.

39
Lady with a Baby

Considering the circumstances, Doug did the most sensible thing he could have done. In the commotion that followed Keedin's flashdance, he grabbed a champagne glass from the tray of a passing waiter, swilled it, tossed aside the empty flute and then roared, 'LADY WITH A BABY! COMING THROUGH!'

It was immensely satisfying for both of us and, in the car on the way back home to pack my suitcase, Doug and I both agreed that we could die happy once we had also used the phrases 'Follow that cab!' and 'Watch out! He's behind you!' in context.

As I packed my bag, I left messages for Jack in every imaginable way. After about half-an-hour, someone from the hospital finally called me back to say that he was still in surgery and would probably be unavailable for several hours.

'Belle, come *on*!' Doug's voice chided me from the kitchen, where he had been putting out food for Rufus. 'I've rung Randolph and Cate and they're both planning to meet us at the hospital.'

'I'm just looking for my lip balm,' I shouted back, frantically scrabbling through my bedside drawer before another contraction started up.

I was starting to feel panicked. All of the books had

listed lip balm as a necessary item during labour. How could I give birth with cracked lips?

In desperation, I pulled open the drawer of Jack's bedside table. And there, right in front of me, was the very first ultrasound photo of our baby. Jack had kept it there, all this time.

For a long moment I stared at the little jelly-bean alien in the photograph. And then, as another contraction began, I replaced the photo and gently closed the drawer.

'OK, little one,' I whispered, placing my hands on my belly. 'We've all been in our own separate worlds for far too long now. It's time for the three of us to become a family.'

An hour later, Doug was bouncing around on the fit ball in my birthing suite while Randolph bustled around doing all of the practical things involved in settling me in. I was between contractions and had started to get changed into my birthing outfit. All of a sudden, Doug stopped bouncing and looked at me with an intense expression. 'Belladonna? Do you know what the date is today?'

'The twenty-first,' I answered, as I pulled on my special labour socks with the rubber bottoms that Fran had sent me. According to Fran, it was very important to guard against slipping over and cold feet during labour. These dangers apparently outweighed the risk of Fetid remaining an only child once the vision of me wearing the socks and my peach taffeta dress had been irrevocably embedded into Jack's mind.

'It's the twenty-first of *November*,' Doug said meaningfully.

'So what?'

'So, if you can hold it in for just a few more hours, it

won't be a Scorpio,' he said excitedly.

I looked at him in complete disbelief, as another contraction started to build. '*Hold it in?* I've been waiting eight and a half months to get to this point and now, when Fetid's using its head as a battering ram against my cervix, you want me to *hold it in*?'

'Well, I'm not the one with an aversion to Scorpios,' Doug retorted huffily. He began to bounce again. 'Ooh, Belle, maybe this is a Theoretical Equation. It could be: is the pain of having a baby worse or equal to that of having a Scorpio child?'

'There's nothing bloody theoretical about it,' I grunted, as another contraction started to build. 'Now, for the love of God, stop bouncing and go home to your lovely partner and child.'

Doug stopped abruptly. 'I thought you needed me to stay and hold your hand until Jack gets here,' he said, looking at me oddly. 'Aren't you terrified now that it's started?'

His question brought me up short. Truth to tell, the contractions hurt like hell and I *really* didn't want to think about how much worse the pain was going to get but strangely – I wasn't scared. Now that there was no going back, it was almost a relief to know that I just *had* to get through it. Huh. Who knew? I might not be very brave but maybe I could be as gritty as the best of the Brazilians.

I waved Doug away. 'Go! I'll be fine.'

He held my gaze and then gave me a sudden grin. 'Do you know, despite being the worst drama queen that I've ever met in my entire life – and that includes a couple of Sydney's finest drag queens who call the emergency number when they break a nail – I really think that you will be fine, you know.'

It was just about the nicest thing he could have said.

He gave me a quick kiss, handed over his four smiley-face T-shirts to Randolph, with strict instructions on when to use them, and then disappeared.

Once the contraction had died down, I turned to ask Randolph a question, just as the nurse who was conversing with him swung around.

'No,' I said in horror. 'Not *you*.'

Nurse Petunia bared her teeth in what I suppose was her version of a smile.

'But what are you doing here?' I stuttered. 'Shouldn't you be in Pathology sucking – I mean, *taking* – someone's blood?'

'They're short-staffed up here and I've had over forty years of midwifery experience. Do you have any objections?'

I let out a long moan as another contraction started to take hold of me.

Nurse Petunia interpreted this as a no. She took my blood pressure while Randolph changed into the T-shirt bearing the image of the smiley face with a straight line for a mouth. One T-shirt bypassed, another one down, leaving two more to go.

'Here's the doctor now,' I heard someone say, and I looked up in relief, dying to see Jack's beloved face.

But it was Dr Bert who was smiling at me instead. 'We're in luck! I'm the obstetrician on duty, so I get to deliver your baby. How are you doing, Belle?'

My face crumpled. 'Where's Jack?' I almost sobbed.

Bert put his arm around me. 'He's coming, Belle. He'll be here very soon. But you're doing an amazing—'

He broke off mid-compliment.

I looked up to discover why. Cate was standing in the doorway of the birthing suite. She was dressed *completely* inappropriately for a labour ward, in a

Collette Dinnigan lace-trimmed slip dress and some rather fabulous kitten heels.

'Cate!' Bert cleared his throat, unable to look away from her.

Cate looked rather taken aback too. 'Bert! Hi. I'd forgotten you were so—' She broke off. I knew Cate very well so I was convinced that she had been about to say 'good-looking', but instead she lamely changed it to 'doctorly'.

Bert laughed. 'It's the white coat. It's comfortable, but it doesn't look half as good as what you're wearing.'

Cate blushed, Nurse Petunia snorted and Randolph looked indignant. 'Oi!' Randolph said, as he gave me some water to sip. 'I don't even know you people. Either stay and help or get a room.'

Recalled to their sense of duty, both Cate and Bert suddenly became very concerned about my welfare.

'How are you doing, Belle?' Cate asked anxiously, hovering over me for lack of anything practical to do.

I groaned in response.

'The contractions are getting much more intense now,' Dr Bert murmured.

'I can *hear* you,' I said crossly, in between grunts.

Bert and Cate's eyes met over my writhing bulk. 'It's very common for labouring women to get a little testy,' Bert said. 'Try not to take anything she says during this time personally.'

'I don't blame her,' Cate said with a shudder, as another contraction tore through me and I roared in pain. 'God, this is horrible. If I didn't already not want to have kids, this would *definitely* put me off for life.'

Bert was looking at Cate in wonder. 'You don't want kids? Ever?'

She looked defensive. 'It's a personal choice, and I'd

rather not hear your views on it if it's all the same to you.'

'No, no, you don't understand,' Bert said hastily. 'The thing is – I don't want to have kids either!'

Cate looked at him, dumbfounded. 'But you're an obstetrician!'

'I know,' Bert said earnestly. 'It's the bane of my life. Every woman that I go out with assumes that I must want ten children because I've chosen this specialisation, but that has nothing to do with it. I'm not paternal in the slightest.'

'You're not?' Cate asked, with growing excitement, patting me absently on the nose in response to another of my shrieks.

'God, no.' Bert gave a merry little laugh as though the idea was hilarious. 'It'd be like bringing work home. And I love travelling to off-the-track places too much. I went backpacking through Bolivia last year. You can't do *that* with a baby.'

A spark was kindling in Cate's eyes. 'Exactly! And I mean, who in their right mind would want to go through *this*?' Cate indicated my moaning form and then quickly said, 'Sorry, Belle. No offence meant.'

'None taken,' I gasped. 'So please don't take offence if I tell you to fuck off. Immediately. I'm very happy for you both but if someone doesn't get me some pain relief and find Jack *now* I'M GOING TO POO ON PURPOSE.'

Cate leaned over and kissed me. 'I won't take it personally. I know you're just in pain. But I just wanted to say that, if it's a girl and you want to name her Mia or Ella, go right ahead. I don't mind at all.'

As Nurse Petunia needed to do some cervix measuring the traditional way, Cate and Randolph decided to exit. With the pleasantries over and a foetal monitor strapped to my belly, Dr Bert departed, promising to return when I was further along. Cate didn't reappear, which didn't entirely surprise me as, judging by the looks in her and Dr Bert's eyes, they had gone off to find an empty supply cupboard in which to more closely examine the positive aspects of purely recreational sex.

'Isabelle, there's a mad woman dressed entirely in black leather in the waiting room who's demanding to be let in here,' Randolph informed me as he re-entered the room wearing an enormous pair of pink rubber gloves and bearing a tub of steaming water. He dipped the washcloth into the bucket, then wrung it out and placed it on exactly the worst aching part of my back. I sighed as the heat penetrated my sore muscles.

'That would be my boss,' I said. 'Assuming that she hasn't fired me. Is there a weedy-looking guy without pants with her?'

He nodded. 'And a couple of police officers. I think they're trying to charge him with indecent exposure. To be fair, he is wearing a tea-towel. I told them that it could be hours yet, but they seem determined to wait.'

'That's because they're waiting to collect Luigi,' I said.

'Who's Luigi?'

'My placenta. I don't care any more. They can have him. I don't need him, do I?'

'Not really, no. But what do they want it for?' asked Randolph, looking utterly confused.

'The scrawny flasher is going to make art from it,' I said. I couldn't resist adding with pride, 'My placenta is probably going to end up in the Venice Biennale. Which is kind of appropriate given the birth-canal metaphor. Anyway, make sure they only get the placenta, OK? Nothing else.' I wanted to be sure that Randolph had very clear and precise instructions. Knowing Cruella, she'd probably have a stab at asking for a kidney or something while she was at it.

As another contraction ripped through me, leaving me shaky and breathless, I roared out my misery to anyone who would listen.

'WHERE'S MY EPIDURAL?' And where in *the bloody hell* was Jack? Although, in all honesty, at this precise moment I would have been happier to see the anaesthetist than Jack.

'Hold on, Isabelle,' Randolph said soothingly, offering me a barley sugar to suck. 'The anaesthetist's with someone else right now but you're next on the list.'

'She doesn't like waiting her turn,' Nurse Petunia remarked dispassionately. 'I've noticed that.'

Randolph ignored her. 'I promise Ethan won't be much longer.'

'Who the hell is Ethan?' I growled.

'He's the anaesthetist.'

Oh dear God, it was descending to the level of farce. In addition to Randolph Reindeer and the inappropriately named Nurse Petunia, I now had to contend with the tongue-twisting Ethan the anaesthetist.

I was about to demand that a message be relayed to Ethan the anaesthetist that if he didn't hurry up I would ask Cruella to step in and knock me unconscious, but at that moment the clouds parted, a shaft of dazzling sunshine lit up the room and small bluebirds started singing as they fluttered around the rainbow that had suddenly appeared. At least that's what it felt like to me. Because, all of a sudden, Jack had arrived.

'Belle, I'm here, I'm here!' Jack ran in, looking wild-eyed, clad in clean surgical gowns.

I burst into tears of relief at the sight of him.

He cradled me in his arms and kissed my sweaty face. 'Belle, I'm sorry,' he said hoarsely. 'I'm so sorry I missed some of it. I came as soon as I could—'

The odd thing was that, even though one of my worst fears had been realised and I had had to go through some of the labour by myself, I simply didn't care. Jack was here *now* and that was all that mattered. Safe in his arms, I already felt happier and stronger.

I spoke over the top of his voice in order to stop his self-recriminations. 'You brought a rainbow,' I said lovingly.

He immediately twisted around to glare at Nurse Petunia and Randolph. 'How much gas have you given her?'

'She hasn't had any!' Randolph protested. 'We're expecting the anaesthetist with the epidural any moment now.'

The mention of the anaesthetist snapped me out of my joyful haze and back to the problem that needed to be sorted out before Fetid's imminent arrival.

I tugged at the sleeve of Jack's gown to get his attention again. 'Jack, I can't bear it!'

'I know it hurts, honey, but I'm here now. Breathe with me—'

'I'm not talking about the contractions! I'm talking about the fact that we never considered our baby's possible vocation and how it might affect their name,' I garbled hastily, as another contraction started.

Jack was brought up short by this, but thankfully Randolph filled him in on the Ethan the anaesthetist problem while I continued to channel Linda Blair from *The Exorcist*.

When the contraction had subsided, Jack took my hand and spoke sternly to me. 'Belle, stop worrying about names. We'll wait and see what sex the baby is and what it looks like and I guarantee the perfect name will come to us.'

'Jack, look around!' I pulled his head closer to mine so that I could whisper. 'We're *surrounded* by people with completely ridiculous and inappropriate names. A thirty-five-year-old Bert. Nurse Petunia, who ought to have been Nurse Venus Flytrap. Randolph Reindeer.' In my agitation I forgot to whisper. 'And what if it ends up like Ethan the anaesthetist? Our child will be a laughing stock!' As I registered the looks on Randolph's and Jack's faces, I already knew. 'He's behind me, isn't he?' I said hollowly.

I swivelled my head and looked into the unamused face of Ethan the anaesthetist. Way to go, me. I'd just pissed off the person who would shortly be inserting a very large needle into my spinal column.

'Er, hi, Ethan,' I said nervously.

'That's *Mr* Ethan T. Sneath,' he snapped.

'You're kidding—' I caved in as Randolph elbowed me in the ribs – which hurts quite a bit when you're in labour.

'I was over at Frances Perry,' he informed the room at large. Rub it in – of course the private hospital patients got preferential treatment.

'I don't suppose your patient's name was Liesel?' I croaked. Although it felt like years had passed since the breastfeeding class, I could tell by the clock on the wall that it was only eleven p.m.

He looked surprised. 'Yes, it was. Is she a friend of yours?'

I avoided the question and asked my own more pressing one. 'Was her partner there?'

Jack shot me a sharp glance, but I was focusing on the anaesthetist.

'Charlie, right? Yes, of course he was there.'

I leaned back and smiled. Good old Nadia. With a bit of luck, she might have permanently cured Charlie of his propensity for taking off when it suited him.

'He was going to leave her,' I informed Jack briefly, not wanting him to think that I had asked about Charlie for any other motive. 'I just wanted to make sure that he hadn't.' I directed my attention back to Ethan T. Sneath. 'How is she doing?' As the pain of another contraction started to build, I felt strangely close to Sleazel, knowing that we were both enduring the same experience. I wished her nothing but good luck.

'She's fine now. I just administered an epidural so she's coping much better.' Whatever else he said was lost on me as the pain roared through me, drowning everything else out.

After a cursory inspection of my vital signs and a brief confabulation with Nurse Petunia, Ethan T. Sneath the anaesthetist took great pleasure in breaking the bad news to me. 'It's too late for an epidural,' he said briskly. 'You're almost ten centimetres dilated. We can give you gas.'

'*Gas? Gas?*' At this point I let fly with a string of obscenities that conveyed to Ethan my feelings regarding the efficacy of gas as opposed to an epidural, my opinion on the procedural processes of a hospital that could fail to administer a painkiller in time, and my thoughts on his character, competence and professional future in general. The warm empathy that I had been feeling towards Sleazel also evaporated. It was all her fault I wouldn't get to have an epidural. I hoped her baby came out doing star jumps.

Ethan T. Sneath listened to me unemotionally and waited for another contraction to grip me before repeating his offer of the gas mask and departing.

While Randolph changed into his frowny-face T-shirt,

I practically ripped the gas mask out of Nurse Petunia's hands. As I took a long deep suck on the gas, I remembered that I had something momentous to impart to Jack. I struggled to find the right words, but unfortunately the black rubber mask had made me feel claustrophobic, so instead I ended up gazing at Jack and whimpering that the walls were closing in.

Then Dr Bert re-entered the room, adjusting his white coat and with his hair looking slightly dishevelled. After a brief examination and a quick discussion with everyone except me, he turned back to me and nodded authoritatively. 'OK, Belle, here we go. You're almost through it. We need you to start pushing.'

With a sigh, Randolph pulled the Edvard Munch-inspired T-shirt out and began to change for the last time.

Hoping that Dr Bert had washed his hands, I tried to respond civilly but somehow ended up screaming instead. Everyone seemed to find this very encouraging, so I did it again. And again, for the next forty-five minutes.

'Jack – it HUU-URTS!' I sobbed. I was going to die from the pain. It was far, far worse than anything I had ever experienced, including the non-medicated bikini wax. 'I can't do this. I can't. Let's just keep it in there,' I begged. 'It'll be like boarding school.'

Tears welled in Jack's eyes but he grabbed my hand and pressed it tight. 'I know, sweetheart, I know, but you're almost there. Do you want our music on? Someone put the music on!' he snapped.

Randolph ran to do his bidding and within seconds the horrible sounds of Gwyneth Paltrow and Huey Lewis filled the room.

'Is Gwynnie's version of "Bette Davis Eyes" on this CD?' Randolph asked chattily, as he efficiently mopped up some of my wee. 'I love that song. That Apple Martin will probably be very musical, given her genes.'

'Ridiculous name for a child, though,' Nurse Petunia chipped in. 'Thirty years ago I was delivering Sarahs and Kates and Jennifers. These days, not a week goes past without the birth of a Madison, Savannah or Cruz.'

'Come on, love – sing it with me,' Jack encouraged me. '*You're gonna fly away—*'

'FUCK OFF! FUCK OFF AND TAKE FUCKING HUEY LEWIS AND GWYNETH WITH – ARRRRRRRRRRGGGGGGGGGHHHHHHH!!!!!'

'That's it, angel – you're doing magnificently. Here comes the second verse ...'

I was going to die from the pain. It was now or never. I had to tell him. 'Jack – I'll marry you,' I wept. 'FUUUUUUUUCKKKKKK!'

'What did you say?' Jack had dropped my hand in shock. He grabbed it again quickly, and looked at me with a gaze that was so deep he could probably see Fetid.

Bert was grinning from ear to ear, and I could only be grateful that he was there to repeat it because I didn't have the energy. He cleared his throat. 'I'm pretty sure she said she wants to marry you.'

'Why?' Jack demanded. 'Why now?'

Oh, for fuck's sake. A long-winded explanation was required and I had neither time nor wind.

'You not like Charlie,' I gasped. 'You no leave me.' Why I had resorted to pidgin English I had no idea, but it seemed to require less energy.

'You really thought I would ever leave you?' he asked in disbelief. 'Belle, don't you get it? I *love* you. I always have. I couldn't leave you if I tried.'

'Me scared. You never around. Like Charlie. And Charlie leave me. But Charlie want leave Sleazel too.' I was channelling either Tarzan, Frankenstein or a pygmy from a lost tribe but I didn't care. The light was back in Jack's eyes when he looked at me, and even the pain didn't feel so bad right now. With a final gasp I managed, 'So that just Charlie. Not my fault.'

Jack was looking at me with an expression that was half cross and half tender. 'Let me get this straight; even though we're having a baby together and I love you more than I've loved anyone in my entire life, you were still scared that I would leave you with no warning, the way that Charlie did? And that's why you wouldn't marry me?'

'YEEEEEESSSSSSSSSSS!!!!!!!' I screamed, as Fetid pushed insistently once again. For the record, being headbutted from the inside is *not* a harmonious match with poignant revelations. But, knowing that I had to get this right and convince Jack, I added, 'Pregnant brain's fault also. Have been insane for past nine months. More than usual. Not my fault either. Fetid's fault.'

Jack looked at me for a moment and then reached under his green surgical smock, into his jeans pocket. To my amazement, he pulled out a jewellery box and opened it to reveal a beautiful diamond ring. I looked closer and a surge of joy filled my heart. It was the same engagement ring that he had proposed with on our babymoon. 'I've been keeping it in my office,' he said softly. 'I wanted so badly for you to have it. I was going to give it to you to celebrate the birth of our baby. But if you're sure . . . ?'

I nodded and, with a Herculean effort, I summoned my last reserve of energy. 'Me. Love. You.'

Jack managed to stop me thrashing around long enough to push the ring on to the fourth finger of my left hand. It was at this point that we both got the fright of our lives when Nurse Petunia suddenly burst into hacking sobs.

'Beautiful,' she said incoherently. 'That was . . . beautiful.' She gathered herself together and quickly resumed her habitual scowl. 'Even if you did put the cart before the horse.'

In an attempt to curb the intense emotion in the room, Randolph waited until the echo from my last scream had abated and then said, 'I know you don't have a name picked out, but what have you been calling your baby up until now? It's almost here. We can't keep calling it "It".'

Jack and I locked eyes and, somewhere amidst the pain, I felt the desire to laugh. He saw the flash of humour in my eyes, and the connection that had been between us right from the very start flared once again.

'Fetid,' Jack said firmly to Randolph. 'We've been calling it Fetid. And, whether it's a boy or a girl, we're naming it Marvin.' Ignoring the stunned gazes of Nurse Petunia and Randolph, he fastened his gaze on to mine and whispered, 'Listen, Belle. Close your eyes and listen.'

Somehow I did as he instructed, and that's when I realised that the dreadful din of Huey Lewis and Gwyneth Paltrow had mercifully ended and that the beautiful melody of 'Over the Rainbow' was filling the room with blue skies and dreams coming true.

'I had a feeling we'd need more music.' The tears in Jack's eyes belied the attempted lightness of his tone. He clasped my hand strongly and looked deep into my eyes. 'You can do it, Belle. I know you can. I'm right here beside you.' He was willing me on.

Hours or maybe minutes or days later, a tiny cry filled the room. Jack cut the cord and then, as he placed our baby in my arms, my tears began to flow.

With a sense of wonder that would never quite leave me, I looked down at our baby and realised that this time it *was* different.

Because this time, Rex Jack Boyd was mine.

Acknowledgements

To: Fairy Godmother
From: Melanie La'Brooy
Re: Borrowing wand. Has been used as follows. Ta.

This book owes its existence to my amazing mother, Marie La'Brooy. Without her endless help I would have long ago been reduced to a snivelling heap. Mum's inexhaustible energy, patience and love set a standard for motherhood that is both inspiring and a wee bit daunting. So with a wave of my fairy godmother's magic wand, henceforth Mum shall always be helped by efficient and friendly sales assistants not named Beatrice.

My wonderful Curtis Brown agents, Alice Lutyens in London and Tara Wynne in Sydney, shall be visited on a weekly basis by the foot-massage fairy in recognition of their spectacular agent-y skills.

To my lovely editor Emma Beswetherick, Donna Condon, Emma Grey and all at Piatkus, I grant you the boon of never venturing into public with unidentifiable stains on your clothes or in your hair: a gift that all new mothers acknowledge as one of the greatest that I have in my power to give.

To my husband Charlie, I grant the blessing of never having to forgo sushi, champagne or seafood. Unless I have to again, in which case you do too. On second thoughts you might have to settle for being eternally loved, even though you do have the worst taste in names and was adamant that you wanted to call our son Rex. (Woof.) Thank you for being the calming, steady presence that I so often need, for being a wonderful father and most of all for giving me the gift of our beautiful baby boy. If you'd just stop losing your keys, you'd be perfect.

And finally to my Dashie. My smile, my naughtiness, my book- and ball- and music-loving boy who, without the aid of a magic wand, transformed this most non-maternal of girls into the most besotted of Mummies. You will always be loved and, curiously, for that I will never need a wand either, even though it's the most mysterious magic of all.